PUBLISHER'S PLEDGE

Shut Up and Kiss Me

Dear Reader,

There's just something about a man in a pink bath-robe.

He put it on after the V8 bath. After the skunk sprayed him. After he crashed his car. After he was forced to return to the Podunk town where he left his one true love.

"Wait, *WHAT*?" I hear you say. Welcome to the world of Christie Craig. Not that Jose is our hero. Heck, Sky's about three thousand times sexier—just ask Shala. But she would have fallen for Jose's brother anyway, even if the Native American lawman wasn't so hunky or protecting her from a killer. It was fate.

That's what you get in a Christie Craig novel: sexy guys in (and out of) uniform, wacky hijinks, and best of all, genuine emotion. There's a reason why critics love her and she's been compared to Janet Evanovich and Susan Andersen. Dorchester's Publisher's Pledge program is our way of identifying particularly special books by giving readers a risk-free guarantee. We feel so strongly about *Shut Up and Kiss Me*, we're willing to pay a full refund to anyone who doesn't find it everything they want in a contemporary romance.

Christie's got a backlist you might not have seen yet. And I'm betting her books and Lay's potato chips have something in common: you can't stop at just one.

Happy glomming!
Christopher Keeslar
Senior Editor

A PRECIOUS WELCOME

"Bo must have given you terrible directions," the voice said. Shala squinted into the darkness. "It took you twice as long to get here as it should have."

"Bo told you I was coming?"

"I've been answering calls about you all night. Tommy Crow called while flipping burgers and said some hot chick was looking for me. Harvey at the Shop and Go said you sounded desperate—and you must have been, to actually walk into the Funky Chicken. Most weekenders stay clear of that place. But you lucked out when you found Bo. There's nothing Bo wouldn't do for a beer and a dance. Bo said—"

"I'm not interested in what Bo said, Mr. Gomez. I get the point. Everyone in town is loyal to you." Which meant they either liked him or feared him. She touched her purse and felt for her Mace.

A growl echoed from behind the swing. Shala saw two big dogs stretched out behind her camera thief. She stepped back.

"Don't worry, you're safe," Sky said.

Shala couldn't help but ask. "From the dogs or you?"

Other *Love Spell* books by Christie Craig:

DIVORCED, DESPERATE AND DECEIVED
GOTCHA!
DIVORCED, DESPERATE AND DATING
WEDDINGS CAN BE MURDER
DIVORCED, DESPERATE AND DELICIOUS

Christie Craig

SHUT UP ᴬᴺᴰ KISS ME

LOVE SPELL NEW YORK CITY

LOVE SPELL®

June 2010

Published by

Dorchester Publishing Co., Inc.
200 Madison Avenue
New York, NY 10016

ISBN 10: 0-505-52799-5
ISBN 13: 978-0-505-52799-8
E-ISBN: 978-1-4285-0884-2

The name "Love Spell" and its logo are trademarks of Dorchester Publishing Co., Inc.

Printed in the United States of America.

10 9 8 7 6 5 4 3 2 1

Visit us online at www.dorchesterpub.com.

To my husband Steve Craig for taking over kitchen duty while I was superglued to the computer keyboard writing about skunks, fire ants, fistfights, and love. And to my son Steve Craig Jr. for eating his dad's cooking without complaining more than twice a day.

ACKNOWLEDGMENTS

I tip my hat to the best critique group in the world; honest, kind, supportive, and pushy broads whose attempts to keep me sane are to be commended, even if they fail: Faye Hughes, Jody Payne, Teri Thackston, and Suzan Harden. To my editor Chris Keeslar, who is probably sweating bullets but doesn't show it when I tell him things like, "Oh, yeah, there's a skunk and a naked man in a bathtub filled with tomato juice and women's douche in this book." To my agent Kim Lionetti, who gives me just enough rope to hang myself, but also keeps a pair of scissors within reach. And finally, to my sister-in-law and fan, Jackie Mathews, who tells me, "Your book made me laugh so hard, even the cows were looking at me funny."

SHUT UP
AND KISS ME

CHAPTER ONE

"Is that war paint or love paint he's wearing?" a female voice rang out from behind Shala Winters.

"Don't care," another woman replied in a Texas drawl. "But I see why they call this town Precious now." There came a burst of raucous laughter.

Shala would have rolled her eyes if her gaze weren't snagged by the group of hard-bodied, almost-naked males entering the arena wearing only headdresses and loincloths. A drop of sweat rolled down between her breasts. Too bad she wasn't in the mood for hard-bodied, almost-naked men—hadn't been for a couple of years. In fact, she wished she'd passed on this powwow altogether. If she'd known photos were outlawed, she'd be in her air-conditioned hotel room right now, washing drool and God only knew what else off her jeans from that humping dog she'd encountered at the park.

Dad-blast it, she needed photographs for her PR project to work. But according to the sign posted at the ticket booth, cameras were adamantly prohibited. In fact, she was supposed to have left hers at the gate. *Right*. Like she would leave a piece of eight-thousand-dollar equipment with strangers. Shala readjusted her shoulder bag, camera included. Why hadn't Mayor Johnson warned her about this?

"Excuse me." A blonde with poufy bleached hair, followed by a tall brunette, pushed into the crowd's front line.

"Look at that," said the brunette. "I always loved playing cowboys and Indians. Now I know why." More raucous laughter erupted.

"Native Americans," Shala corrected.

"Huh?" the brunette asked.

"That's what they prefer to be called: Native Americans."

"Honey, I'll call them anything they want," said Blondie. "This is better than a strip club. Look at those abs."

Shala bit her tongue. For someone to be educated, they needed to be willing to learn.

Focusing on the arena, she let her gaze slip to the men and their abs. Okay, she couldn't blame the women for enjoying the view. Just because she wasn't in the mood, that didn't mean she couldn't appreciate eye candy. However, a fine line existed between appreciating and gawking. According to Mayor Johnson, this was the reason the tribe had only recently opened their powwows to the public: people came to ogle, not to educate themselves in the Chitiwa tribe's culture or history.

The town's economy depended on tourism, however. That was why the tribal council had changed its mind. Precious, Texas, was 65 percent Native American or Native American–Hispanic mix, so they had a vested interest in seeing Precious survive. And now, so did Shala. The town was paying her well to make sure it did. Not that *everyone* wanted her here. That point had been driven home by the mayor, and frankly, it made her a tad uneasy.

Mayor Johnson had suggested she wait for her second visit to set up a meeting with the tribal council, hoping time would soften their opinion of her efforts to increase tourism by publicizing their tribal events. Several of the councilmen moved to the center of the arena and explained that the next exhibition was the "Dance of Love, a ritual meant to lure soul mates together." One of the men, long gray hair flowing down his back, scanned the crowd. His eyes stopped on her, or so it seemed.

"I'm already in love," said the blonde beside Shala, pointing.

Shala's gaze shifted to the dancers and then back to the

councilmen. The one who'd singled her out seemed to nod in acknowledgment. A breeze picked up his hair, but his eyes stayed fixed on her. Did he know who she was? That stare was intimidating. Shala's breath caught.

A lull hit the audience, a reverent pause. The gray-haired man looked away, and Shala drew much-needed air into her lungs. With fresh oxygen recharging her brain cells, she wished again she hadn't come. Heat, hunger, and memory of that overzealous dog kept her from appreciating the show.

The smell of grilled meat, onions, and buttered corn blew past. While the breeze was too hot to cool her, the aromas made Shala's stomach growl. The hamburger she'd bought for lunch had been snatched by her unwelcome and amorous friend at the lake. Just like a man, that canine had been all about sex and food. Glancing around, she considered wriggling out to the concession stands, but then she heard a low thumping in her ears: drums. Her gaze shifted. The councilmen had left, replaced by the dancers. The drums grew louder. The crowd grew tighter. She could swear the temperature increased ten degrees.

A sigh escaped her lips. The sun hung low in the horizon and painted the sky a bright pink and purple. Her gaze eased back to the dancers. The drum tempo increased and the men began to move, tall and proud. The golden sunset cast a glow on them and begged for a photograph. Shala's fingers itched to capture the image. She reached into her heavy tote . . . then remembered the sign out front.

"Stupid rule," she muttered, deciding to address it with the mayor. Powwows would be a big draw for Precious, but visitors would want images.

Her aggravation melted as a low, strange chant filled the air. Sweat continued to collect between her breasts. The line of dancers moved her way: six men, though one stood out. Third to the left. He was eye candy at its best.

"My gawd!" said Blondie. "How much does one of them cost for a night?"

Shala attempted to ignore her, and yet, as another drop of sweat ran from beneath her right breast down into her navel, the trickle of dampness sent a sensual shiver through her body. A shiver she hadn't felt in a long time. For a damn good reason, she reminded herself.

The brunette's drawl carried through the crowd. "Can we shove dollar bills in their loincloths?"

Shala shot her an eye-rolling glance, then refocused on the dancer. Hard. Unrelenting. Muscles corded his arms and legs. His body moved to the pulsing drumbeat. Black hair hung loose, flipping up and down with his motions, and his headdress, with rows of white feathers, shimmered in the sunlight.

His skin, the color hinting at his Native American heritage, caught the sheen of the setting sun. It appeared oiled. *Oiled.* Oiled, slick male skin. The thought took her back to the time she and her husband had ruined a good set of sheets with a bottle of baby oil. Her body recalled with clarity the feel of her oiled body parts moving across his. The experience had been worth the price of good Egyptian cotton. Too bad her marriage had gone the way of the sheets—into the Dumpster.

"Good God, check out his loincloth," Blondie said.

Shala's gaze lowered without thought. The drums continued, and the erotic sound got under her skin, into her blood. *Thump. Thump.* She was staring at that strip of white cloth, vaguely aware of behaving as badly as the two women beside her. Shala closed her eyes. When she reopened them, the man had danced closer. Glancing up, she saw high cheekbones, lips almost too beautiful to be masculine, a chiseled nose—

Her breath caught. His hawklike eyes were on her, and not in a good way. Had he caught her ogling his loincloth? A blush heated her face and she glanced away, but not before she saw his intimidating scowl.

She stared off into the crowd as if looking for someone, despite the fact that she didn't know a soul. Never mind that ever since she arrived she'd had this weird sense of being watched; that was small-townitis, no doubt. But chills ran down her spine. She was an outsider. According to the mayor, an unwelcome outsider.

This dancer's stare was different, though. She could still feel his gaze eliciting strange emotions from her, like loneliness. How could she feel alone when surrounded by a crowd of over three hundred people? *Easy,* her mind shot back. *You don't let anyone get close. Especially men.* But being alone was a small price to pay for emotional safety.

"Hey." The brunette elbowed Shala. "He's staring at you."

Shala ignored her but braved another glance at the dancer. She regretted it. His scowl had grown angrier. Panicked, she dug through her purse—a reason to look away without appearing to be a coward, which normally she wasn't. None of this was normal, yet she couldn't put her finger on why.

The beat of the drums changed, and she sensed more than saw the dancers turn. Tempted though she was to check if the man's backside rivaled his front, escape appealed more.

"Look at those tight asses," the brunette said.

Guffaws broke out. Without looking or laughing herself, Shala swung around, but the strap of her canvas bag caught the brunette's elbow. It slipped off her shoulder, and her eight-thousand dollar Nikon made a break for the ground.

"No!"

Shala dropped to her knees. Picking up the camera, she checked the lens for cracks. No visible damage, thank God. She pulled the camera up close to inspect it and in the corner of her vision saw a flash. Lowering her Nikon, she saw the brunette drop a point-and-shoot into her purse.

More concerned with her Nikon than the woman's illegal photo op, Shala refocused. Sudden gasps echoed from the crowd. Half-standing while raising her gaze from her camera, she found her nose almost against a loinclothed crotch. She swallowed a lump down her throat and rose the rest of the way.

Although she stood only chest high on the man, she tried to appear unaffected, as if she regularly found her nose stuck in men's crotches. Before she could rationalize why the dancer was there, he yanked her camera from her hands. Stunned, she watched his backside—it *was* equally impressive to his front—disappear into the crowd.

Reality hit. Someone had just run off with her eight-thousand-dollar camera. "Stop that man!" she screamed, and took off after him.

An hour later, standing in the hot night air outside the ticket booth and still sweating, Shala teetered on the edge of sanity. Redfoot Darkwater, the tribesman with long gray hair who'd eyed her in the arena, seemed unaffected. He was the fourth councilman paraded down to discuss her missing camera.

Discuss? Ha! The first three had all stood there like rocks, studying her like a high-school biology experiment, not saying more than six words between them. Redfoot was no different, his arms crossed stoically over his chest. She wanted to poke him to make sure he wasn't one of those cigar-shop statues she'd seen as a kid.

"Let me say this one more time, sir. I need my camera."

He didn't blink, but at least he moved. He pointed to the sign. "You read the rules. Yes?"

He talked! "Yes. I read the rules, but I didn't take a picture. I just didn't want to leave my—"

"Sky says you took a picture."

Sky? Oh, Mr. Eye Candy. "Well, Sky's lying. I didn't take a picture. The woman beside me took the picture."

"But you did have your camera. Rule says all cameras must be left at the gate, and if found will be confiscated for one week."

Shala held her breath and wondered if she should tell

him who she was and why she was here. Oh, goodness, this wasn't how she wanted to be introduced! "Look, I accept that I broke a rule, and I'm sorry. But I didn't take the picture, so if you could give me my camera . . ."

"Can't give you camera. Sky has the camera."

"Why does he have the camera? Who is Sky?"

"He handles these things. You talk to Sky."

Shala was dying to let loose with some seldom-used language, but being raised by her grandparents had instilled in her a respect for her elders, even uncooperative, stoic ol' farts. Realizing she wasn't getting anywhere, she decided to be completely honest. "Look, I'm here in Precious, Texas, at the request of your mayor. I'm working for the town to increase tourism. He wants me to find your town 'precious,' and this . . . this missing camera fiasco *isn't*. Do you understand?"

Redfoot's brow creased. "You wait one week. You talk to Sky. You offer donation and he will probably give you your camera. The film, however, I'm sure he's already destroyed."

"Film? Donation?" She took another deep breath, seeking a calm that didn't currently exist anywhere in her emotional zip code. "My camera is digital, and every picture I've taken for the last three days is on it. If that man does something to my memory card, I . . ." She exhaled. "Can I talk to him? Please. Please. Pleeaassse!"

The old man looked tempted. Almost. "One week. You tell Sky you want your camera. Sky is a fair man. He will return your camera. Maybe he ask for donation. One woman shine his boots to get camera back. You do what Sky asks, and he will be fair."

Fury bubbled up inside her. "I won't be here next week. I need my camera, and I need it now. And I am *not* going to polish any man's boots. What I'm going to do is call the police."

"This is Indian land. Police no good here. But you know this, don't you?"

She did, but during conniption fits she often forgot things. And she was smack dab in the middle of one. Why else would she be butting heads with the very people whose cooperation she needed to win? But it was too late. She'd patch up things later. Right now, she needed her camera.

"Look, I'm not going to shine anyone's shoes to—"

"Then you do not want your camera very bad." Redfoot turned to walk away.

Shala called his name, hoping she remembered it correctly. "Please. I really need my camera." As the man faced her, she could swear empathy filled his faded gray eyes. "Please," she repeated.

"You are confusing woman. You seem like nice girl, but you do not obey the rules. You say you not take a picture, but Sky does not lie. You say you want your camera, but you say you won't work to get your camera back. I hope I am right about you, Blue Eyes."

Blue eyes? And right about what? The man talked like a Native American fortune cookie and Shala suspected it was partly an act. "It's my camera. I shouldn't have to work to get it back."

His gray hair stirred in the hot breeze. "All this land was ours, and now the white man is angry because we do not pay taxes on the small piece we have left."

Shala blinked. Somehow her camera had gotten caught up with ancient peace treaties gone bad. She knew then she couldn't win the argument, not with Redfoot, but giving up wasn't in her genes. "Look—"

"You, Blue Eyes, need to learn to follow the rules. I'm sure Sky will teach you." Shaking his head, Redfoot walked away.

Shala turned back to the teenage boy who'd called down all four of the elders to talk to her. He leaned against the counter, his mouth agape, his eyes on her boobs. His attention shot up, but her effect on him didn't go unnoticed. She sent him a smile, not above flirting to get what she needed. "Can you please call . . . Sky? I want to talk to him."

The boy's Adam's apple bobbed. "Mr. Gomez has left. Come back next week. Like Redfoot said, Sky's a fair man."

Okay, the boy was probably in obstinacy training. That, or she'd forgotten how to flirt. Considering she hadn't flirted in years, the latter could be the case. Then she realized: "Sky *Gomez*? That's his name?"

The boy took on the pinched expression of a fish out of water. He started to say something, but Shala didn't stick around to hear.

"Sky Gomez," she repeated as she hurried to her car. Precious, Texas, wasn't as big as a freckle. Somehow, some way, she was going to find this man and get her camera back. That, or she'd bury him in the nearest compost heap.

CHAPTER TWO

The kids at the fast-food joint pretended they didn't know a Sky Gomez. The guy at the convenience store downright refused to talk to Shala. The telephone operator said his number and address were unlisted, and when she asked the woman at the drugstore directions to his residence, the clerk patted her on the shoulder and told her she'd best kiss the camera good-bye for at least a week. Was the entire town in cahoots?

At almost ten, after failing miserably to get someone—anyone—in this godforsaken freckle to tell her where she could find the man, she turned to desperate measures. She drove her Honda Accord down Highway 301 to the last place she wanted to go: the town's only bar.

And what a fine establishment it appeared to be. The watering hole looked like a cross between a biker bar and a dilapidated barn. Of course, the huge demented chicken painted on the metal roof, beer in claw, gave it that real touch of class. But then, the drunken, crazy-eyed fowl did reflect the establishment's name: the Funky Chicken. Of course, someone had painted over the *N* with a *C*. Shala was about to walk into the Fucky Chicken.

She'd passed the establishment several times during the day and put it first on her gotta-do-something-about-it list for the mayor. Hey, she appreciated unique hangouts. Tourists loved them, but this place's appearance wasn't "quirky." Instead, it had that you-take-your-life-in-your-hands-when-entering air. And she was about to enter.

It was for a good cause, she reminded herself: her Nikon. She'd used her inheritance from Nana to buy that camera, and Shala wanted it back. It might sound stupid, but she viewed the Nikon as her grandmother's way of still looking out for her. Yeah, it was sad for a twenty-eight-year-old to still want to be looked after, but everyone had a few flaws, right?

As she pulled into the parking lot, a pair of headlights appeared in her rearview mirror. She turned to see a dark-colored sedan that she'd seen earlier. The car pulled to the side of the lot and stopped. Could it be Sky Gomez? Now, wouldn't that be funny. Not.

Getting out of her car, she approached her stalker. Two steps closer, the car sped off. But as it passed under the streetlight, Shala got a glimpse of the driver—a big guy with short light-colored hair. Not her camera thief.

So who was it? The mayor's warning rang in her ears: *Some people in town, especially the Natives, don't want us turning to tourism. Don't be surprised if you run into some unfriendly folks.* But just how unfriendly could they get?

"Unfriendly enough to steal my camera," she muttered. Then, armed with fake courage and determined to get back her Nikon, she hotfooted it into the Fucky Chicken.

Shala pulled up in front of Sky Gomez's log cabin a short while later. The moon hung eerily low. If she hadn't been so downright pissed, she'd have found the place quaint. Instead, the cabin, nestled between live-oak trees, had creepy music playing in her head.

Leaning against her steering wheel, Shala noticed golden light leaking from the window on the left side of the porch. A truck was parked beside the cabin. Someone was home. *He* was home. An image of the scowling, loincloth-wearing man flashed through her mind. A shiver climbed her spine.

She glanced up and down the dirt road, seeking another light from a nearby home. Nope. Sheer darkness. It was just her and her camera thief, her gorgeous camera thief whom she knew nothing about. He could be a serial killer. He didn't look like a serial killer, but it had been a while since she'd run across one—a while, as in never—so she might have missed the resemblance. She checked her rearview mirror. At least the sedan hadn't shown back up.

She could leave, she told herself, but she hadn't endured that visit to the Funky Chicken to back out now. The bartender had laughed at her twenty-dollar bribe. *Honey, it would take about fifty of those to warrant pissing off Sky.* And if she'd known what she'd end up paying to Bo Eagle, the bar's owner, she might have considered the bartender's offer a better deal.

It had taken two beers before Bo even admitted knowing Sky. Another to sort of recall where Sky lived. But the ultimate price of the exact address had brought her down to a new level. *A little more sweet talk, and one dance, and then I'll cough up Sky's address.* Bo's words bounced through her head like a Ping-Pong ball with spikes. Sort of like how the man danced. She'd have sweet-talked him until the cows came home hungover, but that dance would haunt her. And not in a good way. Who knew disco wasn't dead?

Shala stepped out of her car. The hot night clung to her skin. A hope of sweet-talking her camera from Sky Gomez flitted through her mind, but she quickly dismissed it. Something told her he didn't like women. Or maybe it was just blonde, blue-eyed, all-American chicks ogling his loincloth. Fate wouldn't create a man that drop-dead gorgeous and make him gay, would it? Oh, yes, fate would.

Not that she thought Sky Gomez was gay. Or cared. And him liking her or not liking her? That didn't matter, either. She had one objective: getting her camera.

Stiffening her spine, prepared for this to get ugly, she hugged her bag. If she had to call in the cops, she would. She'd lost her patience back on the dance floor when Bo had flung her between his legs.

Taking a deep breath, checking her bag for her can of Mace, she walked up to the dark front porch. One deep breath later, she knocked. When no one answered, she knocked again. "Please be home," she muttered, rapping her knuckles against the thick wooden door a third time. "Damn it, I had better not have discoed for nothing. Be home."

"I'm home."

Shala jumped and bumped her head against the door-frame. The voice had come from the right, the dark side of the porch, and she aimed her gaze that way.

"Bo must have given you terrible directions," the voice continued. "It took you twice as long to get here as it should have."

"Bo told you I was coming?" She squinted into the darkness, only to make out the shape of a man sitting on a porch swing. A very nice shape that she hoped wore more clothes than earlier.

"I've been answering calls about you all night. James

Stone's son at the ticket gate. Moonshine, Cougar, Wolf, and finally Redfoot. Redfoot had nice things to say about you."

She knew she'd liked Redfoot best. "Look, I want—"

"You managed to meet the entire tribal council tonight. Congratulations."

"Look, I'm here—"

"Tommy Crow called while flipping burgers and said some hot chick was looking for me. Evie, at Walgreens, told me to be nice to you. Harvey at the Shop and Go said you sounded desperate—and you must have been, to actually walk into the Funky Chicken. Most weekenders stay clear of that place."

"I wouldn't know why," she sassed. But she wasn't here to discuss tourism. "I'm not here to—"

"Eduardo, the bartender, said he turned down your bribe. But you lucked out when you found Bo. There's nothing Bo wouldn't do for a beer and a dance. Bo said—"

"I'm not interested in what Bo said, Mr. Gomez. I get the point. Everyone in town is loyal to you." Which meant they either liked him or feared him. She touched her purse and felt for her Mace.

A growl echoed from behind the swing. Shala saw two big dogs stretched out behind her camera thief. She stepped back, having reached her limit of humping for the day. Between the dog and then Bo—

"Don't worry, you're safe," Sky said.

"From the dogs or you?"

"Both." He patted the porch swing. "Have a seat."

"I'd rather stand." Silence rang out. She noticed he wore jeans and a button-down shirt. "You know, it would have been easier if you'd just agreed to talk to me." A hell of a lot easier if he just hadn't taken her camera in the first place.

"Easier for whom?" He shifted. The porch swing creaked, then was drowned out by the intimate silence.

"For both of us. I wouldn't have had to run all over

town, trying to bribe people. And you wouldn't have had to be disturbed with calls."

He crossed his arms over his chest. The pose made him appear solid, strong. Unapproachable. "I wasn't disturbed. They're my friends. I enjoyed every conversation. And I think they enjoyed your attention. I know Bo did. You're the first woman who's danced with him in three years." Shala cringed as she remembered a move that brought back memories of the humping dog. He chuckled. "I would have paid to see that."

A sharp ringing pierced the night. Sky pulled a cell phone from his shirt pocket and answered. "Yeah?" Pause. "She's here."

His gaze moved over her, up and then slowly down, as if to intimidate her. It worked, but she'd be damned if she'd let him know.

"She is that." He chuckled. The deep throaty sound somehow eased her fear but built her aggravation. He pulled the phone away and looked at her. "Bo says hi." Then he refocused on the conversation. "Don't worry, I can handle her." He hung up, and his dark eyes settled on her again.

"I'm not easy to handle," she seethed.

"I'm willing to give it a shot. But if you prefer Bo, I could call him back." He smiled. Really smiled. That confident expression rubbed every bad nerve she had. And a few good ones she didn't want rubbed.

She let go of a deep breath. "I'm here about my camera. If you don't mind—"

"Is that all?"

"All what?"

"All you're really here for? From the way you were looking at me at the powwow . . ."

She blushed. "That's all I want."

"Was it you that wanted to know if you could stuff dollar bills in my loincloth?"

Shala felt her face heat. "No! That wasn't me. I need my camera," she managed to say.

"If that's all you came for, you discoed with Bo for nothing. I have nothing to say that hasn't already been said. You were asked to read the rules before you bought the ticket. You broke the rules."

"I didn't take a picture!"

"The evidence says different."

"What evidence?"

"Me. I saw you."

"You saw a flash. It wasn't mine."

He stood up, and the porch swing creaked again. "Do you take me for a fool, Ms. Winters?"

So, he knew her name. He probably knew why she was here, too. Chances were, he was one of the men who didn't want her here. Was that what this was really about?

He took a step forward.

Fighting the temptation to reach for her Mace, Shala put on a brave front. "Maybe not a fool, but you are jumping to foolish conclusions."

"You think I didn't hear you and your friends?"

"Friends?" She took a step forward, angrier than embarrassed, angrier than frightened. "First, I wasn't with anyone tonight at the powwow. Those women beside me were crude and obnoxious, but I had no part in it."

He actually appeared to be listening.

"Second, the flash you saw wasn't from my camera. It was from theirs. Third—"

"But you had a camera, which is all the reason I need to take possession."

She clenched her jaw. "Third, you know who I am, so you obviously know why I'm here. So hand over my camera so I can do my job."

"Can't do that."

Standing this close, Shala realized something was

different about Sky Gomez. His hair, she realized. Either he'd cut it, or it had been a wig earlier.

"It's an expensive piece of equipment." She took another step, moved so close she could smell his skin. Freshly showered, he smelled of spicy men's soap and something she couldn't put her finger on. Whatever it was, it made her inhale deeply. It made her long for a shower herself.

"Come back in a week and ask nicely, and we'll see if we can't come to an agreement."

"I don't have a week! I'm leaving in two days, and I—"

"That's a shame." And just like that, he stepped to his front door and walked inside, shutting it and leaving her outside, alone in the dark. Alone and furious. Alone and—

A deep growl filled the dark silence.

Okay, not completely alone. "Good puppies," she murmured. When the dogs didn't attack or fall in love with her leg, she let go of her fear but not her anger. "Screw you!" she shouted.

She started for her car, got halfway there, then recalled dancing with Bo. She swung around, shot up the porch steps, got to the door, and almost knocked. Instead—what the hell—she reached for the doorknob, expecting to find it locked, but it turned easily in her hand.

She stepped inside and found Sky sitting on a tan leather sofa. A lamp perched on an end table cast an orb of golden light. Quickly, she allowed herself one look around his place. An open floor plan. The great room held the kitchen and living area. Wood. Lots of wood. Wood furniture, wood floors. A large rock fireplace, and a few colorful rugs. Quaint. Cozy but still masculine. Like him. With his dark hair and devilish dark eyes, he reminded her of one of the Ordóñez brothers, Spanish bullfighters. Only Sky Gomez looked even more daring.

His attention stayed fixed on her, seemingly unsurprised. Almost pleased. His dark gaze whispered down her body the way a man's did while he mentally stripped a woman naked, and she shivered.

He moistened his lips. "Are you sure the only reason you're here is that camera?" His voice had acquired a husky quality that sent sensual shivers down her spine.

"I'm positive." All the moisture evaporated from her mouth as she studied him. With jeans and a white button-down shirt, he looked like a clean-cut, self-confident kind of guy who women fantasized about. But, damn it, she didn't care what he looked like, or that he oozed testosterone. Or that he had just mentally stripped her naked. Well, she cared, but she couldn't control what he did in his mind.

"Look, I want my camera. I need my camera. I have dozens of shots in its memory that I have to have to complete a work assignment. If I can't complete that assignment, I don't get paid. If I don't get paid, I can't pay my rent. I'm trying to be reasonable about this, but I'm not leaving until I get it." She reached into her canvas bag and pulled out her cell phone.

He held up his hands. "Wait."

She wasn't waiting. She opened her phone. "You either give me my camera or I'm calling the police. Right now. This is my last warning."

His expression didn't change. "Well, as luck would have it, we're sort of a one-horse town, and I don't think the chief is on duty tonight."

"Then I'll get him back on duty." Luckily, Sky Gomez's house wasn't on the reservation, and she was tired of being nice. She'd given that up the second time Bo tried to toss her under his legs.

Sky's eyebrows arched. "I can assure you that the chief will agree with me. Let's just say we're—"

"I guess we'll have to see for ourselves, won't we?" she snapped. With the mayor having hired her, the chief would be on her side. Oh, God, please let him be on her side.

Sky crossed his arms over his chest again. His wide chest. She remembered how he'd looked without a shirt on. *Not now!* she screamed at her reawakening hormones.

He reached up and unbuttoned his collar as if he could read her mind. "Do you need the phone book, or would you trust me to give you the number?"

She frowned. "I'll dial 911."

"Well, that's one way."

He shouldered back on the sofa. The small action drew her attention to his body again, to the way his shirt sleeves molded to his biceps. After visually nibbling on that image, she noted the way his jeans hugged his thighs.

Realizing she was staring, and at what, and how that might appear, she forced her attention all the way back up him to the shit-eating grin of a man who knew that a woman found him attractive. Ah, but finding a man attractive didn't mean diddly-squat. Hell, she hadn't given in to her desires in almost two years. Okay, she hadn't *had* any desires for two years. When her heart broke, her hormones had followed suit. And while their choice now to rear their ugly heads was an unwelcome surprise, she could handle it. No way, no how, was she giving in to this egotistical camera thief. In fact, if she had her way Mr. Sky Gomez would be spending the night in jail. She'd see how smug he looked in handcuffs.

"Put the phone down and let's talk about why you're really here." His hand rubbed the back of his sofa as if he was inviting her to sit beside him. The hum of sexual awareness buzzed louder in her ears, and that buzz spread to parts that hadn't been buzzed in a long time.

"I don't think so." That look was *so* coming off his gorgeous face. She dialed 911.

"You really don't want to do that."

She glared at him. "Oh, I do."

He ran his palms up and down his jean-covered thighs. "You realize that if anyone has broken a law here tonight, it's you. Trespassing and—"

"I came to get my—" The voice on the line stopped her dead.

"Precious Emergency," a woman said. Somehow, the two words didn't seem to go together. Before Shala could gather her wits, the voice continued, "Ms. Callan, if this is you again, I'm telling you, being out of Twinkies is not an emergency! Wait, this isn't your—"

"No," Shala managed. "I need a police car here now. Someone has stolen my camera, and I'm at the house of the thief, and he still refuses to hand it over."

"Oh, my!" said the woman, as if she hadn't really dealt with a 911 call before. "Let me see, let me see. First I'm supposed to make sure that this is a real emergency. Is this *really* an emergency?" she asked. "A 911 emergency?"

"Yes! He stole my camera and he refuses to return it. And he's . . . he's making me nervous, if you know what I mean."

"How is he making you nervous?" the woman asked, sounding more curious than concerned.

"As if he might . . . try something."

Mr. Gomez's eyes widened as if calling her a liar.

"Oh, my!" said the woman.

Well, it wasn't a lie. Her body was getting all sorts of messages from him, and not one of them was decent. Every second that passed, in fact, she was finding those messages more disturbing.

Or more tempting, a voice whispered in her head.

Oh, hell. She really needed the police to hurry.

"Okay," said the woman on the line. "I'll contact the chief. But only if you really think it's an emergency. He doesn't like to be disturbed on his days off."

"It's an emergency," Shala snapped.

"Okay, can you stay on the line? I'll get him, and then I'll get your information."

"Yes."

She glanced up, offering Mr. Gomez a little smile of victory, but her camera thief had picked up a newspaper,

feigning total disinterest. Damn him for being so cool.
Damn him for making her feel . . . alive, at least sexually.
She didn't want to feel alive. That fuzzy feminine sensation had led her to saying "I do," and "I do" led to her
heart feeling as if it were stomped on by sharp stilettos,
stabbed by an ice pick, and given to baby crocodiles for a
teething toy.

A ringing filled the cabin. Dropping the paper, her
thief reached over and picked up the phone on the coffee
table. His eyes met hers. "Chief Gomez," he answered, in
his deep, sultry voice. Then he had the audacity to grin
and wink at her.

CHAPTER THREE

Shock filled Shala Winters's baby blue eyes, and Sky
couldn't help enjoying that any more than he could help
enjoy looking at her. While she measured slightly below
average in height, nothing else about her did. Her breasts
were large, her waist small. She had enough leg encased
in that soft, formfitting denim to pull off wearing a short
tight skirt, and wispy blonde hair a man might pay to run
his fingers through. On top of all that, she had the face of
an angel.

Not that faces fooled him. Angels didn't look at men
the way she'd eyed him at the powwow. He might believe
that she wasn't with the other two women, but she
couldn't deny the heated way she'd looked at him.

"Sky? We have an issue. Some woman called 911. I have
her on hold but . . ." It was Martha, his nighttime 911 operator and daytime secretary. Martha excelled at two
things: taking care of her Cadillac and talking.

While Martha jabbered, Sky watched Shala. She hadn't moved. He questioned if she even breathed.

Normally, he wouldn't have minded being blatantly checked out by someone who looked like her, but tonight was a prime example of why the elders in his tribe didn't want the public invited into their private world. Outsiders took something culturally meaningful and turned it into a gawkfest. And this woman was one of the gawkers. She was supposed to be different, supposed to be here to help prevent this very thing. And damn it if he hadn't been the one to talk the tribal council into accepting her.

Of course, that was before Redfoot claimed to have had a *wacoi*—the sacred word—a spirit-sent dream that foretold the coming together of two soul mates. Sky honestly didn't blame his foster father as much as he blamed the chili the man ate before he went to bed. However, Redfoot started spouting off about Shala Winters being Sky's soul mate. Since he couldn't argue with Redfoot, there was only one way to keep the man's nonsense about visions from getting out of hand. Stay away from Shala.

"Sky? Are you listening to me?" Martha's voice brought him back to the issue at hand.

"I'm listening," he answered, but honestly his mind wasn't on the conversation. Instead, it was on the distance he'd sworn he'd keep from Shala and on their close proximity right now. And damn it if he didn't want to be even closer. Unfortunately, knowing the gorgeous blonde was off-limits made her that much more appealing.

Covering the phone, he offered, "You can sit down if you'd like." Shala ignored him.

He thought watching her from a distance had been hard, but coming face-to-face with her tonight took things to a new level. As chief of police—the only law in Precious besides two occasional state troopers—it was Sky's job to make sure her visit to Precious didn't bring out any of the local antitourism crazies. Tonight had him second-guessing his earlier protourism stance. After he'd snagged her camera, he'd been tempted to tell the tribal council he'd made a mistake.

But he couldn't tell the tribal council that. The woman standing before him was the only thing that was going to save Precious, she and other members of the press. The fates of the town and his people were dependent on tourism. But Sky would be damned if he'd let anyone walk onto the reservation and all over his culture. Even Shala Winters.

"Sky?"

"Yes, Martha?"

"What do you want me to tell her?" Martha asked. "If . . ."

Sky waited for Martha to take a breath. "It's okay, Martha. She's here."

"There? She . . . ? You mean the caller." Martha lapsed into silence, which spoke volumes. As one of the mostly white city council, Martha never hesitated to put in her two cents, whether it was wanted or not. Not that he didn't like Martha; he did.

"Yes, the caller. She's here. I'm the one who took the camera away from her—at the powwow. I just haven't had the time to properly introduce myself yet."

"Oh, God, please tell me she's not Shala Winters. Oh, God have mercy on us." Martha sighed. "It's her, isn't it? The mayor is going to skin us alive. First he'll skin you and then he'll skin me. Then he'll go after my Cadillac."

He was going to get the speech again. The one where she pointed out that he had to keep the ways of his people separate from his job. What he'd told her—what she never heard—was that there was no separating who he was from what he did. He was part Native American, part Mexican, and part white, and he was chief of police. But they were all the same man.

"Sky, this is one of those times—"

"I know, Martha. I'm taking care of it."

"You're going to give me my camera back?" Shala asked.

He looked up and raised a finger, asking for patience. Not that it looked as if she had much.

"The mayor left strict orders," Martha continued. "We are supposed to do everything we can to make Miss Winters happy. 'Happy as a lark,' he said."

His eyes returned to the pretty package in front of him, curvy in all the right places. *Make her happy.* He had a couple of ideas of how he'd like to make Shala happy. "Sounds like a good plan."

"Give her the camera back, Sky! Give it back right now."

That wasn't what he meant. "Can't do that, Martha."

"Oh, yes, you can. The wrath of hell will fall down on us if you don't." His middle-aged secretary just happened to be the Baptist preacher's wife.

"I'll deal with that when she shows up," he replied—if hell's minion wasn't already standing right in front of him. Shala would get her camera back in one week and not a minute before. Rules were rules. "Look, Martha, I'd better go." He hung up and dropped the phone.

Shala stood frozen, cell phone still clutched in her fist, staring at him. "You're a real jerk, aren't you?" she asked. He wiped a palm over his mouth to hide his smile.

She dropped her cell in her canvas bag and swung around, and he watched her hotfoot it to his door. Against his better judgment, he savored the view. Damn, but why had Redfoot started with all that soul-mate nonsense? Then it hit him: why the heck did it matter? Sky knew he wasn't soul-mate material. He'd out and out told Redfoot as much. About ten times. So why had avoiding her seemed like the best plan? Just because they were both single and he found her attractive didn't mean they'd hit the sheets. And if they did . . . well, they were adults, and if they saw fit to get naked together, there wasn't a darn thing anyone could do.

There! He'd said it: Shala Winters wasn't off-limits. Part of him hoped her gut-wrenching attraction would evaporate into thin air. But as he continued to stare at her cute, heart-shaped backside, that evaporation didn't happen.

She placed her hand on the doorknob, and he breathed a sigh of relief. He needed to come to terms with what he thought about Shala Winters, against what his gut was telling him now. But when he saw her open the door, he did an emotional U-turn.

"You don't have to go," he said.

"Good night, ol' man!"

Redfoot looked away from the piece of pine he whittled and at Maria Ortega. The young woman was his foster daughter, but she would be his daughter-in-law if only his biological son, Jose, came back home and did the right thing. Jose and Maria belonged together.

"It's Friday night, and you spend your time in bed instead of out with friends, and you call *me* old?" He hoped she'd go out so that he could do the same.

"I'm not going to bed alone. I have a good book."

"You would rather read about the made-up lives of others instead of live yourself."

"I have a life. Matt's just out of town."

"Again?" Redfoot asked.

Maria ignored him. He saw a flicker of concern as she leaned down and placed a soft kiss on his brow, though, and Redfoot could feel echoes of sadness in her touch. Matt had little to do with them. Maria mourned not just for Jose, but for the baby she had lost. Sometimes Redfoot wanted to knock some sense into his son. Next time he saw him, he might just do it.

"Matt can stay out of town," he muttered. He'd bet his best carving knife that boy was up to no good—probably dipping his wick in another candle. He'd never warmed up to the young man's light eyes. True, Redfoot's feeling probably stemmed from his belief that Maria belonged with Jose, but that didn't change the fact that Matt Goodson had *no-good scoundrel* written all over his pale white ass.

Maria shot him a look. "Stop it, *viejo*! Matt is a good man."

"Good as Monopoly money down at the five-and-dime." What was wrong with his son? How could Jose walk away from this soft woman who loved him? And how could Maria give this white boy a second look?

"Don't start." Maria looked at the newspaper on the end table. "Did you read that mustard is good for burns?" She pointed to an article.

"What does mustard have to do with Matt?"

"Nothing." She sighed. "I was trying to change the subject."

She walked off. Redfoot pressed his knife into the pine and removed a good chunk of frustration along with the wood. Since he was already ranting about the young folks, what in damnation was up with Sky? Why couldn't that boy accept that fate had sent him a gift? Was the kid blind? If Redfoot were ten years younger, if his heart weren't already half-taken, he'd go after Winters himself. Half the young men at the powwow tonight had tents in their loincloths from seeing her.

Nope, Redfoot simply didn't get young people today. Sometimes he wondered if his inability to understand them meant he was getting old, or if they were just as stupid as he thought. He let that question sit and finally decided they were just stupid. And fate didn't have much patience. Fate was about to kick ass; Redfoot *felt* it. From the dream he'd had last night, someone was going to try to hurt Blue Eyes. In his dream, it had been a bulldog. Wolves had come to her aid, but there had been blood spilled. Lots of blood.

"Love you, *viejo*," Maria called from the bedroom.

"I'm too mean to love," he called back, then, "Love you, too." And he meant it. He loved both Maria and Sky as much as he loved his biological son.

Not that it had always been that way. Bringing in the foster children had been his wife's idea. A nurturer at heart, she had longed for a big family that fate had not given them. But a few months after getting Sky, Redfoot had realized Estella was right. Then, years later, Estella had gone out and done it again. A year after she found Maria, the spirits had taken his woman home. Sometimes Redfoot wondered if Estella brought Maria into his life because she knew she was going and wanted her family to have a woman's touch. He wondered, too, if she'd known their only son would abandon his people's ways to become part of the white world. That was a choice Redfoot understood but resented. But maybe Estella had been more like her son than she cared to admit.

His gaze shifted to shelves filled with the fine pottery she'd made, pieces the world called art. How much more would his woman have become if she, like their son, had abandoned Precious?

"Did you take your medicine?" Maria called.

"Don't I always?" he answered. And he did, but he hated it—hated that he needed to take the medicines of white men to keep him going. There was only one pill he appreciated, and he took that only when his neighbor Veronica Cloud was in the mood. While it had been over ten years since he'd lost his wife, every now and then Redfoot would think about her position regarding him and Veronica. But then he could see her in his mind, smiling down and saying *You are not dead yet.*

Not yet. Sometimes—like tonight, feeling the passion steaming off Sky after he confronted that Winters gal—Redfoot almost felt young again. And Veronica had been there, dressed in bright colors and looking younger than her sixty years. Her smile had goosed his sixty-six-year-old heart. Maybe, after Maria got settled in, he would go see how Veronica felt. He usually got lucky on Friday nights.

He waited several long minutes, then got up and pocketed his knife. Moving past the hall, he saw Maria's door ajar. "Going to take a walk," he called out. "Thinking I might stop off and see Cougar and play a hand of poker, beat him out of some coins." This wasn't a lie: he had indeed thought about it. Personally, he considered it silly that he had to hide his visits with Veronica, but every time he brought it up, the woman got mad enough to chew leather. No way did she want her children or grandchildren to know. And to her that meant his children should not know, either. Redfoot did not like keeping secrets.

"I hope you get lucky," Maria called back.

"So do I." He grinned, knowing she was talking about poker, but he had hopes for another kind of luck. Starting out the door, he stopped, remembering. Smiling, he went back to collect his bottle of little blue pills.

CHAPTER FOUR

Sky continued to stare at Shala. She stayed frozen for several moments, the door half-open in front of her. Then she shut it, pressed her forehead to the wood, and sighed. He didn't mind; the view of her backside remained nice. He heard her suck in deep gulps of oxygen, saw the tension slowly ease from her muscles. Still facing the door, she finally spoke.

"All I want is my camera. Is that too much to ask?"

"Next week, it won't be. But right now? Yeah."

She swung around. The tension may have eased from her body, but anger brightened her blue eyes. "I'm not leaving. I'm staying here until you hand over my camera." She stomped over to his leather recliner and dropped down.

She crossed her arms over her chest. Now, *that* he minded. He'd rather liked observing the flesh filling out her white tank top. For the last two months, he'd spent every free moment working on the powwow committee, and since his last fling had been flung about a month before that, he'd been without a woman for more weeks than he cared to count.

"I mean it. I'm not leaving until you give me my camera."

He bit back a smile. "Okay."

Her wide eyes widened. "Okay, you're going to give me my camera?"

"No. Okay you can stay. We'll probably be tired of each other before the week is up, but have it your way. I'm not prone to telling beautiful women they can't stay in my house . . . or in my bed for that matter."

"You're a real jerk. You know that, don't you?"

"Sounds familiar." Standing, he stared down at her. She looked good at all angles: back, front, above—and he'd surely like to see her from below.

"Since you plan on staying, can I get you something to drink?" He walked into the adjoining kitchen and opened the fridge. The cool air hit him in the face, and for a second he wondered what the hell he was doing. Even if they hit it off, things always went south eventually. Martha was right: the mayor would skin him alive. And don't forget Redfoot's whole vision issue. If he thought his foster father was giving him hell now, imagine if he and Shala actually got involved. Were a few rolls in the hay worth the cost? The image of her heart-shaped backside flashed into his mind.

"I've got beer. Might have a bottle of wine," he called out, glancing back at her.

"No," she snapped.

"You hungry? Because I'm about to fix myself something."

Her eyes cut to the left. "No."

He recognized the lie. "I make a mean omelet. Cheese, a little ham . . . might even have mushrooms." When she swallowed, he said, "I'll take that as a yes."

She didn't contradict him, so he grabbed the eggs from the fridge and snagged a bowl from the cabinet. "So, you're from Houston, huh?" When she didn't answer, he looked. Her cute rear end remained planted in the leather recliner, and her arms continued to cover her breasts. A shame.

"What did you do," she asked, "have a background check run on me? Maybe see if I've taken other illegal photographs?"

"I'm the police chief. What do you think?" he asked, and couldn't resist a grin. He considered what all he should divulge, then decided what the hell. "You're divorced. You live in a small house northwest of Houston. You have a brother who lives in California with a couple of kids. You have a thing for long baths and lavender candles. You have a quirky sense of humor, and you love animals—cats more than dogs, which was evident on the porch and during the little incident out by the park." He laughed. "Though I have to admit that dog seemed crazy about you."

Her blue eyes narrowed, and for some reason he regretted teasing her. That's when he recalled what else he knew, the thing they shared. "You lost both your parents when you were a kid. You and your brother were raised by your grandparents, who unfortunately have also passed."

She stiffened. He'd clearly overstepped his bounds. Feeling bad, he went for something less personal. "You're damn good at your job. You've helped put over a dozen Texas towns on the tourism map."

She shook her head. Her hair stirred around her shoulders. He itched to touch it.

Her frown deepened. "So you hit my website, read some of my published essays, probably my Facebook page, and checked a few references. Is that supposed to impress me?"

"I was hoping." He smiled. She didn't respond, so he cracked several eggs in the bowl and reached in a drawer for a fork. "I actually was copied on all the e-mails between you and the mayor, which had your personal references. I was forwarded links to your essays by . . . others. But I did check out your website and blog on my own. I'll have to try your Facebook page. Will you friend me?"

She didn't answer. He beat the eggs into a nice yellow froth. The silence hummed. Funny how his cabin seemed quieter now than when he was alone. Which probably explained why he preferred being alone—or at least why he was better at it. Anything more than a casual affair felt like a pair of handcuffs.

"This is a small town, Shala. Your coming was front-page news. By now I'll bet my mailman has checked out your website." He knew for certain the tribal council had.

She stood, and her arms dropped from her breasts, offering that nice view again. "So you know who I am and what I'm doing here, yet you're still pulling this . . . this ridiculous stunt with my camera."

"It's not a stunt." He reached into the fridge for the grated cheddar cheese, mushrooms, ham, and a bag of grapes, then glanced back at her. "The rules were posted. You broke the rules." He rinsed the grapes, dropped them in a bowl and popped one into his mouth. The tart sweetness burst on his tongue.

Anger brightened her eyes again. "I didn't take a picture!"

"Maybe you did. Maybe you didn't."

"Did you check? Did you even look at the shots?"

"Not yet. But either way you broke the rules."

"Your rules are stupid. Tourists coming to the pow-wows are going to want to take pictures. Not that I took one. I just didn't want to risk leaving my expensive camera behind."

He walked to where she stood, halfway between the living room and kitchen. "Tourists coming to the powwows should respect our rules. You obviously have a problem with that. If you're planning on winning over the tribal council, that'll have to change."

"Maybe I shouldn't be working for Precious," she said, not giving an inch.

He held his temper in check and a grape to her lips. He couldn't stop her from walking out on the job, and come hell or high water, he wouldn't give her camera back until next week. But he hoped she wouldn't walk out. The mayor wouldn't be happy. Hell, neither would half the town. And neither would he.

He tapped her lips with the grape. "Take it, it's sweet."

Almost against her will, her mouth opened, and he slowly pressed the fruit inside. He studied her soft pink lips and wondered if kissing her would be stupid. It might possibly scare her into leaving. But wouldn't that be best? He needed to think, to figure things out. So, no kissing, not now. Not yet. He took a step back.

Her expression changed as if she'd had some unpleasant thought. "How did you know about the dog by the park?"

He could lie, but given the choice, he always preferred the truth. It was a bad habit he'd learned from Redfoot. "I was there. By the picnic tables. I was coming to your rescue, but you made it to your car first."

"You just happened to be there?" She looked suspicious.

"No. I've been keeping an eye on you since you got here." He reached for a skillet under the cabinet.

"So you've been stalking me." She studied him as if confused. "Was it you in the sedan?"

"Sedan?" he echoed. "No. Has someone been following you?" When she didn't answer, he put the skillet on the burner, turned that on, and reached into the refrigerator for butter. "Keeping an eye on you isn't the same as stalking. Has someone—?"

"So says the stalker," she interrupted.

He dropped butter in the pan. "Look, some people in town are less than thrilled you're here."

"And you head up that committee, right?"

"Actually, I headed up the pro-Winters side." When their eyes met, something told him she believed him. "I wasn't stalking. I was making sure you weren't bothered while you did your job."

"And you couldn't have just introduced yourself?"

Not without causing all kinds of talk about visions and soul mates. But he couldn't tell her that, so he offered a different truth. "I guess that would have been better, huh?"

He reached for the bowl of eggs and offered her another grape. She took several. They stood there, eating grapes and staring at each other. The melting butter in the pan sizzled and popped. The air between them did the same.

Redfoot took off down the street, his pills in his pocket and his son and Maria on his mind. How could he get Jose to come home before Maria did something stupid and committed to the wrong man? As he turned the corner onto Veronica's street, he heard an owl. Tonight, when he went to sleep, he would ask the spirits for guidance.

Before taking the path cutting between houses, heading to Veronica's back door, he made sure no one saw him, but a flash in the lodge window across the street caught his attention. He stared, thinking maybe he'd just imagined it, but the circle of light flickered across the window again. Someone was inside the lodge, someone with a flashlight. Why, when the lights worked just fine?

Redfoot remembered the nine thousand dollars in cash in the safe from the powwow. He took off at a dead run.

CHAPTER FIVE

Shala watched Sky turn and pour the eggs into the pan. Her gaze lowered to his backside, and she remembered how it had looked in just a loincloth. "Where is it?" she asked, determined to stop thinking about his body parts.

He looked over his shoulder. "Where is what?"

"My camera."

"It's safe," he said, and retrieved a spatula from a drawer.

"You realize how ridiculous this is."

He turned. "Why don't you put in some toast for us? Toaster's on the counter." He gestured with the spatula. "Bread's in the pantry."

Shala closed her eyes, fighting the need to scream. "You do realize, when the mayor gets back in town he's going to chew you up and down for this."

"Yup, I know that," he said.

"And he's going to make you hand over my camera."

"That I don't know." He gestured again to the pantry. "I'm cooking the omelet. You could do the toast."

She stood there staring at him, trying to decide whether she should (a) go bat-shit crazy on him, (b) storm out of his house, or (c) try to talk some sense into him. Maybe because she could smell the eggs and her stomach was tired of sucking on her backbone, she chose (c). And maybe it was because in spite of how insane it felt, she had accepted the truth: she'd been a little wrong. When she took her camera into the powwow, she'd broken a rule. She just had to get him to make this situation an exception . . . and perhaps convince him that the rule needed to be axed altogether.

Wasn't that part of her job, to make the town more tourism friendly? Befriending the town's chief of police would help. But to do the job she'd been sent to do, she needed her camera. Surely he could see that—or he would once they both calmed down and she got him to see reason.

Finding a loaf, she popped bread into the toaster. The aroma made her mouth water, and her stomach rumbled. She looked at Sky, hoping he hadn't heard. He grinned, damn it.

"You like cheese, ham, and mushrooms, right?"

"Yes."

He pulled out a cutting board and started cutting. The man knew his way around the kitchen. She'd never known a man who could or would admit to being so domesticated, especially one so outwardly masculine. Maybe that's why he could do it. It sure wasn't hurting his macho image.

She studied the way his muscles moved beneath his shirt as he chopped, then shifted her gaze to his straight black hair resting above his collar. "Did you cut your hair, or was that a wig you were wearing?"

"It's part of the headdress," he answered. "The plates are in the cabinet." He pointed with his knife.

She opened the cabinet door and stared at the row of plates. Top shelf. She had to push up on tiptoes to reach them.

"Here. Let me." He stepped behind her. "I didn't realize you were so short."

"I'm not short." Feeling him against her, she stared into the cabinet.

"Okay, petite. It wasn't meant to be an insult." His words brushed the back of her right ear, hot breath against the tender skin. He didn't reach for the plates.

"I'm five foot three. That's not petite," she said, almost afraid to move. With him behind her, several inches over six feet, she did feel petite . . . and feminine.

"Am I picking up on a Napoleon complex?" He chuckled.

"No." *Okay, maybe a little,* she admitted to herself. She'd always longed for a few more inches of height.

Fighting the sensations caused by their proximity, she considered which way to step to avoid physical contact. Then his chest moved against her shoulder as he reached for the plates. The warmth of his body invaded her space. She held her breath, and his nice clean scent tickled her nose and made her wish she'd had the chance to shower. Not that her deodorant was failing, but standing this close made her want to be . . . fresh.

That's when the absurdity of this entire freaking situation smacked her right in the face. She'd come to retrieve her camera, not to have the man cook her dinner and for them to play house. What was she doing?

Redfoot reached the door. The lock had been broken. He pushed inside the lodge and moved as quietly as he could through the darkness. The scent of rosemary filled his nose. Maria, who did the accounting for the tribal council, constantly burned scented candles at her desk. He could see a flashlight moving across the floor in the next room.

Was this some wayward teen? Maybe one of his own tribe. In the bad economy, people got desperate. Desperation drove people to do bad things, and so Redfoot's gaze shot to the safe beside the desk. A safe in plain sight. A safe that appeared untouched. What was the thief looking for, if not money?

Pulling his carving knife from his pocket, Redfoot took another step. A loose piece of pine flooring creaked. Shifting, he bumped a wooden chair. He caught it, but books on the seat tumbled to the floor. The orb of light in the next room shut off. The thief had heard.

Redfoot's hold on his weapon tightened. He hoped the intruder was one of his people, someone he could convince to walk away, nothing taken, no harm done. But standing straight, prepared to defend himself, he felt every one of his sixty-six years.

The intruder shot toward him. Redfoot raised his knife and stared. The man wore a ski mask. His large body did not seem familiar, but for some odd reason Redfoot remembered his dream of a bulldog. The man shifted, and Redfoot noticed pale skin where the intruder's collar met his mask. This wasn't one of his people.

The man's hand rose, and Redfoot realized his mistake: never bring a knife to a gunfight. He remembered his dream and all the blood. What he hadn't realized last night was that the blood spilled would include his own.

CHAPTER SIX

What the hell am I doing? The question bounced around Shala's head. Sky's proximity as he reached for the plates had every one of her nerve endings standing on its head, kicking its feet in glee, and singing "God Bless America." She could smell him. She could feel him. Oh, mercy, could she feel him!

His chest brushed her shoulders, his knee pressed against her thigh. His pelvis fit against her backside. Finally, he had the plates in his hand. He lowered the dishes for her to take and then stepped away.

Shala drew in a mouthful of mind-cleansing oxygen. *What the hell am I doing?* The question ricocheted back at her. The oxygen must have worked, because somehow she answered. *My job.* That's what she was doing. And right then she decided to stop acting like a schoolgirl around a star quarterback and more like Shala Winters, owner of Winters Tourism. Owner and entrepreneur who, in spite of insinuating that she might walk out, needed this job almost as much as Precious needed her.

The bad economy meant small towns were looking to tourism to keep them afloat. Unfortunately, the bad economy also meant fewer towns had money to throw around. And plain and simple, she didn't come cheap. Not that she wasn't worth it. As Mr. Gomez implied, she had a good résumé.

Another gulp of oxygen, and she decided she could do this. She was smart, a good communicator, and she excelled at negotiating. Standing a little taller, she set the plates on the oak table.

"Silverware?" she asked, looking back at Sky to catch him studying her. She completely ignored his hooded gaze. Yup, best to ignore that.

"Top drawer."

He focused on the stove again. She focused, too. Hopefully, over dinner she could establish a reasonably pleasant, purely platonic relationship with him—one that led to his returning her camera. Yes, that was a damn good plan.

Aware of the silence, and remembering something he'd said earlier, she pulled utensils from the drawer. "Were you actually in favor of my coming to Precious?"

"Yes," he replied.

"Really?"

His right eyebrow arched, as if he didn't like to be questioned.

"It's not as if I don't believe you. I just know Mayor Johnson said most of the Native Americans were against my coming."

"I'm not most of the Native Americans."

"Right." She smiled but wasn't sure it came off well, because he didn't react. Her nerve endings started to twitch again, so she turned around and went to work collecting the toast. "I appreciate dinner. I'm starved."

"You should taste it first," he said.

"It smells wonderful. Do you want butter? For the toast?" She glanced back and tried to smile again.

He nodded. "It's in the fridge."

She retrieved the butter—real butter, not margarine—and set it on the table. The silence grew awkward, and she realized it was easier being angry with him than playing nice. But damn it, she could and would do this.

"Should I get us something to drink?" She put a hint of cheeriness in her tone.

"There's milk." He leaned against the counter and continued to study her. "Glasses are in the cabinet over the toaster."

She got the milk, poured it, and set the glasses on the table. Uncomfortable with his perusal, she looked around. "You have a nice place. Did you decorate it yourself?"

"You're not getting your camera back tonight." He picked up the frying pan and delivered half an omelet to one plate and half to the other. Putting the pan in the sink, he faced her.

"You think I'm just being pleasant to get my camera back?"

"Not only do I think it, I'd stake my right eye on it." He dropped into a chair and motioned for her to do the same. "Not that I'm complaining, but I wanted to be up-front."

"Perfect."

Maria Ortega read the last line of the last page, sighed, and closed her book. She smiled and set it on the bedside table beside the six others waiting to be devoured, then fell back on her pillow. Her day job of running a small accounting business often gave her plenty of reading time. Other than creating pottery, books were her favorite pastime.

Okay, so she might be slightly addicted to romance novels. Yet considering her heritage and past, there were worse things to be addicted to. A lot worse. And it wasn't as if she honestly believed in happily-ever-afters; life had already disproven those. She placed a hand over her navel, where she had once carried a child. Jose's child.

Don't go there. She pressed a hand to her forehead.

Letting go of things she couldn't change, she sat up and reached for another novel, thumbed through the pages. No, life wasn't perfect. Not that she expected it to be. But was it too much to ask for it to be pleasant? Was it too much to ask that she find someone who wanted the same things in life as she did—a home, someone to lean on when the not-so-perfect times came crashing down? Maria remembered Redfoot and his wife Estella before her brain aneurism. They'd been happy, their love good. Maria hoped she and Matt could find the same kind of happiness.

Thinking about Matt, she eyed the clock. Matt sold tools to engineering companies, and his job required lots of travel. But . . . on the weekends? *No!* she told herself. She had to trust him, didn't she? Yes. But it was late. He'd said he would call. Had he gotten busy with his client? Did he miss her?

Did *she* miss *him*? She closed her eyes and saw his green-eyed smile. She missed him. She knew Redfoot didn't like Matt, but her foster father wouldn't like any man she brought home. Which was too bad. Redfoot was going to have to accept Matt. The relationship was going places.

Her cell phone rang. Rolling over, she snatched it up. "If you were here, I'd have you naked so fast you wouldn't know what happened."

The answering chuckle made her feel fuzzy inside. "What if it hadn't been me?"

"Oh, is this Matt?" she teased.

They chatted about silly things, like what Matt had eaten for dinner, and then she told him about Shala Winters and how Sky had confiscated her camera.

"Does Redfoot still think she's Sky's soul mate?" Matt asked.

"I think so," she replied.

"Does he ever have dreams of us being soul mates?"

Matt paused. "Wait, don't answer that. He probably has visions of scalping me."

"Matt!"

"I know, bad joke. Sorry. I just don't know what he has against me."

Maria knew: Matt wasn't Jose. Redfoot had been so sure that she and his son would come together. And they had, only it hadn't meant anything to Jose. Maria also knew that sooner or later she needed to tell Matt everything. He had a right to know, but . . . not now. She could only hope it wouldn't change things between them.

The front door opened and then slammed. A loud thud followed, as if someone hit the wall; then the light in the hallway went out.

"Hold on a second," she told Matt. "Something doesn't sound right."

"*Viejo?*" she called to Redfoot. When he didn't answer, she got up to go see.

CHAPTER SEVEN

Sky watched Shala drop down in a chair.

"You know, I thought we could talk about this in a reasonable manner. Obviously I was wrong."

He took a bite of omelet and studied her. The spark of anger in her eyes was back. Much better. Not that he liked angry women, but her play-nice routine had been as believable as a sock-stuffed bra on a bearded crossdresser. And knowing that he could rile her so easily was thrilling. He wondered if she was as easy to rile in the bedroom.

"Your omelet is getting cold," he pointed out.

She pushed her plate away. "I'm suddenly not hungry."

"That's a shame. I make a mean omelet."

"Look, Mr. Gomez. I'm in town to do a job. I can't do that job without my camera."

"I can see how that might be difficult."

"It wouldn't be if you'd just . . ." She closed her eyes. "If you'd just accept my sincerest apology for overlooking the rule."

He picked up his toast. "I can't do that."

Her eyes popped open. "You mean you *won't* do that."

He considered. "You're right. I won't do that."

Her mouth tightened. "You are impossible. It can't be legal to just steal someone's camera!"

"I didn't steal it. I confiscated it, just as the rules stated I would." His cell phone, still on the coffee table, rang. Sky decided to just let it go to voice mail. Fighting with Shala was fun. "Seriously, you should eat before it gets cold. Nothing's worse than cold eggs."

His home phone rang. He debated answering, but the woman with fury in her eyes tempted him more. The answering machine picked up and played his outgoing message. Then a frightened voice spilled out.

"Sky, answer, damn it! It's Maria. Redfoot's hurt. Bad! Oh, God, there's so much blood."

Sky shot out of the chair so fast that it slammed backward onto the floor. He ran across the room and grabbed the phone.

"Maria? What happened?"

"Someone broke into the lodge. Redfoot caught them."

"Christ! Have you called an ambulance?"

"He won't let me. He said to call you. He keeps muttering about having to tell you something."

"How bad is it?" Terror constricted Sky's chest.

"I don't know. He's conscious, but . . . there's so much blood."

"I'm on my way. I'll call the ambulance." He dropped the phone and ran across the living room, snatching up his keys and cell phone and dialing 911.

"Precious Emergency. Ms. Winters, is this you again? I'm—"

"Martha, get an ambulance over to Redfoot's. He's been hurt. Get it there now!" He flipped the cell phone closed before his secretary had a chance to ask him any questions, then started out the door. "Damn!" he swerved around as he remembered the silent woman at the kitchen table. "I've got to go."

She nodded, eyes wide. "I understand. I hope he's okay." She stood up as if to leave."

"I have to go," he said again. "I . . . I'll call you." His gaze shot to the food on the kitchen table. "Feel free to finish eating."

Shala stood in the same spot until she heard Sky's truck start and the sound of his tires slinging dirt outside. She noticed the omelet. Her stomach grumbled, but her mind shot to the old man she'd just met, and she tried to imagine him hurt and bleeding. She also remembered getting a call very similar to Sky's from her grandmother's neighbor. Nana had fallen. Before Shala got to the hospital, her grandmother had died.

Shala's chest clutched, and she hoped Sky's emergency ended better than her own. Then she wondered who Redfoot was to him. Was he family?

Picking up the two plates, she emptied the food into the garbage and put the dishes in the sink. She didn't feel comfortable enough to clean much more, but at least he wouldn't come home to a dirty table.

Putting the butter back in the fridge, she emptied the milk from their glasses and rinsed them out. Then she went to the living room.

Shouldering her purse, she got halfway to the door before she remembered why she'd come. To get her camera.

* * *

Sky slammed his truck into park and jumped out before the vehicle came to a full stop. As he made his way to the front door of the home he'd lived in since he was twelve years old, the memory of his arrival hit hard.

He'd been full of anger and resentment back then, certain Redfoot and Estella would grow tired of him like the two foster homes before. They hadn't, even when Sky made their lives hard. Estella hadn't given up on him because she was too kind, and Redfoot had hung in there because . . . well, he'd said he was too stubborn to let a twelve-year-old boy win a battle of wills. In so many ways, Redfoot had been right. It *had* been a battle. Not so much because Sky hadn't wanted them to love him, but because he hadn't thought they could.

"Maria?" He heard voices coming from the kitchen and took off almost at a run. Logically, he knew Redfoot couldn't live forever, but he hadn't come to a place where he could let the old man go. *Not yet,* he prayed, *and especially not at the hands of some murderer.* Rage filled him.

"In here," Maria called.

Redfoot sat at the kitchen table. Maria sat in front of him, her hands gently separating the old man's hair. He pushed her hands away. "I am fine. Leave me be."

Sky's gaze shot to the blood-soaked towel in Maria's hands. "You're not fine," he said. Then, to Maria, "An ambulance is on its way."

"I'm not getting carted off in some noisy van like a cripple!"

"Yes, you are. I don't care if I have to handcuff your ass."

"Stubborn ol' Indian," Maria muttered.

"I do not need an ambulance." Redfoot waved Maria's hands away. When a new stream of blood flowed down his forehead, she pressed the cloth back to his brow.

"How bad is it?" Sky asked.

"Not as bad as I thought," Maria admitted. "But he needs stitches and to be checked for a concussion." She gazed down at her foster father with tenderness and concern.

"I am not a child to be coddled!" Redfoot's gaze shifted to Sky. "We have bigger problems than the scratch on my head. This person who broke in, he—"

"What's important is that you're okay." Sky moved closer, but his gut clenched as he thought about the work he and the others had put into the powwow and their plans for the money in the lodge safe. No doubt that was what the intruder had come for—and had probably taken. But did he want to rub salt in the old man's wounds by discussing it?

"I need to get dressed," Maria said.

Sky noticed her nightgown for the first time, and thought of the woman he'd left at his house.

"Watch him," Maria commanded. "I'm going to change before the paramedics show up." She handed her towel to Redfoot. "Keep that on that cut to slow the bleeding," she said, then tenderly touched his cheek.

As Maria walked out, Sky sat down in her chair. "Do you feel up to telling me what happened?" he asked. The money didn't matter, but catching this creep did.

"I was walking and saw a light through the window of the lodge."

"Why didn't you call me?" Sky asked.

"By the time you got here, they could have robbed us blind."

"It's just money. Your life is worth more than that."

Redfoot pulled the towel from his head. "The intruder was not there for money. This is about Blue Eyes."

Sky flinched when he saw a stream of blood flow down the old man's face. "What about her? Why don't you lie down?"

"I'm fine. I told you of my dream of the mad bulldog? For some reason, I think this man is that dog."

Redfoot had gone on and on about the dream that afternoon. It hadn't made sense then, and it still didn't.

"Why do you think this has anything to do with her?" Sky took the towel and pressed it to Redfoot's head.

"Because the thief wasn't there for money. All he wanted was Blue Eyes's camera."

"Her camera?" An ambulance siren sounded in the distance.

"He asked me where we keep the cameras we take. I pointed to the cabinet. We still have two small ones that people never came back for, but he opened the cabinet and got mad. He said he wanted the one from today."

Sky tried to wrap his mind around all this. Had Shala gotten someone to steal her camera for her while she distracted him? The thought rolled around his brain but he didn't believe it. She'd come to him looking for the camera, and she hadn't known he was chief of police. Sky supposed someone had seen her with it and, knowing its value, had simply wanted to steal it from the lodge.

"Did he take anything?" he asked Redfoot.

"Nothing."

"The money?" Sky pressed.

"The safe was in front of him. He was big enough he could have carried it out with him. He didn't. I'm telling you, he came for her camera. That's all he wanted."

"I guess it's good that the camera wasn't here," he said, almost to himself.

"I know." Redfoot swayed a little in his chair. "You need to listen, Sky. Your woman, she needs you. This man is after her."

Why would anyone be after Shala Winters? Because of her work bringing tourism to Precious? He recalled the troublemakers in town trying to stop the Chamber of Commerce from hiring her.

"Did you get a good look? Recognize him?"

The sirens seemed to stop in front of the house.

"He wore a ski mask. Big guy. Light eyes. Don't think he's from around here."

The doorbell rang. Sky got up to answer.

"I'm not getting in that noisy . . ."

Redfoot's words faltered, and Sky looked back. His foster father had stood up. "Sit down!" he ordered, but too late. Redfoot stumbled. Sky managed to catch him before he hit the floor, and said, "I got you," but when he laid the old man down, he realized Redfoot was unconscious.

Maria came running into the room. "What's wrong?"

"He passed out," Sky replied.

"Dios!" Maria said, and Sky saw her tears.

"Open the door," he ordered. "The paramedics are here."

When Maria ran off, Sky looked back at Redfoot. The man had been more than just a foster father; he'd been the only real father Sky ever knew. His chest swelled with emotion, and for the first time ever he wondered if he'd actually told the man thank you. Had he ever said the words *I love you*? Probably not.

"Redfoot, don't you dare die on me."

CHAPTER EIGHT

Shala felt the moral heaviness in her chest expand, but this wasn't wrong. It was her camera, damn it!

In the kitch   nd pantry, she found all sorts of cooking appliances   in spite of searching every nook and cranny, she did   find her Nikon. She did, however, learn the man had a fixation on Lucky Charms cereal. Three boxes made it a fixation. Considering her cabinet at home held two—she'd just finished one—she couldn't judge.

With the kitchen deemed Nikon-free, she searched the television armoire in the living room. In there, she discovered Sky's DVDs. She expected to find a few porn flicks, but nope, adventure movies, mostly. Amazingly, she'd seen all but two.

By the time she got to the computer room, she'd made up her mind to only take the memory card if she found her camera. She should have asked him for that in the first place. She would have, too, if she hadn't been so distracted. This way, she could still download the images and get some work done. She'd even eventually pay the fine to get her camera back, though, come hell or a freaking huge tsunami, she would not shine his shoes. None of this meant she felt Sky had any right to keep her camera, but she didn't feel right searching his house for it while he was gone.

Closing her eyes, she sent up a small prayer that Redfoot would be okay. She remembered how he had called her Blue Eyes, and she liked the idea that he'd given her a nickname. Her granddad had called her Pumpkin. Her dad, when he was alive, had called her Princess. Something about being called by a nickname made her feel special. She vaguely remembered asking her ex if he had a nickname for her. He'd laughed and said, "Yes—my fuck bunny." And she hadn't even been his only fuck bunny!

Pushing the past into a mental Dumpster, she poked around the computer room. Lots of drawers and file cabinets, lots of places to hide a camera, but they held only documents and old files. She didn't take the time to check each out; her goal wasn't to snoop. However, shutting the desk, she accidently jarred the computer awake. She heard it yawn, spit, and come alive. The screen lit up with a picture of her. Well, not just a picture of her, but her web page. He hadn't been lying about visiting her site. He'd definitely done his own checking out, so maybe she shouldn't feel as bad about searching his place.

The Internet isn't the same as rummaging through his home.

She ignored the nagging guilt and bounced out of the chair. As she turned to leave the room, she spotted framed photos on a shelf: pictures of Sky with a family. Shala looked closer, and she realized the man in the picture was Redfoot. Was he Sky's father? Again her heart clutched with hope that everything turned out okay.

Shala next found herself standing in the door of the master suite. She could smell him here. The scent of sleepy male skin filled her nose, and light from the hall sprayed inside. Her gaze caught on an unmade king-size bed with dark tan sheets and a darker, mussed comforter. For just a second, she allowed herself to imagine Sky in the bed. Her imagination took it one step further and she saw herself in that bed with him.

Oh, hell! What in freaking frack was wrong with her? Had being humped by that dog turned her into a divorcée on the make? Shaking off her desire, she stepped into the room. "If I was a camera where would I be?" But her gaze stayed on the bed. The low lighting created an intimate setting.

Did Sky bring a lot of women home? *I'm not prone to telling beautiful women they can't stay in my house . . . or in my bed.* That's what he'd said. Of course Sky brought a lot of women home.

"If I were a camera, I wouldn't be in that bed." She hit the light switch, hoping to chase away her lascivious thoughts. Like the rest of the house, the room's decor stood out—not like an interior decorator had spent time pulling it together, but the owner was a person of good taste.

Forcing herself to get it over with, she went to the pine chest of drawers and opened the top. It contained underwear, socks rolled into balls, and a box of condoms. The second drawer held folded shirts and shorts—neat, but not to the point of obsession. None of the other compartments held her camera, either.

She next attacked the dresser. There she found some

sweats and another box of condoms. Okay, the man liked sex. She'd already figured that out, thank you very much. Slamming the drawer, she stood straight and faced herself in the dresser mirror. "It's my *camera* I'm looking for. And I just want the memory card."

Shaking off her sense of guilt, she headed to the bathroom. All sorts of dirty little secrets lurked in a man's bathroom. Standing inside it, she glanced around. He clearly had someone who came out and cleaned his house. Men didn't keep house this well.

She checked below his sink. Only cleaning supplies. No condoms. What, he didn't keep them in every room?

Opening the medicine cabinet, she stared at a row of over-the-counter meds. Aha! Finally. She knew the man couldn't be perfect. There, between the Advil and peroxide, rested a tube of athlete's foot cream. Then she looked at the john and found his second flaw. The seat lid was up. Arrest the guy right now. She knew he couldn't be perfect.

That's when it hit her, and hit her hard. She hadn't been looking for her camera in here. Damn! Damn! Damn!

She stormed out of the bathroom, ready to storm out of his house and out of his life, eager to outrun the crazy feeling that her emotional insurance was about to be tested. She almost got out of the bedroom before she spotted the closet door.

"If I were a camera, *that's* where I'd be."

She pulled open the door. Clothes hung in neat rows, more jeans and casual shirts than dress clothes, but the three pairs of Dockers, dress shirts, and two blazers said Sky Gomez wasn't afraid to get dressed up. On several of the hangers hung plastic covers, as if he used a dry cleaner regularly. Then her gaze hit a box tucked in back. It seemed unlikely that he would have hidden her camera there, but then again, who knew?

She found the light switch and got on her hands and knees to retrieve the box. Pulling it away from the wall, she removed its top. Her breath caught as her eyes lit on a metal object inside. Not her camera, a gun. An old gun, resting on some old photographs. Why the weapon surprised her, she didn't know. Sky Gomez was the chief of police.

She started to close the lid when one of the photographs caught her attention. Reaching in, she pulled out the faded image of a family of three: mother, father, and young son. Sky? She studied the boy's face. Yes, Sky. The boy still had a baby face. Probably no more than four, he clutched the hand of his mother. The father, whom Sky mostly favored, stood a foot apart. There seemed to be some meaning to the distance. Shala studied the father, who looked part Hispanic and part white. The mother must have been where Sky got his Native American heritage.

Reaching back into the box, she pulled out the next image. This one was of just Sky, older, maybe seven, posing beside a new bike. A Christmas tree stood behind him. Shala stared at the young boy's eyes and saw happiness in his expression. He'd really liked that bike. She recalled that the year before her parents died, she'd gotten an Easy-Bake Oven. Somewhere at her house she had a picture much like this, a smiling girl thinking everything in the world was perfect because she'd gotten what she wanted for Christmas.

Her next foray found not a photograph, but a clipping from a newspaper. The image was of a firefighter, arms tight around a struggling child. The boy had dark straight hair and the saddest eyes she'd ever seen. Sky's eyes. Shala read the article beneath the photo.

Desperate young boy attempts to save parents from fire. Paramedics had to restrain the ten-year-old to keep him from running into the flames. Unfortunately, the recovered bodies of both father and mother showed that the cause of death was not by fire but gunshots. Police suspect a murder-suicide.

Shala's breath caught, and a knot crawled up her throat. She stared at the gun, then again at the image of Sky. How did a child get past something like that? He didn't, she realized. To this day she remembered being pulled from the car, still remembered walking behind that curtain to see doctors and nurses trying to bring her parents back to life.

Dropping the photographs and newspaper article back into the box, she shut the lid and scooted as fast as her backside would go out of the closet. She stood up and hugged herself, wishing she hadn't gone in there. Eager to leave Sky's bedroom, eager to leave his house, super eager to shake the feeling that she'd done something really wrong, she forced herself into high gear. She shot down the hall, grabbed her bag from the sofa, and headed for the door. Her hand gripped the knob just as she heard the dogs' insistent barking from outside.

Great. All she needed to do was get mauled or humped again. Then she heard the sound of a car engine. Light beams sliced though kitchen windows, and the engine cut off. Was Sky already back? Guilt flashed through her. Should she confess what she'd done? Apologize?

She hurried to the window to see if it was Sky's truck. Nope. It wasn't even a truck, but a dark sedan. A dark sedan just like the one she'd seen following her earlier. Okeydokey. Panic fluttered inside her.

A man got out of the car, reached back in, and pulled out something else. An article of clothing? A ski mask. He pulled it over his face. And since Shala felt certain Mayor Johnson would have mentioned a ski resort if one existed in Precious, and since the heat index of a hundred precluded any snow in the forecast, her flutters of panic changed from butterflies to bats.

The man started toward the porch. The dogs started some serious growling. Shala's stomach stopped fluttering and all the wings seemed to bolt up her throat.

* * *

Sky pulled into the ER parking lot five minutes after the ambulance. Fear of losing Redfoot had been sitting shotgun as he drove the six miles to the hospital.

He'd stayed behind at the house to call Jose, then run by the lodge. When he found the lock on the door broken, he'd called Pete, one of the state troopers who assisted him, to come and park by the lodge to make sure whoever had shown up wasn't coming back to finish the job.

As Sky made his way to the hospital entrance, he thought about Jose. He didn't judge his foster brother's need to leave Precious. Small-town life wasn't for everyone. And that was without even factoring in the reservation. As one of the elders' sons, Jose was expected to follow in his father's footsteps. Only problem was, Jose wanted an entirely different path. An architect, he wanted the glitz and glamour of the big city.

In the last two years, Sky's foster brother had come home twice, both short visits. But at least he'd come back. In addition, he'd sent plane tickets to Redfoot to visit him on three different occasions. Redfoot had packed a bag and gone to New York to visit his son, but Sky saw the hurt in the old man's eyes every time Jose's name came up. Redfoot wanted his son home. Of course, Redfoot wanted a lot of things for other people's lives. As much as Sky loved his foster father, he knew the old man's expectations were often too much.

Walking into the hospital, Sky spotted Maria sitting in the corner looking extra worried. She shot up and across the room, wrapped her arms around his waist, and pillowed her head on his chest. The woman was a hugger, something Sky had to continually work at accepting.

"How is he?" Sky feared the tight embrace meant bad news.

Maria pulled back. "The doctors haven't announced anything yet. The paramedics said he has a concussion. He came to on the way here. I thought they were going to have to strap him down when he realized he was in an ambulance." Her brown eyes welled up with tears. "I tried to go back with him in the ER, but they wouldn't let me. I'm scared. I love that old man so much."

Sky pulled her in for another hug. Not for him, but for her, though he'd be damned if he didn't find some comfort in it. He closed his eyes and let himself hope that everything was going to be okay. Then he stared at the door toward the back, wanting to storm through it but knowing he'd only be in the way. "We have to believe he's going to be fine."

He released Maria, but she held on for a second longer. Like him, Maria had known hard times. Unlike him, the experience had made her needy.

"Did you call Jose?" she asked.

He nodded.

"And?"

"He's booking a flight. Supposed to call and let me know when he has a time. Someone may have to pick him up at the airport tomorrow."

"Can't he just rent a car?" Maria asked.

Sky saw the emotion in her eyes. "He didn't mention renting a car, but don't worry, I'll pick him up." He moved Maria back to her chair.

Of all the flaws of his foster brother, this one stuck in Sky's craw. Maria had been in love with the boy a week after she arrived to live under Redfoot's roof. Jose, nineteen to Maria's sixteen, hadn't given Maria the time of day. He'd gone off to the university the next year, coming back on summers and holidays. While Maria remained crazy about him, he'd treated her like a sister, though Maria never missed the opportunity to point out that they weren't blood related. Jose remained aloof, parading his college girlfriends home to meet the family, almost as if to discourage her. When Sky asked Jose about it, his foster brother got his nose all bent out of shape, protesting a little too much, in Sky's opinion. And then the summer before Jose moved to New York, Sky noticed looks passing between Maria and Jose. He had no proof, but he'd wager that the baby Maria lost had belonged to Jose.

His foster brother didn't know how damn lucky he was that New York wasn't a few hours away. There had been a night or two Sky might just have driven to Jose's uppity high-rise apartment and beaten the holy shit out of him. Not just for Maria, but for Redfoot. Sky figured that if he suspected the truth about Maria's child, so did the old man. The only thing that kept Sky from removing a couple of the boy's lower body parts was that he didn't think Maria had ever told Jose about the baby. She had avoided ever seeing Jose on his visits back to Precious.

"Sky?"

Sky turned to see Ms. Gibson, a nurse and a friend of his secretary, walking out of the back. "How is he?" he and Maria asked at the same time.

"Doctor just got to him. But he keeps fading in and out of consciousness."

"Oh, *Dios*."

Maria reached out and clutched Sky's arm. Sky didn't blame her. He didn't care for the nurse's tone, either.

CHAPTER NINE

Air caught in Shala's throat. She hated jumping to conclusions, but for the life of her, she couldn't think of one damn good reason anyone would be wearing a ski mask when just a few hours ago you could smoke a roast on the pavement. Okay, she could think of *one* reason, but she didn't like it one iota! The reason being, the man didn't want anyone to recognize him because he was about to do something bad. Something illegal.

The dogs' growls grew louder. She could hear footsteps moving up the walkway and slapped a hand over her mouth to stop a scream from spilling out. Her gaze cut to the door, which was unlocked. Dropping on her hands and knees, she crawled forward and turned the latch. The sound seemed to clatter through the silence, and she prayed the stranger hadn't heard.

"Oh, shit," she muttered under her breath. Breathing wasn't coming easy. "Think," she added. She remembered her cell was in her bag. Her bag was on the chair in the living room. But if she ran now, he might see her through the window. For some reason, staying hidden felt safer. Of course, if he decided to break a window or kick the door down, her little hiding place wouldn't be so safe.

The dogs' growls intensified. Shala's gaze shot to the purse in the living room, which held her phone and her Mace. She remembered Sky's phone on the counter beside the pantry. That was closer. Every instinct in her five-foot-three frame screamed for her to run to Sky's phone and call 911, to insist once again that this was a Precious emergency.

Footsteps thudded onto the porch.

Along with a couple other people, Sky and Maria sat in the ER lobby and stared at the TV. It had only been ten minutes, but it seemed longer. Sky studied the door leading into the back and fought the urge to storm back there. He could tell Maria felt the same way.

"If they're going to put a TV in a waiting room, why don't they give us a remote control to change the channels?" his foster sister fumed.

Sky eyed the screen—the *Tonight Show* played—then Maria's worried face. "Isn't that the senator who they say is going to announce his candidacy for the next presidency?" he asked, hoping conversation would help ease the wait.

"Yeah, I think so," Maria replied. "But I don't like the looks of him."

Sky glanced back at the screen. "I've read some good things," he offered, not caring particularly but glad for the distraction. When he wasn't thinking about Redfoot, he was thinking about the woman he'd left at his place.

"I've heard 'good things' about Hitler, too," Maria said. "He's got one of those faces. Reminds me of the guys my mom used to date. All talk, no substance." Maria glanced back at the ER door. Sky reached over and squeezed her hand.

"I agree," offered the woman sitting across room. "He has one of those faces. I could swear I saw that same weaselly face on a man pumping gas today."

Maria offered the woman a smile, and then said to Sky, "What's taking them so long? Maybe we should go check."

Right then, the door into the back swung open and Dr. Henry Michaels walked through. Sky and Jose had gone to high school with him, and Sky liked knowing Henry was looking after Redfoot.

Both he and Maria jumped up, and Maria clutched Sky's arm.

"Relax." The doctor seemed to read their faces. "He's fine for now."

Maria let go of Sky's arm, and Sky had to remind himself to breathe. They sat.

"I'm not going to lie to you. It could still be serious," Henry amended. "His blood pressure's low. We know he has a concussion. I'm going to get some CT scans to make sure there's no bleeding in his brain. Whoever hit him wasn't playing around. It could have killed him."

Sky felt his own blood pressure rise.

"Redfoot's no spring chicken." Henry hesitated, then offered them a smile. "Then again, I thought he was going to kick my ass when I told him that."

"Stubborn ol' coot," Maria snapped.

Sky grinned. "I think he did that once, didn't he?"

Henry laughed. "You mean the time he caught Jose and me getting into his whiskey? He didn't lay a hand on me, but I don't think I've ever been so scared." The doctor paused. "Anyway, once we have the results from the scan, I'll know more." He stood. "Oh, he's asking for you, Sky. He won't let the nurse undress him, and he says he's not getting the test done until he sees you."

"What about me?" Maria asked.

Henry offered her a sympathetic gaze. "He said just Sky."

The sound of the dogs' snarling seeped through the door.

"Motherfucker!" a deep voice rumbled. "You bite my ass, I'll kill you, too!"

Too?

A large popping noise sounded. Shala jumped. Oh, God, had the man shot one of Sky's dogs? It could have been a car backfiring, she told herself. She forced herself to shift ever so slightly, to look out the window. The man, dressed all in black with his matching ski mask, stood staring at Sky's two dogs, and in his hand was a . . . Well, it sure as hell wasn't a backfiring car. But both dogs were still snarling.

The larger beast glanced in the window at her. Shala slammed back against the wall and heard her heart thump in her ears. In all her twenty-eight years, she'd never danced once with the grim reaper. To whom, she wondered, did she owe the pleasure of this dance? The mayor's warning rang in her ears: *Some people in town, especially the Natives, don't want us turning to tourism. So don't be surprised if you run into some . . . unfriendly folks.* Did trying to kill you fall under the "unfriendly" umbrella? Her knees gave way and she slid down the wall like a scoop of flung ice cream.

The growls grew closer as the dogs got between the door and the man. Was this really happening because she was trying to bring a little tourist economy to Precious?

Was that really worth killing someone over? Was it worth dying over? No! It didn't matter that she needed the money. She'd eat beans and rice for the next six months if she lived through this. She would renege on her contract. She'd send it and the fat little check back to the mayor wrapped up pretty in a pink bow. If she lived through this.

If!

Redfoot lifted his head off the narrow hospital bed as Sky walked into the room.

"Let's get your clothes changed," Sky said. "Then you're going to let the doctors do their tests. You got that?"

Redfoot leaned on one elbow. "Come closer." The old man dropped something in Sky's hands. "Take this stuff home."

Sky stared at the bottle of pills. "What's this?"

"Medicine I had on me. Just put it away," Redfoot insisted. "Take it to my place. Don't want it mixed up with what they give me here."

"They may want a list of medications." Sky turned the bottle over in his hands.

"Put that damn medicine away and help me change my clothes! The nurses keep coming for me."

Sky saw the seriousness in the old man's eyes, so he stuffed the pills in his jeans pockets and then helped Redfoot sit up and remove his shirt. A few minutes later, Sky was tying the back of Redfoot's gown. His foster father reached over and squeezed Sky's arm. "Now, go find Blue Eyes. I saw her again when they were bringing me here. She's in trouble. Your woman needs you."

Shala refused to die.

She needed a weapon. She thought of the gun she'd seen in Sky's closet, but was it loaded? Remembering the knife Sky had left in the sink, she crawled to the kitchen counter. Behind her, she heard someone trying to open the door.

She rose to her knees and reached into the sink. Something heavy hit the front door, like a big shoulder or foot. Panicking, she felt her hand close around what felt like a knife, and the blade sliced into her palm. Well, it passed the slice-through-human-skin test. Ignoring the pain, she pulled it toward her.

"God damn!"

Screams came from the porch, along with a loud thud like something heavy falling. Something heavy, as in a big man wearing a ski mask. Feeling brave—or maybe just stupid—Shala stood and ran to the window. The intruder lay on his back, kicking violently at Sky's dogs. Finally, he rolled. The dogs moved after him, growling, their lips curled and their teeth bared. Shala saw what looked like the gun lying behind them. The man rolled off the porch. One of the dogs followed. The man scrambled to his feet and took off back to his car. Shala stood frozen, holding her breath, the knife still gripped in her hand. The car fishtailed off the curb and sped away down the dirt road.

Collapsing against the wall, Shala kept her eyes on the porch, where the second dog joined the first. Both beasts turned around. Two pairs of eyes met hers, two pairs of bright gold eyes. Shala had never come face-to-face with a wolf, but she'd seen enough pictures to recognize one. These animals on Sky Gomez's front porch were more wolf than dog. They'd saved her life, but she wasn't eager to confront them. Not after seeing them in action.

A question derailed those thoughts: how had this hardened criminal learned where she was? He hadn't followed her here tonight; she'd been looking out for him. She remembered Sky Gomez's sudden supposed emergency that had left her here alone. Sure, he'd said he was on the pro-Winters side, but hadn't Mayor Johnson claimed most of the Natives were against her? If he was on her side, why was he taking her camera?

Something wet and warm oozed down her palm. Blood spattered the wood floor.

Sky bit back the retort that Blue Eyes wasn't his woman. Arguing with the old man now would be futile. Then they took Redfoot away, and it was almost an hour before Henry came back and informed Sky that his scan was clear. But to be safe, they were keeping Redfoot overnight.

"He's sleeping now," Henry explained to both Sky and Maria. "But there's a cot in his room if someone wants to stay with him."

"Since you're picking up Jose, I'll stay here," Maria offered. Jose had called right after Redfoot was carted off to be tested. He'd be flying in at nine A.M.

While his foster sister stepped off to call her boyfriend, Sky peeked in on Redfoot. The old man was asleep. Sky eased toward the bed, remembering his thoughts when the old man had passed out in his arms.

"Love you," he whispered.

He was a step out the door when he heard, "Me, too. Now find Blue Eyes."

Shaking his head, Sky started out to his truck. Emotion filled his chest, but when he climbed into his cab, he leaned his head back and relaxed for the first time since he'd received the call.

Now find Blue Eyes.

He remembered leaving Shala at his place. Remembered wanting to kiss her. Remembered wanting to do more than kiss her. Then his mind hit instant replay, and he recalled something she asked: *Did you check? Did you even look at the shots?*

He'd been damn sure at first that she was the one to take the picture, but he hadn't seen her take the shot. Then, three minutes after she insisted on her innocence, he'd believed her. Reaching down to the floorboard of the passenger seat, Sky lifted Shala's camera. It took him a few minutes to figure out how to see the images. He didn't find any shots of the powwow. It felt good to be right.

Not that this made her entirely innocent. She'd still broken a rule. Of course, looking at the expensive Nikon, he could almost understand why. Especially since someone had broken into the lodge to steal it.

Maybe he should bend the rule for her. *Maybe.* He'd see if she played nice tomorrow—real nice, not the fake approach she'd tried before he left. Yeah, he'd make his decision tomorrow when he saw her.

Anticipation stirred in his chest. But would he have time to see her? Between investigating an attempted robbery, picking up Jose, and checking in on Redfoot, could he fit her in?

I'm not leaving. I'm staying here until you hand over my camera.

He hoped she hadn't been lying. A vision flashed through his mind, of finding her naked in his bed, warm, willing. It was a very nice vision. His body reacted, but shouldering back in his seat he gave his libido the soul-crushing news that it wasn't happening. If by some far-fetched chance she was still at his place, she'd probably be sleeping on his sofa—if she was sleeping and not waiting for him with murder and her camera on her mind. He headed home to see.

He hadn't gotten down the block before his cell phone rang. "Hello," he answered, his head and heart already back on Redfoot.

"Sky, it's me."

Sky recognized his friend Sal's voice, the owner of the one and only hotel in Precious. It should have put him at ease, but it was after midnight. Since Sal had married Jessie, late-night calls weren't his thing.

"What's up, Sal?"

"There's trouble. That Winters chick stormed into the

office and woke me up squawking about how someone broke into her hotel room. I checked, and they really did a job on it."

"Damn it!"

"She said she found her room like that, but she was bleeding pretty bad and I'm not sure if she's telling me everything. Maybe she caught whoever was breaking in."

"How bad is she hurt?" Sky couldn't help but remember Redfoot's warning.

"I don't know. She wouldn't let me touch her. I think it's just her hand, but she left a trail of blood in and out of my office. I gave her another room."

"I'm on my way."

"Uhh . . ." Sal sounded nervous. "I'm not sure that's a good idea."

"Why not?" Sky asked.

"Because when I said I was calling the police, she went wonky on me and said if you showed up without her camera, your ass was hers. She said all she wanted was a different hotel room and her freaking camera back by morning. As she left she said that Precious could 'freaking figure out how to bring tourists here on its own.' And while she did say 'freaking,' she looked mad enough to eat her young."

It hit Sky that whoever had gone after Shala was the same asshole who'd broken into the lodge and hurt Redfoot. He made a quick turn toward the hotel, glancing at the camera on the seat next to him. The thing was expensive, but was it worth this much effort? He didn't think so.

Sal continued. "I'm guessing her camera was stolen in the break-in . . . ? Not that she was making sense, but she muttered something about being trapped by a pack of wolves and 'I'm not finding Precious so precious.'"

Wolves? Redfoot's vision? Damn, he didn't believe in all that shit. Unless . . . His dogs. Had Shala had a run-in with Butch and Sundance?

"I gave her the key to a different room, and she shot out

of here like a chicken with its feathers on fire and a stick of dynamite up its butt. I hope like hell the mayor hasn't given her a check yet, 'cause I'm thinking, when she's out of Precious, she's not coming back."

Sky didn't want to think about her leaving. He looked at her camera. Suddenly, handing it over to her didn't seem like a good idea.

"I'm on my way," he said. "Just do me a favor and keep an eye on her room. Make sure no one gets to her."

"Shit, man. You think someone is *after* her? I mean, I was thinking this was just a random break-in. Kids or something. Hey, maybe it's someone who signed the petition. Or even Charlie, the guy who's heading the whole campaign. He showed up here six times trying to convince me to sign the damn thing. He's got a temper on him, too."

Sky snapped, "Just watch her, okay? I'll be there in ten minutes." He had a sudden thought. "Sal, do you think she's hurt bad enough to need an ambulance?"

"Ambulance? No. But with that much blood, I'd be surprised if she doesn't need stitches. I offered once to take her to the hospital, but the look she gave me . . . Well, I didn't offer again."

When he reached the hotel, Sky circled until he spotted Sal leaning against a light post. He grabbed Shala's camera and his Glock from the glove compartment, and parked.

"Which room is she in?"

"Thirteen." Sal motioned a couple doors down and studied the camera in Sky's hands. "Is that hers?"

"It's hers. I'll explain later, but for now do me a favor and put this in your safe." He passed Sal the Nikon, tucked his gun into the the back of his pants, and pulled his shirt out to cover it.

"Wait," Sal said, as if he'd just figured something out. "This is the camera you confiscated tonight, isn't it? I didn't see who you snagged it from."

"Yeah." Sky walked toward Shala's hotel room. Sal followed.

"But why did someone break into—?"

"Maybe they thought we gave it back to her. I don't know." Sky needed a couple of hours to mentally go through everything.

"No wonder she went wonky when I mentioned you." Sal chuckled and elbowed him. "You know this isn't any way to treat your future wife and mother of your kids."

Sky scowled. Damn it, he'd known that sooner or later that whole soul-mate thing would leak out. If Sal's wife had the word, the whole friggin' town would be talking about it by noon tomorrow. "I'm armed," Sky muttered. "Don't piss me off."

Sal's grin widened. "Okay, pretend I didn't say anything. I just thought you should know what's blowin' in wind."

"So Jessie knows, huh? Where'd she get her information?"

Sal shrugged. "She and Maria had lunch yesterday. But don't blame my woman. Gossiping is her only sin."

Sky shook his head. Damn it, Maria knew better. Sure, she and Jessie were friends, had been since high school, but one word spoken to Jessie and even the Pope in the Vatican would know it in less than an hour.

"But just for the record," Sal added, "you could do worse. She's *hot*. Then again, after seeing her all worked up . . . she might be a handful."

When Sky stopped at the door to Shala's room, Sal said, "Let me know if you need anything." Then he stepped a few feet away and waited.

The first thing Sky noticed was the bloody handprint on the outside of the door. His gut clenched as he envisioned Shala bleeding, and he hoped like hell she was okay. Leaning forward, he knocked. "Shala? It's Sky. Can you open the door?" When he didn't hear anything, he knocked again. "Shala?"

"Do you have my camera?" came the reply from the other side.

Sky looked back at Sal, who moved her camera behind his back. "No, I don't have your camera. But I need to talk to you."

"I'll talk to you tomorrow when you give me my camera. It's late. I'm tired and I'm already dressed for bed."

Sky leaned his head against the door. "Shala, there's blood out here and Sal, the hotel manager, said you were bleeding. Please open the door so I can check on you."

"I'm fine!" came her sharp reply.

"You're not fine. Open the door."

"Okay, let me put it this way. I don't trust you. I don't know who is behind this . . . this attempt to get me to leave Precious, but it's working. I'm leaving tomorrow. But I swear to God, you are going to give me my camera back or I'll get a lawyer and bring the wrath of God down on you."

Sky closed his eyes in frustration, then walked over to Sal.

"And here I thought you could talk your way into any woman's hotel room," his friend joked.

Sky wasn't laughing. "Get me the key."

"Really?" Sal asked.

"Just do it!"

Sal headed for the office, and Sky edged back toward Shala's door. "Listen to me, lady. I'm the chief of police. It's my job to make sure you're okay. I'm not 'behind' anything. Let me in so that I find out what happened." When she didn't answer, he frowned. "Shala, you were at my place tonight. If I was behind this, wouldn't I have done something then?"

"Yeah, but it happened at your place. Who else knew I was there?"

"What happened at my place?" he asked, confused but desperate to make sure she was okay. "Shala, seriously, I need you to open the door."

"He didn't follow me to your place, because I was look-ing. So someone had to have told him I was there."

Sky ground his teeth. "Who didn't follow you?" He put a few of the pieces together, but . . . "If you think just be-cause something happened at my place that I'm behind it, you're wrong. And let me remind you, you told half the town that you were looking for me." When he didn't hear anything, he added, "Come on. Open the door. Do you really think I'm behind this?"

Sal's footsteps sounded at the same time Sky heard Shala releasing the lock. He thrust out his hand to keep Sal away.

CHAPTER TEN

The door inched open. Shala's eyes were puffy and wet. She'd been crying. Damn, if that didn't send tremors right to Sky's gut.

"Can I come in?" he asked, respecting the fact that while her suspicions made as much sense as fat-free but-ter, to her they made sense.

She hesitated, then eased back. Sky stepped into the room and shut the door.

She wore boxer-bottom sleepwear with pink hearts and a matching tank top. They weren't indecent or overtly sexy, but they made his knees weak. The cotton material fit her curves to a T, and the thigh-length boxers gave him his first peek at her shapely legs. Then he spotted the bloodstain on her shirt and, rightfully so, his libido was sent packing. She had a washcloth wrapped around her right palm.

"Can I see your hand?" he asked.

"It's fine," she replied.

"Please let me look at your hand."

She extended her arm, and he carefully removed the washcloth. He saw a two-inch slice across her palm.

"How did this happen?"

"A knife," she said. His gut went hard again.

"Someone came at you with a knife?"

"No. I cut it going for a knife to protect myself."

"To protect yourself from who?"

"Well, darn." Some sassiness returned to her tone. "I didn't introduce myself, and neither did he. But it obviously has to be someone who doesn't want me working for Precious."

Sky would deal with that accusation later. Meeting her eyes, he brushed his thumb over the back of her injured hand. "Are you hurt anywhere else?"

"No."

Okay. He believed her. "What happened?"

"A guy with a ski mask and gun tried to break into your place."

A ski mask. So it was definitely the same guy who'd attacked Redfoot. But what exactly did that mean?

He looked back at her hand and pulled carefully at the cut to see how deep it went. The deep gash oozed blood. Frowning, Sky wrapped the washcloth back around her hand and commanded, "Get dressed. I'll take you for stitches. You can tell me everything on the way to the hospital."

She pulled her hand back. "It's not that bad."

"It needs stitches."

"I don't think so. It's a straight cut. It will heal."

"It's on your *hand*. Every time you move, that cut will open up." He looked around and spotted her jeans on the back of a chair. Picking them up, he handed them to her. She tossed them on the bed.

"I don't think I need stitches."

He let go of a deep breath. "Shala, change your clothes. I'm taking you to get your hand sewn up. This is not a debate."

"But—"

"Fine. You want to go in your pajamas." He put his hand on her back and nudged her toward the door. "They actually look rather nice."

She put on the brakes, digging her heels into the tan carpet. Sky's gaze flew to her feet, which were bare, petite, feminine. Her toenails were painted a soft pink and the big ones had daisies. "You have pretty feet." He wasn't sure why he said it, but he did.

She looked down at her toes. After a pause she asked, "Do you really think it needs—?"

"Yes." He ran a finger along her chin and raised her gaze back to his. "You need stitches."

She sighed. "But it's so late, and I'm so tired and hungry, and all I want to do is go to sleep." She paused. "I'm sounding pretty pathetic, aren't I?"

He chuckled. "Terribly so." Food sounded damn good. And a bed—not necessarily to sleep. Inhaling, he got a whiff of clean woman, kept his two fingers under her chin, and grinned. "Don't make me toss you over my shoulder and drag you in."

"You'd do that?" A hint of tease touched her tone.

He winked. "I'd probably enjoy it." He sure as hell enjoyed touching her right now. Deep down he knew he should be thinking about getting information about the attack and not about how soft she felt. He should be mentally trying to solve this mystery, not measuring how his hand would fit the curve of her waist. He should be pondering why all this went down, not wondering how she would taste if he slipped his tongue inside her mouth. And Heaven knew he shouldn't be thinking about those sexy naked feet running up his bare leg.

She rolled her eyes and she gave the tiniest of smiles.

"Well, we certainly wouldn't want you to enjoy anything, now, would we? Let me change clothes."

He gave her cheek one more brush with his index finger, then pushed a couple wispy strands of hair behind her ear. Maybe because she was tired or scared, he didn't know which, she'd let her guard slip. He wasn't above taking advantage of it just a little. Something told him it wasn't going to be easy to get this close again. He stared at her mouth and considered . . .

That would be pushing it. Wouldn't it?

Maria eased open the door to Redfoot's hospital room, careful not to wake him up. She still couldn't reach Matt. When she'd first found her foster father, in a state of panic she'd told Matt she would call him back, but now his phone kept going to voice mail.

"He's still not answering your calls, is he?" Redfoot asked.

His tone implied more, but Maria refused to let the old man make her start doubting. Matt cared about her. She believed that. Okay, she'd admit his frequent business trips often left her wondering, but she trusted him.

She moved to the edge of Redfoot's bed. "You should be asleep."

"I would be if I was home. I've slept on rocks more comfortable than this bed. Tell you what: you go see if you can find out where that nurse hid my underwear, and you and I—"

"You're staying, *viejo.*"

"Come tomorrow, woman, I'm going home. I don't care if I have to walk out of here and cross the town square with my bare ass winking at the entire Precious community."

Maria grinned. "And risk sending what little population we have left for the hills?"

"My ass won't run anyone out of town. It might convince a couple to stay."

Maria chuckled and rested her palm on his hand, which was gripping the bed rail. "Get some sleep." She leaned down and kissed his forehead.

"He's not good for you, daughter."

Maria hesitated. "He makes me happy."

"Is that happiness making that wrinkle in your forehead?"

Maria sighed. "I'm just worried because I can't reach him."

Redfoot sighed. "I know what you worry about. And I believe your worries have merit. You should listen to your heart."

"My heart says you should be sleeping," she said.

"You and Sky both fight this devil, but in different ways. Sky runs from things because of his past. You run *to* things."

She sighed. Was Redfoot right? Did she rush into things? Was she pushing the relationship with Matt? As much as she wanted to deny it, his words hit home. Hadn't she run too fast to Jose? She sure as hell had jumped in his bed the first time she saw him look at her differently.

For some reason, she'd assumed sleeping with him would change things. It hadn't. When the job offer from New York came, he'd jumped on it like a hungry kid on ice cream. The day she realized she'd missed her period and went to tell him her concerns, she'd found him packing his bags. He'd said he intended to tell her before he left, but tell her what—good-bye?

She gazed at Redfoot. "Okay, wise one, tell me: what do your dreams say I should do?"

He reached up and touched her cheek. "I have had no dreams of you. It is—"

"Ah, but you've had visions of Sky," she teased, hoping to escape the subject of Matt. "I always knew you loved him more."

Redfoot frowned. "I have no control over my dreams.

It is with my heart that I know you are on the wrong path."

"And is your heart as reliable as your dreams?"

"No," he admitted. "But *your* heart should be. Listen to it."

"Go to sleep now." She moved to the cot and sat down. Her cell phone was still in her hand.

What was her heart saying about Matt? She closed her eyes and remembered him walking her past the jewelry-store window. *Which one would you pick for yourself?* he'd asked her. She could still remember how solid he'd felt standing behind her, solid like someone she could always lean on or count on, someone unlike her own parents. But was he? Or was she just rushing into things again, feeling things she wanted to feel?

Was reading romance novels filling her head with silly dreams, blinding her to the truth and maybe Matt's flaws? If she'd had her eyes open with Jose, she wouldn't have made the mistakes she'd made. Maybe it was time to take a new look at Matt.

"Change your clothes, Blue Eyes."

Shala blinked those sky-colored orbs at him, which were full of concern. She reached for the jeans on the bed. "I'm so sorry. With everything that happened I forgot to ask, how is Redfoot?"

"He has a concussion but is going to be okay. They're keeping him overnight at the hospital. Maybe we can peek in on him while we're there."

"How did he hurt himself? Did he fall or something?"

That reminded Sky of his need for answers. "I'll explain on the way." He motioned her to the bathroom. "Go."

When she emerged a few minutes later, Sky realized how right he'd been about her guard being down only temporarily. One look showed her emotional barriers had been reerected. He had his own, so hers shouldn't have bothered him. But they did.

She glanced at the door, then him. "It just occurred to me how silly this is. There's no earthly reason why you should have to take me. It's late. I can drive."

"Your hand is cut," he pointed out.

"I drove back from your place. I can make it to the hospital. Seriously, I'm fine by myself. I can—"

"Shala," he interrupted.

"There's no reason why . . ."

She didn't stop talking as he snagged her purse, pushed her out the door and all the way to his truck. Half of what she said didn't even make sense. Jabbering was either naturally part of her personality, or she was extra tired or nervous. He hoped it was the latter. Sky would walk uphill naked and barefoot through the snow and a bed of porcupine needles to avoid a jabbering woman.

As he crawled behind the wheel, she lapsed into silence. He glanced over and saw she had tears in her eyes. Real tears. Those beautiful baby blues of hers were glassy and sad.

He leaned over and put his arm against the back of the seat. "You okay?"

She shook her head, blinked, bit her lip as if fighting a battle over tears, and then nodded yes. He didn't like tears, but he could handle those a hell of a lot better than jabbering.

It hit him then. The woman had been attacked tonight. If jabbering made her feel better, he could endure it. He'd be an asshole not to. "Can you talk about it?"

She shook her head again. "No."

She'd gone from jabbering to silence, and he needed her to talk. "I have to know what happened tonight. You're going to have to tell me."

"Oh." She blinked a few more times. "I can talk about *that*."

What? If tonight's events weren't what had her in tears, what the hell had? He almost asked but stopped himself. "So, what happened?"

She pulled her purse into her lap. "The dogs started barking. I heard a car pull up. When I looked out the window, I saw that black sedan that's been following me."

He recalled her mentioning the sedan and realized he should have asked about it. But he'd followed her most of the day and hadn't noticed anyone. "When did you first see it?"

"When I left the railroad museum."

That had been after Sky left to get ready for the pow-wow.

"And again when I was driving to the Funky Chicken."

He had to tell her she probably shouldn't go there. It was a rough place. "What time was it when the car showed up tonight?"

She bit down on her lip, and her brow crinkled. "After you left."

He sighed. "I know it was after I left. How much after?"

"I don't know exactly."

Why was he suddenly getting the feeling she was fudging the truth? "How soon after I left did you leave?"

Something close to guilt flashed in her eyes, and just like that, he figured things out. "You went looking for your camera, didn't you?"

She nodded. "I was just going to take the memory card!"

Sky started his truck and pointed it toward the hospital for the second time that night, not sure how he felt about her searching his place. But he needed to get the facts about the attack. He'd chew on the other details later.

After several blocks of listening to the sound of the wheels against the pavement and watching her squirm, he asked, "So was it maybe an hour after I left?"

"Around that," she agreed.

"After you heard the car pull up, what happened?"

She went through her story while he drove. Sky's heart raced, realizing how close she and Redfoot might have come to dying. But why? Apparently, someone wanted Shala's camera. But again, why? It wouldn't bring *that* much money at a pawnshop. Could it be someone wanted to stop her from doing her job? Yes. But Redfoot hadn't recognized the man. Granted, Redfoot didn't know everyone in town. And why, then, would the guy be set on getting Shala's Nikon?

When she paused, he asked, "Do you know of anyone who might have a vendetta against you?"

She snorted. "Half of Precious, from what Mayor Johnson said."

"No, I mean someone personal," Sky explained.

"No."

"What about a boyfriend?"

"No."

He smiled. "No, you don't have one, or no you don't think he'd try to take your camera?"

"No to both."

Something akin to relief stirred in his chest.

A new thought occurred to him, though it was kind of crazy. Could Shala have taken a picture of something or someone, and that was why someone wanted the camera? It didn't seem likely. Precious wasn't without crime, but in the three years he'd been chief, he'd had one accidental shooting, a dozen break-ins, and his all-time least favorite, a rash of domestic-violence cases. Ninety percent of his workload involved dealing with DUIs or fights at the Funky Chicken.

"So, back to tonight," he said, realizing he'd lapsed into silence. "What happened after you heard that gunshot?" She must have been terrified.

"At first I felt paralyzed, but then I got mad."

He chuckled. "Gunshots do that to me, too."

"That's when I went for the knife," she said. Tension thickened her voice, and she gripped her hands together. The white washcloth wrapped around her palm turned red.

It could have been a lot worse, Sky reminded himself. If his dogs hadn't taken a disliking to the intruder, the woman beside him could have . . . He made a promise to himself that he'd catch the asshole and make him pay.

Knowing he needed to keep his emotions in check to do his job, he focused on the case and not his need for revenge. Shala continued. "He must have dropped the gun on the porch when the dogs attacked him. He couldn't get to it, so he ran to his car. And then—"

"Wait!" He pulled into the hospital parking lot and hit the brakes. "He left the gun on my porch?"

"Your dogs—or I should say wolves—chased him away."

"Only *part* wolves," he muttered, and asked his question again. "Are you saying—?"

"Aren't they dangerous?"

Sky frowned. "When you left, was the gun still on the porch?" He pulled his cell phone out to call Lucas. It was after midnight, but before he'd gotten sober the man had hauled Sky's butt out of bed numerous times to drive his drunken ass home from the Funky Chicken. Paybacks were hell.

"No, I put it on top of the refrigerator. I was afraid the dogs might somehow shoot themselves."

"That's good." Although he hoped like hell she hadn't messed up any prints. Also, he worried the perp might go back looking for it.

Dialing Lucas's number, he explained briefly to his neighbor about his needs, the attempted break-in, and the gun, and he told Lucas to watch his back. Not that Sky worried too much about the man. "Call me once you get there."

He hung up the phone, parked, and cut the truck engine. Half-turning to Shala, he asked, "You ready?"

Her gaze shifted toward the hospital, her blue eyes rounded with fear.

"Have you never had stitches before?"

Her frightened gaze flipped back to him. "Of course I have." Her face paled, making her blue eyes even bluer.

"They numb you before they stitch." Funny, after all she'd endured tonight, this was the most fear he'd seen from her.

"I know that." But she didn't move to get out.

"Let's get this over with. Come on." He reached over her to open her door. Unintentionally brushing his chest against hers was a thrill. Pushing the door open, he leaned back and tried not to enjoy it too much. "Let's go."

She got down and took baby steps around his truck. When she finally met up with him on the other side, she looked up with huge, doelike eyes. Given the right situation, those eyes could bring a man to his knees.

Staring at her hand, she said, "I'm just not sure I need stitches. Honestly, if we bought some of those butterfly bandages, I'll bet—"

Sky chuckled, put his hand on her back and nudged Shala forward. "I'll give you a bullet to bite on. Seriously, it doesn't hurt that much."

She didn't move. "I'm not afraid of stitches."

"Right." This time he latched his arm around her shoulders before pushing forward. "For real, I'll hold your hand. And you can squeeze it as tight as you want. I promise not to call you a scaredy-cat. *Meow*," he teased.

She came to sudden stop. Her tennis shoes scraped against the pavement. "I—I don't like hospitals," she admitted.

"Because they give stitches?" He chuckled. "Or is it the needles?"

"It's not because—"

"Come on, I'll make sure you get a sucker when you're done." He forced her onward.

"I don't like hospitals, because when I was eight, I watched my parents die in one."

Her voice was tight, from anger or angst he didn't

know. Sky's footsteps faltered, his chest grew heavy, and he felt like an insensitive jerk. The look on her face was one of alienation and pain. He'd known those feelings since the day his father killed his mother and then turned the gun on himself. Life had changed when he went to live with Estella and Redfoot, but the loneliness never completely went away.

He tightened his arm around her shoulders. "I'm sorry. I thought—"

"I know what you thought." She moved out of his reach and walked through the hospital doors.

CHAPTER ELEVEN

Jose Darkwater blinked, forced his eyes open, and wished he'd grabbed another cup of coffee at the service station a few miles back.

After he'd gotten off the phone with Sky, he'd called the airline back and learned they had a late flight going to Houston. He could fly there, rent a car, and drive into Precious. What Jose had forgotten was that he'd been pulling a week of late nights at the office, and driving while exhausted was inadvisable for one's health. When he spotted the Precious sign proclaiming the population to be 893, he almost pulled over to close his eyes.

Eight ninety-three? He'd bet it was less. They probably hadn't counted the two or three deaths of the old-timers he'd been informed of by his father. Jose just hoped like hell the number didn't drop again. With his ass-backward ways and beliefs, Redfoot drove Jose crazy, but in every way it counted, Jose could never have had a better father. Problem was, he wasn't sure Redfoot was similarly proud of him.

No doubt about it, he'd disappointed his ol' man. To remedy that, he'd have to change everything he wanted in life and become a carbon copy of Sky. And while he respected his foster brother, he also knew he could never become him. In fact, he resented the hell out of him—resented the relationship Sky had found with his father. At the same time, he was thrilled Redfoot had someone close by. If not for Sky and Maria, he would never have been able to leave. Being stuck living in Precious was about as pleasant as stepping in a bed of fire ants.

Jose looked at his speedometer. Seventy. He glanced at his watch. He'd made good time. But at almost one in the morning, he wondered if he should go straight to the hospital or to his dad's place to get some sleep. He'd called the hospital after landing, and a nurse had said his dad seemed okay. Maybe a nap and a shower were the better option.

His thoughts shot to Maria. She'd avoided him on his last several visits, so he hadn't seen her in two years. That hurt, but he'd also been relieved. Jose's mind created a snapshot of Maria. As always, thinking about her brought a mix of lust, love, and something akin to shame. God knew she wasn't blood, so being attracted to her wasn't a cardinal sin, but his mother hadn't seen it that way. And the very last conversation he'd had with his mother had been about Maria.

No doubt his mom had noticed the way he and Maria looked at each other. *She's family, son. And you're older than her. Promise me that you won't do something to cause a ruckus.*

Jose had promised, never realizing it would be the last promise he'd ever make to her. And he'd kept that promise to his mother until two years ago when, somehow, he'd convinced himself that they were older now and all bets were off. But they weren't. And it sure as hell had caused a ruckus.

He'd gotten the call about the job in New York only a month after throwing caution to the wind with Maria, and the day she found him packing and he'd told her about it had made two things crystal clear. The first was that he loved Maria, loved everything about her: her smile, her positive outlook, her sweet nature—and damn him if he didn't love her hot little body. But loving Maria was like stepping in concrete, tying him to Precious the rest of his life. To Maria, the town was home.

He suspected she would have come to New York if he'd insisted, but she would have hated it for all the reasons he loved it. So Jose had done the right thing. Well, it had *felt* like the right thing. After two years of comparing every woman he dated to Maria and having them all fall miserably short, he sometimes wondered if he'd been wrong.

A loud popping filled the darkness—a front tire, possibly. His car swerved. Fishtailed. He jerked the steering wheel to the right and he thought he had it under control, but when he looked up, all he saw was a tree coming right at him. He slammed on his brakes.

Too late. He prepared himself for the impact.

Shala, heart pounding, walked to the front of the emergency room.

The semitransparent glass window opened. "Can I help you?" a middle-aged woman asked.

It took Shala a second to be able to talk. "Yes, I . . . I need a doctor."

The woman's brow wrinkled. "Are you hurt? Sick?"

Shala didn't appear in any distress, which meant she had missed an opportunity in life: she should have been an actress. Because frankly, she was a millimeter from a full-fledged, fall-to-the-floor, cry-your-eyes-out panic attack. She raised her hand, pulled off the bloody washcloth, and held out her palm. Several steady drips of red oozed onto the counter.

The woman shot backward in her seat as if she'd never seen blood. "Oh, my! You walk around back and we'll get that taken care of."

Shala felt someone beside her. Sky. She didn't say a word but moved toward the door.

He dogged her footsteps, so she turned around. He looked serious and apologetic. A lump the size of a small frog took up residence in her throat, but she managed to say, "I can handle it from here. Thank you."

"But I—"

"I'm fine." She pushed away through the door.

The desk clerk stood at the end of the hall, putting on rubber gloves as if afraid she might get blood on her just by showing a patient to the examining room. Shala walked toward her, listening to see if Sky had followed. He hadn't. Relief whispered through her. She wasn't angry with him. She really wasn't. Unfortunately, with an emotional storm threatening to engulf her sanity, she didn't have the capability to deal with him. Not when she had to deal with the past.

Oh, God, the smell. That antiseptic scent, with a hint of Lysol—it threatened to take her back. She drew in a deep gulp of air that suddenly felt thicker. Forcing herself to keep moving, to put one foot in front of the other, she kept her gaze on the woman's face. Just her face. Because if she dared look around, Shala knew what she'd find. The details would be same. This small-town emergency room would look just like the one she'd found herself in at eight years old.

"Right this way," the receptionist said.

Shala followed the woman into a curtained-off space just like the one she'd been in at eight, alone. Just like the one her dying parents had occupied a few curtains down.

"I'm going to get our insurance person to take your information here. We wouldn't want to get her office bloody."

Shala nodded.

The woman motioned toward the bed. "The nurse and Kelly from insurance will be right in." She looked at Shala's hand. "That's a nasty cut. What happened?"

"A knife."

"Cooking?"

"Sort of," Shala answered, not wanting to explain.

"Okay, deary. We'll have you fixed up lickety-split." She walked off, her footsteps tapping against the tile floor, and left Shala alone. Alone. Just like before.

Shala stared at the bed and tried not to see the curtain. Tried not to remember getting off the bed and moving two sections down, pulling the curtain back. Tried not to remember seeing her mama's and daddy's bloody bodies lurching off the tables as doctors filled them with electricity. Shala's heart thumped against her chest bone. Feeling the fuzziness of panic, she had one of those good old-fashioned come-to-Jesus talks with herself, the kind Nana had been famous for dishing out whenever necessary. Damn, but she missed Nana. Blinking, she swallowed the lump in her throat and continued talking herself down.

She told herself it had happened a long time ago. That it was time she moved past everything. Get over it! Yeah, her parents had died, and yeah, she'd seen something an eight-year-old shouldn't, but she wasn't eight anymore. Breathing in through her nose and out through her mouth, she moved to the bed, sat down, and stared at the bloody cloth around her palm.

Footsteps sounded. They stopped at her curtain. Looking up, she expected the nurse. Sky Gomez stood there, arms crossed, posture hard. He stared sternly down at her as if daring her to tell him to go.

The hospital cot was about as comfortable as camping out. Maria hated camping out.

After an hour of tossing and turning, she fell into a semisleep. The sound of the hospital door swishing open pulled her back. The nurses came in and out, though, checking on Redfoot, their footsteps soft and their voices feminine. She didn't have to acknowledge them, she told herself. The sweet darkness of sleep lured her back. But as she rolled toward the wall and almost drifted back into slumber, something tickled her awareness.

A hand brushed over her shoulder. A warm comforting hand. "Maria?" A masculine voice whispered in her ear. "I came back. I had to make sure you were okay."

He'd come back? An image of Jose filled her sleep-hazed mind. He'd left her. Hurt her. She'd lost his baby and maybe her ability to ever have a child. Now he wanted to know if she was okay? Wasn't it too late for that?

"You awake?"

The soft baritone and the comforting touch weren't Jose's, she realized. Rolling over, she threw her arms around Matt.

He smelled the way he always did. His soap always left a hint of something like rosemary and the earthier scent of fresh-cut hay. She pressed her face into his shoulder. For the first time that night, she felt everything would be okay. It felt so good when he held her. Like home felt after you'd been away too long. Then she recalled having thought he was Jose, and guilt flashed through her.

She sat up. Matt sat beside her and put his arm around her shoulders. "You're okay," he whispered. "Thank God, you're okay."

She brushed hair from her face. "I tried to call you."

"I'm sorry. You scared the shit out of me when you hung up without explaining what was happening. I got in my car and left right away. I was an hour out of Dallas before I realized I'd left my phone. I pulled over at the pay phone and tried to call you, but you didn't answer."

"I didn't know that was you. I didn't take the call."

He brushed a hand over her cheek. "I was so worried. All you told me was that the lights went out. And then right before you hung up, you screamed something about someone breaking in. I didn't know what the hell was happening."

"I'm fine. Someone broke into the lodge. Redfoot caught the intruder in the act and was hurt. He made it back to the house, but he fell against the wall and hit the light switch. I panicked. I'm sorry I didn't explain better . . ."

She leaned against him and was enjoying every moment until she remembered the talk she'd had with Redfoot. Hadn't she warned herself to stop feeling so much and start thinking? Maybe even ask some questions about Matt's business trips to Dallas?

But he was here. He'd driven all the way home just to make sure she was okay. That meant something, didn't it?

"How is the old coot?" Matt asked.

"The old coot is fine!" Redfoot called gruffly from his bed, and Maria had to put a hand over her mouth to stop from giggling. "Which is why you, Maria, should go home, now."

"Sorry. Did we wake you?" Maria went and stood by the bed.

"Actually, the squeaking of that cot keeps waking me up. I know you want to stay for me, but if you'd go home I'd be better off."

Maria frowned. "But—"

"Don't 'but' me! Go home."

Maria sighed. "Let me check with the nurses, and if they think you're fine I'll consider it." Looking back at Matt, she motioned for him to follow her out.

"No," Redfoot said. "He stays behind so I can have a word with him."

Matt's eyes widened.

Maria shook her head. "Now isn't the time, Redfoot."

"Feels right to me."

Matt stood up and winked. "It's fine, Maria. You go talk to the nurses, and I'll be out in a minute."

Maria admired Matt's courage. Redfoot had a way of

instilling fear in people. She just hoped Matt knew Redfoot's bark was always worse than his bite. Of course, the
people who got bit never stuck around to compare.

Then again, if she and Matt were really going to make
it, Matt would have to learn to deal with Redfoot. Difficult and stubborn though he was, her foster father was
family. And family was sacred.

The lump in Shala's throat returned, but she would not
cry.

"I apologized," he said, and stepped into the room.

"I know." The stinging in her sinuses increased. After a
few deep breaths, she added, "I'm not mad."

"Good." He slipped into the room.

For some crazy reason, she got the impression he didn't
apologize often. Maybe he didn't have to. She recalled
rummaging through his house, assessing him as perfect.
Well, *near* perfect, with the exception of having athlete's
foot. Her gaze slid to his feet, and that's when she remembered what else she'd found—that newspaper clipping. She continued to stare at Sky's feet while a wash of
empathy cascaded through her.

At last she felt brave enough to glance up, and the emotions in his eyes seemed to mirror her own. Her gaze
shifted to his chest, which looked ideal to lean against.
She imagined him wrapping his arms around her, offering comfort as she did the same in return. Realizing she
stared, she shot her gaze back to his feet.

"Something wrong with my shoes?" he asked.

"Nope. Just safer to look at." Oh, hell. Had she really
said that out loud?

"Safer?"

His cell phone rang. From the ensuing conversation,
she assumed it was the man Sky had asked to go to his
place and retrieve the gun. "Great," he said into the phone.
"I'll pick it up in the morning. Thanks."

He hung up and eyed Shala without speaking. After a

moment, the silence felt intimate. Luckily, a woman came in to get her insurance information.

Instead of talking to Shala, though, her attention found Sky. "How's your foster dad doing?" Foster father? Even feeling half out of it, Shala was able to file away that information.

When the woman asked for Shala's insurance card, Sky pointed to her injured hand and then her purse, lifting an eyebrow. She nodded. While she answered questions, she noticed Sky flipping through her wallet, looking for her insurance card, but paying particular attention to the pictures. Oddly, she didn't mind, yet it felt odd having him peek into her personal world. Then, as she recalled her search of the man's home tonight, turnabout seemed fair play.

The insurance woman left and the doctor walked in. "Sky? I thought that was you. You like hanging around here, or what?"

Sky introduced Shala to Dr. Henry Michaels. The doctor smiled at her. "I think Redfoot mentioned you."

"He did?" Shala asked.

"Yeah." Sky shot the doctor an odd look. "He got hit pretty hard on the head. Was talking a lot of nonsense."

"Nonsense about me?" It seemed better to concentrate on this conversation than on her tragic history with hospitals.

"About everything." Sky continued to stare at the doctor.

The doctor, still smiling, reached for her hand. "I just went to check on him. He's sleeping, and his blood pressure is normal. I think he's going to be fine. Should go home tomorrow." The doctor gently removed the washcloth from Shala's wound. "Ouch," he said.

After cleaning the gash and making sure none of the ligaments were cut, he had the nurse bring in the needle and sutures. Amazingly, that's when Shala realized she'd managed to get through being in a hospital without falling apart. Of course, her final experience had been worsened by the news that Nana was dead. That hadn't been a good night. Shala had been alone.

Unlike tonight, she realized. Her gaze went to Sky. Had his presence helped? He turned his head, his dark eyes meeting hers.

"I'm going to deaden it first," the doctor announced. "It might hurt for a few minutes. You ready?"

Shala lay back on the bed, held out her hand, and closed her eyes. She felt the first stick of a needle, and pain shot up her arm. She tried not to flinch, then she felt a masculine palm slip into her other hand and squeeze. She almost pulled away, but Sky's hand felt so warm, so comforting, that she decided that for just this little bit, she'd allow it. Just for this little bit.

CHAPTER TWELVE

Redfoot watched the white boy edge up to his hospital bed. He hit the button to raise his mattress and turned on the light. Redfoot had seen himself earlier when he'd taken a piss, so he knew how he looked. One eye was bloodred; both eyes had shiners.

The boy's green eyes widened in surprise. "Wow, you must have taken quite a hit," he said.

"Yeah, but I'm tough," Redfoot replied. The white boy needed to know someone was watching out for Maria, someone who would whup his ass if he hurt that dark-eyed little angel. Sky would do it and so would Jose if he asked either of them, but Redfoot planned to take care of it on his own.

"Maria is special," he said.

The white boy smiled and a donned a goofy, lovesick expression. "I know that."

"Too special for you." Redfoot glared at him. "It's best if you move on down the road, if you know what I mean. 'Cause nothing is worse than pissing off an Indian daddy."

Matt actually took a step back. *Good*, Redfoot thought. "That's all I have to say." He pressed the button to level out his mattress.

"But it's not all *I* have to say, sir." Matt moved to the bedside. "I care about your daughter. I'm glad we're having this talk, because I'm thinking—"

"I don't give a dog's chapped ass what you're thinking about. Maria is—"

"Maria is special. And I care about her," Matt insisted.

Redfoot didn't like it, but he respected the boy's courage. Not that respect made him right for Maria. Jose was Maria's soul mate.

"I'm not perfect," Matt said. "But—"

"Maria deserves someone perfect. Not some guy who'd rather spend his time doing God only knows what in Dallas every few weekends! And from the guilt flashing in your eyes right now, I would say that God doesn't want to know what you've been up to in Dallas!"

"Sir, it's—"

Maria walked back through the door. Her gaze shot to Redfoot, then Matt, then back to Redfoot. "We can go," she said.

Redfoot knew Maria didn't like the fact that he'd had a talk with her young man, but Maria hadn't liked it when he wouldn't let her stay out past midnight at seventeen. She hadn't liked it when he'd forbidden her to wear those itsy-bitsy bathing suits the guys always liked. Point was, sometimes fathers had to do things that didn't make their daughters happy.

* * *

Jose pushed the air bag out of his face and sat there for a good five minutes assessing every twinge and pain he felt. He could taste blood, but he was pretty sure it was dripping into his mouth from where he'd hit his head.

Reaching up, relieved he could move without agony, he felt his scalp. From what he could feel, the cut was small, the goose egg not so much. But he hadn't passed out. He didn't feel dizzy. Probably no concussion. He moved all his limbs, and nothing felt broken.

"Damn lucky," he muttered, realizing he'd ended up about twenty feet into the woods. He opened the car door. The entire car leaned to the left.

Still dazed, he half-rolled out of the vehicle and landed in a patch of thick vegetation. He pushed himself up, perched on his hands and knees, and stayed like that for a second, making sure his back and neck weren't hurt. No serious pains shot through his body. Then he felt it: a stinging in his ankles. A burning sensation that crawled up his pant legs.

"Shit!" He recognized that pain. Leaping up, he kicked off his shoes and started slapping at his legs. Luck would have it that after a damn car accident he'd find himself belly-up in a freaking fire-ant bed.

He took off running, stopping every few steps to slap at his calves, hoping to stop the ants from moving upward—ants that were at this moment sending shots of painful poison into his skin. The stinging made its way up his thighs. Sneaky bastards traveled at amazing speeds in tight places. Not wanting to suffer the bites to his crotch, he started shucking his pants. Unfortunately, his foot got caught in the leg of his jeans. He fell. Hard. Landed facedown in a briar bush. Luckily, the thorns missed his eyes, but his nose wasn't so lucky. And that's when he heard it: a slight rustle in the bushes right in front of him.

He pushed up on his elbows and came nose to nose with a pair of beady eyes. The animal did a half circle in a flicker of a second. Jose recognized the black-and-white markings. He screamed and rolled over three times, landing on his back, but it was too damn late. The skunk spray got him and got him good. He closed his eyes to fight the nausea. When he opened them, he saw the town's water tower lighting up the sky like a beacon. He read the words painted upon it in huge purple letters:

WELCOME TO PRECIOUS

Jose dropped his head back in the dirt. Lying there with thorns sticking out of his nose, his head bleeding from what could have been a fatal crash, his pants around his knees while fire ants munched on his balls, he tried to not puke from the smell of the skunk. His gaze shifted back to the water tower. "Good to be home," he seethed.

Sky studied Shala in the passenger seat, her head leaning back against the headrest, her eyes closed. He couldn't tell if she was sleeping, but he didn't doubt it. She'd had a hell of a day. They'd given her a pain pill to help her sleep.

Remembering her earlier remark about being hungry, he'd dropped about ten bucks in the vending machine and gotten chips, cheese and crackers, a candy bar, and a pack of cookies before they left the hospital. Shala had devoured the cheese and crackers before they even got to his truck. He remembered the dog snagging her lunch at the park, and he wondered if she'd eaten anything all day. She hadn't eaten the omelet he made her. Too bad the closest all-night restaurant was an hour's drive away.

Feeling the hole in his stomach, he opened the Snickers bar, ate, watched Shala, and drove. Admittedly, he did more watching her than anything else, which caused him to almost run one of the two stoplights they had in town. But damn, she looked sweet sitting there. He fought the urge to reach over and pass the back of his hand over her cheek, fought the idea of driving her back to his place and insisting she stay with him. He'd sleep on the sofa, if she wanted. Not that the other option wouldn't be a lot more fun.

He'd bet she wouldn't be in the mood, though. Women weren't like men, who'd never let something as small as twenty-six stitches get in the way of sex. Especially first-time sex. A man could lose a foot and still be up for some first-time action. And if it was good, he'd be up for more.

Realizing his thoughts were affecting him more than he wished, he adjusted the crotch of his jeans and attempted to push back his inappropriate lust. But his gaze caught on Shala again, asleep, warm, soft, and so damn touchable, and he decided that maybe he should cut himself a little slack. It was—he glanced at the radio's clock—two A.M., and beside him slept a woman who was hotter than Helios. Considering he hadn't had sex in months, he deserved some slack. And she found him equally attractive. Wasn't that a good thing? But again came that voice from earlier, the one that said he was playing with fire. And his concern didn't all stem from Redfoot's soul-mate nonsense, but also from how easily and powerfully she'd gotten under his skin.

His phone rang. Shala's eyes shot open and she sat up, looking disoriented. He touched her shoulder and then grabbed his cell. "Just my phone."

He glanced at the clock again. Who would be calling at this time? He'd checked in with the nurse before he'd left, so he doubted the call involved Redfoot.

"Damn." The caller ID said it was Martha on the 911 number.

* * *

Jose, wearing one shoe, with a cloud of stench following him, his lower extremities on fire from ant bites, and his forehead bleeding, made his way the mile and a half to Redfoot's home. There, he rang the doorbell and prayed.

No one answered. Thank God and hallelujah. As he'd hoped, Maria had stayed at the hospital. Walking off the porch, looking for the fake rock in the flower bed, he removed the spare key from its hidden compartment. It had lain in the same rock for sixteen years. His mother's idea.

God, he still missed his mother. She'd been the one sane thing in the otherwise-crazy life here.

Letting himself in, he headed right for the kitchen and prayed his dad's liquor cabinet was stocked. He pushed the Jack Daniel's, the tequila, and the expensive bottle of scotch to the back and thanked the heavens when he spotted the V8. But there were only two bottles, not nearly enough to kill the skunk stench.

Damn. He started to close the door when, on second thought, he grabbed the whiskey, unscrewed the top, tossed it across the room, and took a big gulp. It didn't burn near as bad as his balls.

Stumbling to the master bathroom, he stood staring at the shower. He needed a tub. He needed to soak in what juice he had to get the smell off. Thus, he turned around and headed to the bathroom with the tub: Maria's.

One step into her room, his gaze shot to the bed where they'd made love numerous times. It had been good, too. A smile threatened to wipe the scowl off his face when he spotted the romance novels on her nightstand. She'd never change.

He moved into the bathroom and stripped off his clothes, stuffed them into the plastic bag that lined the garbage can, and tied it in a knot. He hoped like hell he could find some of his old clothes, or he'd be making the hike back to his car wearing the pink nubby housecoat that hung on the door.

Two measly bottles of juice he had to bathe in. He needed more. At last he remembered hearing another remedy for removing skunk smell: women's douche. Something about the vinegar and odor eliminator. Desperate, he looked toward the cabinets. Maria had regularly used one after having sex. What was the chance she'd have some now? Was she having sex? Even though he could really use the stuff to remove the stench, he hoped like hell her cabinet was douche-free.

He opened the first cabinet and smiled when all he saw were tampons and her makeup case. He moved to the second. His smile took a hike, and he took a swig of whiskey. There, lined up like soldiers waiting for action, were six Summer's Eve bottles, in the Sweet Romance fragrance. The real kicker, however, was tucked in the back: a thirty-six pack of extra-large strawberry-scented French-tickler rubbers.

Extra large? Who *was* the bastard? Jose considered all the men living in town that he thought were available. Couldn't be more than six possibilities. Then the craziest thought shot through his head. Sky? No, Sky wouldn't do that. Sky was her foster brother. "Just like you are, idiot!"

He took a two-shot swig of whiskey, then another when he saw his reflection in the mirror. What a fucking reflection. Leaning against the counter, he touched the blood-streaked goose egg on his head. Ouch! Both his eyes had half-moon bruises, and he counted at least a half dozen thorns sticking out of his face. He tried to pull one out, but that seemed to only push it deeper. He needed tweezers.

He'd just started to search the bathroom when he remembered he really needed to get the skunk off him. Grabbing all six douches, he tossed them beside the tub and placed the whiskey down, too. He set the stopper in the tub and climbed his bare ass inside.

Opening the V8, he poured one bottle of juice and then the other over his head, then scrubbed it into his scalp. He didn't know if it was cutting the smell or not, but he wished he had a shot of vodka, celery stick, and a lime. He reached for a bottle of douche, found the whiskey instead. Good enough.

After two more good long swigs, he leaned back in the tub and started thinking about Maria again. Was her relationship serious? Shit! He hadn't decided that trying to patch things up was right, but he'd sure as hell wanted the option. Realizing how egotistical that sounded, he downed another long drink. The buzz of the whiskey through his veins made the fire-ant bites on his legs and balls hurt less, so he downed a few more swigs.

Remembering what he was supposed to be doing, he grabbed the first bottle of douche and squeezed the fresh-scented liquid over his chest. It actually smelled pretty good, so he went for the second. That's when the bathroom door swung open, and Maria and some white boy with sandy-colored hair—obviously the extra-large-tickler-condom wearer—stood gaping at his naked ass soaking in a half-inch tub of V8 juice, holding a bottle a Jack in one hand while squirting himself with Sweet Romance–scented douche with the other. Oh, and don't forget the thorns in his nose or the black eyes.

From the cleaning materials the pair held over their heads, he figured they expected to find a rabid skunk and not a naked man. Maria dropped the mop, but white boy held tight to his broom. Jose drew the whiskey back to his lips.

Welcome to fucking Precious, he thought.

Sky stood two feet away from Shala, who stood in the hotel parking lot staring at the smashed windows of her Honda. He expected her to start crying at any minute. Not that he considered her weak or an easy crier, but she'd come close several times, and this just might be what tossed her over the edge.

Sal's wife Jessie had called 911 when she saw what was going down in the parking lot. Martha had called Sky. Sal was now standing a car length away, as if scared Shala would turn on him for having allowed this to happen at his hotel. Who'd known his friend was a wuss?

"You okay?" Sky asked Shala.

She continued to stare, her arms folded tight across her chest. She slowly met his eyes. "Whoever named this town Precious needs to friggin' be castrated."

Maybe it was the blue fire in her eyes, maybe it was the emotion she put in the word *friggin'*, but odds were, it was probably the word *castrated*. Sky instantly decided Sal was simply being cautious.

Shala took a step toward Sky, and it took courage not to retreat. If looks could kill, he wasn't sure anyone would find enough body parts to identify him.

"I want whoever did this to pay!" she said. "I want him caught. I want him arrested. I want him castrated right along with the person who named this town!"

Yup, it was definitely the word *castrated*.

As she spun and shot off toward the hotel, it might not have been smart, but he caught up with her. "Shala, we need—"

She stopped so fast that her shoes probably left skid marks. She swung around to face him. Her arms remained locked around her middle, which had to hurt, considering the stitches in her hand, but maybe the tight grip held her together. If she stopped hugging herself, she might fall apart.

"Look," he said.

"No, you look. It's two in the morning. Today, I've been stalked, robbed of my camera, vandalized, almost killed, twirled around a dance floor in an establishment named the Fucky Chicken by someone who thinks he's Travolta, and—oh, yes—I've been leg-humped by the very same dog who stole my hamburger."

She drew in a deep breath. "In case you don't get what that means, my point is, I've had it! I'm not dealing with this right now. Tomorrow, when you give me my camera back—which you *will* do—I'll fill out a report or sign a statement or whatever it is that I need to do to have this bastard put away for life. But right now . . . right now I'm going to bed."

She turned on her heel and stormed up the stairs. Sky watched her go, and while he saw the fury in her, he also didn't miss the vulnerable little girl who needed someone. And damn if he didn't want to be that someone. Not forever, he amended. He simply wasn't the forever kind, but maybe for longer than usual.

He walked back to Sal, but before he could ask questions, his friend started in. "See, that's what I saw this afternoon! Seriously, man, you give that woman even a mild case of PMS and she's Lorena Bobbitt."

"Give her a freaking break," Sky snapped. "She's had a hard day. As hard as they come."

Sal studied his expression. "Well, I'll be damned. Redfoot's right. You're already in love with her."

"God damn it, Sal!" Sky growled. "Stop it"

His friend shook his head. "Don't worry, I'm shutting up now. Everyone knows that once two people have been selected as soul mates, God forbid the poor sap who tries to come between them. Forget I said anything bad about her. Go for it. Like I said earlier, she's hot—even if she's a real handful."

"Would you please—?"

Sal belted out laughter. "If there's anyone who can handle her, though, it's a man who's always locked and loaded. That's you, man. Just don't expect us to have you guys over for Sunday dinner."

Sky clenched his jaw. "Shut. Up."

"I'm just sayin', if you love her like I love Jessie, then I get it, man. You got my blessings."

Sky shook his head to clear it. "What happened here? Did you even see the guy who did this?" He'd almost asked what kind of a joint his friend was running, but he knew the answer. Sal and Jessie ran a small-time hotel that barely paid their electric bills, and Sal also ran housecleaning and eBay businesses on the side.

"It's just like I told you on the phone."

"You didn't make a damn lick of sense on the phone," Sky growled.

"Okay, I may have been shaken up. That asshole nearly killed me." Sal paused. "I got this call from some guy wanting Shala Winters's room number."

"Tell me you didn't give it to him."

"No. I never give out room numbers unless . . . well, let's just say I don't do it. Anyway, I heard the train rolling by, and that's when I realized that I could hear the train on the phone, too. Don't ask how I knew, but I got a feeling the guy was calling from *here*. I stepped out of the hotel and saw this man on the phone standing next to your chick's car. And I could see the broken glass. I yelled and started walking over. He jumped into a running car and—"

"What kind of car?" Sky asked, though could have guessed.

"A dark sedan. I hoped to get the license plate, but damn if he didn't aim right at me, full throttle and everything. I swear, his bumper was kissing my ass when I climbed up that there tree." He pointed to an oak with low-hanging limbs. "We really must be related to chimpanzees, because I instinctively knew how to climb, and I never did that as a kid." Sal leaned close and added, "Don't tell a soul, but I had to change my shorts."

Sky glanced up at Shala's hotel room. The lights were still on. He doubted she'd let him in this time. Not that that was going to stop him. Whoever was after her camera had gone to extreme measures, and Sky doubted he would stop now. He wasn't about to let the asshole get close to Shala again.

"Do me a favor, Sal. Give me her room key and bring me her camera."

"Room key? You sure you want to do that?" Sal asked. "With her talking about castration? I'd let her cool off."

"Just do it!"

CHAPTER THIRTEEN

Maria paced from one side of the living room to the other, questions, concerns, and emotions doing somersaults in her chest.

"Calm down," Matt said.

"Calm down?" Maria snapped. "My house smells like skunk and he's being impossible. He needs to be seen by a doctor. He looks as bad as Redfoot. You saw his black eyes!"

"I wish that was all I saw." Matt laughed.

"This isn't funny!"

Matt wiped his smile off his face. "Maria, you can't force him to see a doctor."

"He's just like Redfoot: stubborn, hardheaded, and—"

"Is this normal for him?" Matt asked.

"Is what normal?" Maria's head and heart swam.

"The drinking," Matt explained.

"What? Because he's Native American, you just assume—"

"No." Matt held up his hands and stepped back. "I didn't say that, Maria."

"You implied it," she accused.

"No, I didn't imply it. I'm asking because he's obviously drunk off his ass right now." Matt shook his head and studied her. "What's wrong? You're supersensitive and acting crazy."

She shook her head, torn in so many ways. She could still remember her talk with Redfoot. She could still remember admitting she needed to ask Matt about his weekends in Dallas. She remembered how good it had felt when he wrapped his arms around her at the hospital. But on top of that, she had to deal with Jose. About Jose not knowing about her pregnancy or the miscarriage. About Matt not knowing about Jose. About Matt not knowing that she might be infertile. "You know, I think it might be best if you left."

"Left?" His eyebrows shot together. "You asked me to stay."

"It's just . . . awkward."

He stared at her. "Why is it that I get a feeling that when you say awkward, you mean more than just your brother smelling like a skunk, being drunk and naked in your bathroom, and bathing with your douche?"

The denial lay on her tongue but she couldn't lie. Not when she knew sooner or later she would have to tell him. But not tonight. Not when she couldn't understand whatever her heart was telling her. She needed to think before she spoke. She needed Jose far away when she came clean.

"What is it you're not saying?" Matt asked.

"I'm saying we need to talk. I . . . need to tell you things, but not now."

"What things? What are you saying?" He glanced down the hall toward her bedroom. "You know, I really wish you would explain, because my head is coming up with things that I don't like."

"Please, let's talk later."

He raked a hand through his hair. "I drove like an

idiot to get back to you, and now you send me off as if . . . That isn't your brother, is it? Who's in your bedroom, Maria?"

Her patience snapped. "What did you leave in Dallas? Or who? *Who* did you leave?"

He stood stunned. Emotion played on his face—oh God, was it guilt? His expression echoed what she felt inside.

Tears came to her eyes. "It's true, isn't it?"

"I don't know what you're suggesting," he said, but his voice was fraught with meaning.

"I'm suggesting the same thing you are."

Matt shook his head. "Who is he?"

"It's Jose. There is no blood between us. But he is Redfoot's son."

"So what you're saying is—"

"Go!" she ordered.

He did.

Although she'd asked him to go—*insisted* he go—when the front door slammed behind him, Maria felt her heart crash against her breastbone. Pain exploded in her chest and she felt certain her heart curled up in a mangled mess and died. Oh, God, what had she done?

"I think I love you," she said to the slammed door.

She moved to stop him, but before she even got to the door his tires were spitting gravel out in the drive.

She ran to the phone, ready to call him to come back. Then she remembered Dallas. Walking to the sofa, she dropped down and let herself just sit there. The emotional pain was almost too much, pain like on her fifteenth birthday, as she'd watched her mother pack her bags to go to Vegas with her new boyfriend with no intention of coming back.

She recalled that look in Matt's eyes when she'd asked about Dallas . . . Oh, God, did it have to hurt this much? Of course it did. Didn't it always? Hadn't it when her mother walked out? When Jose walked out? Why would Matt's leaving be easy? And why the hell had she expected it to end any differently?

Because you believe in the fantasy.

No more. That was it. She was throwing away every romance novel she had.

"You don't look too good," said a deep voice.

Maria looked up. Jose stood before her, whiskey still in hand. "Neither do you. You're drunk off your ass."

"Nah, I'm not drunk. I'm working on getting that way, but I'm not there yet."

"Really? Then why in the hell are you wearing my robe?"

He looked down at the pink terry cloth and laughed. "Maybe I am drunk." His gaze shifted around the room and he whispered, "Is Monsieur Le Tickler still here?"

She frowned. "You need to be seen by a doctor."

"Not happening," he said with defiance. Then he gave her that bad-boy grin Maria remembered so well. The one she'd watched him offer to other beautiful women when she was young. The one she'd swooned over when he finally offered it to her. Of course, with his beat-up face, it didn't have quite the same appeal.

He took a step closer. She took one back. He still smelled of skunk—which meant so did her robe.

He waggled his brows. "Why don't you just take care of me?"

"Why don't you go to hell!" She shot up from the sofa.

"I already have," she heard him say as she walked away. "I'm in Precious. And the only thing precious about this place is you."

Maria slammed her bedroom door.

"Shala?"

She heard Sky at her door and rolled her eyes. Slipping her pajama top on over her head, she frowned when saw blood on it and went to grab a clean set from her suitcase. "Go away!" She got dressed.

"I can't."

Maybe if she just ignored him, he'd leave. She went to the bed. But just as she had the covers pulled back, she heard her door opening. She swung around, seeing the chain dangling on the door, which she hadn't locked. Duh! She had a crazed stalker after her and she hadn't even taken precautions. Not smart. So not smart.

Sky stepped into the room. She got over being angry with herself and focused on him. "You can't just walk into my hotel room!"

"I think I should stay here, in case this guy comes back."

Shala shook her head. "I'm dead tired. I'm going to sleep. You can't stay here."

He looked around the room. "The chair looks comfortable. You won't even know I'm here."

She closed her eyes for a second. God, she was so tired. Probably, it was the pill the doctor had given her. Opening her eyes, she studied him. "I can take care of myself."

"You didn't even have the door bolted."

"I'll do it right when you leave. You can stand out there and listen," she offered.

"That wouldn't stop someone who *really* wanted to get in."

"So why did you chastise me for not bolting it?" she snapped.

"Because it should be a clue that you're in no shape to take care of yourself."

She knew he was right, but . . . "Can't you stay in the room next door?"

"I'll feel better in here."

"But I won't. If this were any other town, I could call 911 and have you arrested."

"You already tried that, remember?"

She dropped back on the bed and pressed her hands into the mattress. Pain flared in her stitched palm.

Sky sat in a chair and pulled another close to put his legs up. "I will ask for a pillow, though."

She turned her head so she could see him. "You're serious?"

"One hundred percent." He paused. "Just go to sleep. But don't snore."

Even in her exhaustion she noted the way he looked at her—with heat—and she felt the stirrings of desire. She tossed him a pillow.

He caught it and stuffed it behind his head but didn't stop looking at her, and she didn't stop feeling looked at. His gaze dropped to her feet. She recalled him complimenting her feet earlier. She stared down at her toes and found herself happy she'd gotten a pedicure before coming to Precious.

Realizing what she was thinking, she spotted her purse beside the bed and rolled over to pick it up. She dug into the bag with her left hand, grabbed something, and held it out for him to see. "I swear to God, if you try anything, I'll Mace you." Then she set the can and her purse on the nightstand.

"I'll remember that." He adjusted himself in the chair, tilted back his head, and stared at the ceiling.

She reached over and turned out the light. Then she rolled all the way to the edge of the bed, as far away from him as possible. Closing her eyes, she heard him shuffling around, standing up, and unloading his pockets. The chair creaked as he sat back down.

Staring at the ceiling, she just listened to him breathe. She had to admit she felt better not being alone. The day's events were rolling through her head, her heart beating like the drums at the day's powwow. She recalled seeing Sky for the first time, the way he'd moved to the beat of the music. Then she recalled the way Sky had held her hand as the doctor stitched her up.

"Thank you," she said into the darkness.

"You're welcome."

"I mean for holding my hand at the hospital."

"I know." His voice was soft. A minute later he said, "Shala?"

Her eyes fluttered open. "Yes?"

"I'm sorry about your parents."

Yours, too, she almost said. But she wasn't supposed to know that. "Thanks."

Sky continued to stare at the ceiling, his mind flipping through the images he'd seen on her camera earlier. She'd done an excellent job of capturing the town. Blue Eyes was a damn good photographer. Of course, he'd known that from her website.

He hadn't seen one image someone would be willing to kill for. And yet, his gut told him that it was there. Tomorrow he'd retrieve the camera from the safe where he'd had Sal store it again, and he'd comb through the images. He also needed to get that gun from Lucas, run a check on its serial number, and dust for prints.

He heard the bed shift. He sat up, leaned his elbows on his knees, and studied Shala. She wore a different pair of pajamas, but the same style. Her blonde hair lay scattered on the pillow. She rested on her side, and the soft curve of her waist made him yearn to run his hands over her.

She was asleep; he could tell by the way she breathed. Leaning back, he turned away and tried to reposition his pillow behind his neck. Christ, he must be getting old—there had been a time he could sleep standing up. Or maybe it wasn't his position keeping him awake. He took another deep breath. The soft feminine scent of lotion filled his lungs.

He turned his head and eyed her again. She looked so small in that bed, he couldn't help but imagine her against him. Under him. On top of him. His body responded, the crotch of his jeans felt like it shrunk, and damn if his balls didn't feel cramped. He pulled at the inseams of his jeans and loosened another button on his shirt. Cursing under his breath, he stood up and removed it. Before he realized, his habit of stripping naked to sleep had taken over and he'd unzipped his jeans. He stopped, glanced at her, and remembered her feeling comfortable in her boxer pj's. Oh, hell, he could at least lose his jeans. She probably wouldn't even know. He'd set his phone's alarm to go off at six. He'd be up and decent before she ever rolled over.

But then what? Would she be okay here by herself? Would the asshole who tried to run down Sal and who'd hurt Redfoot come back?

Dropping his jeans beside his chair, he recalled he had to pick up Jose at the airport. How easy would it be to convince Shala to go with him? And how hard would it be to convince her to stay in Precious while he tracked down the culprit? He recalled her saying something about leaving in the morning with her camera.

Would she leave without the Nikon? If keeping her camera meant she'd stay, that's what he'd do. But what if she decided to go back without it? And what if whoever was after the camera followed her home? He recalled how lonely she'd looked walking into that hospital last night and walking up to this room afterward. Alone, she'd be easy prey. Somehow he had to keep her close to protect her.

He sat back down and closed his eyes, intending to sleep, but his body longed to be horizontal. Almost an hour later, he turned his head again and studied her unconscious form. She was only taking up only a few inches of that king-size bed. But damn, he needed some rest.

He saw the fancy tubelike pillows she'd tossed from the bed against the wall. Picking them up, he lined them down the middle of the bed, creating a barrier.

If she got mad, he'd deal with it in the morning. After he'd had a couple hours of sleep.

CHAPTER FOURTEEN

An odd sensitivity tickled Shala's mind, while something else tickled her backside. A warm body lured her closer, seeking safety and comfort. The back of her arm found skin. A slight movement against her hip brought a new thought wiggling into her half-slumbering brain: it felt like . . . She hadn't felt one of *those* in a long, long time.

"Get that thing away from me!"

She bolted straight up, standing on top of the mattress. Sky Gomez, shirtless, jerked into a sitting position, uncovered, staring at her with unfocused eyes. His gaze shot to the door as if someone had broken in.

"What is it?" He wiped his palm across his face.

That's when she noted that in addition to being shirtless, he was also without pants, wearing only boxers. And poking out of the slit was his bald-headed hermit! The dang thing had decided to come out to play and was standing at attention. It had been knocking on her shorts, no doubt thinking Shala's boxers might be his ideal playground.

"What is it?" he asked again, dazedly.

"That!" She pointed to his crotch.

His gaze shot down. While he grabbed for the covers, she sprinted across the bed, jumped to the floor with a loud thump, and attempted to arm herself with her Mace. Unfortunately, she bumped the nightstand. The Mace, a gun, and some other stuff all went tumbling to the floor. Dropping to her knees, she latched her injured hand around the Mace and pointed it up at him.

"Whoa!" He held up one hand and shifted to the other

side of the bed, making sure to keep himself covered. He peered down at her. "I wasn't trying anything. I swear to God."

"You got in the bed!"

"Yeah . . . well, the chair wasn't as comfortable as it looked." He motioned to the mattress. "It's a king-size bed, and you didn't take up a fifth of it."

She frowned harder.

"And . . . look," he searched the mattress and held up one of the oblong bed pillows up. I even put up a barrier." When she held the Mace higher, he frowned and said, "If you'll notice, I was still on my side. You broke over the barricade."

"You didn't have a side!"

"My point is that I wasn't . . . uh, wasn't trying anything. So just put that down."

She nervously shifted the can.

"Shit, Shala, can you at least let me have a cup of coffee before I get Maced? Come on, put it down. Please."

"You took off your pants."

"I couldn't sleep with them on. But I wasn't trying anything."

"That's not how it appears." She motioned to the tented blanket over his crotch.

He brought his knee up to hide the evidence. "It's morning. That happens. Besides, I'm wearing the same thing you are. Minus the shirt."

"Well, *I* manage to keep my body parts inside my clothes." The shock of waking up to . . . *that* was beginning to wane. She recalled drifting off to sleep last night actually thinking he was a decent guy. She also recalled shifting closer to him when she first woke up.

As more of her early-morning fog cleared off, she saw he was telling the truth. He hadn't been trying anything. Which meant she didn't have a good reason to Mace him. Not that she had to admit that. Not yet.

"Are you giving me my camera back?" she asked.

"We need to discuss that."

She raised the Mace higher.

"Damn it, put that down," he growled.

"Promise me you'll give me my camera back."

"I don't make promises I can't keep. But if you spray me, I swear I'll—"

"You'll do what? Bring out your bald-headed hermit again?"

His eyes widened. "Put it down."

She shifted, and her knee hit something that rolled across the floor. She looked down and saw a pill bottle. Her eyes widened. She snatched it up and . . . Yup, it read just what she'd thought it read.

She pointed to the covers. "If you've had that problem for over four hours, you need to call a doctor." She threw the bottle at him.

"What do you mean . . . ?" He looked at the pills and went pale. "Oh, hell no!" he said as she retreated into the bathroom. "These aren't mine!"

She slammed the door and locked it. Standing frozen, she stared at herself in the mirror. Her face was bright red, her pupils dilated. She recalled with clarity that brief, half-asleep moment when she'd felt him against her and she'd wanted to give in to her body's desire, to answer the tapping on her boxer shorts and let him play all he wanted.

Her gaze shot to her cell phone, which was on the bathroom counter. Picking it up, she saw she had a voice mail message. Lillian, her neighbor. Why would Lillian be calling her now?

Calling her voice mail she heard, "Hi, Shala. I hate to be the bearer of bad news, but when I walked by your house tonight I saw your front window was broken. I called the police. They said it must have been a burglar, but something must have scared them away, because the only thing it looked as if they got was your computer."

Shala gritted her teeth. "Only my computer?" She had

homeowner's insurance, but what was this, Crap on Shala Week? Was the universe trying to do her in? What had she done to it?

Remembering her reason for storming into the bathroom, she pushed down her pajama shorts and dropped onto the toilet. Only the seat wasn't down. She dropped her ass right into the toilet bowl of cold water. *If* it was just cold water. Who the hell knew if he'd even flushed?

Seething, she stood. "I should have Maced you!" she yelled at the door. "I really, really should have Maced you!"

"They're not my pills!" he yelled back.

Sky grabbed his pants, poking his legs inside them as fast as he could. "They aren't mine!" he said again.

He heard the shower start and frowned. As luck would have it, he had to piss like a racehorse. Hence the hard-on that persisted even after she threatened to Mace him. Right then his phone rang, and the damn thing was somewhere on the floor with all the stuff Shala had sent flying as she went for her Mace—a huge overreaction, if you asked him. It wasn't as if she'd never seen a penis before, right?

"Bald-headed hermit, my ass!" he muttered.

He moved the clock radio and saw the time. Five forty-five. Who the hell would be calling at this ungodly hour? Snatching up his phone, he answered before even looking at the number.

"Sky, you need to do something."

He recognized Maria's voice, and his thoughts shot to Redfoot. "What's wrong?"

"He's passed out on the floor wearing my robe, which isn't tied securely, thank you very much, and he still stinks."

"Say what?"

"You heard me," Maria snapped.

Sky dragged a hand down his face. "I'm sure I didn't. Redfoot's in the hospital. Aren't *you* at the hospital?"

"Not Redfoot. Jose! Redfoot made me leave last night. And I was going to go back to the hospital, but my car's there because Matt drove me and was going to take me back this morning, but then we found Jose in the bathtub and then Matt left."

Sky tried to make sense of it all, but nothing computed. He heard sniffling. Was Maria crying? He shook his head. "Maria, Jose's flight doesn't come in until nine."

"Well, then, he just had Scotty beam him down, because he was here when I came home last night. Actually, he had Scotty beam him into my bathtub with V8 juice, a bottle of Jack Daniel's, and my douche." She took a few deep breaths and sniffled. "Oh, and he said he hit a tree."

"He hit a tree while being beamed down?" Sky scrubbed his palm over his face to make sure this wasn't one of those crazy dreams that didn't make an iota of sense.

"I need my suitcase," Shala yelled through the bathroom door.

"Who's that?" Maria asked.

"Nobody." Sky looked around the room. He spotted the suitcase beside the closet and grabbed it just as Shala yelled again.

"Either get out of my room or pass me the suitcase. And for God's sake, get your clothes on!"

" 'Nobody' sounds pissed," Maria remarked.

Frowning, Sky set Shala's bag beside the bathroom door and covered his phone's mike with a finger. "Here's the suitcase. By the way, those aren't my pills," he said one last time, just in case she'd missed it. When Shala didn't answer, he backed away from the door and moved his finger. "So, Jose's there?"

"What pills aren't yours?" Maria asked.

His finger must have been in the wrong place. Sky

groaned and watched Shala's hand creep out to snag the bag. "Is Jose really there?"

"Yes. So, can I stay at your place for a few days?"

Sky had entertained the notion of Shala staying there, but Maria was family. "Look, I'll be there in—" His mind wrapped around something else she'd said. "He's wearing your robe?"

"Yeah. Probably because his clothes are ruined. But now my robe is ruined."

"Why are his . . . ? Never mind. I'll be there shortly."

He hung up and called the hospital to check on Redfoot. The news was good. He'd just gotten off when Shala came out of the bathroom and tossed her suitcase onto the bed. Unable to wait any longer, he darted into the bathroom.

Shala was stuffing her pajamas into her suitcase with her injured hand as he came out, putting her shoes on with the other. She looked great. The shorts she wore fit her backside like a glove, and her sandals showed off her painted toenails.

She caught him staring and frowned. "Bet you didn't lower the seat this time, either," she muttered.

He shook his head. "Don't tell me. You're definitely a morning person."

"Bite me," she growled.

Sky considered doing just that, studying the back of her neck where she'd pulled her hair up into a ponytail. Realizing that his thoughts would get him nowhere, he asked, "What are you doing?"

"I'm packing."

He had to stall, had to think up something fast. "Why?"

"Why? Because I'm getting the heck out of town. But don't think for one minute that I'm not coming back for my camera. As God is my witness, if you don't give it to me, I'll—"

"I have a problem with that." His mind reeled.

"It's my camera!" she almost shrieked.

"No, I don't have a problem with *that*," he explained.

"Good, then you can give it back now."

He shook his head. "No. I mean, I can't let you leave just yet."

Her eyes narrowed. "Why?"

Why? That was an excellent question. "Because . . . because you haven't filled out any reports about what happened." That had some truth to it.

"I *told* you what happened."

"But it needs to be official."

"And what makes it official?"

"A report signed at the station, and probably more questions. And—"

"You already asked me questions."

"I'm sure I'm going to have more."

She was shaking her head. "Then let's go to the police station and you can ask your questions. Since my car window is broken and it's going to get hot, I'd like to do most of my driving before noon." She did up the latches on her suitcase.

Sky let out a deep breath. "Somebody tried to kill you," he reminded her.

"Yeah. That's why I'm getting the hell out of Dodge. You don't want me here."

"Yes, I do." The moment he said it, he knew it was true.

"Not you. The town, or whoever, doesn't want me bringing in tourism."

"I don't think that's what this is about," he remarked.

"Then what is it about?"

"If I had to guess, I'd say it's about your camera."

"My camera? It's not worth killing for. It's not *that* expensive."

"Which is why I think that it's something you have in it."

"In it?"

"You took a picture of something that someone doesn't want exposed."

That made Shala stop and think. "The only thing on my camera is what I've taken while here in Precious or on my way here."

"I know, but you took the shots, and I need you to stay in town until I figure it out. To go through the pictures with me."

She studied him. "You don't mean for just another hour or so, do you?"

"No. Give me a couple of days. Give or take." He got a vision of her standing over him on the bed, and couldn't help but imagine many different kinds of giving and taking.

"You're joking, right?"

"No, I'm very serious."

She shook her head. "No. You can call me with your questions. I've got a problem at home that—"

"What if whoever wants that camera thinks you have it when you leave?"

She eyed him. "I'll put a sign in my rearview window. 'Sky Gomez stole my camera!'"

"Get real, Shala."

"I am real. The mayor said people didn't want me here. Chances are, the person doing this is trying to scare me into leaving. And the truth is, they're doing a damn good job. I want to go home and you can't stop me." She moved to her suitcase and closed it.

He didn't really want to play this card. Truth was, it was a wild card. Oh, it was a real law, but he was about to bend it to hell and back. For Shala's own good, of course. "That's where you're wrong. I can keep you here. You're part of an ongoing investigation, and as the chief of police I can—"

"I freaking don't believe this," she muttered. "You're arresting me."

CHAPTER FIFTEEN

"No," Sky explained, in what he hoped was a calming voice. "I'm not arresting you, I'm detaining you. There's a difference."

Shala shook her head. "Do you have any idea how much I'm growing to hate this town?"

"Yeah, Precious could really use some work on its image," he joked.

"Good luck with that. I quit." She flinched, looking guilty. "Don't worry, I'll return the town's check in full. And I'll be happy to give you the number of one of my competitors."

He didn't want her competitors. He wanted Shala—in more ways that he wanted to admit to her. So he decided to ignore the whole quitting issue. Later, he hoped to change her mind. "I want you to go through your pictures with me, but first I've got to take care of something. And I need you to come with me."

"What? Why?" She dropped down on the bed as if worn out. He spotted smudges of exhaustion under her eyes, a fatigue which his own body echoed. She let out a deep huff. "If I'm detained, I think I'll go back to bed. *Alone* this time."

Alone? What fun was that? "The problem is, I don't know if it's safe for you to be alone."

"So it's not safe for me here alone, but you won't let me leave town." Shala nodded as if it all made sense. Then she said, "Would you explain that to me again?"

Sky exhaled in frustration. "Shala, this is more than someone trying to scare you out of town."

"You don't know that." She sounded hopeful.

"No, I don't," he admitted. "But let's look at what's happened. He went looking for the camera at the lodge. There's no way he thought you would have been there. He broke into your car. It's your camera he's wanting. And whoever did this knows who you are. Thanks to your Internet presence, all it takes is a few clicks to find out your home address. If you leave Precious—"

"Crap!" she said.

"What?"

"Nothing." Her brow crinkled.

"What?" he asked again.

"I'm sure it's just a coincidence." But Shala's face looked grim.

"What's a coincidence?"

"I had a message on my phone. My neighbor called last night. On top of everything else, my house was broken into yesterday."

This announcement sent a jolt of alarm through Sky. "Anything taken?"

"She said it looked as if it was just my computer."

"See! Your pictures are digital. You save them on your computer, don't you?"

"Yes, but I'm not there," she said.

"Don't you ever e-mail the images home?"

"Yes, but I haven't sent . . ." She frowned. "Why is this happening to me?"

She stood up and hugged herself tight, the way she'd hugged herself last night. Was this foreshadowing another mini-meltdown?

"I friggin' can't believe it. What the heck could I have taken a picture of that is worth all this? For someone to go this far, I must have caught something really bad on film. But I didn't notice anyone burying a body or anything. I think I'd have noticed that."

Yes, it was another mini-meltdown. But by the time she

finished, her eyes looked sane again. She just looked tired.

He hadn't seen anyone burying a body in those pictures last night, either, but they'd go over them again. "Whatever it is," he promised her, "we'll figure it out together." He really liked the last part.

She flopped back down on the bed and shook her head. "Staying in Precious doesn't solve anything. They could get to me here just as well as at home."

"Like hell," he rumbled. "*I'm* here. I won't let anything—"

"I can go to the cops in Houston," she interrupted.

He growled inwardly. "Small towns come with perks that big cities don't have. I can make you my personal project. The most a Houston cop'll do is send someone by your house every eight hours."

"You don't know what a Houston cop will do," she accused.

"Yes, I do. I worked for almost a year in San Antonio until this job came open. I know how big-city cops work. They don't have time to really watch out for one person." Unless said cop was single and took a personal interest in Shala. His inner growl deepened.

"But I need—"

"You need to stay here." He studied her. "This guy isn't playing. He wants your camera, and he's willing to do whatever it takes to get it. If my dogs hadn't intervened last night . . ." No, he didn't want to say that. "He nearly ran down Sal with his car. He could have killed Redfoot and—"

"What?" Shala's eyes widened. "Redfoot was hurt because of this?"

Sky realized he hadn't told her those details. Seeing the sympathy in her eyes, he wasn't above using it a little. "He caught the guy breaking in. The guy was after your camera. Look, Redfoot really likes you. He's worried."

But he wasn't going to explain how his foster father felt Shala was future family.

She looked apologetic. "I'm sorry. He's going to be okay, right?"

"Yes. I thought we might go by the hospital to see him after I . . . after I take care of this other problem."

"What other problem?"

"Family," he said. Because for the life of him, Sky still didn't understand the details of what was going on with Maria and Jose.

"I know Redfoot would like to see you. Then I need to go to Lucas's place to get that gun and see if I can get any prints off it. I figure by lunchtime we can go to the police station and start going through your Nikon." She bit her lip as if considering. Encouraged, he said, "Stay. Please."

She sighed. "Promise me it's only for a few days."

"I'll do the best I can."

It was the first straight-out lie he'd told her—or anyone—in a long time. Yet he didn't think she could handle the truth right now. He was just coming to terms with it himself. The truth was that Shala Winters intrigued the hell out of him. And not just in a sexual way. She triggered a "protect and serve" instinct that went far deeper than the one that had got him into law enforcement in the first place. Not for one second did he buy into all that soul-mate crap, but a few days would never be enough with her.

"You ready?" He offered his hand.

She hesitated, then slipped her uninjured palm into his. When she stood up, he didn't let go and she didn't pull away. The feel of her palm against his gave him a shot of confidence.

She met his gaze. "Why are you doing this?"

"What?"

"Making me your personal project."

Yeah, why are you doing this? He pushed back the feeling that the answer had layers of truth and told her what he wanted to believe. "I'm chief of police. It's my job. And when you're not trying to get me arrested, aiming Mace at me, or talking about castration, I find you sort of likeable."

She smiled. Then, looking down at their locked hands, she lost that smile and released him. That's when he recalled another matter that needed clearing up.

"About this morning."

"I'm trying to forget that." She took a step, then spun, her expression defensive. "Which, by the way, won't happen again. You're not staying in my hotel room."

He nodded, hoping she'd relocate to his place. Guessing that humor would maybe help the mood, he offered, "Was it really that bad?"

She cut him off with a glare. But while those blue eyes said "Don't go there," they also said "Come get me." He wondered if she knew what she wanted. He knew that he did.

He held out his hands. "I really wasn't trying anything." When she didn't appear convinced, he added, "Come on, you were married. You have to know that men in the mornings have a tendency to . . . 'get up' before they get up."

"You shouldn't have gotten in bed with me," she replied, "or removed—"

"Okay, I'll admit that I might have crossed a few lines. I wasn't thinking."

"Really?" Her voice held a teasing quality, which made him happy. "The almighty Chief Gomez admits he wasn't thinking."

"I made a mistake," he agreed. "I don't have a problem admitting when I'm wrong. Not that it happens a lot." He grinned. Nothing beat being in the presence of a witty and beautiful woman—except perhaps being in the presence of a witty and beautiful *naked* woman. But give that time.

"Right." She grabbed her purse and started for the

door. "Other than your athlete's foot and toilet-seat issues, you're perfect."

"What?"

"Wait." She glanced back, her blue eyes twinkling. "I'm forgetting about your ED issues." Then she walked out the door.

He grabbed his phone and followed. "My . . . Oh, hell, I do *not* have erectile dysfunction!"

Sky would have done just about anything—including dance naked in the street with a party hat over his privates—to take his words back. Jessie, Sal's wife, the gossip queen of Precious, stood right outside. She was grinning from ear to ear, and mentally he could see her rubbing her hands together in glee, desperate to announce to every man, woman, and child in Precious, their brothers, sisters, and probably their pet guinea pigs, that Sky Gomez had been discussing his inability to get it up.

Redfoot woke with a start, and the dream pushed him to focus. Where the hell was he? His mind tried to absorb the white room. Had the spirits taken him? No, he was in the hospital. But pieces of a dream flashed in his head.

He closed his eyes, trying to capture it. The bulldog had reappeared, bigger, more powerful than before, but after that the images were fuzzy. Obviously the sleeping pill had made his dream harder to remember. He saw images of Jose and Maria, but then the white boy, too. Why was Matt involved?

He couldn't grasp enough to understand the spirits' entire message, but another part of the dream was crystal clear: the river of blood, Shala Winters standing nearby. Blue Eyes still wasn't safe. And she hadn't been standing by the river alone. Others were in danger, too. But who?

Trying to wipe the smile off her face, Shala watched Sky gaze around the parking lot as they walked to his truck.

Did he really expect the crazed ski-masked man to appear in broad daylight? Not smiling suddenly became easier.

"You enjoyed that," Sky accused as they slipped into his truck.

"Enjoyed what?" she asked innocently, knowing full well what he meant.

"You know," he growled.

"You embarrassing yourself with your erectile-dysfunction comment in front of that hotel owner? Maybe a little." She smiled again. When she looked at him, his black hair glistened in the sun and his dark eyes showed frustration but amusement. Damn, if his smile wasn't the type to jump off a man's face and curl up inside a woman's heart. The kind that made a woman want to run her fingers across a man's lips, the kind that made a woman feel the expression was for her alone. It was the kind of smile that made a woman answer, "Yes, hell, yes!" without considering the specifics of the question.

"I hope you enjoyed it, because I'm going to pay." He shook his head. "By lunch today, this whole town will be thinking I can't . . . man up when I want to. The only time Jessie isn't gossiping is when she's sleeping or has her mouth full of food. Wait. I take that back. At the community picnic, she gossiped while eating a hot dog."

Shala's gaze fell to Sky's chest, appreciated the way it filled out his white button-down shirt. She remembered seeing him without it, stretched out on the bed like a lover. She could also remember that fraction of a second where she'd wanted to lie down on top of him and feel the heat of his body against hers. Inside hers.

Her heart did a little tap dance, *clickety-clacking* her down the path toward a real, full-fledged attraction. It was a place she hadn't been in so long, a place she wasn't sure she was ready to visit. And yet for the life of her she wasn't ready to call it quits. Not that she'd stay around for the long haul. No way was she planning on losing her head, her heart, or even her clothes. But was it so wrong to just enjoy flirting? To enjoy feeling alive?

Sky sighed. "That woman can get information passed around town faster than the five o'clock news."

"Then why didn't you just explain, tell her it was Redfoot's medicine?" Shala asked.

He opened his mouth to answer, then closed it. "You knew they were Redfoot's pills all along? So why were you giving me such a hard time?"

"I'm not responsible for your hard time. You got that all by yourself."

"You know what I mean!"

She did, but she was having fun. She shrugged. "I saw his name when I picked them up, but just because they were prescribed to him doesn't mean you don't take them to—" He squinted and made another growling sound, one that reminded her of an angry bear waking up after a long winter, and she almost laughed. "Okay, I probably did it because it was funny, and because you deserved to be teased for taking off your pants and climbing into my bed. But you have to admit—"

"I admit nothing. Redfoot handed me the pills last night and asked me take them home. I sure as hell didn't know what they were. I didn't even know he was . . . in a position to need . . . happy pills. And I couldn't tell Jessie, because then she'd go announcing *that* to the world. Knowing Redfoot, he'd kill her, and then I'd have to arrest him."

"So you'll allow people to think you have ED to protect Redfoot?" Her question was humorous, but she found his affection for his foster father touching.

Sky's gaze shot to the hotel office. "God, I'll bet she's already on the phone." He shook his head. "Maybe Redfoot's method is better. I could kill her and you could help me bury her body." He scrubbed a hand over his face and then started the truck. "I seriously don't see what Sal sees in that woman."

Shala grinned. "She's pretty."

"She's a menace to society."

"She seems sweet."

"She is," he admitted. "And I'm going to feel guilty killing her, but I think I can still do it."

Shala laughed wholeheartedly. Sky turned to look at her and stared. The frustration melted from his expression and he said, "Damn, you're beautiful when you do that."

Was she so desperate for a man's attention that one little comment could send her high-stepping it up to the clouds? Yes. The compliment, delivered with heat both in his gaze and voice, sent Shala's heart soaring. But while the trip to that light and fluffy feel-good place was fun, God knew falling could hurt like hell. Caution flags started waving in Shala's head. She really, really needed to stay grounded.

Maria sat on the bed, tapping her foot on the carpet and waiting. She wanted out of the house before she had to face Jose again, before she lost her temper and did things she had no right to do—such as blaming him for the death of a child he knew nothing about.

Realistically, she knew Jose held no responsibility for the baby's death, but a part of her dealt in feelings, not facts, a part which believed that if Jose hadn't left for New York, she wouldn't have miscarried. But she couldn't just trust feelings. Take Matt for example. Her feelings swore they had something special, yet last night he'd walked out on her. He hadn't offered any excuse for his long stays in Dallas—probably because his reasons weren't excusable.

He'd wanted her to explain Jose, of course, but she hadn't done that only because it felt wrong to talk about Jose while he was there. And while Matt might have assumed the worst, he would have been wrong. Although . . . he would have been only a shade off. The truth was, at one time she had indeed been having an affair with him. But that didn't mean she didn't care for Matt, and it didn't mean she was cheating on him.

Instantly, she questioned if her own assumptions about Matt were faulty. Could he have a reason for staying in Dallas that might not include a lurid affair? Her heart said yes, and she let the possibility take a few laps around her head, but then she reminded herself that she was at it again. She was letting her feelings guide her.

Her cell phone rang. Hoping it was Sky, she checked the caller ID and almost didn't answer. She wasn't in the mood for one of Jessie's gossip sessions. Then again, sitting around thinking about Matt held zero appeal as well.

"Hello," she said.

"You are never going to believe this," Jessie began, giggling.

"What?" Maria asked.

She really didn't have to; Jessie would have told her either way. Jessie loved telling things. The only way the woman wouldn't blab something to hell and back was if she pinky-promised not to. Not that Maria asked for any pinky-promises from Jessie. Not lately. Not since the miscarriage and her secret affair with Jose. Her relationship with Matt had never been a secret. She hadn't cared if the whole world knew they were together.

"He stayed the night with her at the hotel," Jessie said.

Maria's heart clutched. "Matt stayed at your hotel with some woman?"

"Matt?" Jessie repeated. "No, not Matt. *Sky* stayed at the hotel with . . . Ah, *Dios*. Something happened between you and Matt."

Maria let out a deep breath. "I'm not ready to talk about this." But the words came out anyway. "Jose came home."

Jessie gulped. "Does he know about the baby?"

"No," Maria said. "It's just . . . It was unbelievably crazy and I must have been acting guilty, because Matt somehow knew Jose is more than just my foster brother."

"You need to tell him," Jessie announced.

"Tell who?"

"Both, *chica*. Tell Jose so you can move past this. Tell Matt so you can stop feeling as if you are lying to him."

Maria closed her eyes. "You know you can't repeat this, right?"

"I promise on my pinky," Jessie said. "Are you okay?"

"No, I'm not okay," Maria growled, and tears filled her eyes. "I'm pretty sure it's over."

"But you told me yesterday that you thought he was the one! If he loves you, he—"

"I guess I thought wrong." Maria wiped her eyes and tried to pull herself together. "Really, I'm not ready to talk about it yet."

"Okay, but you know that when you are, I'm here for you."

"You always are," Maria said. "And I love you for it."

There was a pause. "Now, do you want to hear about Sky's shenanigans?"

"Sure," Maria said. "What did he do?"

Jessie began with the whole hotel break-in and her husband's near-death experience with the black sedan. She ended with something about Sky having erectile dysfunction. Maria didn't believe it, but the delivery was funny and she found herself pushing her own problems aside to laugh with her best friend.

"I'm cleaning their room now. The bed is messy—"

"Sky left?" Maria asked.

"Just a few minutes ago."

Maria breathed a sigh of relief. "Good. But you have to let me go so I can get Redfoot's things together."

After a few more words, the two women hung up. Maria tiptoed down the hall to Redfoot's bedroom. With luck, Jose would stay incapacitated until she left for the hospital.

CHAPTER SIXTEEN

Sky hadn't explained where they were going or what "family issue" he needed to fix, and Shala didn't ask. She wanted to, but those caution flags kept waving in her head. Sky Gomez, with his mouth-watering body and wit, his bedroom smile, and his caring approach to life had her working overtime at putting up barriers.

Oddly, she hadn't worried about barriers before. She hadn't needed them. It wasn't as if the men weren't knocking on her door. They were, but sending them packing had been a piece of cake. She hadn't even needed barriers. Until now.

"You okay?" Sky asked.

She cut her gaze toward him. "Fine."

"You got quiet," he said. "Where did you go?"

"I have a lot to think about," she answered vaguely.

"Your hand's not hurting, is it?"

"It's sore is all." She looked at her bandaged palm, remembering the fear she'd experienced while huddled on the floor at Sky's house. "What's the chance of this freak just giving up?"

Sky's right eyebrow rose. "Not knowing exactly what it's about, it's hard to guess. But my instinct says that he's gone to too much trouble to just throw in the towel."

Her stomach gurgled with frustration. "What the hell could I have photographed that's worth hurting people over?"

"I don't know," Sky said, "but we'll go over your pictures and maybe find something."

"And if we don't?"

He frowned. "Then we catch him when he tries his next move." His gaze softened, and he reached over and brushed a strand of hair from her cheek. "I won't let anything happen to you, Shala. I promise."

His words rang so sincere, his touch was so tender, but as she felt herself warming to him, common sense kicked in and immediately she went back to barrier-building.

They drove past the arena where the powwow was held, onto the Chitiwa reservation. Shala had driven around here yesterday while trying to get a feel for the place. It mostly consisted of well-kept middle-class homes, although she'd spotted a share of empty or rundown buildings, early signs of a town's downhill slide. According to the mayor, more and more of the younger Native Americans were moving away. The bad economy was blamed for the tribe's losing its sense of community and culture. Shala figured it was the way of the world for the youth to move on, but a bad financial situation was hardly enticement to stay.

Yet with just a little cooperation from the locals, Precious could really turn its economy around. The town had so much to offer vacationers. With several lakes and a river, the town center's quaintness, the historical buildings, Precious had so much promise. Add the appeal of tribal history, and with just a little work, she really could see the town becoming a weekend vacation spot as popular as Fredericksburg.

She remembered one of the questions she'd wanted to ask the mayor, and it slipped out of her mouth. "Does Precious have an art community?"

"Community?" Sky echoed.

"Local artists, galleries, studios?"

"We have lots of artists. No galleries. As for studios . . . it depends on what you mean. Most of the locals work out of their homes. Estella, Redfoot's wife, was well-known for her pottery before she passed away. She had shows everywhere, including New York. She even had exhibits in Paris. She used to teach classes at the lodge. Maria still does a class every summer."

Shala heard the hint of grief in his voice. "How long ago did Estella pass away?"

"Ten years ago." He paused. "But it seems like yesterday. She was one hell of a lady. Redfoot knew how to pick them."

Shala smiled. "Precious should promote this, maybe open up a few studios for tourists. Offer weekend art classes. Make it a memorial to her."

He glanced over, and a satisfied smile tickled his lips. "That's a wonderful idea. Maria still does some pieces, and she paints. I personally think she's as good as Estella, but she hasn't tried to sell anything. Do you want me to tell Maria to get a meeting of the local artists together, so you can speak with them?"

The question reminded Shala that she'd told him she was quitting. She'd been serious about that, hadn't she?

"Who's Maria?" A Maria had called Sky last night when Redfoot was hurt. Was the woman Sky's girlfriend? The thought stung, but only because he'd been flirting with her. Not because she was interested.

Keep telling yourself that, a voice whispered in her head.

"She came to live with Redfoot and Estella when she was sixteen, as a foster child. She still lives with Redfoot."

Shala nodded, relieved if not wanting to admit it. Then other questions formed. Personal questions. Yet if she asked too much, Sky might question the source of the information she'd obtained while snooping through his house. Then she remembered, "The nurse at the hospital last night called Redfoot your foster father. Is—?"

"Yes." Sky looked out the side window, as if to escape any more questions. A minute later, he parked in front of a white brick home. "Actually, you can ask Maria about the art community yourself."

"Maria?" Sky called out as he and Shala stepped into Redfoot's entryway. It smelled strongly of air freshener and scented candles.

"In Redfoot's room, gathering a few of his things," came a very quiet reply from down the hall. "I'll be ready in a snap."

Sky's gaze went to the huge mirror in the hall and studied his reflection. Shala stood next to him. Damn, if she didn't look good there. He was dark; she, light. His solid frame contrasted with her curvier one. And while he had a good ten inches on her—the top of her head only came to his shoulders—something about her size felt perfect, as if she'd been molded to fit his body. He'd never been particular about a woman's size before, but suddenly he wondered if he'd overlooked a fetish for petite girls.

Her gaze locked with his in the mirror. He recalled how quickly she'd shut down when he'd complimented her in the truck. Right then, he knew there was more than just her camera standing in the way of them getting close. Or getting naked.

His gaze lowered to the cotton-covered breasts filling her pink T-shirt. There was nothing petite about those. Looking back at her eyes, he saw their warning: *Don't come any closer.* But while Shala Winters kept herself locked away, he was good at picking locks.

Their staring had reached the awkward stage, so he looked away from the mirror and directly at her. Their gazes met and locked again.

"Why don't you wait in the living room while I speak to Maria," he suggested, motioning to a room down the hall. "On the shelves are some of Estella's and Maria's pieces. Feel free to check them out."

Nodding, Shala walked away.

He enjoyed the view of that perky ass. Her shorts hugged all the right places. But when he felt his body responding, he forced himself to move down the hall. When had he reverted to instant hard-ons? *Since you haven't had sex in a month of Sundays,* he told himself, not wanting to think it had everything to do with Shala herself.

Moving down the hall, he found Maria gathering a clean change of clothes into a bag. "Hey," he said.

His foster sister turned, and the moment he saw her face, he sensed that whatever was going on was more serious than he'd feared.

"You didn't wake him up, did you?" she asked.

"Wake who up?"

She rolled her eyes. "Jose."

"No." Sky took a few more steps. "What's going on, Maria?"

"He still stinks," she replied.

Right then, another smell, one that lingered beneath the air freshener, penetrated Sky's senses. "Is that skunk?"

"Lovely, isn't it?" Maria snapped. "You're going to have to deal with him, because I just can't."

"What the hell happened?"

"Leave it to Jose to come back and screw everything up."

"Screw what up?" Sky had never really seen Jose as a troublemaker.

"Everything." Tears filled Maria's eyes. "He screwed up everything."

She came barreling at him, Redfoot's underwear clutched in her hand, and wrapped her arms around him. When Maria needed a hug, she didn't ask, she took. When she thought you needed a hug, she gave without permission, too. Fighting it was like fighting Mother Nature. So Sky just endured.

"I can't stay here while he's home," she sniffled. "Please tell me I can hang out at your place."

"Of course you can." Visions of Shala danced in his head, but he simply couldn't tell Maria no.

Of course, an idiot with a gun had gone to his place. His home might not be safe for Maria or Shala. But he also had a lot of stuff to work through, and he really didn't have to time to stand here hugging his sister in a skunked-up room.

He'd just opened his mouth to speak again when a scream from the other room split the air.

CHAPTER SEVENTEEN

Shala had been admiring the pottery on the entire wall when her foot bumped into something, but she was so awed by the glazed pottery that she ignored it. These were gorgeous pieces with smooth rising lines. Sky's foster mother had indeed been an amazing artist. Or were some of them Maria's? But then that something her foot had struck—or rather, that some*one*—wrapped a hand around her ankle. It was a dark-haired man, eyes closed and stretched out on the floor. He wore only a woman's pink bathrobe. And—

"Holy moly!"

For the second time that morning, she found herself staring at an erection. And while Shala had no problem with male anatomy, having gone visually penis-free for so long, the sudden wealth of phalluses was a shock to her system.

She jerked her leg, but the grip tightened. The man

opened his eyes and glared up at her. She loosed a scream and took off in a dead run—not an easy task when someone has a death grip on your ankle. Before she knew it, she found herself facedown on the carpet. The man still held her ankle, so she kicked, hard. Her foot made contact.

The hold on her ankle fell away. A few choice words sputtered out behind her, but she didn't look back. On her hands and knees, Shala crawled like a baby on speed across the living-room floor. She moved at such amazing velocity that she plowed right into another pair of jeans-clad legs. She didn't even bother looking up, but barreled right between the knees and took a sharp left into the hall.

The front door was now in view, so she lunged to her feet and took off. But she didn't make it. Someone snagged her arm.

"What's wrong?"

Sky. Her heart hammered in her throat, and she couldn't answer. Swinging around, she pointed to the living room.

"What?" Sky asked. The near-naked, cross-dressing ankle-grabber lay hidden behind the sofa.

"Oh this is freaking great!" said a dark-haired woman behind Sky—Maria, Shala assumed. She stood with her hands on her hips, frowning toward the living room. Something about her expression said she knew what had Shala so panicky.

"Please, stop yelling." The ankle-grabber stood up, holding both his palms over his ears. Blood was running from his nose. Unfortunately, with both his hands being used as earmuffs, he couldn't hold the ill-fitting pink robe over his privates. At least the thing wasn't still standing at attention.

"For Christ's sake, Jose!" moaned Sky. "Cover yourself."

The man flinched, then lowered one hand to pull some

pink material over his crotch. "Just stop yelling and"—he pointed at Shala—"keep her away from me." He wiped his other hand under his nose. Slowly, bloodily, he moved past them down the hall.

It couldn't exactly be called a graceful exit. Not just because each step appeared to pain him, but because with the robe pulled tight in front, the back of the pink robe rode up above his naked buttocks. And right before he stepped out of view he muttered, "Welcome to fucking Precious."

Sky frowned at Shala, who quickly explained. "He grabbed my ankle and wouldn't let go. I was trying to get away. I didn't mean—"

"Stop," Sky said. "I'm not blaming you." He placed an arm around her shoulder. "You okay?"

"I'm fine." She noted the easy manner with which he touched her, and questioned if she should step away. "I wasn't the one bleeding."

"Yeah, but he scared the crap out of you." Sky stared down the hall. "What's he thinking, running around like that?"

Shala shot him an accusing look. "*Now* nudity is a crime?"

"Yes. Indecent exposure. But I'm talking about that pink robe." Then, as if just realizing her meaning, he added, "This isn't the same thing as the hotel." He raked a hand over his face and looked at his foster sister. "What the hell is going on, Maria?"

"You tell me, then we'll both know. He's pretty much been like this since I found him in my tub, bathing in douche."

"Douche?" Shala gasped, certain she'd misunderstood.

"Yes. I'm sorry. My name is Maria, and I swear my house isn't normally occupied by hungover, nearly naked men giving peep shows. And it doesn't always stink like a skunk, either."

"Skunk," Shala repeated. She caught herself inhaling,

and past the air-freshened scent she picked up a hint of stink. "Oh, my!"

"Terrible, isn't it." Tears filled Maria's eyes. "It's been a hard night."

Shala nodded. Awkward silence filled the room, and then Maria offered, "Have you guys heard that mustard is great for burns?"

"Yellow mustard?" Shala asked, not knowing what else to say.

"Yes. I read it in the paper a few days ago."

"What the hell does mustard have to do with this?" Sky asked.

"Nothing," Maria snapped. "I was just hoping to break the awkward silence."

Shala grinned. "You didn't get that?"

"No, I didn't, but I'll let you guys discuss mustard on your own." Sky moved around the two women. "Excuse me just a minute." He walked down the hall and disappeared into the same room as the ankle-grabber.

Jose heard someone moving down the hall, and his head pounded in unison. Those footsteps sounded like a jack-hammer striking concrete. He just managed to pull the front of the robe over his dick before the door swung open.

He blinked, causing extreme pain to his eyeballs—who knew eyeballs could hurt?—and stared at Sky in the doorway. "I'll give you twenty bucks if you don't slam the door," he begged.

His foster brother apparently wasn't in the same financial straits as during his teen years, because he slammed the door and yelled, "What the hell is going on?"

Jose held up a hand. "I think I drank too much."

"You think you drank too much? What was your first fucking clue—your headache, smelling like the bottom of a whiskey barrel, or waking up wearing pink lingerie and attacking an innocent woman?"

"I didn't attack her. I thought she was Maria and I was just going to . . . I wanted . . . Oh, hell, I had a wreck and then there were fire ants, and thorns, and then that skunk came out of nowhere. Then I found out Maria is sleeping with some white boy with a big dick. Then the dick and Maria came in, and I was naked and almost drunk. I guess I didn't see the point in stopping then."

Sky just stared. Jose didn't blame him. If he hadn't experienced it all, he'd think the whole story was a crock.

He scowled. "Hell, I've still got the ant bites on my balls, if you care to check. I'll bet you can still find a few thorns in my nose, and the damn house still smells like skunk. And don't forget the car. You'll find it over by Old Man Jacobs's place, wrapped around a tree."

"You were driving drunk?"

Jose ground his teeth. Sky looked ready to pull out a pair of handcuffs and drag his ass to jail, and that pissed him off. Sure, he didn't carry a badge and protect the good people of Precious, he hadn't stayed behind to be the son of Redfoot, but he designed friggin' buildings that each alone could house more people than populated this town. Didn't that count for anything? Why did Jose always feel as if he stood in Sky's shadow?

"I wasn't drunk when I hit the tree," Jose said. "I was rushing home to check on my father."

Sky shook his head. "Well, if you plan on seeing Redfoot this morning, you'd better clean up your act and fast. Even suffering from a concussion, he sees you wearing that pink robe and he's likely to kick your ass and ask questions later."

Jose clenched his fist. Maybe it was still the whiskey, but damn if he didn't want to pound Sky Gomez's face in. How dare his foster brother come in here and explain his father? Just because Jose and Redfoot were nothing alike didn't mean Jose didn't know his old man.

"Just leave," Jose snapped, his shoulders slumping in defeat.

The tension faded from Sky's expression. "I don't mean to start shit, Jose, but damn it, you . . ." He raked a hand down his face. "Don't you want a ride to the hospital? I think Maria said Redfoot has the only keys to his car."

"I'll find my own way."

Sky stood there as if intending to argue, but his cell phone rang and he pulled it from its case and checked the caller ID. A worried expression crossed his face as he answered. "What is it now, Martha?" he asked.

The tension in Sky's posture had Jose listening.

"No!" Sky bit out and turned around and leaned against the wall. "How serious is it?" Sky paused. "Damn it, this is my fault!" He leaned against the wall. "I'm on my way. Call Pete and Ricardo and get them over there." He pulled his phone from his ear.

Jose's heart leaped in his chest. "What is it? Dad?"

Sky turned, and the look on his face was grim. "Not Redfoot," he said. "It's Jessie."

"Jessie Lopez, Maria's friend?" Jose asked.

Sky nodded, turning toward the door.

"What happened?"

Sky glanced back. "She was shot. And it's my damn fault. I should have never left the camera there."

Shala sat between Sky and Maria, both of whom were giving off so much tension and fierce concern that it filled every nook and cranny of the truck, making it hard to breathe. Jessie had been shot.

She didn't really know Jessie, and the few encounters the two had shared were short, but Shala could still recall the smile the woman had worn this morning when Sky made his ED comment. She recalled Sky's frustration about her being a gossip, but even then, Shala had heard genuine affection in his voice, as if Jessie were a family member who drove him crazy but he tolerated because, deep down, he cared.

Yup, Shala had heard that in his voice. She'd almost

envied it, too. It had been a long time since she'd had a circle of family and friends. She accepted that her solitary lifestyle was her choice. After the divorce, most of her friends had pulled away—some because they were more Brian's friends, and others because . . . well, because they were married and having a single friend, bitter about men, wasn't good for their own relationships. Then came Nana's death, and after that the new business. It had just seemed easier to focus on work than on outside relationships. Easier, but lonely.

Glancing from Sky's scowl to Maria's soulful expression, she felt the guilt blossom twofold in her chest. People Sky cared about were getting hurt. Was it her fault?

"I'm so sorry," she muttered. "I swear I have no idea why this is happening."

"This isn't you," Sky said, and continued to make his way through the traffic, doing about seventy miles per hour. "If anyone is to blame, it's me. I should never have left that camera at the hotel."

"No one is guilty but the person who shot her," Maria said. Sky had given her a short synopsis of everything they knew. "We just have to believe that everything is going to be okay. Jessie is going to be fine." She cupped her hands together, and her eyes grew moist.

Shala turned from Maria to look at Sky, and what he said suddenly sank in. "My camera was at the hotel?"

"In Sal's safe."

She felt terrible asking, but the camera did hold an emotional connection to her Nana. "Does this mean it was stolen? I mean, I know it's not really important now, but—"

"I don't know," Sky said. "From what Martha told me, Jessie was shot while cleaning your room. So I don't think so."

"My room . . ." Shala stared at her lap. Deep down she'd been hoping this would turn out to be about something else. Such hope was shattered. "God, first Redfoot and now this." She closed her eyes. "I should just take the camera and go back to Houston. Let the police there try to sort this out."

"Like hell," Sky said.

"I don't want anyone else hurt!"

"So you're going to go off and get yourself killed?" he asked.

"I won't get hurt. I'll go straight to—"

"Damn right you won't get hurt, because you're not leaving."

The mixed emotions in her chest found a leader: anger. Anger at Sky. "You can't force me—"

"The hell I can't. I told you earlier, you're being detained. If you try to leave, I'll arrest your ass."

Shala scowled right back at him and then looked at Maria. "Is he always so downright, frustratingly, overwhelmingly, pigheadedly difficult?"

"Gosh, could you have thrown in a couple more adverbs?" he asked.

Maria raised her eyebrows, glancing at Sky and then Shala as if making an assessment. "No, he's not always that way. Only with people he really cares about."

They drove the next five minutes in silence. Sky chewed on everything he knew about the shooting, and on everything he didn't know. He needed more information and to make some decisions.

Maria leaned forward to look at him. "I thought we were going to the hospital."

Sky parked in front of Sal's hotel. When he saw both the black-and-white cruiser and Ricardo's red Chevy, he found he could at least breathe a little better.

He glanced at Maria, saw the worry in her eyes. Damn, if he didn't know just how she felt. The weight of the world was on his chest right now, a big part of it guilt. He'd totally screwed up by leaving Shala's camera.

"I need to stop by for just a few minutes. Can you two wait here?" He wanted to be able to keep them in sight. God forbid, the asshole who'd shot Jessie was still around. His gut said that was next: if the perp couldn't find the camera, he'd go after the photographer.

"Can't you drop me off at the hospital?" Maria asked.

"I need to do this, Maria. I won't be—"

"Nothing you can do here is more important than Jessie." Tears filled his sister's eyes.

"I'll only be a few minutes."

"Why now?"

"It's my job," he explained, careful to stay patient. He'd already lost his cool with Shala. Later, when some of the pressure had eased, he'd apologize for sounding harsh about her wanting to leave. But protecting her was his job, damn it!

"Promise me you two will stay right here," he demanded.

Maria and Shala both nodded. Maria's sorrow cut deep, but he didn't have time or the words to console her. As he got out of his truck, however, he saw Shala reach over and take Maria's hand. He stood beside the window and stared, unprepared for the emotion swirling in his chest. He wouldn't let this nutjob get to her.

"Sky?" called Pete, one of the state troopers. Sky headed across the parking lot toward him.

He didn't waste time on idle chitchat. "You got it closed off? Where's Ricardo?"

"He's up there checking out the crime scene. It's ugly. Lots of blood. But yeah, we got it shut off."

That was Jessie's blood all over the hotel room. Sky's gut clenched. He let out a deep breath and said, "Do me a favor. Keep your eye on this truck. Shala Winters is in there with Maria. If this creep is still around, he might go after her."

"You got it." As Sky started to turn away, Pete added,

"Hey, you think this is going to end up a murder case?" He actually sounded excited.

Sky clenched his fist. It would have felt damn good to let loose on Pete, but deep down he knew the person who deserved to be on the receiving end of his fury was the guy who pulled the trigger. Besides, Pete lived in the next town over. He didn't know Jessie. To him, this was just another case. "I don't know."

"You calling the rangers to do the crime scene?"

"Yes." He didn't like the idea, not even when the ranger he'd call was a friend, but Sky knew his limitations. He couldn't do around-the-clock protection of Shala and also work this case correctly. And this creep needed to get caught. Not that he planned to stop working the case.

"Hey," Pete said, motioning. "Is it true that Shala Winters is a sight to behold?"

"Just watch the friggin' truck!" And Sky left before the man earned himself a black eye.

As he walked up to the hotel room, he pulled out his phone and called Lucas. "Hey, I need you to come over to the hotel," he said when his neighbor answered. "Like, now."

"What's going on?"

"I need you to keep something safe for me." He gave Lucas the lowdown on the camera and on Jessie's getting shot, then he hung up and made his next call. Part of him hated doing it, knowing he'd lose most of his control on the case, but damn it, a smart man knew when he needed a hand. Sky needed help.

Phillip Freeman, senior captain for the San Antonio department of the Texas Rangers, answered on the third ring. "It's good to see your number on my phone. You planning another poker game?" he asked.

"This is business."

"Damn. You know I hate business."

"We got trouble in town."

"Someone run your traffic light?" he teased.

"There's been a shooting," Sky replied in total seriousness.

"Okay, let me make it easy for you. If the person is married, look at the spouse. Marriage makes people want to kill each other. If I thought I could get away with it, I'd kill my ex-wife."

"It's not like that." Sky bypassed Ricardo and entered Shala's hotel room. The blood on the wall had his gut in knots. "And it's someone I know."

"Sorry. Was it a murder?"

Sky closed his eyes. "The victim is in the operating room. From what I heard, it could go either way." From all the blood, Sky was afraid to hope.

"Do you have a suspect?"

"This is where it gets weird." Sky filled him in on Shala and the camera.

"Damn, you got a mystery on your hands!" Philip sounded glad to help. "Just tell me what you need, and you got it."

"For starters, I need someone to do the crime scene."

"It will take me a few hours to get the van and my people there. I'll give you a call when I get close. You can meet me."

"Yeah. I'll be at the hospital."

"Sky," Philip said, "be careful. If this guy's shot one person, he won't hesitate to shoot another." His big-city friend sounded worried.

"Believe it or not, Phil," Sky said, "I figured that one out myself."

CHAPTER EIGHTEEN

"Open your eyes and tell me you're okay, you stubborn old Indian."

Redfoot felt a soft, feminine palm against his face, and his first thought was of Estella. When he opened his eyes, he found Veronica.

"Oh, my. Your eyes are both black."

Redfoot's pride cried out, *You should see the other guy!* But that was a lie, so instead he said nothing and just looked at her. He took in her soft brown eyes, concern swirling in their watery sheen, and right then he knew that although Veronica would never take Estella's place, somehow his heart had grown her a separate location. She belonged there. She belonged with him. Now, if he could just convince her of that.

He understood that her husband had been gone only two years, but two years was a long time to be lonely. And while Veronica swore that her reservations were because of her children, sometimes Redfoot wondered. If rumors were true, she had reasons not ever to commit herself fully to another man. But for several months now, she had given him her body. Now he wanted more. He wanted her to stand beside him, not just lie with him a few nights a week. He wanted her heart. And he was tired of keeping their relationship secret from his family and friends.

"Are you okay?" she asked.

"I'm not okay," Redfoot answered. "I had plans last night to be with a beautiful woman, and instead I had to sleep alone in a cold hospital bed."

She grinned, but it faded. "I didn't hear until this morning. I waited for you last night."

But she hadn't called. He knew, because after Maria left last night he'd checked his messages. The reason she hadn't called was probably because she was afraid Maria would answer. Afraid someone would discover they were seeing each other.

He patted the bed. "Lie beside me and remind me what I missed." He gave her hand a tug, but she resisted.

"There's not enough room."

"I'll make room."

She grinned like a schoolgirl. The bright blue of her blouse made her look young, as did the scoop neck that hinted at her figure. For a woman her age, she had beautiful breasts. Redfoot stared at the tiny buttons—at least ten—that held the blouse together. His mind created the image of her taking it off.

"You are a crazy man. What if someone comes in and catches me in bed with you?"

"Then I'll smile really big and pretend we were just resting."

She rolled her eyes. "You know I can't."

He frowned. "If you're not careful, I'm going to think you are ashamed to be seen with me."

"I'm not ashamed!"

"Then why don't you want anyone to know about us?"

She took a step away. "We've discussed this, Redfoot. I just . . . I can't."

"I mean so little to you."

She moved back toward the bed. "No. I care for you. More than I should. It's my children."

"Your children are not in this hospital, Veronica," he pointed out. "As a matter of fact, when I look around, I see only us."

He patted the bed again.

* * *

Shala sat in the waiting room, her hands in her lap, watching everyone pace. Over a dozen individuals had shown up, a mix of family and friends. Jessie, obviously loved by many, was in surgery. Shala had heard someone say it was touch-and-go. Tears filled everyone's eyes. Even Shala's eyes burned.

Having fought off the sorrow, Shala now tried to breathe through her mouth so that the hospital smell wouldn't get inside her senses and start messing with her head, wouldn't take her back to the past. Whenever she felt panic inch closer, she told herself to grow up. This wasn't about her; this was about a woman who'd been shot in part because of something Shala had done—even if that something was taking an unintentionally wrong picture. It was still her fault.

She also knew that if it had been her in that hotel room, it would have been her in that operating room. This waiting room would be empty—no friends, no family close enough to show up. Her gaze moved around the crowd and she wondered what it would feel like to have so many people in her life.

She heard her name. When she looked up, Maria waved. Someone must have asked who she was. Suddenly Shala felt as if she didn't belong here. She was a stranger, the outsider to everyone but Sky. Closing her eyes, she recalled arguing with him about staying at the hotel. His pigheaded demand had probably saved her life.

Opening her eyes, Shala looked for him. When he'd returned from the crime scene, he hadn't said a word. Shala surmised it had been emotionally difficult. Coming here wasn't an easy feat, either.

She'd watched him flutter from person to person. He'd approached the most anxious people, touching them, offering words of comfort. Whenever anyone extended him the same courtesy, he pulled away. No, Chief Sky Gomez could give comfort, but he couldn't accept it. Was it just for professional appearances, or was there something more?

She remembered how Sky had approached Sal when they'd first come into the hospital. Sky had worn guilt like a second skin. Sal, with tears in his eyes, had shaken his head, and while Shala couldn't be sure, she felt certain no blame had been assigned. Remembering Sky's past, the newspaper article in that box at his house, that ten-year-old Sky struggling against the firefighter's hold, it somehow made sense that Sky would want to save other people because he hadn't been able to save his parents. She wondered if he somehow blamed himself for their deaths.

While her own past had left Shala with a boatload of emotional issues, guilt wasn't one of them. The fault lay in the hands of a drunk driver. Nana had made sure Shala and her brother understood. Shala could still remember how, less than a week after her parents' funeral, her grandmother had marched her and her brother into a courtroom. They'd faced the drunk driver and the judge, and guilt had been clear. If not for Nana, there was no telling how much more of a basket case she and her brother would have been.

It occurred to Shala that Sky had gone into the foster program, which meant Sky hadn't had a grandmother. He hadn't had anyone to ease the transition from loved child to orphan. She couldn't fathom dealing with her parents' deaths and also a relocation to a home with strangers at the same time. Empathy for Sky filled her chest as she searched the crowd again, wanting to make sure he was okay. He wasn't there. Had probably stepped outside to take another call. She'd heard his cell ring at least four times since they arrived.

Leaning back in her chair, she stretched her neck, hoping to relieve some of the tension building in her shoulders. The sound of the intercom calling for a doctor filled her ears. Shala closed her eyes, and instead of thinking about her past, or even Sky's past, she tried to remember the different photographs she'd taken in the last few days. What could she have caught on film that had brought this on?

Someone's hand moved between her tightened palms. She popped her eyes open. Sky sat in the empty chair next to her. Her heart swelled at the sight of him, and she had to fight to keep from hugging him. Not so much to hug the stubborn and difficult man he'd grown to be, but the boy she knew he'd been.

He stared at her, looking almost as guilty as when he'd faced Sal. "I'm sorry," he muttered. "Christ. I completely forgot." He took her left hand in his.

"Forgot what?"

"Your aversion to hospitals. You okay?"

"I'm fine."

He ran a finger over her cheek. "No, you're not. Come on, let's take a walk."

Pulling her up, he laced his fingers through hers and led her across the room. Shala didn't have any will to deny him the touch. Not just because she needed it, but because she felt he needed it, too.

Jose lay in bed, fighting his headache and berating himself for everything he'd done since he crossed the Precious city line. When he heard Sky and the others leave, he picked himself up and went in search of a pain reliever and clothes.

He found some aspirin in the cabinet and a box of his old clothes in a closet. The jeans felt a little loose; he'd obviously lost a few pounds living the city lifestyle. The room in his jeans was a good thing, since he'd be going commando. There'd been no underwear in the boxed clothes, but that wasn't altogether a bad thing, because he had at least seven fire-ant blisters on his family jewels.

Finally armed with clothes that weren't pink, feminine, and didn't smell like Maria, he almost felt human. Almost. Sitting down to make a few calls, he rang the hospital to check with the nurses about his dad. Next, he contacted his insurance company, and then Ramon's Service and Wrecking Company. Ramon was an old high-school buddy from a few houses down who now owned and ran one of the two mechanic shops in town.

Sky had already called and asked them to bring in Jose's car. Leave it to Sky to take care of things. Jose knew he should be appreciative—and damn it, he was—but his foster brother's ability to always do the right thing made him feel inadequate.

"Who's going to be driving the wrecker?" Jose asked.

Ramon paused. "I am, as soon as my other employee comes in."

"Is there any way you could swing by Dad's place and give me a lift to the hospital?"

"You bet," Ramon said. "How is Redfoot? Mom told me this morning that he caught some guy breaking in and got hurt."

"Yeah. According to the nurses on his floor, he's doing fine. They said he'll probably come home today." Jose had yet to actually talk to his dad, preferring to do that in person. He knew he was procrastinating, but his dad never failed to mention his moving back home, and Jose never failed to feel guilty. With Redfoot hurt, his guilt would reach new heights.

"I'm glad he's okay. I'm sure Sky is going to catch the bastard."

Jose pressed a hand to his throbbing temple. "Yeah, that's Sky for you."

"Did you hear about Jessie getting shot?" Ramon asked. "You know Sal and she got married last year. He's crazy about her, too. I know he's in a world of hurt right now."

Jose remembered her. She'd always been vibrant. "Didn't know they got married, but I heard about the shooting. I hope she's okay."

"Me, too. I just can't believe this shit is happening here. Did you bring some of that big-city crime with you?"

"I hope not." Jose's mind shifted gears, and he wondered about the blonde with Sky. Who was she? He'd made a complete jackass of himself in front of her. Reaching up, he touched his nose. Damn, she could kick. "Hey, is Sky seeing anyone?" he asked. "He was here this morning with a blonde."

Ramon's laugh spilled out of the phone receiver. "Funny you ask. My sister dropped by this morning with a wild-ass story about him staying at Sal's hotel with the tourism specialist that's in town—the one Redfoot claims is his soul mate. Not that I blame Sky for going after her. She's wet-dream material. I saw her at the powwow. She brought her camera in and took a picture, and Sky yanked it right out of her hands. Then, damn it, he goes and gets lucky with her!"

"Sky's soul mate?" Jose scoffed. "He beds and leaves 'em."

"Yeah. Though from what my sister said, he's got a problem with the bedding part. Supposedly he was talking to the blonde about erectile dysfunction."

"*Sky?*" Jose chuckled. Was it terrible of him to take pleasure in the almighty Police Chief Gomez having trouble getting it up? Yeah, it was terrible, but it soothed his ego just a bit.

"Yeah, Sky. But you know how those rumors go. It probably doesn't have a lick of truth. Next we'll hear he's into cross-dressing."

No, that will be me, Jose thought dispiritedly.

"Hey, Jimmy's here. I'll be over there in about ten minutes."

Jose hung up the phone and went to collect Maria's robe to toss in the washer. It was the least he could do. But when he walked by her room, he stopped and stared at the bed. He recalled how she'd looked last night: soft, sexy, unchanged.

But no. She had changed. She used to look at him with so much affection. Damn it, he still loved her. Was she serious about this new guy? Did he stand a chance of winning her back? Hell, was winning her back even the right thing? Had two years changed anything? Was she still determined to stay in Precious? He was still determined to leave.

Wasn't he?

Sky, his heart swimming in guilt, entered the elevator with Shala. How in God's name had he forgotten her issue with hospitals? Sure, he had a hundred things on his mind, but if anyone could understand how difficult this was for her, it was him. To this day, the smell of smoke turned him inside out.

The doors to the elevator closed and low classical music filled the space. He recalled seeing Shala sitting there in that chair, apart from everyone else, and again he'd been hit by her vulnerability—and by his need to make it disappear.

He gave her good hand a squeeze, hoping she understood she wasn't alone. "Seriously, I'm sorry. I should have remembered."

She stepped in front of him and rested her hand on his chest. The touch, completely innocent, sparked a sensation that bordered on pain.

"You don't have to do this. You can stay with your friends. I'm doing okay. I'm dealing with it."

Without thinking, he cupped the back of her head and brought his mouth to hers. They'd barely touched lips when she tilted her head back. Her big blue eyes blinked up at him.

"I don't think that's a good idea."

"It seemed like a good idea to me," he said, aware that her hand remained on his chest. The pain had faded, and now the touch was simply warm, comforting, and he found himself wishing that he could feel her fingers on his skin.

She shook her head. "I could name ten reasons why it's

a bad idea. For starters, I'm just in town for a while and . . ." She rattled on, and he heard something about an ex-husband before he stopped listening. The moment a woman started talking about her ex, he shut off.

"Shh." He pressed a finger to her lips.

She kept talking. Those sweet lips moved against his finger. God help him, she really was a jabberer. He really didn't like jabbering woman. But that didn't stop him from wanting her.

"Shala?"

"What?" She inhaled deeply as if she'd forgotten to breathe.

"Stop talking."

She didn't listen but went right back to jabbering. When she mentioned her ex again, which he had no desire to hear about, he noticed two things. First, the elevator wasn't moving. They obviously hadn't hit a button. Not that he minded. He could and would use it to his advantage. Second, while she worked awfully hard telling him they shouldn't kiss, her eyes told him just the opposite. Added was the fact that her sweet palm remained against his chest.

"Shala?" He tapped his finger on her ever-moving lips.

"What?" she asked again, but didn't wait for him to answer before starting another sequence of jabbering.

"Would you please? Just . . . shut up and kiss me." He leaned down and claimed her mouth again. He could taste the toothpaste she'd used this morning. And he tasted more: he tasted *her*. Intoxicating. Like good wine or ripe, exotic fruit. Something to be savored.

She didn't resist this time. The kiss wasn't meant to be pure lust, and it wasn't. It was soft. It was giving. And it was more intimate than he wanted to admit.

Not that lust didn't enter into it.

He slipped his tongue into her mouth and she moaned. Her breasts, soft mounds of flesh, pushed against his chest right above where she kept her hand. Her nipples were hard, begging for attention. He felt himself thickening. Yet lust still placed second in what was happening here. Sky didn't even completely understand it, but the experience had something to do with wanting to help her, to soothe her, to chase away the nightmare he knew existed in her head about her parents and about hospitals.

A deep clearing of a throat sounded. Since Shala's lips were occupied, as were as his own, it had to be from someone else. How he'd missed the sound of the elevator door opening, he didn't know. Yet now they had company, so he had to pull away. And he would. In just . . . one . . . more . . . second.

Okay, two seconds.

Pulling back, he was rewarded by Shala's sweet weight falling against him. He smiled. There was nothing like knowing you'd turned a woman's knees to jelly. He took her by the shoulders to steady her before focusing on the uninvited guest.

It was the frowning, stern face of a balding man that watched them through the open elevator doors. Shocked but refusing to be intimidated, Sky nodded. "Mayor Johnson."

Shala didn't bounce back as quickly. Her eyes widened with panic. Her mouth, swollen from his kiss, opened, but when no words came out, she closed it. Then she opened it again. Then she closed it.

Words finally spilled out, not that they made much sense. "Hi . . . I was . . . Sky and I were . . . I mean, Mr. Gomez and I were . . . We were—"

Knowing Shala could go on babbling for a good ten minutes, and God only knew what excuse she might produce for them kissing, Sky intervened. "Have you and Ms. Winters been officially introduced yet?"

The mayor glared at Sky before seeming to come to his senses. "Only on the phone."

Sky watched Shala and the mayor shake hands. Then the mayor's all-consuming frown was again aimed at him. "Can I have a minute of your time, Chief Gomez?" he asked.

"Just one," Sky insisted.

"What the hell are you doing?" the mayor seethed in the first second of his minute. He had only a minute—Sky was timing him.

Sky glanced from his watch to Shala, who was standing beside the elevators a good thirty feet behind him, looking as if she wished to fade into the hospital's white walls. He needed to get her out of here. Or kiss her again. Then she'd forget her embarrassment. The second option was more appealing.

Sure, kissing her might appear inappropriate to some, but he'd kissed her for the same reason he'd hugged Maria: to give comfort.

"Do you have something to say, Mayor? Because your time is running out." Sky tapped his watch. Phillip would be calling soon.

"Do I have something to say?" he bellowed, then lowered his voice. "You have an attempted murder, three breaking-and-enterings, one attempted burglary, one attempted vehicular homicide, an important tourism specialist—who is our last chance at saving this town— and what are you doing? Playing kissy-kissy with her in the elevator."

Sky frowned. "As I already told you on the phone, I have Pete and Ricardo standing guard at the crime scene. The Texas Rangers are on their way. I have the gun that was found last night waiting to be checked for prints." He motioned down the hall toward the waiting room. "The woman in that operating room is my friend, and as soon as I get the update on her condition, I'm going to be combing though Shala's images again, trying to figure out why this is happening."

The mayor started to bluster, but Sky checked his watch again and kept talking. "I've secured a place for Shala to stay in case this asshole comes after her again. I've spent the last twelve hours running around town dealing with all the crap that you just pointed out, while also trying to keep her safe. Unlike you, I haven't been playing golf with a bunch of buddies, claiming to have a family emergency while you're supposed to be working. Still, if you have comments about how I do my job, I'll be happy to listen to them later. But my personal life is . . . personal."

"You can't be . . . seeing a victim. It's against policy."

"Thing is, I was seeing her before she became a victim. Now, if you want me to resign . . . ?"

"Seeing her *before*? She's only been here two days."

"I work fast," he said. "But as I said, if you want—"

"No." The mayor groaned, but Sky knew him well enough to know he wouldn't back down completely. "You're good at your job—that's why I hired you. But Ms. Winters is . . . Damn it, Sky, you're going to mess this up for us. Your 'love 'em and leave 'em' ways are going turn us into a ghost town. We don't need you breaking her heart and then—"

"Your minute's up. I'm taking her out for fresh air. I'll be right outside the hospital if you need me."

He started back toward Shala with the mayor's warning, along with a few of his own, echoing inside his head. However, one look at Shala and the warning faded. They were adults, damn it!

"Am I fired?" she asked as they stepped back into the elevator.

"Hell, no." Sky pushed the down button. "He's just jealous that it wasn't him in the elevator. He's been drooling over that photograph of you in your bathing suit with your essay on kayaking since he hired you."

"You're joking." She looked appalled.

"Nope," Sky answered truthfully. "He even printed it out. Not that I blame him. My printer is broken or I'd have done the same." Smiling, Sky brushed a strand of hair from her cheek.

She caught his hand. "Don't even think about kissing me again."

The elevator doors opened. With a hand on her back, he ushered her out. "I don't think either of us can forget about it."

"Watch me," she said.

"I will." He fitted his palm to the soft curve of her waist. "Watching you is one of my favorite pastimes."

Her pace slowed. He gave her a little nudge, leading her outside through the hospital's automatic doors. While it was only nine in the morning, the heat radiating from the pavement promised the day would see record highs. Sky gave the parking lot a once-over, looking for black sedans. There weren't any.

His cell rang, and he checked the number, worried it was the mayor. "It's Maria," he told Shala, and his gut tightened. Keeping one arm around her, he answered the call. "Please tell me it's good news."

"She's out of surgery. The doctor said it looks good."

"Thank God!" The weight in his chest faded. He smiled at Shala, who smiled back. "I'm going to grab a breakfast sandwich from the deli," he told Maria. "See if anyone else needs anything and I'll bring it up."

"Why don't you bring a dozen doughnuts?" Maria said. "Oh. Have you told Redfoot about Jessie yet?"

"No. Didn't want to worry him. But speaking of Redfoot, I'm going to have to meet someone in a little while, so can you get him home?"

"You bet. See you in a few minutes."

"So, Jessie's going to be okay?" Shala asked when Sky hung up.

"Doctor said it looks good." He nudged her forward again. "Come on, there's a diner across the street that sells breakfast sandwiches. You hardly ate yesterday; I'm sure you're starved." He glanced at his watch. "Unfortunately, we're going to have to wolf them down. I need to get you situated and going through those images while I meet the Texas Rangers at the crime scene. They're going to want to take the camera, so I need copies on my computer before they get here."

"Get me situated where?" she asked.

"A friend of mine, military and an ex-cop, lives a couple miles from my place. He'll be keeping an eye on you while I work."

She frowned. "Do you really think that's necessary?"

He arched an eyebrow. "Don't start." Although she continued to frown, he saw her mentally throw in the towel, so he promised, "He's a good guy."

At the sidewalk, and between the sounds of birds and chatting people, he heard a car's engine revving. Turning, he saw a silver SUV barreling right at them.

CHAPTER NINETEEN

Shala saw Sky turn, and then she felt him swing around, hard and fast. His forearm, thick and corded with muscle, smacked right across her abdomen. It knocked the air from her lungs and hurled her several feet off the ground and across the sidewalk. Her back slammed against the ground before she felt another blow—something heavy smacked on top of her, then rolled off. Wait. Not an it—a he. Sky rolled off of her.

The roar of an engine rang in her ears, followed by the squeal of tires. The smell of exhaust made her aware of how close the car had come to hitting her. She gasped for air, but the oxygen wouldn't travel down her throat.

Sky was scrambling to his feet and pulling something from inside his shirt. A gun. He pointed but didn't shoot. "God damn son of a bitch!"

Sky's words bounced around inside her head. Then the realization hit: someone had tried to make roadkill out of her. Still gasping like a fish out of water, she saw Sky towering over her. At last her lungs cooperated, and she sucked in much-needed oxygen. She probably sounded like a strangled elephant.

"You okay? NJ6328. NJ6328 . . ."

Breathing got easier, but talking was not yet feasible, so she just nodded.

"NJ6328," he repeated. "The tag number was NJ6328. Can you stand up?" He knelt down, concern flickering in his eyes.

"I think so," she managed to say.

He helped her up and pulled her against him. Tight. She sensed people milling around. She didn't care, only wanted to stand there and absorb Sky's strength.

"It's okay," he said.

"I know," she whispered, then realized he wasn't talking to her.

"I've got it handled," he told the gathering crowd. "Move away. It's handled."

He appeared calm. She knew better; she felt the tension in his body. His heart thudded in his chest, right where her cheek rested. He continued to hold her, and she continued to let him. She felt him shifting one arm and heard him pushing a number into his phone.

"Martha, it's Sky. I need a license number pulled. NJ6328. Call me as soon as you have it. Just do it! And call Ricardo and Pete and have one of them head out toward the hospital looking for a silver SUV with that plate. Just do it!" he repeated.

Hanging up, he gently raised her face from his chest. A huge scowl beetled his eyebrows. "Christ. You're bleeding."

A coppery taste filled her mouth and she remembered. "I bit my lip when I landed."

"Come on, let's have a doctor look at you." He had his overbearing, in-charge voice going.

She stepped out of his embrace. "I'm fine. Look." She pulled her lip out to let him see. He pushed a hand down his face, then started moving her toward the hospital.

"I hit you hard, Shala." He wore guilt like a cloak again.

"You knocked me out of the way of a speeding car. Having a bleeding lip is a small price to pay. And it does not warrant being seen by a doctor."

He didn't stop moving until the hospital doors swished closed behind them. "You swear you don't hurt anywhere else?"

"I swear."

He looked back out the doors.

"Do you need to go after him?" she asked.

"No, he's gone by now. And I got a trooper out looking for him."

"That's disappointing," she said, hoping a bit of humor would help the tension.

"What is?"

She grinned. "It's just that the cops in the movies—you know, Hollywood cops—would chase them down on foot, commandeer a motorcycle or a Porsche, and after an exciting high-speed chase, they'd jump on top of the moving vehicle and get their guy."

Humor flashed in his eyes. "Yeah, I was going to do that, but I didn't want to show off. We just started dating."

"Funny," she said. But just as suddenly, her amusement faded. As he moved her to the elevator his words replayed in her ears, the feel of his hand on her waist tingled down her body, and the memory of their kiss played like slow music in her brain.

The music came to a screeching halt as she heard another of her emotional barriers crash to the ground. She couldn't do this. She pulled away from his touch. "What's really funny is the lie about us dating."

"Why is it a lie?" he asked.

"I told you why." She stared at the closing elevator doors, attempting to close the doors to her heart.

"I must have missed that. Was it right before you kissed me?"

She stared at him, her emotions running amok. "*You* kissed *me*. I didn't kiss you."

"Semantics." He moved closer, and his arm brushed hers. Leaning down, he touched his lips to her temple. "Because you enjoyed it as much as I did."

"Says who?" she snipped. He was right, but she'd never admit it to him. Or to herself. Yup, lying to oneself was often recommended by the surgeon general. Or at least it was favored over cigarette smoking.

"Me. I say so." Sky laughed. "And I'll bet if you ask the mayor, he'll agree."

"See, is this so hard, woman?" Redfoot asked Veronica, craning his neck to lock eyes with her. It had taken almost an hour to talk her into his bed.

"For one minute only. I swear, if someone catches us I'll say you forced me."

"You would not." He smiled and pressed his lips to hers. The kiss lingered, the kind that told a man a woman wanted him. That she cared.

He moved his hand up to her breasts. Her lips tasted sweet, like a woman should. He moved his mouth to her neck. And damn if he didn't feel things moving down south in an appropriate way. Maybe he didn't need the pills anymore. Maybe with his feelings growing into something more than lust, his body would cooperate.

As his fingers began to toy with her nipple, she removed his hand from her breast. "I think your minute is up, *viejo*."

He laughed and gave her cleavage a kiss. She wrapped her arms around his neck and squeezed him tightly to her breasts.

"You are such a bad man, but you make me feel young and daring."

"We *are* young and daring." He went to pull back, but his hair had gotten tangled in the tiny buttons on her blouse.

"Redfoot, I should get up before someone comes in."

"I would let you, but I think you have my young and daring hair caught in your buttons."

She pushed him up, but the hair tore at his scalp. "Wait," he said. "Let me get on top and then you can see to pull it free."

He rolled on top of her, and the cool air of the room bathed his bare buttocks as the covers slipped off.

"Raise your head," Veronica said, and giggled.

"I'm showing my ass," he complained with a laugh.

"It's not a bad ass," she teased. "Raise your head a bit."

He tried, but the hair was too tangled. He dropped his face back to her breasts, then tried again.

"Not yet." Her fingers worked in his hair. "Now try."

She gently pushed him up, but the pain quickly brought his nose back to her cleavage. She tugged him up; he pushed back down. If he didn't feel certain that the game would leave him bald, he would have enjoyed it. And that's the position they were in—ass showing, pushing up and down, both of them muttering and giggling and occasionally groaning—when the door swept open behind them.

Redfoot reached to conceal his posterior with a blanket. Unfortunately, this brought his head up, tearing hair from his scalp, and he immediately pushed back down. Veronica tried to wriggle away from him, but with half his hair attached to her bosom, there was no escape.

"Mom?" A voice echoed in the room. Veronica froze, and Redfoot heard words he'd never heard her say before.

"Dad?" Another voice sounded, and Redfoot recognized his own son.

"Leave!" Redfoot bellowed out. He heard a scramble of retreating footsteps.

Veronica, using what only could be described as maternal force, pushed him off her, removing a good portion of his scalp. She lunged out of bed. "My son!" she accused. "You said he would not be at the hospital! Now he sees me and . . . he knows. Oh, my. What have you done to me, Redfoot?"

Jose looked at Ramon, who was standing stunned outside Redfoot's hospital room. "Tell me we didn't just see that. Tell me it didn't happen."

Ramon had his hands over his eyes like a child forced to watch a scary movie. "I don't know what I saw. But I swear I didn't see *that*."

Jose closed his eyes, hoping it might help. But the vision of his old man's ass moving up and down like a bad porn flick played in his head. Then the humor of the situation bubbled up inside him. He opened his eyes. "I'll make you a deal. You poke my eyes out and I'll poke yours."

Ramon looked up. "Poke my eyes out? I'm blind. I'll never see again."

Jose laughed. "I tell you . . . it's good to know that we can still do that at that age. Did you see them going at it!"

"Not funny," Ramon said.

"Yes, it is," Jose crowed. "They were going at it like rabbits!" Only then did he note what little humor had existed on Ramon's face was gone.

"That's my mother, damn it! I'm going to kill your father." His friend took a step toward the door.

"No. Leave them be." Jose grabbed him by the arm. Ramon turned, and his expression was ugly.

Sky had just hung up with Lucas, who was waiting for them at the emergency-room exit, when Martha called. The silver SUV belonged to Dr. Henry Michaels. Sky didn't for one moment believe the doctor was behind this.

"That asshole must have stolen Henry's car."

"I don't want to sound un-Christian," Martha said,

"but if he touches my Cadillac, I'm personally sending him to Jesus to have a talk."

Dropping Shala off with Lucas, Sky combed the hospital parking lot. There he found a black sedan. The run-down on that vehicle told him the car was stolen yesterday right outside of San Antonio. While that gave him nothing further on the perp's identity, it did give him a time frame. The man couldn't have gotten into town until midmorning yesterday. So if it was a picture taken by Shala that had caused all this mess, it had to have been taken after that—unless this guy wasn't the one in the photograph, but hired by the one who was. Shit, this wasn't doing him any good. Sky just prayed the vehicle had a fingerprint that would lead somewhere.

He called Ramon next. The mechanic was somewhere in the hospital, because his wrecker was parked not two cars away from the black sedan, with what Sky assumed was Jose's smashed rental car.

Ramon didn't answer, but Sky ran right into him as he walked back into the hospital.

"Hey, I just tried to call you."

"And I didn't answer for a reason." Ramon kept walking.

Sky followed him back into the parking lot. "What's up?"

"Your fucking dad's up, that's what. And I'm telling you right now, if that old man thinks he's gonna do wrong by my mother, he's got another think coming."

Sky started to speak but didn't have a friggin' clue what to say. "I . . . What?"

"Your ol' man is banging my mom, that's what, and Jose and I just got to witness it!"

"Whoa." Sky held up a hand. His mind didn't want to wrap around those words, or the visual they created. *"What?"*

"You heard me. He's banging my mom in his hospital bed! While you might not be able to get it up, your old man doesn't seem to have a problem."

"What? I don't have a probl—" The rest of what had been said filtered through his brain. "Redfoot would never . . ." Words failed Sky again, though he continued to walk beside Ramon.

"Look, I'm sure there's been some mistake, and right now I need you to do something for me."

"Yeah, well, I'm not feeling very cooperative right now," Ramon snapped. He pulled his keys from his pocket. "Just ask Jose."

"No," Sky said. "I need you to drop the car you're carrying and take that one"—he pointed to the black sedan—"down to police headquarters. You can come back for this one later."

"Like I said, I'm not feeling very cooperative," Ramon repeated.

"It's important," Sky said. "It's about Jessie's shooter."

The fury faded from Ramon's expression. "Fine. But I swear to God, Sky, the next time I see your ol' man, I'm belting him."

"We'll work that out later," Sky said. He'd knock the shit out of anyone who touched Redfoot, Ramon included. But he couldn't help but assume some huge misunderstanding had taken place.

Sky suddenly remembered the pills Redfoot had passed off to him last night. Well, maybe Redfoot and Ramon's mother *were* sharing company. But no way would Redfoot be having sex in a hospital room where anyone could walk in. The man was too private.

Ramon started his wrecker and set the release on the car. When he got out to unhook the Mustang, Sky asked, "Is this Jose's rental?"

"Yeah, and when you see him, tell him I'm sorry for punching him. He's not responsible for Redfoot."

Sky shook his head. Jose was having a hell of a bad day.

CHAPTER TWENTY

"Son of a bitch!" Jose muttered, eyeing himself in the hospital bathroom mirror. His forehead sported a gash and a goose egg, and he had two black eyes. His nose still exhibited splinters from the thorn bush and was bruised from the blonde's Reebok. Now he had a swollen lip. And the vision of his dad humping his neighbor. He splashed some water on his face. "Welcome to fucking Precious."

After drying off with paper towels, he stepped out of the bathroom and eyed his father's room down the hall. Not knowing if Ramon's mother was gone, he decided to shoot back up to surgery to check on Jessie and see if he could find Sky. He sure couldn't face his old man now. The only positive side to this was that they'd have something to talk about other than his moving back to Precious.

So Dad, how's sex in a hospital bed with ol' lady Cloud?

In the surgery waiting room, he didn't see Sky or Maria, but he got some strange looks. He knew by name most of the people he saw, though others he just recognized. Growing up in the same small town, he'd seen them dozens of times at the grocery store or diner.

Spotting Cheryl, another friend of Maria's and Jessie's from high school, he asked about Maria.

"I think she said she was going to the café on the third floor to grab something to eat," Cheryl said, staring at his face. "What happened to you?"

"Just bumped into something," he said.

She grinned. "It looks as if you bumped into a lot of somethings." She motioned at the blood on his shirt.

Ignoring her, he headed for the cafeteria. When he

stepped out of the elevator on the third floor, he saw Maria standing in front of a window, her nose pressed to the glass like a kid looking into a candy store.

Wanting to get past the awkwardness, he went and stood beside her. She didn't even turn to look at him, just stared at the baby sleeping in the bassinet. "Is that the kid of someone we know?" he asked.

She jumped and faced him. He saw the emotion in her eyes. Having already heard that Jessie was okay, he knew something else had made Maria so sad.

"You okay?" he asked.

"Fine." She swiped at her cheeks. Her gaze shot to the blood on his shirt. "What happened to you?"

He shrugged, not sure he could say it aloud. "You wouldn't believe it."

A crease appeared between her eyes. "I don't know. After what I witnessed last night and this morning, I'm not sure it would take a stretch."

Okay, he deserved that.

Sighing, he shoved a hand into one of his pockets and started fingering his keys. "I guess I owe you an apology."

"You think?"

"I'm sorry."

Her gaze shot back to the nursery window and more tears filled her eyes. "For what, Jose? What are you apologizing for? For last night, or for two years ago?"

He held his breath, not sure he was ready to have this conversation. Hell, he wasn't even sure what he wanted to say. Should he ask for a second chance? Or was he kidding himself that he had any chance at all? If one thing had been made clear in the past twelve hours, it was that he and Precious didn't mix. Still, he knew this was a necessary conversation.

"Would you have come with me if I'd asked?" he blurted.

She stood quiet, as if the question didn't make sense. Finally, she answered. "I don't know. But I guess what you're saying is that your job was more important than me."

He shook his head. "I didn't say that."

"But it's true, isn't it? You chose New York over me."

"I chose New York over Precious. It's more than the job, Maria. It's this place. I hate Precious. I hate its small-ness, I hate its heat. I hate being expected to be a carbon copy of my old man—that I need to put on a costume and perform stupid rituals that I don't believe in. I hate disappointing my father while watching you and Sky do everything right."

A tear rolled down her cheek. "Don't you dare blame us for your relationship with your dad."

When she turned to walk away, he grabbed her. "Stop. I didn't mean . . . I don't blame you and Sky. I blame my-self, and being here just reminds me of it." He pulled her into his arms and held her. Damn, if it didn't feel a hun-dred different kinds of right. He buried his nose in her soft black hair.

"Maria, you have no idea how many times I picked up the phone to call you and ask you to join me. But I didn't think it was fair. To ask you to give up this place when I know how much it means to you. So I waited to see if you would come on your own."

She answered without pulling away. "You were the one to leave. Why should I come after you?"

He swallowed down the knot in his throat while the answer vibrated in his head. *Because then I would have known that I meant more to you than Precious.* But he couldn't say that. He pressed his hand to the back of her hair. He didn't have an answer he could tell her, but one thing he knew: she felt good in his arms. He heard the ringing of the elevator opening its door. Footsteps sounded, but he wasn't ready to let her go.

She pulled out of his embrace. Jose looked up and saw the man at the same time he heard Maria's breath catch. It took him a second, but then he realized that the sandy-haired guy staring daggers at him was the same one who'd caught him naked, drunk, and bathing in Summer's Eve last night.

Without saying a word, the man turned to walk away. Maria watched him take a few steps. Jose's heart rejoiced that she didn't go after him, but he rejoiced too soon, because seconds later she took off.

"Matt?" she called.

You were the one to leave. Why should I come after you? Jose remembered what Maria had just told him. That rule must not apply to Matt, because Maria chose to give chase.

The elevator doors opened again. An elderly gentleman walked out as Matt went in. Maria followed. When the doors closed, Jose was left alone. And for the second time that morning, he felt as if he'd been coldcocked.

Maria's heart thumped against her breastbone. What was she doing? She'd told herself that it was over with Matt, that he obviously had another woman in Dallas. That she'd been a fool to hope. But she'd seen the way he'd looked at her with Jose. She'd seen the hurt in his eyes. He was wrong about her and Jose. Was it possible that she was wrong about Dallas?

"I heard about Jessie," Matt said, without looking at her. "I thought you might need me. I forgot you had someone else."

"It's not how it looks," she said.

"Then how is it?" He frowned at the elevator doors. Why wouldn't he look at her?

"It's over," she said. "It's been over for a long time." But even as she said that, it felt like a lie. And just like that, she knew why: it wasn't over yet. Before it could be over, she had to tell Jose the truth.

Jessie had been right—she had to tell Jose about the baby. It was the closure she needed. Then she had to tell Matt. She had to explain that she'd lost Jose's baby, and because of it she might not be able to have another child.

Maria suddenly realized that Matt was staring at her. He stared as if trying to read her thoughts.

"You're right," he said. "It's not how it looked. Because from what I just saw, it didn't look over."

"He hugged me. That's all." That much was truth.

Matt shook his head. "I've been through this once. I loved a woman who loved someone else. I paid the price. I'm still paying, and I refuse to go through it again."

"It's not like that," she repeated.

"Really? Look me right in the eyes, Maria, and tell me you don't love him. Tell me that he doesn't matter to you anymore."

She opened her mouth to say those words, but they didn't come out. Jose mattered. She wasn't in love with him, but could she really say she didn't love him? Her feelings for Jose were so mixed up. There were two Joses in her heart: Jose, the man, and Jose, Redfoot's son. Could she explain to Matt when she didn't understand it herself?

Her time ran out. The elevator doors opened, and Matt walked out. Maria had the feeling he wasn't ever coming back.

Jose reached his father's floor the same time Maria walked out of the other elevator. She'd been crying again.

"Everything okay?" he asked.

She looked at him with a mix of anger and grief. "No, it's not okay, Jose. It will probably never be okay."

Was she talking about Matt? Jose wasn't sure if he felt happy knowing they had possibly broken up, or if he felt guilty for instigating it. He followed her down the hall. "I didn't mean to cause problems."

When they got to Redfoot's room, she reached to push the door open. He grabbed her arm. "Knock first."

She rolled her eyes. "What's he going to do? Come answer it?"

"Uh, it just seems like a good idea," he replied, giving a knock.

"Come in," Redfoot called.

Jose and Maria walked in. Redfoot nodded at them. Jose nodded back. Silence followed.

"You look like day-old crap," Redfoot finally said.

"So do you," Jose answered.

"I just love the way you two show your affection. Men." Maria gave Jose a shove. "Give your father a hug."

Jose did as Maria said. The old man's arms reached up and awkwardly squeezed him.

"I didn't know you were coming down," Redfoot said.

"When I heard about the accident, I was worried."

"If you lived here," Redfoot said, "you wouldn't worry so much."

Well, hell. Jose thought catching his old man screwing his neighbor would have at least bought him a few minutes' reprieve. Obviously not.

"Have they said when you're getting out?" Maria asked.

"Doc just left. I got my walking papers. He said I was fit as a fiddle. Up for anything."

"I could have told him that," Jose said.

Maria gave him a strange look before returning to Redfoot. "Did he restrict you from any activities?"

"It's too late if he did," Jose muttered. When Maria turned and stared, he shrugged. "I'm just saying he looks as if he could . . . hit one out of the ballpark."

"You just said he looks like crap."

Jose glanced out the window. "Yeah, well, that's after he told me *I* look like crap."

"I wasn't 'hitting one out of the ballpark,'" Redfoot spoke up. "I was stuck."

Jose choked.

Maria's gaze shot back and forth between the two of them. "Stuck where?"

"I've never heard of anyone getting stuck," Jose said with difficulty.

"What are you talking about?" Maria asked.

Redfoot slapped his hand on the mattress. "Would someone get me some pants so I don't have to show my ass as I walk the hell out of here?"

Jose snapped. "You didn't worry about showing it a few minutes ago."

CHAPTER TWENTY-ONE

Sky had gotten Shala's images copied to a flash drive and then got her settled at Lucas's place with his laptop to start combing through her images. He was confident that she was safe. Not that he hadn't called to check on her four times.

"What? You afraid I'm going to make a play for her?" Lucas had joked.

Sky hadn't considered the possibility until Lucas mentioned it. Then he found himself feeling territorial. That was new for him. Sure, no man wanted a guy trying to steal his woman, but jealousy? He didn't do that.

Not that he was even doing it now. It was just that he hadn't gotten started with Shala yet, and it would be easy for some other guy to step in and put an end to his start before he got to the finish. The finish? What was that? His thoughts ricocheted around in his head.

We don't need you breaking her heart.

The mayor's warning rang in his ears. Sky didn't go

around breaking women's hearts. Most of them listened to him in the beginning. Most of them knew from the get-go that he wasn't long-term. He and the ladies enjoyed each other's company, and when the fun was over, one of them walked away. The fact that he usually walked first didn't mean anything.

You afraid I'm going to make a play for her? He dialed Lucas again.

"Hey," he said when his friend picked up.

"Yeah?" Lucas said. Sky heard laughter in the background.

"What are you guys doing?"

"Playing Scrabble."

"You finally got someone to play Scrabble with you?" Before Lucas sobered up, every time he got drunk he'd begged Sky to play. The man loved word games.

"I have to tell you, your woman cheats."

Your woman. Sky's territorial feelings relaxed.

"How does she cheat?" Sky figured he needed to know this information for future reference, but he wished like hell it wasn't coming secondhand. He wanted to be discovering all these little things about her himself.

"She's trying to convince me that *stanky* is a word. I told her *that word* is what's stanky."

"Which confirms it's a word," Shala called out in the background. She laughed again, and Sky remembered how she looked while doing it. His pangs of jealousy might have evaporated, but he was up to his eyebrows in envy. He wanted to be the one seeing her laugh, making her laugh . . . His gut said she didn't do it near enough lately. He wanted to be the one to change that.

"Has she gone through the photos?" Frustration rang in his voice, and he hated it.

"All freaking day. I'll bet she's got over five hundred shots. I made her take a break."

Sky wanted to be the one taking care of her, insisting she needed breaks, being her hero even if she'd pointed out he didn't hold a candle to the Hollywood cops. Who could know pushing her out of the way of a moving car wouldn't be enough? Yeah, he'd seen she was joking, but it had dinged his ego just the same.

"Before you ask: yes, I fed her dinner."

"Good," Sky replied, and forced himself to stop acting like an idiot. "I'll be finished here in a bit. See ya then."

Sky almost told Lucas to have her wait up for him but stopped. The only stupid thing he hadn't done was to call Shala himself like a swooning teen.

He heard Lucas disconnect, and tucked his cell back in his pocket. What the hell was wrong with him? He told himself it was the case. For eight hours he'd been working with Phillip and the rangers, and for what? Nothing. Eight hours of trying not to think about Shala and their kiss, and about how much he wanted to kiss her again. And he wanted more. How long had it been since he'd wanted a woman this badly? How long since he'd wanted more than simple sex?

Sure, he wanted sex with Shala, but he looked forward to simply getting to know her, learning what she liked to eat and cooking it for her. Before, all the getting-to-know-you periods had been steps on the road to sex, or to keeping the sex. Now he was actually looking forward to the journey. Which led him back to his original question: what the hell was wrong with him?

"Everything okay?" Phillip asked.

Sky nodded. "Late night last night."

"A woman?" Phillip guessed.

"Not what you think," Sky replied, in no mood to share.

"Why don't you head on out? I don't think we're going to get anything this go-round, either." They'd returned to the hotel to give the room one more check. But after ten minutes of milling around, even the two eager CSI guys looked bored.

The only thing that had turned up today was Henry's

car. Without prints. The black sedan and the gun had yielded nothing, too. Whoever this creep was, he'd managed to do a few things right. Which meant he was either professional or lucky. And since his cars were impounded, the guy was either running around on foot or had stolen something different. Or he could have someone working with him.

Questions. A lot of damn questions and no answers.

Sky's gaze flickered across the bloodstain on the wall. The sight still made his gut churn, though less now that Jessie was going to live. His eyes shifted to Shala's suitcase. Sky knew Phillip wouldn't allow anything out of the room right now. Which meant Shala would need to go shopping. He imagined going with her, learning what she liked . . .

Dear God, when had he ever wanted to go shopping with a woman?

Then he realized she wouldn't even have a toothbrush tonight, or anything to sleep in. That was a visual he liked: her, soft and sexy in bed, an artfully arranged sheet—

"We're going to want to talk to Winters tomorrow," Phillip said, interrupting Sky's daydream. "I've had someone go through those images, looking for the obvious. Nothing's jumping out. I'll go through them tomorrow morning myself, and then I'll call you with a time to meet."

"Fine," Sky answered. "Do you want me to bring her to the station, or do you want to go to her?"

"Where did you say she was staying?" Phillip asked, eyeing the blood and frowning.

"With a friend of mine."

"Is this guy able to protect her if he has to?"

"He's ex-military, ex-cop," Sky explained. He didn't mention the present job, which was for the government—supposedly training special-ops, but Lucas remained vague with the details. Whatever he did those few weeks every six months, it afforded him his rather nice toys. Along with those boats and cars, it had also turned him into a drunk until he pulled himself together last year.

"Why don't you bring her down to the police station?" Phillip suggested. "Unless you're worried she'll be followed."

"I'll bring her." Shala would probably be getting cabin fever by then, and he couldn't keep the woman locked up forever. As long as he or Lucas was with her, she was safe. Sky looked at his watch—it was almost nine o'clock. He still needed to go by Redfoot's and his own place before he could get back to Shala. "I think I'll head out."

He nodded his good-byes and walked out to the truck Lucas had loaned him just in case the perp had decided to track Sky's. As he did, his phone rang. He checked the caller ID. For a crazy moment he hoped it might be Shala needing to talk to him—or better, just wanting to talk to him—but it wasn't. It was Maria. His foster sister had called a couple of times already today. He'd already dropped the bomb about her not being able to stay at his place because of the danger. She hadn't whined, but she'd told him the tension at Redfoot's was thick enough to serve over pancakes. And neither Redfoot nor Jose would explain.

Obviously, being around Jose was difficult for Maria. Which was a prime example of why Sky wanted no part of the everlasting kind of love that Maria had set her heart on. Well, not the prime example, he admitted. That honor went to his parents.

Shala watched Lucas play his last two letters and declare himself the winner.

"You don't give a girl a break, do you?"

"Just because you're female?" While probably the same height, approximate weight, and only a little older than Sky—meaning around thirty-five, over six feet tall, and carrying close to two hundred pounds of lean muscle—this was a very different man. Lucas's build reminded her more of a football linebacker, while Sky's seemed more suited to baseball or soccer.

"I stopped giving girls breaks when they started getting equal pay. Plus, I hate losing at Scrabble." Lucas laughed and ran a hand through his hair. The thick mane was short and chestnut brown. His eyes were hazel, where Sky's were black. But there was no question that Lucas's charming grin, a little crooked, only added to his good looks.

"I never would have guessed," Shala teased. She liked Lucas—felt comfortable around him. Safe. Unlike how she felt with Sky.

Not that Sky didn't make her feel safe physically. Hell, the man had saved her life twice: getting her out of the hotel room when that wannabe camera thief came calling, and then getting her out of the way when the SUV called back. No, the unsafe feelings she got around Sky involved desire. Kissing, touching . . . wanting to reopen herself to romance and love. But that meant opening herself to the possibility of being hurt again. Was she ready to go there?

Her cell phone rang inside her purse. Her heart felt a little yank and tug, hoping that it might be Sky. He'd called Lucas several times but hadn't called her, even though he'd gotten her number before he left.

Not that she expected him to call, and not that she wanted him to. Okay, she did *want* him to, just like she wanted his kisses and all the stuff that went alongside falling head over heels for a guy. Because she was falling, damn it. She was falling for Sky Gomez. In spite of how unsafe it felt, in spite of the fact that she hadn't known him long enough, she wasn't sure she could stop herself. For that matter, she didn't know if she wanted to stop herself.

"Hello?" She answered without looking at the number.

If it was Sky, maybe it would be a sign that she should take a leap of faith.

"What size underwear do you wear, Blue Eyes?"

Sky's voice made her smile. Then she realized what he'd asked. "What?"

"I didn't know there were so many types of panties."

"What the heck are you doing?" Shala saw Lucas stand up and motion to the front door, indicating he would give her some privacy.

"I'm at Wal-Mart, trying to pick you up a few essentials before they close."

"Can't you bring my suitcase?"

"It's evidence, and it will be at least a few days before they release it." He paused. "Do you wear bikinis? Thongs?" His voice was husky.

She grinned, imagining him standing there daunted. "Don't tell me you've never bought a woman underwear before."

"Sure I have. Just not at Wal-Mart."

"So you're more a Victoria's Secret kind of guy?" she teased.

"Is that where they sell the kind that come in flavors?"

Their laughs spilled through the line at the same time, and she pulled her knees to her chest and hugged them. Her mind was full of unexpected and erotic images. Her heart rate increased, and she felt her cheeks burn.

She fought back the images. "I wear a size four."

"What type? There's the high tops, the low tops, the boy cuts."

"I'm not picky."

"You'll wear a thong?" His voice was husky again.

She hated thongs. Deplored them.

"Will you?" Heat laced his voice.

"Sure." As soon as she answered, she smacked herself on the forehead. Then his low growl had her smile spreading into her chest, bringing on a giddy feeling.

"Okay, now the next problem. What size bra?"

"You're getting personal," she teased.

"Okay, let me guess. I'd say . . ." He paused. "Wow, I like this one. Will a red one do?"

She chuckled again. "Red's fine, but not if I'm wearing a light-colored top."

"I'll get one of each. This size looks right. Thirty-four C. Right?"

"Amazing. You're really good at that," she said honestly. "Do you guess birthdays, too?"

"Yours is November fifteenth," he said. "But I found that online. Oh, I already picked you out something to sleep in."

She wrapped a strand of hair around her finger. "I'm afraid to ask."

"Yeah, I saw a few things I liked, but I was good—picked something similar to your other pajamas. But this one is blue to match your eyes."

"Lucas told me he'd loan me a shirt," she spoke up, realizing her bank account was a tad thin.

"You're not sleeping in that man's shirt. I'll bring one if that's what you prefer."

Was that jealousy? A little was good, because she'd already felt a pinch herself. How many women had worn flavored underwear for Sky?

"I was also going to pick up a pair of shorts and shirt, just to get you by. Hopefully, I can take you tomorrow to pick out some things for the next few days."

Next few days? That brought her back to reality. She only had a few days. She and Sky only had a few days. She lived almost two hundred miles from here. Was she ready to jump headfirst into involvement with Sky Gomez, willing to do a long-distance relationship? And what if she got involved with him and things went south?

"They have some khaki shorts and tank tops similar to what you wore yesterday. Is that okay?"

"That's fine, but nothing too expensive. I'm on a budget."

"These are gifts," he said.

"You shouldn't be buying me gifts."

"Are you always so difficult?" he asked.

"Are you?" she countered.

"Probably," he admitted.

"Me, too."

He chuckled. "I've got to go by Redfoot's place and mine, but I'll see you as soon as I can." A silence followed. "If you're in bed, do you want me to . . . come in?"

"To talk?" she verified.

"Did I push myself on you last night?" he asked.

"Do I need to remind you of what happened?"

He chuckled. "I'll make sure it doesn't happen again."

"Okay," she said, then wondered what she'd agreed to.

There was an awkward silence, as if something else needed to be said. Something, as in "I miss you" or "Hurry home" or "Love ya," but none of those fit. Obviously their relationship was in a strange place. If it even was a relationship. Had she made up her mind that it was?

" 'Bye," he said, as if he felt the uncomfortable pause.

" 'Bye," she replied.

She hung up and hugged her legs even tighter. The awkwardness faded, leaving her with only a sense of giddiness. That's when the absurdity of it hit: she'd been stalked, had her camera taken from her, barely escaped death twice, had to have her hand stitched up, had to deal with being in the hospital twice, and yet she felt happier right now than she had in years. Amazing, what a little human contact could do for one's spirits. That, and a prospective romance. She'd forgotten how much fun it was to flirt. Forgotten what it was like to feel sexy.

The front door opened, and barreling in with Lucas came Sky's two dogs. Correction: Sky's two wolves.

Shala drew her knees up closer. The dogs stopped and stared at her. "How did they get here?" she asked.

Lucas glanced from her to the dogs. "They've been here all day. Sky probably told them to watch out for you."

Shala chuckled nervously. "Right. He said, 'Go on over to Lucas's place and protect Shala,' and they just came barreling over."

His eyebrow rose. "You don't think they understand English?" He called out several commands—sit, lay, and roll over—and the pair complied to his every request. "They're smart dogs."

"You mean wolves?"

"Part wolves," Lucas agreed. "This one here is Sundance." He pointed to the lighter of the two. "And that one is Butch. And they are so smart that right now, they know you're scared."

"And for a good reason. They're part wild animals."

Lucas dropped down beside Sundance and patted his flank. "Yeah, but don't all of us have a little wild animal inside?"

"I'm pretty tame. Isn't it against the law to keep them as pets?" A shiver tiptoed up her spine as Butch's golden eyes met hers.

"I've never heard of that law."

"I'll bet Sky has," Shala muttered. "I'm surprised he didn't think before taking in these mixed breeds."

Lucas stood up. "Maybe he did it because he's a mixed breed himself."

Shala swallowed a lump of embarrassment. "I haven't thought about it like that."

"It's okay." Lucas smiled. "Don't worry. I think for the most part, Sky has his wolf under control."

"I didn't mean—"

"I'm teasing you," he laughed.

One of the dogs approached her. No doubt, Lucas saw the uneasiness in her eyes. "Hold your hand out and let him sniff you. He'll be your best friend before you know it."

"I was bitten by a big dog when I was young," Shala said, feeling the need to explain.

"Today, when I stepped outside, I got shit on by a bird. But I'm still going back outside tomorrow."

Shala laughed and carefully extended her hand. Both Sundance and Butch eased up to her. Their noses were wet, and their fur not as wiry as it appeared.

"See, they like you."

Sundance pushed Butch out of the way to get petted. Shala laughed. "I guess they're not as scary as I thought."

"Things generally aren't."

Shala bit her lip, wondering if a relationship with Sky would be less scary if she let him closer. "So you and Sky . . . are close?"

Lucas, now in the kitchen, poured some dog food into two bowls and placed them on the floor. Both dogs ran to be fed. "I like Sky. Respect him. Don't know if I'd call us close."

Shala grinned. "Is that because of him or you?"

"Good question," he said, but didn't offer a good answer.

"How come I get the feeling that you don't like a lot of people?"

"I like plenty," Lucas said, chuckling. "It's the respect part I have a hard time with."

"But you respect Sky?" She realized that she'd already begun to respect him, too.

"Yeah, I do." Lucas stared at her. "But I'm a guy."

"What does that mean?" she asked.

He looked away. "Not a damn thing."

She wanted to ask him to explain. She wanted to ask more questions about Sky, but Lucas didn't seem like the type to dish out information, and she didn't want to make him uncomfortable. He was being more than kind just to let her stay here.

She stood up. "I think I'll go look through some more of my pictures until I fall asleep."

"I left a new toothbrush and toothpaste in the bathroom

off of your room, and one of my shirts to sleep in." He picked up a crossword-puzzle book and dropped into a leather recliner.

"I'm not running you out of your bedroom, am I?" she asked.

"No, I have three bedrooms. I've always slept in the back one."

Three? So when Sky showed up, he didn't have to share the room with her. That realization left her with mixed emotions. She started toward the bedroom but turned around. "Lucas?"

He looked up. "Yes?"

"Thanks for letting me stay here, and for being good company. I had fun tonight."

He smiled. She got a strange feeling he was a loner like herself. And like Sky. She remembered seeing Sky at the hospital, surrounded by people, and then with Maria and Lucas. Funny how even while surrounded by people who cared about him, people he cared about, he still came across this way.

But perhaps being lonely was a state of mind. Perhaps it was time she changed her mind.

CHAPTER TWENTY-TWO

Sky eased himself into the room where Shala slept. The bedside lamp was left on, but she was out cold. Even his laptop in the bed with her had fallen asleep. He dropped the bag of his purchases on the room's chair and then just stared at her.

She slept in the same outfit she'd worn all day, but he spotted her bra folded on top of the second bedside table.

He could smell soap, as if she'd showered. Too bad he hadn't gotten here in time to give her the pajamas—or maybe the red bra and matching thong.

Then again, he'd purposely taken his sweet time arriving. When he'd gone home and found the light in the closet on, and the box with his childhood things pulled out as if someone had gone through them, he remembered she'd searched his house. It pissed him off to know she'd gone though that box. Not that the past was some big secret. Hell, half the town knew—but that pissed him off sometimes, too. And the town hadn't gone snooping through his things.

He didn't like snooping women. He didn't like jabbering women. Shala Winters wore both those labels, and yet he liked her. Liked her too much.

That's when he realized that, more than angry, he was feeling scared. All Redfoot's babbled nonsense about soul mates for the last month must have messed with his head. Why else would he be staying away from a woman who'd spent five minutes on the phone taking about her underwear with him? A gorgeous woman who was sleeping alone and admitted to liking thongs.

With one knee on the bed, he carefully closed his laptop and set it on a bedside table. He removed his shoes, shirt, and jeans. Glancing down, he gave his new underwear a quick inspection, making sure all the buttons were secure. He sure as hell wouldn't have picked this pattern for himself, but Wal-Mart had a limited supply of button-fly boxers. His gaze went to Shala, looking so damn sweet. She'd practically said he could sleep here. Okay, it had been slightly vague, but considering he didn't plan on trying anything . . . He pulled back the covers and climbed in beside her.

Reaching over, he turned out the light. The darkness enhanced his sense of smell. He inhaled a breath of freshly showered woman. Damn, if he didn't want to pull her to him. *I didn't try anything last night,* he'd told her.

Which implied he wouldn't tonight. Sky worked hard at keeping his word. But give him just a little more time and he'd stop making those implications.

Redfoot lay in his bed at home, staring at the ceiling. Veronica hadn't returned any of his calls. Part of him wanted to stomp over to her house and force her to admit to herself and the world what he believed to be the truth: she cared about him as much as he'd grown to care about her. Any of his forefathers would simply have gone to her teepee and brought her back, fighting, screaming, and most likely loving it. In the old days it had been an honor to be carried off by a man who loved you. Today's women didn't play along.

But there had to be a way he could convince Veronica to openly admit she cared about him. If not that, then how could he steal the woman from her teepee without Sky coming after him with handcuffs?

His mind and heart went to Sky and Blue Eyes. Tonight, when the boy came by, he'd had that look in his eyes. Love had that boy by the neck, which fit nicely with his predictions. But the rest of his dream still weighed on Redfoot's mind. Sky had to watch his woman carefully, for the dog still waited.

Sky had listened to this advice, as Sky always listened, but listening and believing were two different things. Redfoot knew that Sky did not believe in the ways of the spirits. But unlike Jose, there was a part of Sky and even Maria that remained open. They might not embrace it, but they did not turn their backs on their heritage, either.

As he closed his eyes, Redfoot's mind went to Jose. His heart ached for the distance he felt growing between them. He thought about Maria and the sad weight that both she and his son carried on their shoulders. How could he help these two find their way to each other?

At least it appeared that Matt had run off. The boy was

wiser than Redfoot had imagined. The spirits never looked kindly on anyone trying to stop the union of two soul mates. While so many people tried, love could not be overlooked. How could he make these young people— Veronica, too—understand that romantic love was what life was about? Alone, a person's soul grew old and sad, but with the love of another person it grew. It found laughter instead of sadness, answers instead of questions. One had soft touches instead of loneliness. Love meant hope. Without love, life held no promise.

Folding his arms over his chest, Redfoot willed the spirits to help him. A dream would show him the way.

Maria rolled off her bed, her heart and head twisted in so many painful directions. Standing in the middle of her room, she toyed with the hem of her nightshirt. She'd promised herself she would tell Jose about the baby. To find the closure she needed. That she *deserved*.

Some promises were hard to keep. She'd sat in the living room tonight across from Jose and Redfoot, both men with black eyes and bruises, neither of them speaking, both wallowing in their self-made worlds of misery. Maria had stared at the television, not really watching. Her heart was breaking for Matt, the man she thought she loved. It broke for Sky, who had jumped out of his skin at the mere mention of Shala Winters's name. Obviously, Redfoot was right: Sky was already half in love with the woman. Knowing his past, Maria knew her foster brother would fight it.

But mostly, Maria's heart broke for Jose and Redfoot—a father and son who loved each other, but whose lives led them down different paths.

She kept hearing Jose tell her, *I hate Precious. I hate its smallness, I hate its heat. I hate being expected to be a carbon copy of my old man. That I need to put on some costume and complete some stupid rituals that I don't believe in. I hate disappointing my father while watching you and Sky do everything right*. In all these years, she had never once imagined that her presence and Sky's had made Jose's life harder, but it had made the differences between him and his father more obvious.

She also realized how much Jose was like his mother. Estella had loved Redfoot, her town, and her family, but she had hungered for more. Estella's art had assuaged her hunger. Jose had no outlet. Estella had understood him, but with her gone, Jose had lost the one thing in Precious that made him feel accepted. More importantly, he'd lost the bridge to his father.

Not that any of this changed Maria's circumstances. However, it did explain her infatuation with Jose. She had always loved Estella's zest, her flair, and Jose exemplified those. Add his sexy male body to the mix, and how could she not want him? Yet Jose had been right today. She could have gone after him when he left for New York. She hadn't. Not just because he'd been the one to leave, but because going would have meant leaving Precious, Redfoot, and home. It would have meant leaving the very first place she'd ever felt safe and loved. The truth hurt, but she hadn't loved Jose enough.

Understanding was good, but she still had to tell the truth about the baby. Putting on a silk robe and tying the sash around her waist, she went to face the music.

She got to Jose's bedroom door and stopped. Her heart pounded in her ears. Would he be angry? Didn't he have the right to be angry? Her hands started shaking, and she hurried away down the hall. When she got to the kitchen, headlights flashed in the front window.

Matt? She went to peer outside, hoping and praying. Instead, she saw Ramon Cloud getting out of his car. He brought a suitcase and dropped it at the front door, then left. She recalled that Jose's suitcase had been in the car Ramon had towed.

Ramon left, and she collected the suitcase. On the way back to her room, she set it outside Jose's door. Tomorrow, she'd talk to her foster brother. Tomorrow, she'd have more courage.

Jose pulled the pillow to his face. He wondered if Maria had slept on it, because he could smell her. As much as he loved her scent, he wished he were back in New York, in his own apartment, using his own pillow, living his own life. Missing her had been hard, but seeing her hurt worse. When she looked at him, he saw only anger and disappointment. Before he went to New York, she'd always looked at him with affection, desire, and warmth. Acceptance.

He punched the pillow with his fist. He wanted that back. He wanted *her* back. Was it even possible? *Not if you don't even fucking try*, he told himself. But what if she said no?

When had he become such a wuss? A surge of courage shot through him, and he decided to act. Now.

Jumping out of bed, he shot across the room, flung open the door, burst through, and tripped and fell. Face forward. Floundering, he tried to catch himself, but only air stood between him and the wall. He hit headfirst, hard. The impact jarred his brain and instantly blinded him. Wait . . . not blinded him. Blinking, he saw and felt a chalky substance fluttering around his eyelashes. Only then did he realize his position. He stood on his knees, his head completely punched through the Sheetrock.

It took a moment to regain his bearings. Bracketing his head with his hands, he pulled himself out of the wall. Spitting chalky substance from his mouth, he looked right and left. He saw his father armed with a baseball bat and Maria holding a vase of flowers over her head as if ready to throw.

"What the hell happened?" Redfoot asked.

"Oh, my." Maria lowered her weapon at the same time as her foster father. "I think your nose is bleeding again." She turned on the hall light.

Jose looked down. "Who put this friggin' suitcase in front of my door?"

"I did," Maria said. "Ramon brought it. I thought you'd see it in the morning."

"Well, I didn't."

Maria covered her mouth and giggled. "I'm sorry. It's not funny, but you should have seen yourself with your head inside the wall. And now the hole in the Sheetrock is the same shape as your head."

"That's because my head went through it!" he snapped, not seeing the humor. His face was covered in powder. He even had some on his teeth.

Redfoot let go of a laugh. "Look." His father pointed to the outline in the Sheetrock. "You can even see his nose."

Maria laughed and waved a hand between them. "*Viejo*, you can't laugh too hard. *Both* of you look like you've been beaten with an ugly stick."

Jose wanted to get mad, but his gaze slid to the hole in the Sheetrock, and damn if he didn't see the shape of his head and nose. A chuckle spilled out of him. Then, there in the hallway, all three stood and howled until they had tears in their eyes.

Maria was the first to retire, but only after she made Jose move his neck to make sure he wasn't seriously hurt. Her concern and the gentle touch on his chin felt wonderful, and that reminded him why he'd left his room. But it was too late. He and Redfoot watched her leave.

His dad clapped him on the shoulder. "It's good to see you, son."

Jose reached up and covered his father's aged hand with his own. "It's good to see you, too."

They stood there and looked at each other for several seconds. Jose couldn't remember the last time he'd felt this close to his old man. Then he grinned. "You know, Maria is right. We both look as if we've been beaten with an ugly stick."

"We should have a picture made," Redfoot suggested. "So we can laugh at this later."

"We will," Jose said, and gave his dad's hand one more pat.

"Son," Redfoot said as he turned.

Jose looked back. "Yes?"

"What you thought you saw today at the hospital—"

"Don't worry, Dad. Mom's been gone for a long time. You're an adult. And I don't think Ms. Cloud can get pregnant."

"That's just it, son. What you thought you saw wasn't . . . what you saw."

Jose had never known the old man to lie, and if he hadn't been there, he might believe his father hadn't been having sex with the woman. "As I said, Dad, I'm fine with it. Ramon, on the other hand, isn't." He rubbed his chin. "I'd stay away from him for a while. He throws a mean right."

"You fought with Ramon?" Redfoot asked.

"He was upset and said he'd . . . Well, never mind."

"He threatened me?" Redfoot asked. "You took a punch because of me?" He grinned. "I'm sorry, but I'm also proud."

Jose's chest expanded. He couldn't remember his father ever saying that before. Maybe it wasn't because of his career, but it still felt damn good. "I'm sure you'd have done the same for me."

"You know I would," Redfoot agreed.

Jose walked back to his room, and for the first time since he'd arrived home, it felt good being there.

Sky had been awake for an hour, but he hadn't moved. It was morning. Shala lay still, her head pillowed on his chest, her uninjured hand resting low on his belly. It felt like heaven. It also felt like hell.

What he wouldn't give to slide her hand down inside

his buttoned boxers. What he wouldn't give to slip his hand underneath her tank top and touch the soft flesh and pebbled nipple that rested against his ribs.

All of a sudden, she flinched. He heard her catch her breath and felt her lashes flutter open against his chest. He crooked his neck to see. Her blue eyes were open, and she stared down at her hand and probably the bulge beneath his underwear.

"Don't panic," he whispered in her ear. "I bought the boxers with buttons."

CHAPTER TWENTY-THREE

He caught her as she started to pull away. "Please don't," he said seriously. "Just give me a few more minutes."

Her warm breath spilled out on his chest, and she didn't pull away. "Lucas has a third bedroom." The huskiness of sleep laced her voice.

He could tell from her lack of tension that she wasn't angry. "Yeah, there was a little problem with it."

"What was that?"

"You weren't in it," he answered.

"You're terrible." She shifted to look at him. The slight shift in position brought her breast and that nipple pressed tighter to his side. He really liked how it felt.

"Terrible because I want to be close to you?" He met her sleepy blue eyes, and his gut tightened with a sudden realization. Never before Shala had he slept with a woman who wasn't his mother and not had sex. Never would he have wanted to, either.

"Why didn't you wake me up when you came in?"

"Because you looked exhausted. And . . . because I was

afraid, even though you'd sort of agreed to let me sleep here, that you'd tell me I couldn't."

She leaned up on one elbow. "Do you always tell the truth in hopes it will get you out of trouble?"

He considered that. "Probably." He smiled. "A bad habit I picked up from Redfoot."

She grinned, and it was the prettiest sleepy smile he'd ever seen. "Bad, aren't you?"

"Not all bad." He stared at her. "You do mornings well." He ran a finger over her chin.

"What?"

"Mornings. I was a little afraid after yesterday—you know, waking up with Mace aimed at me—that you're one of those nasty chicks when you first wake up."

Her gaze shifted down to his boxers. "What is that?"

He laughed. "If you don't know, I'm not telling."

She slapped his chest. "I meant, what's that printed on your boxers?"

"Nope." He pulled her against him and rolled atop her. "That's not going to happen," he said, placing an elbow on each side of her head. God, it felt good being on top of her.

"What's not going to happen?" she asked, wriggling. Damn, if that didn't feel good, too.

"No making fun of my shorts."

Her eyes lit up, and she craned her neck again. "Those are little devils, aren't they?"

"It was devils or hearts. Wal-Mart doesn't carry a large selection of button-up boxers. I think these are left over from Valentine's Day." When she laughed, he stared at her. "You'd better stop that."

"Stop what? Making fun of your little-devil under-wear?"

"No. Stop laughing."

"Why?"

"Because it makes me want to do this."

He leaned down and took her lips with his. There

wasn't a moment of hesitation; she opened up, and her tongue slipped inside his mouth. Her kiss said yes. Her kiss said, *Go for it.* So he did.

Adjusting his weight, he slipped his hand underneath her tank top. His palm moved over the softest skin he'd ever felt, up over her tight little abs until he found the pleasing weight of her breast. He sighed and rubbed his thumb back and forth over her tight nipple, and his mouth started moving south, needing to taste the treasure he'd found under her shirt.

He kissed the curve of her neck. Her pulse fluttered against his lips. He ran his tongue up and then down the column of her neck. The sound she made—half sigh, half moan—gave him courage. He lifted himself and pulled her shirt up toward her face, slowly, teasing both of them. Uncovered, he saw his right hand on her breast. His skin was dark compared to hers. Her nipples were light pink, tight peaks that begged to be touched and tasted. He lowered his mouth and took one of the sensitive nubs in his mouth, circled it with his tongue.

He felt her hands move down his back, then up to his shoulders. Soft hands, exploring. She touched with pleasure; she touched for pleasure. And she gave it. But he knew where he wanted those hands next.

Pulling away, he slipped the tank top over her head and took a second to look at her. Holy hell, but he loved what he saw. Her breasts were perfectly shaped and large. His gaze shifted to her face. Her blue eyes looking up at him were filled with need, desire, and passion. Her mouth appeared soft and still wet. What else was wet?

He leaned down again, pressed his lips to hers, and felt her hips rise up to slightly brush against his swollen cock.

"Yes," he muttered into her mouth, and slipped his hand down her abdomen past the waistband of her shorts. He nudged his fingers under her silky underwear, past the triangle of hair and lower, at last finding the softness of her sex. Exploring the folds of her tender flesh, he found the moisture he craved.

He growled and slid his finger down into that tight little core in which he longed to bury himself. "I want to taste you." Pulling his fingers out, he left a trail of dampness over her lower abdomen. Unsnapping the waist of her shorts, he lowered the zipper.

He had one side of her shorts off her hip when he heard, "'Jeremiah was a bullfrog! Bom-bom-bom!'" Since the words were sung in a deep baritone and off-key, he pretty much knew it didn't come from Shala. "'Was a good friend of mine.'"

Sky shut his ears and went back to concentrating on getting Shala's shorts off. But in the back of his mind he made himself a promise: if Lucas's little song came between him and getting Shala naked and satisfied, the man had sung his last.

He caught the top of Shala's shorts, was about to lift her to remove them and her panties in one swift move, when she caught his hand. "Sky?"

"What?" he growled. He hoped Lucas had his will signed, sealed, and delivered.

"I can't . . . I . . . Lucas is up."

"I'll get rid of him." Sky bounced up and off the bed.

She called his name, her tone impatient. "Sky, this is his house. You can't throw him out of his own house."

"Watch me." He took another step.

"Please."

He stopped and raked a hand over his face. The musky scent of her made his already stiff cock as hard as petrified wood. "Please what?" He kept his eyes closed, knowing without question what she was going to say, but he had to hear it before he could begin to accept it. And acceptance wasn't going to be easy.

"I can't do this. Not now."

He turned around. She held her shirt up over her breasts. She looked mortified, her face flushed, her shorts unzipped and open. The look suited her. She was sexy as hell.

" 'Joy to the world!' " sounded outside.

There's no joy in my world, Sky thought. He'd been robbed. He fought the desire to walk into the kitchen and permanently remove his friend's voice box. Instead, he went over to the bed, sat down, and flopped back on the mattress. He didn't move, just stared at the ceiling and waited for the blasted ache in his cock to subside. It was going to take a while.

"You aren't mad, are you?" Shala asked. He felt the bed jiggling. She was obviously putting her shirt back on.

"Furious, but not at you." He flung his arm over his face. When he smelled her scent again, he moaned and changed arms.

"It's not Lucas's fault," she said. "I should have stopped you earlier. I'm not quite ready to . . . I mean, we barely know each other. What's it been? I mean, I know we've been through a lot, but . . ."

God, she was jabbering again. Nope. There was no joy in his world. He waited until she took her first breath, so he wouldn't come off like a total ass, but then he popped up. "I'm going to take a shower."

Ten minutes later, the water still hitting him in the face, he realized what a complete jerk he'd been. He'd crawled into bed with her last night knowing he'd practically tricked her into agreeing to let him sleep there. He'd told himself it was okay because he wouldn't push her, that just sleeping beside her was enough. Obviously, it hadn't been. He'd taken a chance, seen her good mood, and turned it into something more. She'd given him a little taste of heaven, and when they'd gotten interrupted—which wasn't her fault—he'd just up and walked out, left the room without so much as a hug or an "I liked what I saw, can I have a rain check?" Yup, he was an ass.

He pinched the bridge of his nose and tried to think. Damn, he had zero ideas on how to get out of this mess, zero knowledge of how to get out of jams with women, because he'd never tried to get out of one before. Not because he hadn't been in any; he just hadn't cared about getting out of them. When a jam arrived in a relationship, that's when he knew it was walking time. But it wasn't walking time with Shala. He had to find a way out.

He cut the water off and pushed back the shower curtain to stare at the bathroom door. Was she waiting out there to lash out at him? God, would she start jabbering again? He deserved it, he supposed. This time he'd sit there and take it.

He got out of the shower and eased the bathroom door open a bit. She wasn't outside. A big pain hit his gut. Was she so angry that she'd run to Lucas to complain? Was she at that very moment squawking to his friend about how much of an ass he'd been? Was she asking Lucas to help her leave town? Oh, hell. She couldn't leave.

Rushing out of the bathroom, scrubbing the towel over his chest as he did, he hurried to his clothes on the chair. At the clearing of a throat, he turned around. Shala sat at the tiny desk behind the bathroom door, laptop open, one hand now covering her eyes, but her two middle fingers had a wide vee of separation and one blue eye was checking him out.

He let her look a few seconds before moving the towel from his chest to his crotch. "I looked out and didn't see you. I thought you'd stepped out," he explained.

She moved her hand. "Still here," she said. A blush turned her cheeks a pretty pink color.

He studied her expression, blush and all. Was she not angry at him?

She glanced back at her laptop. "I wanted to show you a few things I found when I went through my pictures. I'm not sure if it's anything but . . . it might be something."

He wrapped the towel around his waist, moved closer. "Show me."

He leaned down, put his hand on her shoulder. Emotion churned his gut just from the contact. It hurt like hell, but it also felt wonderful, because she was still there. And obviously she wasn't furious with him, either. Or was she just hiding it?

"Let me find it again." She clicked through the images.

He leaned down close, his cheek pressed against hers. "I'm sorry, Shala."

Her fingers on the keyboard stopped moving. She glanced over, uncertain. "For what?"

"For being a jerk just now."

"You weren't really a jerk."

"Yes, I was. I thoroughly enjoyed what happened." He waved toward the bed. "You're beautiful, and I really would like to enjoy it again . . . and enjoy more. Instead of telling you that, I got frustrated and ran."

Her blue eyes studied him. She bit her lip, as if debating her next words. "I enjoyed it, too." She held up her unbandaged hand, her fingers pinched close together. "I just need a little more time."

"And maybe some privacy?" He looked toward the door, beyond which Lucas had started another song.

"That might help, too." She smiled.

He kissed her. Her mouth was warm and sweet. Careful not to let things progress to a place where he'd end up apologizing again, he pulled back.

Shala went back to flipping through the images. He remembered he'd already apologized to her twice before: once in the hospital, when he'd been giving her a hard time about being afraid of stitches, and again when he'd forgotten about her hospital issue. All three times she'd accepted his apology without giving him grief. All three times he might have deserved a little grief. Which meant Shala Winters wasn't the type to hold grudges. Not very many women managed that. It was a nice quality. It somehow made up for the jabbering and snooping.

"Here's one of them," she said, and pointed to the screen. "I'd stopped off on my way to Precious to get a few shots of other accommodations around the area. I think this shot is around Bueford—I could check my notes and tell you for sure. But the Chambers gave me directions to a few of local cabins that are rented out. They said I couldn't take shots of the inside because a couple of them were leased, but I could take a few outside shots. Look in the car parked in the driveway. I didn't notice it when I took the shot, but look, it has two people, and I don't think they're just talking, if you know what I mean."

He shifted to study the picture.

"I mean, it's sort of odd that they've got a whole cabin and they're doing it in the car, but . . ." Her hands started tapping some keys. "Let me blow it up and you'll see." Then she looked up at him. "I thought maybe someone is cheating and think I'm like a PI or something. I know it's not much, but . . ."

He smiled. "As you said, it's more than before."

"There are three others." She tapped a few more keys. An image taken at nearby Cypress Pond appeared. A couple of men were fishing, and to the right was a family having a picnic. It was a very serene portrait of Precious. "This is the one I got the most excited about."

"It's a great picture, but I don't see—"

"Here," she said, and pointed to a small area in the background that showed the parking lot. "Do you see the car?"

Sky moved closer. "The black sedan?" He kept his tone even. He didn't want to disappoint her, but a picture of the car wasn't going to do them any good.

"But look when I blow it up," she told him, and the screen filled with the section that contained the car. "It's not the clearest shot, but look."

"At what?" he asked, thinking she meant the license plate. Hadn't he told her they had the car? That they—

"Look at the guy standing to the right of the car. I'm pretty sure that's him. That's the guy who was driving the sedan."

Smiling, he squeezed her shoulder. "You are quite a detective, Ms. Winters!" He tugged at the towel around his waist and went to grab his cell. Then he remembered she'd said she had two other images for him to see. "What else did you find?" He went back to stand behind her, wanting to give Phillip the whole story.

She already had another image on the screen. "These might not be anything, but I found him in two different pictures, on two different days, and it just sort of gave me the creeps." She pointed to a small figure in the background at the railroad museum.

"Can you make it bigger?"

"Yeah. I think this is the one where you can almost make out his face. The other one, he's standing in the shadows, but I'm almost certain it's the same guy." She hit a few keys and the image expanded. Sky saw a man in jeans and a navy polo shirt.

When he didn't say anything right away, Shala glanced back. "Do you know who he is?"

"Yeah," Sky said, and he didn't like it.

"Who is it?" she asked.

"His name is Charlie Rainmaker." Grabbing his phone, Sky started dialing Phillip. "He's the main guy who was against trying to bring tourism into town. He started a petition against it."

"Do you think he might be behind *this*?"

"I think he's got a lot to explain."

When Phillip answered his phone, Sky said, "Phillip, it's Sky. Shala went through the images and found a few things that might help."

"I'm looking at the images now," the ranger said. "She's a damn good photographer."

"I know. She's good," Sky agreed, feeling a sense of pride. Oddly, he couldn't ever remember being proud of any of the women he'd dated. Well, there was the one who'd been a centerfold in *Playboy*, but that was different.

"What are the file numbers?" Phillip asked.

"Just a second," Sky said and then asked Shala, "Can you write those file numbers down?"

"Already have." She handed him a piece of paper, then quickly looked away as if she didn't want to eavesdrop. Hoping to let her know she wouldn't be intruding, he placed a hand on her shoulder while he talked.

"Okay, here's what we got . . ." Sky explained to Phillip what Shala had found and then gave him the file numbers. "No, I'll pay a visit to Charlie," he insisted when Phillip offered to send someone. Before he hung up, he set up a time to bring Shala in to be interviewed.

Dropping the phone on the table beside the laptop, he studied her sitting there staring at the wall. "You're okay with going in and talking to Phillip, aren't you?" He moved to the edge of the desk. She turned her head.

"That's fine," she said.

"Hey." He pulled her from her chair, turned her around, and leaned his forehead against hers. "You okay, Blue Eyes?"

She nodded ever so slightly, and a slow grin pulled at her lips.

"What?" he asked.

Her smile widened. "You lost your towel."

Redfoot lay in bed, staring at the ceiling. The images of the dreams flashed in his head. He'd asked the spirits to tell him what to do. He had never understood the saying "ignorance is bliss" until now. If he could go back and un-ask the spirits, he would. This was not going to be easy.

Unfortunately, the spirits had given him a plan. He didn't have to like it, but the spirits would no doubt be angry if he ignored their messages. Angry spirits were not a good thing. A man would have more luck milking a bull than soothing angry spirits. Redfoot had tried as much in his younger years, when he'd been stupid from too much whiskey and his friends had set him up to be the fool. He still had the scars the bull had given him. And sometimes, when the elders of the tribe got together, they still told the story.

He wished he had time to stay in bed and reminisce about the past, but he needed to help make the future right.

He closed his eyes and thought of all the things he wanted to see happen in the lives of those he loved, all the things he had believed were destiny. A man never liked to be proven wrong, but accepting his mistakes and making them right were part of being a man. He got out of bed and made his way to his closet. He pushed away one shirt and then another—trying to find one that he didn't mind getting stained with blood.

CHAPTER TWENTY-FOUR

"You look good in this kitchen," said a husky voice.

Maria swung around. Jose stood in the doorway, watching her. She felt his gaze move up and down, taking in her new sundress, which clung in all the right places—a dress she'd bought to impress Matt. The appreciation in Jose's eyes toyed with her feminine pride. How long had she waited to see him look at her with desire? For years, before he'd finally noticed her.

"How's your neck this morning?" she asked, noticing how his fitted and pressed jeans and expensive button-down business shirt showcased his body and conveyed his personality. Jose had never been a faded-jeans-and-

T-shirt kind of guy. Even his clothes had always set him apart from the laid-back lifestyle of their small town.

He moved his head from side to side. "Amazingly, it doesn't hurt at all."

"Good." She motioned to the counter. "There's coffee."

"Thanks." He shifted, and she listened as he served himself.

Closing her eyes, she wondered how she should start this conversation. Or if she should start it now. Redfoot would be out shortly. She didn't want him to overhear.

Sometimes, she got the feeling that her foster father knew about her and Jose; other times she wasn't sure. Redfoot never pushed people to talk. He just studied them, offering little advice, but sometimes she felt as if he could see right through her.

She turned around and found Jose leaning against the counter, studying her, reminding her of his father. She recalled that she needed to talk to him about Redfoot, about what he'd said about them. Last night when they had all been laughing in the hall, the tension had subsided, but she knew it would return if she couldn't make both of them see that their differences shouldn't stop them from loving one another. She needed to reconstruct the bridge that Estella had been for them. But how?

"Later," Jose said, glancing toward the door, "when we won't be interrupted, I'd like for us to talk."

Surprised, she managed only to nod.

Redfoot walked into the kitchen. He stood by the table, frowning, and eyed Maria and then Jose.

Maria watched the two men acknowledge each other's presence. Nodding. They were back to only nodding. "There's coffee."

Redfoot sighed. "I'll grab some while I'm out."

"Out? Where?" Maria asked. "Shouldn't you take it easy today?"

"The doc said I was fine."

"Yes, but . . . where are you going?"

198 CHRISTIE CRAIG

A frown formed between his eyebrows. "To talk to a man about a horse."

Maria recognized Redfoot's pat answer that meant none of her business. She wanted to push, but pushing Redfoot was like training rocks to tango.

The stubborn old man moved across the room, snagged his keys from the hook beside the door, and looked back at Jose. "You coming?"

"Me?" Jose asked. "I . . . need to come with you to talk to a man about a horse?"

"Yup. You got a dog in this fight, too."

"What dog?" Jose asked.

"What fight?" Maria added, but Redfoot had one foot out the back door.

"What's going on?" Jose asked Maria.

"How the hell am I supposed to know?" she said. "But go watch out for him."

Jose dropped his cup in the sink and hurried after his father.

"There's coffee," Lucas said as Shala and Sky walked out of the bedroom.

Shala hadn't considered being embarrassed about sleeping with Sky until she faced Lucas. Now she had the overwhelming desire to belt out "Nothing happened." But something *had*. Well, almost. But the "almost" felt like something. It had felt wonderful and it had felt wrong. But the wonderful outweighed the wrong.

"I'm going to have to pass," Sky said. "I need to have a little talk with Charlie Rainmaker."

"I thought that was him when Shala showed me those pictures," Lucas said.

Shala moved away from Sky and filled one of the cups for herself. She recalled Sky's mouth on her breasts, his hands slipping inside her panties. She recalled telling Sky that she just needed a little more time. Which basically meant she'd agreed to eventually sleep with him.

Which basically meant she'd decided to toss her emotional insurance to the wind.

What in God's name had she been thinking? Wait, that was it: she hadn't been thinking. She'd been feeling. Bringing the mug to her lips, she saw Sky studying her. He smiled and winked. She felt her cheeks grow warm.

Yup, she'd been feeling all right—sexy, wanted, alive, and a heck of a lot happier. The only question was if she could feel her way through this without getting her heart shattered.

"Cream's in the fridge, if you take it," Lucas said, then looked back to Sky. "Do you think your friend will be able to get you something on the sedan driver?"

"I don't know," Sky replied. "I just called Phillip, and he's looking at the images now."

"If you need help, let me know," Lucas said.

"I'll remember that," Sky said.

"Are you a cop, too?" Shala asked Lucas. She'd asked him what he did for a living, and he'd told her he did odd jobs here and there after being mostly retired from the military. Did a former military career earn him enough to afford this place and the nice furnishings? And wasn't he too young to be retired?

"Nah," Lucas said. "Just know a few people." He turned back to Sky. "I'm going to have to make a run to the store. We ate up all my rations yesterday. What's your schedule?"

Sky looked at his watch. "How about you two head over to the diner? I'll meet you there as soon as I finish up with Charlie, and I'll buy breakfast. Then I'll take Shala over to talk to Phillip. Depending on what Phillip and his guys are doing, I might drop her back off here after that."

"Do I really have to be babysat twenty-four/seven?" Shala asked.

Sky and Lucas looked at each other and then at her, and they said at the same time, "Yes."

She rolled her eyes.

Lucas eyed Sky. "We'll be at the diner, then."

Sky started to leave, but he stopped when he reached the door. He turned, walked right up to Shala, and pressed his lips to hers. His tongue swept inside her mouth, his hand moved slightly down her waist to her bottom, and the kiss rang all of her bells.

"See you later."

His smile, sexy as sin, had Shala forgetting about inappropriateness and Lucas altogether. Emotional insurance be damned; she wanted to experience this. Wanted Sky. Sure, she might end up getting hurt, but what if she didn't? What if Sky was her someone special, special like her father had been special to her mom? Shala could still remember them putting on music every Friday night and dancing and laughing. She could remember her granddad and Nana going through life, through sickness and health together, for sixty years. Shala wasn't stupid. She knew true love was hard to find. But these last few years, she'd somehow forgotten it even existed. And if she could just remember that, then maybe she could believe it was worth risking her heart to try and find it.

Sky drove through the reservation toward Charlie's house, mentally tallying up all he knew about the man and trying to forget how he'd lost his head and kissed Shala in the middle of Lucas's kitchen. *Yeah, think about Charlie,* he told himself.

Charlie had a temper. He loved being a rebel. At any meeting, be it the town council or an open-house tribal-council meeting, Charlie arrived ready to cause havoc. His long-winded speech about not wanting strangers in town had struck a chord with a lot of the townspeople. And when, after several more meetings, the town voted in favor of bringing in Winters Tourism, Charlie hadn't been happy and had started holding meetings to try and stop it.

Temper ran in Charlie's family—and a bad one. Charlie's brother was doing life for murder. Did that make Charlie capable of murder? Sky sure as hell hoped not, because his own family history made Charlie's sound pretty good.

Sky's old man had been a mean and miserable son of a bitch. The only thing he'd loved was Sky's mom. His mom must have loved his dad back, because she'd put up with more from him than Sky cared to remember. Of course, Sky couldn't remember everything, because his old man had knocked him out once when he'd gotten between them. To this day Sky wondered what might have happened if he hadn't been spending the night with his next-door neighbor, if he could have stopped his father from killing his mom. He wouldn't have tried to stop the old man from turning the gun on himself, though. No, Sky would have loaded it for him.

Sky pulled up in front of an old house with chipped paint and pushed his personal issues aside. He had other problems. Would Charlie have hired someone to steal Shala's camera? Did Charlie even have the money to hire someone? If Charlie's intent had been to scare her out of town, why take it so far? It didn't make sense. Then again, he'd clearly been following Shala.

Charlie's old Chevy wasn't parked under the carport. Getting out of the truck Lucas had loaned him, Sky knocked on the front door.

Mrs. Rainmaker answered, and Sky immediately noticed her bloodshot eyes, unkempt hair, and clothes that looked slept in. Her drinking was no secret, especially to Sky, who'd arrested her twice and personally made sure her driver's license got revoked. It was a sad condition, too common among his people. Sky had insisted to the mayor that Precious offer free counseling to anyone who needed it. He'd even told Bo and the bartenders at the Funky Chicken to call him, night or day, if anyone needed a ride. He had zero patience with anyone who would drink and drive, especially after a local drunk two years ago had taken not only his own life but also the life of an innocent teen.

"Why do I think you're not here just to shoot the shit, Chief?" The woman leaned against the door frame.

"Wish I could I say I was," Sky said.

"Well, it ain't me you're here for this time. I haven't driven a lick."

"And I appreciate that. I need to talk to Charlie. Is he around?"

"Can't say he is. What's he gone and done this time?"

"I just need to speak with him." No need to alarm the woman. "Does he have a cell phone?"

"Sure does. Not that it'll you do any good. I tried calling him all last night and he's not answering. I figured I got lucky and he ran off with that slut he's been seeing at the Funky Chicken."

Good ol' marital bliss.

"Well, if you don't mind giving me his number, I need to talk to him."

She went back inside and brought out a scrap of paper with the number scratched on it. "If you get him, tell him he still has to pay the rent."

Sky started to leave.

"This isn't about that tourism woman, is it?" Mrs. Rainmaker asked.

Sky stopped, tucked the paper in his pocket, and faced her again. "You know something about that?"

"I know he was following her around. Keeping an eye on her. Is that a crime?" She wore a smirk he didn't understand.

"It could be considered stalking," Sky said.

"Then you might want to slap some handcuffs on yourself. Because he said he spotted you playing Peeping Tom, too." She laughed. "Of course, with her being your soul mate and all . . ."

Sky bit back a retort and said, "Have a good day, ma'am."

When he got into his truck, he dialed Charlie's number. The man didn't answer. Damn. He'd come here for answers and all he'd gotten was another long list of questions.

"Aren't you going to tell me where we're going?" Jose asked his father. It wasn't like his old man to play tricks like this.

"See for yourself." Redfoot pulled into the diner parking lot. It was the only restaurant in Precious that was open on Sundays.

Jose looked around. Why had Redfoot been so secretive about coming here? "So, where's the man and the horse?"

"He's here." Redfoot surveyed their surroundings. "They both are."

Jose followed his dad's gaze to the end of the parking lot. "Oh hell, no!" he snapped, and looked back at his old man.

Too late. Redfoot had one foot out of the truck.

Reaching across the seat, Jose grabbed his arm. "Are you looking for trouble?"

His dad sighed. "Sometimes you just have to stare trouble right in the face and spit in its eye." He slid the rest of the way out of the truck.

"Dad, get back in!"

Redfoot slammed the door and started for the diner.

CHAPTER TWENTY-FIVE

The smell of bacon grease greeted Redfoot at the door. He saw Ramon and a couple of friends in a booth in the back, while Matt sat alone at a table. The boy looked miserable, and it was about to get worse.

"Hey, Poncha," Redfoot called out to the waitress. "Bring me some coffee." His voice carried, causing Ramon to look up and frown.

Redfoot dropped into the booth beside Matt's table. The bell over the diner door jingled. Redfoot knew without checking that it was Jose, because Matt looked up and fury splashed the white boy's face.

"Jose?" Poncha squealed, and Redfoot remembered that Jose had dated her in his senior year of high school. She threw herself into his son's arms. Obviously, she hadn't quite gotten over him.

"You look fabulous," the waitress was saying as Jose set her back on her feet. "Well, most of you looks fabulous. What happened to your face?"

"A . . . an accident." Jose didn't pay Poncha the attention she'd clearly have liked. Instead, his gaze shot around the room. Eyes fixing on Ramon he said, "Excuse me." He moved to the booth where Redfoot sat. "Let's get out of here," he said.

Redfoot shook his head. "Sit down."

"Dad."

"Sit down!" Redfoot commanded.

His son was grown, but he plopped his ass down like a five-year-old.

Poncha reappeared, carrying two cups of coffee. "Did you want a cup, too, Jose? I brought one." She smiled sweetly.

"That's fine." Jose, apparently remembering his manners, met the woman's eyes. "How're you doing, Poncha?"

Her smile widened. "I'm fine. Finally going back to college. How is life in New York?"

"Crowded," he said.

"Your dad showed me the article about the building you helped design in Vegas."

"He did?" Jose looked surprised.

"Can you bring us two breakfast specials?" Redfoot asked, ignoring the unspoken question in his son's eyes.

Poncha nodded and moved away. Right then, Redfoot heard a cell phone ring and watched Matt pull out his cell.

"Did you see him?" Redfoot asked Jose, keeping his voice low.

"Yes, I saw him. Which is why I think—"

"Not Ramon. Him." Redfoot nodded toward Matt.

Jose turned, and a frown appeared on his face. He picked up his coffee and eyed Redfoot over the rim. "They broke up."

"I don't think so," Redfoot said. "It's pretty serious. I'm pretty worried about her."

"She told me they broke up." Jose glanced again at Matt.

"I'd bet you're wrong," Redfoot said. "She's got it bad for him." He paused. "Listen to him. I'll bet he's talking to her now. He's got something going on in Dallas. Poor Maria, she's suspicious and it's breaking her heart."

"He's cheating on Maria?"

The fury in his son's voice saddened Redfoot. His son unquestionably cared. "Listen," he told Jose.

"I love you, too, babe." Matt's words were barely audible,

but from the muscle popping out in his son's cheek, Redfoot knew Jose had heard.

Jose set down his coffee, got up, and dropped into the chair next to Matt. "Who the fuck do you think you are?" he growled.

"One down and one to go," Redfoot muttered. Looking at the booth where Ramon sat, he rubbed his chin and went to spit trouble in the eye.

Sky pulled up at the diner. Lucas and Shala were on their way, and he was meeting them here.

Getting out of his truck, he spotted Redfoot's truck. Strange. Redfoot generally only visited the diner on Wednesdays. Sky was about six feet from the entrance when a chair crashed through the front window and bounced against the sidewalk. Swearing, he ran inside. He was barely through the door when he spotted Jose going toe-to-toe with someone—no, not just someone, but Maria's Matt. Two Texas Rangers, Phillip's men, stood to one side trying to break them up.

A loud crash echoed from the back of the room. Sky's attention shifted. His heart plummeted. Ramon Cloud had Redfoot's shirt bunched up in his grip and had his right fist drawn back as if ready to strike. Shooting across the room, knocking down a few chairs, Sky grabbed Ramon by the arm.

"Don't even think about it!"

Ramon's eyes widened. He ducked. Redfoot's fist shot forward and hit Phillip, who was standing behind him. The blow took the ranger square on the nose. Phillip, caught totally off guard, lost his balance and landed in the middle of a table where three men had been eating and enjoying the fight. Scrambled eggs and coffee cups flew.

"Stop this!" Sky yelled at Redfoot, then turned to help Phillip up. When he saw one of the CSI guys grab Redfoot by the arm and draw back his fist, he jumped in the way. "No! He's my dad!"

The man started to drop his fist, but before he relaxed all the way, Jose charged. Sky spun and grabbed his brother's arm. Jose swung without looking, clipping him on the jaw. He staggered backward, knocking Phillip down again, this time onto a different table, right into a plate of grits.

"Sorry!" Jose leaped over him to grab Ramon, who had Redfoot by the shirt again.

Out of the corner of his eye, Sky saw the new diners shoving Phillip off their table. They looked none too gentle. Sky's own jaw was stinging, and he wasn't sure at first where he was most needed. Jose was physically removing Ramon from Redfoot, so he decided to help his friend.

Turning, he saw Phillip reaching inside his shirt. Realizing his friend was going for his firearm and knowing that would only lead to disaster, Sky yelled, "No guns!" Then he jumped in the middle of the fight. More fists flew. Grunts and groans and the sound of shattering plates filled the room. Then a voice boomed over the loudspeaker.

"She's taking her clothes off, guys! And she's *hot.*"

After a few final bangs and clatters, Sky could have heard a pin drop. Every head in the place turned, Sky's included. Shala Winters, fully clothed, stood on the counter. She shot the crowd a nervous smile and waved, then grimaced at Lucas standing behind her, his mouth pressed to the diner's microphone.

"Now that I got everyone's attention," Lucas continued. "I want you all to take a deep breath. We've got your chief of police and I'm counting at least four Texas Rangers in the room. If this goes on for much longer, it's going to end ugly. None of you want it to end ugly, do you?"

"Is she really going to take her clothes off?" someone

called out. It was the first guy Sky yanked by the arm and tossed out of the diner.

"What are you doing?" Phillip asked as Sky began directing people to leave.

"Cleaning house," Sky replied. "Before things start back up."

"Oh, hell no." Fury radiated from Phillip as he wiped blood from his mouth and knocked egg from his hair. "A few of these guys are getting booked and charged. We can start with *that* one."

He was pointing at Redfoot.

CHAPTER TWENTY-SIX

Maria shoved into the police station. Her heart raced as she chewed on the bits and pieces of information Sky had given her. Redfoot and Jose were in jail. Why in the hell would Sky put them in jail? All he'd told her was that he thought he could talk the rangers into letting them go, but for now they were incarcerated. He hadn't enlightened her on why they were locked up, just that she should stay home and not come rushing up to the station like a mother hen.

Well, good luck with that. She *was* a mother hen when it came to her family. And this was her family. The day Estella died, Maria had stepped willingly into the role and never looked back. And after her talk with Jose at the hospital, Maria realized that she'd failed in some ways. Her own issues with Jose had blinded her to what was happening, but she could see clearly now. God have mercy on anyone who stood in her way.

The door swished shut behind her. After leaving the

bright sunlight outside, the front room appeared dark. When Maria's eyes adjusted, she saw people everywhere milling around, which was odd for a Sunday. She recognized the two highway patrolmen who sometimes assisted Sky, but the other three men standing there staring at her, two of whom looked as if they'd been in a fight, were complete strangers. Not that it mattered. The person she wanted to see was absent. He was probably in his office.

As she started moving, one of the strangers stepped in front of her. "Can I help you?"

"Yes. Get out of my way. I'm here to see Sky."

The man must have spotted her determination, because he stepped back. Maria moved down the hall and shoved open Sky's office door. Her foster brother stood in the middle of the room arguing with a new stranger. Another beat-up stranger. Sky's own face appeared slightly swollen.

She snapped a hand to her hip. "What the hell happened?"

Sky scowled. "Phillip, this is my foster sister, Maria. Maria"—he motioned to the man—"meet Phillip. He's with the Texas Rangers."

"So he's the one who wants to keep dad and Jose in jail?"

"That would be me," Phillip replied.

"What did they do?"

As Maria stepped closer, scowling, the ranger stepped back. "They started a brawl at the diner."

She notched up her chin. "Redfoot wouldn't start anything."

"My face says differently," said the ranger.

"He didn't mean to hit you," Sky inserted. "He was aiming for Ramon."

"Ramon?" Maria asked. "Ramon Cloud?"

Sky nodded.

"Why would he go after Ramon?"

"It's complicated," Sky answered.

"Well, uncomplicate it! I swear to God, I'm not leaving without—"

"Redfoot is seeing Ramon's mom," Sky blurted.

Maria rolled her eyes. "No, he's not."

"He admitted it," Sky said.

"You misunderstood. I want to see him." She swung around to go upstairs to the jail cells, but Sky grabbed her.

"I can't let you go up there."

She jerked away. "Watch me."

Sky got between her and the door. "It's locked."

"Then, unlock it!"

Sky scrubbed his palm over his face. "You don't want to go in there."

Maria's heart burst. "Oh, God, is he hurt? How bad?" Her gaze shot to the man beside Sky. "I swear to God, if you hurt him . . . He's almost seventy years old!"

"No," Sky said. "It's not . . . He's not the only one back there. Just go home."

"Is *Jose* hurt?"

"No one's hurt!" Sky snapped. Then his shoulders collapsed and he seemed to give up. "Aww, crap. Matt is back there, too."

"Matt Goodson? My Matt?"

"Yes, your Matt."

Maria's mind reeled. "How is he involved with Ramon and Redfoot?"

"He's not. His problem was with Jose."

That didn't quite compute. "Jose and Matt fought? Why?"

"I don't have a friggin' clue. But it's best if you just stay—"

Maria stared her brother right in the eye. "You open that door, Sky Gomez, and let me get to the bottom of this, or I swear to God and every spirit Redfoot believes in that I'll spend every second of my life finding ways to make the rest of your days holy hell."

"I'd let her go back there," Phillip suggested. Sky turned and glared, but the ranger said, "Hey, they're locked in the cells. What's going to happen?"

Sky shook his head, turned, and stomped up the stairs. Maria followed.

"You don't eat enough to keep a bird alive."

Shala looked up at Lucas. The two of them were sitting at his kitchen table. "I'm sorry. It's not the food. I just . . . Guilt and turkey sandwiches don't go well together."

"Dare I ask what you're feeling guilty about?"

"Everything. Redfoot gets attacked. Jessie gets shot. And now that fight—"

"Whoa. I guess I can see—*maybe*—taking some blame for the first two, but I don't see any correlation between you and what happened at the diner. Why is it that women have the need to take on guilt?"

Shala selected a potato chip from her plate, broke it in half, and fed it to Sky's two dogs. They sat on each side of her. Lucas had been right about them; they'd become her constant companions.

"Maybe the fight isn't my fault, but . . . a man at the diner told me that ever since I came into town crazy things have been happening." She frowned. "Then he asked if I needed a map to see how to leave."

Lucas frowned. "You should have told me that while we were there. Which one was he?"

"I don't know. He had on a navy shirt. But he didn't threaten me or anything." She picked up another chip and popped it into her mouth. Glancing at Lucas she said, "Sky looked furious when he saw me on that bar."

Sky's friend sipped his tea. "Yeah, I've never seen that side of him. But, don't worry. He knows I put you up to it."

Shala grinned. "I have to admit, I never saw a fight end so quickly. How did you know it would work?"

"It's a trick I picked up in the Gulf War. I know how to say those words in five different languages. Works every time—except once, and I had no idea it was a gay bar." He laughed. "Live and learn."

"You're an intriguing guy, Lucas," Shala said. When he didn't reply, after a moment she asked, "Did you ever get to talk to Sky? I think he was hit pretty hard."

Lucas chuckled. "It's going to take more than that to take Sky down. He's tough as nails."

Shala recalled the newspaper picture of him, ten years old and standing in front of that house fire. Something told her that Sky wasn't as numb to pain as everyone thought. She reached down to pet Sundance, who nudged her leg with his nose.

"Do you mind if I borrow Sky's laptop?" Lucas asked. "I'm going to shoot a couple of your pictures to someone else to run a check."

"Not at all."

He was halfway across the room when the dogs jumped up and barked. Lucas swung around and froze.

"What is it?" Shala asked, staring. Lucas and the two dogs seemed primed for action.

Sky's friend pressed a finger to his lips and cocked his head to the side. A second passed, and then Shala heard it, too. She said, "Please tell me that was just a car backfiring."

The dogs barked again. Lucas didn't answer. Instead, he walked over to a cabinet, touched a keypad lock, and pulled out a huge rifle that looked like something Rambo would have carried. When he glanced up at her, gone was the joyful man she'd been staying with. He looked rock hard and deadly serious.

"Go sit in the hall bathroom for a while. Now!"

* * *

Before he moved aside and let Maria pass, Sky yelled through the door. "Everyone better be decent—a woman's coming in!"

Maria stepped through. This wasn't the first time she'd been here. Last summer, the women's club had decorated the jail's top floor and held a dinner in the seventy-five-year-old cells as a fund-raiser to help support art classes. Dinner Behind Bars had brought in over five hundred dollars. This time, though, it wasn't charity. Men she loved were imprisoned.

She saw Jose and Redfoot standing in one cell. Across the way were Matt and Ramon. Ramon had blood all over his shirt from his nose. Matt lay stretched out on a cot, staring up at the ceiling. One of his eyes looked swollen shut.

Maria looked back at Jose and Redfoot, unsure if their face bruises were new.

"You shouldn't be here," Jose said. "Damn it, Sky. Make her leave."

The cot squeaked in the cell across the way. Matt sat up and studied Maria with his one good eye.

"What the hell happened?" she asked everyone.

Someone began calling Sky downstairs. He gave both jail cells a firm look and said, "I'll be right back. Behave."

"Someone please explain what happened," Maria insisted. Sky's footsteps tapped down the old stone stairs.

"Your old man happened," Ramon said. "With my mom."

Maria looked at Redfoot, unbelieving. "Just tell him he's wrong. You're not dating Veronica."

"Oh, he's not *dating* my mom. He's just screwing her!" Ramon's voice bounced around the old stone walls.

"Do not talk about your mom like that," Redfoot ordered.

"Really, ol' man? I can't say it, but you can do it?"

"Respect her, damn it!" Redfoot said. His tone had Maria second-guessing her earlier claim.

"Respect her?" Ramon bellowed. "Is that what you were doing in the hospital—respecting her?"

"Stop it!" Maria shouted. She sensed Matt looking at her, and she wanted to yell at Sky to bring the keys to open the door so she could check on him. His eye had to be hurting like the devil. But would he welcome her concern? At the hospital he'd seemed determined to believe the worst.

"We weren't doing anything in that hospital bed," Redfoot growled.

"I know what I saw." Ramon struck the bars with his hand. "I can't believe you have the balls to stand there and say you haven't slept with her."

"I didn't say I hadn't slept with her," Redfoot replied.

"So you're admitting it?"

"Yes." Redfoot stood straight. "I admit it."

"You do?" Maria asked, stunned.

"You arrogant son of a bitch," Ramon snarled. "You're going to do right by her. I'm going to go to the tribal council about this. You're supposed to be one of the respected elders."

"Sit down and shut up, Dad," Jose said. "And Maria, get your ass home."

"I don't take orders from you!" Maria retorted.

Matt let out a laugh. "You tell him."

Jose leaned toward the bars. "Don't you even start."

Maria stared at the two men. "Why in God's name were you two fighting?"

"Why don't you tell her the truth?" Redfoot spoke up, directing his question to Matt. "Tell her the things you are hiding from her."

Maria looked from Matt to Redfoot. "What's he hiding?"

"That he's cheating on you," Jose snapped. "The scum—"

"That's bullshit," Matt said. "Why don't you tell her about that waitress you had all over you this morning?"

Maria glanced from one cell to the other, confused. Then she heard footsteps behind her. Turning, she saw it was one of the troopers.

"Sky had to run out on an emergency," the man told Maria before eyeing the occupied cells. "But which one of you is Matt?"

"I am," Matt said.

"Your wife just called and said your lawyer is on his way."

Maria grabbed the trooper's arm, shell-shocked. "His *wife*?"

The cop looked concerned. "Uhh, that's what she said."

"You no-good piece of shit!" Jose yelled.

Everyone starting talking at once. Redfoot was saying something unintelligible, Ramon yelled something about his mother, and Matt just kept repeating Maria's name. It all seemed to echo, bouncing to and fro across the rocks of the old building. Slapping her hands over her ears, Maria swung around and left.

Sky entered Lucas's place, gun in hand. His friend sat facing the door in his recliner, a rifle at his side.

"Anything?" Sky asked, looking around for Shala. She was at the kitchen table, setting up a game of Scrabble. Their gazes met and held, and he fought the need to grab and kiss her. He didn't do public displays of affection. His kiss good-bye this morning had been a spontaneous act that still had him questioning his sanity. Holy hell, these last few days were mixed up.

"Nothing," Lucas replied. "I said that you didn't have to come. I heard two shots. Could've been someone shooting a rattlesnake for all I know."

"How close? Which direction did it come from?"

"An educated guess, a mile, maybe a little more. There's

a wind blowing. It sounded as if it came from the north-east."

Sky nodded, his gaze on Shala again.

Lucas added, "Someone threatened her at the diner."

"What?" Sky eyed Shala. "Who? Why didn't you tell me?" He walked over to her.

"It wasn't really a threat," she answered. "He wore a navy shirt, a button-down, and I remember some kind of logo. And I think you had enough on your plate right then." She reached up and touched his jaw. "Is it sore?"

"I'm fine." He took her hand and held it, then looked back at Lucas. "I've got Pete combing the area. I'm sure Phillip is going to want to talk to Shala, but not before things calm down at the station."

Lucas nodded. "Just call and I'll bring her down."

Sky was staring at Shala, fighting another urge to kiss her. He let go of her hand. "I'll see you," he said at last.

"Later," she said, and Sky took off before he cratered and did something like kiss her again in front of Lucas.

After he left, he went about his business. There seemed to be a heck of a lot of business to attend to. Not that it stopped him from thinking about Shala.

Still unable to reach Charlie Rainmaker, Sky put a BOLO out for the man's truck, telling other law enforcement agencies to be on the lookout for him. He also asked around and learned the only person wearing a navy shirt with a logo at the diner today was Donny Chavez, Charlie's neighbor. Sky knew Donny, and he seriously didn't think the man was a criminal, but he went by and had a long talk with him. Donny admitted to telling Shala to go home. He'd been out of town with his wife and kids the last few days, however, so he couldn't be Shala's stalker. After telling the guy to mind his own business, Sky left.

Next, having heard about the whole fiasco at the jail and also being in the neighborhood, he stopped by the house to check on Maria. She'd been crying. She insisted she didn't want to talk, but when Sky hugged her good-bye she broke down and told him everything—all about Matt being married. All Sky could do was hold her. He didn't have any glib words to toss at bad relationships.

He next visited Jessie at the hospital. As expected, Sal was at her side.

"Tell him to go home and get some sleep," Jessie commanded.

Sky didn't even try. It would have been easier to bite through a diamond than to get Sal away from her. The two of them reminded Sky of Redfoot and Estella—which made Sky wonder about Redfoot and Veronica Cloud. It had been ten years since Estella's passing, so Sky didn't begrudge his foster father a need for company, but was the relationship serious? Redfoot deserved to be happy, so he supposed he would support him no matter what.

Unfortunately, Jessie couldn't tell Sky anything other than that the guy who'd shot her was big and wore a ski mask. And Pete, the trooper on duty, hadn't turned up anything on the shots fired out by Lucas's place. Maybe it really had been just someone shooting a snake. Dead ends. That's all Sky was getting.

He went back to the station, and it was almost seven before he finally was ready to close down. Phillip had conceded to letting everyone go home with no charges. He'd also rescheduled his talk with Shala. Right before he left, he told Sky that he'd sent an image of the man suspected of driving the sedan to his headquarters, but he warned it could take weeks to find a name to go with the face.

Starting his truck, Sky thought about Shala. He wanted some time alone with her, and he almost called and asked Lucas to spend the night on his boat—his friend normally slept there a couple of nights a week, so asking didn't feel like too much of a favor. But while the idea of getting Shala alone and naked tempted the hell out of him, the push and pull Sky felt every time he got close to her was confusing. Probably just that soul-mate crap.

His phone rang as he pulled out of the parking lot. Taking it out, he looked at the number. It was Martha on the emergency line again.

CHAPTER TWENTY-SEVEN

"What's up?" Sky asked, sighing as he answered the call.

"It's Candy Peterson again."

Sky's gut knotted. He hated domestic disputes with a passion, but he especially disliked getting called to the Peterson house. Candy's drunken slob of a husband regularly beat her. What Sky couldn't figure out was why the woman continued to let him.

"God damn it, Martha. Tell me she didn't let that son of a bitch come home."

"It sounds bad, Sky. It's her daughter on the phone."

Sky considered calling Pete to meet him, but there wasn't time. "I'm just a few blocks away."

In less than a minute he was parked in front of the house. Pulling out his gun, he went to the door. He didn't have to knock; the door was off its hinges and he could see Peterson standing over Candy, who was lying on the floor bleeding. The sight took Sky back twenty-two years. He gripped his gun. What he wouldn't give to take the bastard out! But pulling himself back from the abyss, he stormed into the room.

"What happened here?" he asked, and wasn't surprised when Peterson glared at him. He grabbed the asshole by the hair and slammed him into the wall, half-hoping the drunken bastard would come at him.

Peterson didn't disappoint. He raised his fist and swung. Missed. Sky didn't. His blow caught the asshole on the chin, hard. Holstering his gun, Sky grabbed the barely conscious brute by his shirt, flipped him over, put his knee in his back, and handcuffed him. Then he turned to Candy. Her face was bleeding, but she didn't look as bad as last time.

"Mama?" a young voice called, low and scared. Sky looked up to see Candy's eight-year-old daughter peering out from a bedroom, tears and raw fear in her eyes.

"It's okay," he told the child, his gut turning inside out. "Go on back to your room. Nothing else bad is going to happen." When the child did as he requested, Sky addressed Candy, who was still on the floor. "Is anything broken?" he forced himself to ask.

She shook her head. "No. You got here just in time."

"Should I call an ambulance?" He already knew what she'd say, but he always asked.

"No. I'm fine."

She wasn't, though. She was as messed up as her husband. And for the first time, Sky found himself hating his mother. For years he'd blamed his old man, but his mom had played a part. Just like Candy.

"You let him come back, didn't you?" His mom had. Let his no-good father come back time and time again.

Candy wiped blood from her lip. "He said he'd changed."

"He said that last time, and the time before that. For God's sake, woman! Go look at your daughter. Look at the terror you just put her through. You call yourself a mother, but you do this to your child?"

Candy was shaking her head, crying. "I know I was wrong."

"I swear—if this happens one more time, I'll see to it that little girl is placed with someone else. I'll personally take her away from you. Do you understand me? I swear to God, woman, I'm serious." Taking a deep breath, he stood, grabbed Peterson by the arm, and jerked him to his feet. Then he asked one last futile question. "You pressing charges?"

Shala lay in bed, wearing the light blue pajamas Sky had bought her, unable to sleep. Instead, she thought about Sky. He'd claimed these pajamas were similar to her others, but this tank top had lace on it; the boxers were shorter and a tighter fit. The outfit was sexier than her others.

Or maybe she just felt sexier. She'd showered—even borrowed a razor from Lucas to shave her legs. Then she'd used the few cosmetics she had in her purse to make herself feel ready. *But ready for what?* a voice inside her head asked. She'd argued with it all evening, telling it that wearing lipstick and blush didn't mean she was ready to sleep with Sky. Now, facing disappointment, she recognized her lie: she'd been ready to take that leap. Only Sky wasn't here to leap with. At least, he wasn't in her room.

Deciding she needed something to drink, she got out of bed and inched the door open. The kitchen and living room looked empty. Disappointed, she went out and poured herself some milk. Where was Sky? Was he sleeping in the other bedroom? The idea of opening that door seemed too brazen, so she took a sip of milk and moved to the front window to see if his truck was visible. Unfortunately, she could see only part of the driveway.

She opened the front door. Hearing the crickets and night noises, she edged onto the porch to see the driveway. The darkness made her remember the guy in the ski mask, and she froze.

"You shouldn't be—"

The voice had come out of nowhere. Startled, Shala swung around. Heart thudding, she recognized Sky sitting on the porch, his back against the rough exterior cabin wall. He wiped milk from his head and face. Had she . . . ? She looked at her empty glass. Yup, she'd doused him with her glass of milk.

"—shouldn't be out here." He wiped his hand on his shirt and tried to dry off the rest of the way.

A giggle almost escaped her throat. "I'm sorry! You scared me."

"Good thing I'm not lactose intolerant."

She laughed, and a light and airy feeling filled her chest, the feeling that always seemed to hit when she was around Sky. "What are you doing out here?"

He smiled, but the expression was forced. She eased closer and noted a haunted look in his eyes.

"Besides waiting for a milk shower?" he asked.

"Yeah, besides that." Her gaze flickered down to the bottle beside him. She caught a whiff of whiskey.

"Just thinking. What are you doing out here? You shouldn't come outside alone when—"

"I couldn't sleep. I thought some fresh air might help." Okay, she was lying, but admitting that she'd been looking for him seemed too bold. She stared down at Sky, and he looked away.

"Lucas said you had another emergency," she prompted.

"Yeah."

"Did it involve me or the camera?" she asked.

"No."

"Was it something . . . bad?"

"Yes."

His voice was bleak, so she hesitated. "Do you want to talk about it?"

"It's just business."

She didn't believe it. Searching for the right thing to say, she asked, "Do you mind company, or do you prefer to think alone?" When he failed to answer she announced, "I'll just leave." Saying nothing was answer enough.

She walked back into the house, the light and airy feeling he'd evoked fading with each step. But when she reached the bedroom, she recalled the look in his eyes. Then she remembered trying to push him away in the hospital, and how he hadn't let her.

Shala swung around. She wasn't going to let him push her away, either. He might not want to talk—men seldom did—but she bet she knew something that might help.

Sky stared at the door through which Shala had just disappeared. God Almighty, she looked good in those pajamas he'd bought her. The image of that tight little body in that light blue tank top and those short blue shorts had his libido grabbing him by the neck and trying to force him to race after her. Instead, he closed his eyes, leaned his head back on the rough wooden wall of the house, and took another sip of the whiskey.

He hadn't had near enough yet. He wasn't drunk. He still had too much crap running through his mind. Boozing wasn't his habit, but tonight he needed a distraction. And if Shala Winters got too close, he'd be too damn tempted to let her become just that: a distraction, something to lose himself in, something to help him forget. She deserved better, so he'd best stick with the alcohol. Plus, he hadn't gotten around to asking Lucas to leave.

The front door swung back open and Shala walked out. She stopped directly in front of where he sat, placing one bare foot on each side of his outstretched legs. His gaze shot to her painted toenails and then to those perfectly shaped legs, then up to the sweet little spot where the hem of her shorts hung just loose enough to give him a peek at the tender skin of her thigh. Sky gulped, the whiskey still stinging his throat. He fought the need to lean forward and press his lips to that spot, fought the memory of how wet she'd been that morning.

Like some kind of erotic dancer, she lowered herself.

Sky adjusted his legs, and she sat on his lap, her knees bent by his sides, her thighs spread. His hands itched to move along those knees, up between those thighs, and inside those shorts. Her scent—feminine, clean, and slightly minty, like toothpaste—filled his nose.

"Shala . . ."

He wasn't sure what he intended to say, but her weight shifted, pressing her closer to his cock, and suddenly logic didn't exist. He dropped the whiskey bottle and his hands moved to her waist, drawing her closer, bringing her weight against his crotch. She came against him without any hesitation. She didn't wait for him to kiss her, either. Instead, she pressed her mouth to his. Her tongue slipped between his lips and brushed his, ever so lightly. Her hands came to rest on his chest, spanning out, and one slipped up around his neck and into his hair.

The kiss, wet and wanting, had things happening fast. She unbuttoned his shirt and slipped a soft palm inside. Her warm touch brushed his chest and sent pleasure whirling down his abs, tingling into his balls. His mind begged for her to slow down, but his body would have none of it. He was as hard as a rock.

Thankfully, he recalled himself enough to know that he couldn't take her on the front porch. Latching a hand under her bottom, he stood up. She weighed next to nothing in his arms, and her legs wrapped around his waist. She didn't stop kissing him, and he didn't want her to. Carrying her inside, he had enough brain cells left to remember to lock the door. Then he walked her right into the bedroom. He didn't give a damn if Lucas was here. He didn't give a damn that three minutes ago this hadn't seemed like a good idea. He wanted Shala Winters. She wanted him, and he needed to lose himself in something sweet.

He shut the bedroom door behind them. The bedside

lamp was on, giving ample light to enjoy the view. Moving to the bed, he lowered Shala onto the mattress. He had to slip his hand back to get her to release her legs from around him, and with one knee on the mattress he half-stood, loosened two more buttons, and yanked his shirt over his head. He unsnapped his jeans and pushed them and his underwear down in one swift motion. His dick appreciated the freedom. Hard and ready, it sprang free and pointed toward the ceiling.

Stepping out of his jeans, he stretched out beside Shala. She ran her hand over his face and then lower, to his chest. He took her hand and moved it. But the moment her soft fist wrapped around him, he realized his mistake: if she so much as stroked him, the night was over. He pulled her away from his crotch and got busy getting her naked.

Her skimpy tank top slipped with ease over her head, her breasts jiggling ever so slightly as they were released from containment. Hooking his thumb into the waistband of her pajama shorts, he pulled them down her legs, loving the silky skin he brushed against. A moment later, his hand slid up from her knee to that hot little spot between her legs. Moisture met his fingers and he moaned. His body ached for release, to bury himself inside her, deep and then deeper, fast and then faster. So much better than whiskey.

Remembering he needed a condom, he stood. There was one in his wallet. But before he reached for it, he looked back. The air locked in his lungs. He didn't move. He couldn't move. She mesmerized him. She lay stretched out on the bed, naked, his for the taking, and he couldn't remember any woman ever being so beautiful.

Her hair was a golden halo around her head. Her eyes stared up at him, her light blue gaze fraught with desire— the desire to please him. He somehow sensed she was offering herself as a gift. That she somehow knew he needed an escape. And just like that, the need to fulfill his lust took a backseat to the desire to fulfill hers.

He lay back on the bed, brushing the back of his hand down her cheek, kissing her with the patience of a man who had all night. And he did. Five minutes. Ten . . . He wasn't sure how long they kissed, but long enough that she shifted closer. He felt her melt into him with no reservation, no hesitation. He lowered his mouth and took her right nipple, suckled it ever so lightly. Only when he heard her breathing increase did he slip his hand back between her thighs.

She moaned, and the sound sent pleasure cascading over him. He ached to hear more—more moans, more of those little noises that told him he was doing everything right. Slowly he traversed her body, kissing a path along her abs to her navel, easing down toward her moist center. The surrounding triangle of hair felt soft. He slid his finger inside, separating the soft nether lips of her sex, and he moved his finger back and forth, brushing across the little nub that he knew drove women wild.

When he touched his lips to her, she shuddered. Positioned between her legs, he looked up and slowly brushed his palms up and down her outer thighs. "You okay with this?" She opened her eyes but didn't answer, so he took a chance and lowered his mouth and passed his tongue over her again. Her hips rose to meet his mouth, giving him her answer.

He listened to the sound of her breathing while he pleasured her, and he adjusted his pace to match the gentle shifting of her hips. When her orgasm neared, he knew because she started making those soft little sounds again, that mix between moans and sighs. Oddly enough, hearing them sent a swell of emotion to his gut, and he found himself smiling.

When she came, her thighs tightened, she raised her feet, then pressed her heels into the mattress. Sky studied her, and all he could think about was making her come again. He rose above her, took her face in his hands, and said, "You're beautiful."

She opened her eyes, and the sweetest smile twisted her lips. Right then and there, Sky felt something in the world shift. He didn't know exactly what it was or what consequences it would bring, but he'd deal with them later.

"I was supposed to be the one seducing you," she said.

He grinned. "Yeah, what happened to that?"

She ran her hands over his back and down across his butt. He felt the bandage on her palm, and he reminded himself not to forget and grab her hands.

But then somehow she'd maneuvered him so that she was resting slightly to the side. She inched her fingers down his chest to his rock-solid hard-on, and for some reason he felt even more in control than before. Her palm wrapped around him and she moved it up and down, her hand tightening and releasing with just the right pressure. He closed his eyes and concentrated on not exploding with pleasure.

Finally, unable to take it anymore, he drew her hand away from him. "Condom," he gasped.

"I wasn't finished," she replied, her voice innocent and yet so damn sexy. "I had other plans." She licked her lips, taunting him. It worked. His dick stood taller, and the thought of her sweet mouth on his cock had his balls tying themselves in knots. Then he recalled how wet and warm she was between her legs.

"Rain check," he growled. "I want to be inside you." He rolled to the side and found his wallet and the condom he'd placed there for this very moment. Unwrapping the package, he covered himself. Then he grabbed the pillows and stuffed one behind each bedpost.

"What are you—?" She looked as if she expected him to whip out some chains. Not that he minded introducing a pair of handcuffs now and then, but that wasn't his intent.

"So the bedposts don't hit the wall," he explained.

"Oh." She actually blushed and looked at the door, as if she'd just remembered Lucas.

Oh, hell, she wasn't going to stop now, was she?

CHAPTER TWENTY-EIGHT

She wasn't.

"Good idea," she said. A laugh caught in Sky's throat, a mixture of pleasure and relief. She wasn't going to stop this. Even the possibility was a hardship beyond imagining.

He stretched out beside her and pulled her closer. Shala's blend of seductress and innocent enthralled him. Staring into her eyes, he moved his fingers over her lips. She opened her mouth and took one finger inside. She nursed the digit, as if reminding him what she might be doing to his throbbing shaft, but the warm wetness of her mouth reminded him of another place—a place he had to be, or explode.

Rolling her onto her back, he positioned himself between her legs and eased inside her. Pleasure spiraled low in his abdomen as he pushed deeper. Shala's slick, tight opening welcomed him. Holding back the urge to slam against her, to take her all at once, he eased himself out and then slowly back in. Their gazes met. Held. She wrapped her legs around his waist, and they began to move together.

He felt his world shift. Suddenly, he was on his back and she straddled him. But while she moved, it wasn't fast enough. He needed speed. Depth. *Now.* But when he opened his eyes and saw her riding him—up and down, her breasts jiggling with every motion, and lower, where her soft sex gripped him like velvet—the visual took his pleasure to new heights.

She placed her uninjured hand on his abs, bracing herself and rising up to the point that his swollen sex almost slipped out of her. There she paused, and then she lowered herself again. Somehow, in the downward swoop, she managed to take him deeper than ever before. And then she did it again.

He grabbed her hips to encourage a faster pace. She didn't seem to mind, even let him guide her. In. Out. Up. Down. It was fast and furious, and everything he wanted. She closed her eyes and her head fell back, and as he watched, he heard those soft sounds again: she stood on the cusp of another orgasm. He stood there with her.

Flipping her onto her back, he pumped inside her, hard. A moment later, he felt himself take flight, and every nerve ending in his body focused on that shattering pleasure—pure, awesome pleasure. His orgasm hung on longer and took him higher than ever before. And when he passed its peak, he fell atop her, all two hundred pounds of his dead weight.

Remembering himself at the last moment, he rolled to the side, taking her with him. That's when it hit him that he wasn't altogether sure she'd finished. He recalled thinking she was almost there, but . . . Still unable to catch his breath, he attuned every ounce of his being to her body. He heard her short, deep breaths, felt the spasms of her slick flesh where his sex was still buried inside her. She'd come. He hadn't let her down.

Relief and then happiness filled his chest. Drawing her closer, he held her. He felt her cheek against his shoulder, felt the air leaving her lips brush against his chest. "Was that not . . . fu . . . fabulous?" he breathed into her hair.

"It was," she gasped. "But do you think Lucas heard?"

He didn't give a flying fuck. Of course, she probably

did. He looked up at the bedpost. Both the pillows had fallen. Remembering how hard he'd pumped into her, he wouldn't be surprised if they'd need to repair the Sheetrock. He drew back for a moment to take care of the condom; then he lay down beside her again.

"Were we loud?" She raised her head just a bit to look at him. Embarrassment flushed her cheeks.

"You mean, the bed? I don't remember," he answered honestly, shifting a little closer. With a smile he added, "I'll try to listen next time. Of course, I'm not sure I'll be able to hear. Not with you screaming like that."

She giggled. He rolled on top of her again, almost forgetting her bandaged hand as he grabbed her wrists and held them over her head. When he looked down, her eyes lit up and he found himself wondering about the men who'd been lucky enough to be in this place, the men lucky enough to know her body, her smiles, and the sounds she made when she orgasmed. A new feeling—jealousy, an emotion he didn't do—took up residence in his chest. He recalled Shala talking about her ex during one of her jabbering sessions, and damn if he didn't wish he'd listened.

"What did he do to you?" he asked before he could stop himself.

"Who?"

"Your ex." When she didn't answer right away, he got a terrible feeling. "Please tell me he never hit you."

She shook her head. "No. It wasn't . . . Should we be talking about this now?"

"No," he admitted, but then he couldn't let it go. "Yes. What did he do?" He released her hands and settled beside her.

She released another deep breath. "It's just . . . you love someone and then they're gone." The words were cryptic, but he saw the hurt in her eyes. He wondered if she meant her ex, or her parents and grandparents.

"You left him?" he guessed. He couldn't freaking believe he wanted to know. He'd never wanted to know a girl's past before. Not seriously.

"He cheated with a friend of mine. He actually thought that would make it okay. He wanted us to become this big happy family . . ."

Sky almost laughed and told her that was every guy's dream, but her ex was an ass for hurting her as he had. He wondered if the ex regretted it—and if he'd ever tried to get her back. "Does he ever contact you?" he asked.

"Some. Less now. It's been almost two years. I don't answer his calls."

"You're better off without him," Sky said.

"I know."

He held her close, savoring her warmth. Her sudden bout of laughter caught him by surprise, and he asked, "What's so funny?"

She bit down on her lip. "I just remembered your expression when I accused you of having erectile dysfunction the other morning."

"A total error on your part, as now you well know. Admit it!" he teased.

Her grin was shy and sweet. "I guess I'll have to give you that."

That wasn't all she'd give him, Sky thought. He lowered his mouth to hers.

The leg sprawled atop his thighs shifted, and Sky came awake. He didn't have to stop and wonder whom it belonged to; memories of last night brought a smile to his lips. They'd had sex twice, but with his dick saluting the ceiling in its early morning ritual, he wasn't above going for number three with Shala. Or even four. Did he have anything pressing this morning that would prevent them from—? A whistling began in the next room, and Sky's mood took a downward turn. Somehow he sensed

Shala would be disinclined to get down and dirty with "Yankee Doodle Dandy" being belted out nearby.

The 911 emergency he'd handled last night popped into his mind. Candy Peterson had brought back a barrel of unwanted memories. After all this time, he couldn't understand why the memory still tore him up inside, but it did. Sex with Shala had chased those thoughts away.

The idea that he might have used her just to cope tugged at his conscience, but he pushed that aside. Last night had been about more than just forgetting. It had been about pleasure and sex. Hell, it had been about *more* than just sex, it had been—

That's when his mood took another nosedive. Sex had never been about anything else for him. He always kept his emotions disengaged; he always kept himself free and clear. But the memory of last night tiptoed through his mind and, son of a bitch, if he didn't feel emotional footprints all over it. Last night hadn't been just about sex. It had been about Shala—about making her smile, about making her happy. It had been about making her forget her demons. He'd wanted her to forget that her parents were dead, that her husband had hurt her, that some freak was after her for God only knew what reason. Last night had been about protecting and caring for her. It had been about much more than just sex.

Her hand resting against his chest suddenly felt as if it weighed ten pounds. Shala's leg over his felt confining. Her sweet smell filled his nose and he couldn't breathe. He wanted away, *now*.

He forced himself not to leap out of bed. Instead, he slid slowly free, grabbed his jeans, had them on in record time, and hurried out of the bedroom.

"Hey," Lucas said.

Sky didn't answer. He went straight outside. Trying to breathe, he leaned both palms on the porch railing and fought a claustrophobic feeling that had nothing to do with small spaces and everything to do with the small blonde he'd just left in bed. He heard the front door open behind him.

"You okay?" Lucas asked.

"Fine," Sky said without turning.

"You two have an argument?" Lucas asked.

"No." Sky felt in his pockets to see if his keys were there. They were. He could run to his house for another shirt. Glancing down, he saw he needed shoes, too. He didn't have to stay here. "I need to . . . go to my place. Could you bring Shala in to talk to Phillip around ten?" He'd have Phillip tell her he'd gone to revisit the crime scene. "Stay to bring her back afterward. I probably won't be there."

Turning, he saw his friend frown and nod. Lucas started to go back inside, then said, "Oh, fuck it. Do you know what I do for a living, Sky?"

Confused, Sky said, "Train special-ops?"

Lucas nodded. "Yeah, I do that sometimes, but mostly I make sure innocent people don't get hurt."

"So?"

Lucas pointed at the cabin. "Shala Winters is about as innocent as they come. Don't hurt her."

Sky took a few steps forward, reacting without thinking. "You hot for her yourself? Is that what this is about?"

Lucas looked taken aback. "No, damn it. It's nothing like that."

"Then stay out of it," Sky snapped. A moment later, he wished he hadn't.

Lucas's eyes were hard. "I normally do," he said. "I'm good at staying out of other people's business. But you brought her here. You got me involved. And yes, I know you didn't ask for advice, but I'm just saying she's different than the gals you usually go for. Remember that."

He slammed inside, leaving Sky feeling like an ass.

Jose stood in the doorway of the kitchen, still dressed in his thin pajama bottoms and T-shirt, watching Maria move from counter to counter. Her tired eyes told him she hadn't slept well. When he and Redfoot had gotten home from jail, she'd been in her room. He'd almost knocked on her door to check on her, but Redfoot had stopped him with a question: "Do you love pain?" Jose hadn't understood, and he'd gone to bed worried.

"You okay?" he asked her now.

His foster sister swung around, coffeepot in hand. "Fine," she lied. Her eyes told the truth.

"You offering?" He nodded to the pot. When she motioned to the cabinet, he pulled himself out a cup. Looking around the room, he asked, "Where's Redfoot?"

Maria shrugged. "I think he went to see the tribal council. He told me it was 'about another horse.'"

Jose shook his head. "You know, they might try to force him into marrying Veronica."

Maria scoffed. "I can't see anyone forcing Redfoot into something he doesn't want."

"Perhaps." Jose edged closer. "Is it really over between you and Matt?" he forced himself to ask.

Her chin lifted a notch. "He's married. What do you think?"

"If it makes you feel any better . . ." Jose made a fist and gave it a swing. "I did get in one good punch."

"Hitting people doesn't fix things."

"I don't know, sometimes it feels good." Seeing her frown, he added, "Guess it's a man thing."

Her eyes filled with tears. "It's a stupid thing."

Jose nodded. "Women make us stupid." He stepped closer and found himself looking into her eyes, longing for the look of adoration she'd always worn before. "You make me do stupid things. You make me crazy."

Her eyes widened, and her mouth dropped open as if his words perplexed her.

Jose took the final step, which brought him right in front of her. He stood so close he could smell the shampoo she used. He held his cup out. She stared at it and then started pouring. Steam rose and swirled between them.

"I think I'm still in love with you, Maria."

Her eyes snapped up, confusion swirling in their cinnamon depths. "What?"

Unfortunately, she didn't stop pouring. Jose yelped as hot coffee overflowed his cup and burned his fingers. He dropped the cup, which hit his abdomen, and scalding liquid soaked the front of his T-shirt and thin cotton pants, practically burning the skin off everything in its path. Groaning with pain, he yanked the elastic waistband, pulled back his pants, and started blowing.

Maria swung around to the fridge. The next thing Jose knew, she stood in front of him, had his pants pulled out a good six inches or more, and she was squirting an entire bottle of mustard down them. The cool liquid was soothing, but his mind couldn't quite wrap around what she was doing.

He grabbed her hand. "I'm not a damn hotdog!"

The beginning of a smile tickled her lips. "Mustard is good for burns."

"Don't you dare laugh," he hissed—but he didn't mean it. He'd much rather see laughter in her eyes than pain, even if he was in pain himself.

She released his pants, slapped a hand over her mouth, and giggled. It became a chortle, and even with his balls burnt clean off, he forced himself to say, "Give me another chance, Maria."

The laughter in her eyes faded. She pressed a finger over his lips. "I can't."

"Why?" Jose asked.

"Because she loves me," a voice stated from behind them.

Jose and Maria both swung around. Matt and Redfoot crowded the kitchen doorway. Jose stood frozen, his nether bits still burnt and swimming in the yellow mustard that was now oozing down his legs. His dad shrugged as if in apology.

Maria approached Matt. Jose's gut tightened, and he prepared himself to see her embrace the white boy. Instead, she drew her fist back and coldcocked him.

"Damn," Jose said.

"Damn!" Matt grabbed his nose.

"Damn," Maria said, and shook her wrist.

Matt caught her hand. "Did you hurt yourself?"

Scowling, Maria jumped away from him. Looking over her shoulder at Jose she said, "Maybe it isn't just a man thing." Then she grabbed her purse and keys from the table and ran for it.

The back door swung open, halting her, and Veronica Cloud stormed in. "You!" She pointed at Redfoot, her gaze filled with all kinds of lethal intent. "Don't you dare go before that tribal council. I'd rather be branded as a whore than forced into another godforsaken marriage." And without another word, she swung back around and walked out with Maria.

"Damn," Redfoot said.

Jose's balls still burned. Mustard oozed down his ankles. "Excuse me," he said. And fighting the temptation to throw any punches, he headed to the bathroom, leaving yellow footprints in his wake. One thought echoed in his mind: *welcome to fucking Precious.*

CHAPTER TWENTY-NINE

Sky didn't budge as Lucas left; his emotions held him paralyzed. Standing frozen, he stared out into the woods at nothing. Absolutely nothing. Even when the front door opened again he stood frozen, though he was scared shitless it was Shala.

At last he overcame his paralysis and turned. His friend stood in the doorway. "The fact that you haven't run yet is pretty telling, friend." Lucas brought a coffee cup to his lips and studied Sky over its rim. "Damn. Never thought I'd see the day."

Sky wanted to deny it, but he didn't quite know what he'd be denying. All he knew was that Shala Winters had him tied in knots.

Lucas lowered his mug. "Here's my advice. Pour her a cup of coffee. She takes it with cream. There are some croissants on the counter. Put a slab of butter on the plate and then some preserves. She likes the peach better than the raspberry. Oh, and try to get that 'I'm fucked' look off your face before you do." He chuckled and headed back inside.

Sky gave his truck one more glance. He could still run, could still get the hell out of there. Lucas would take care of Shala. But then Sky realized Lucas knew what type of preserves Shala liked, and he himself didn't. That disturbed the hell out of him.

His gaze shot back to the cabin door. He didn't have to leave. He could take Shala a cup of coffee and a croissant, just as his friend suggested. But the claustrophobia with which he'd woken up that morning was playing scary music in his head—something like "Here Comes the Bride" mixed with the theme from *Jaws*. He took a step toward his truck.

What the hell was wrong with him? Stopping, he raked a hand over his face. Shit. They'd had sex. Yes, it had been good sex, maybe even great sex. It probably had been more intimate than any he'd ever experienced . . . and yet it was still just sex. Which meant that this next step . . . ? It was just breakfast. Hell, it wouldn't even be a full breakfast, simply a cup of coffee and a piece of bread— good bread, like it had been good sex, but still just bread. He'd personally cooked a three-course breakfast for almost every woman he'd ever slept with, so why in the heck was he behaving like this? What made this so different? Nothing, damn it.

He shot inside and got the coffee. Got the croissants. And the preserves. But the moment Sky walked into the bedroom and saw Shala sitting with the sheet wrapped around her naked body, he knew what was so different: *everything*. Shala was different. The sex was different. With her, *he* was different.

She smiled up at him, and he had flashbacks of hearing her moaning little half sighs, recalled with pleasure how it had felt to enter her that first time: tight, awesome, and so damn right. And just like that, he decided the differences didn't mean crap. They didn't change a thing. She lived over two hundred miles away—she couldn't smother him with talk of relationships or commitments. What the hell was wrong with just enjoying this? Whatever "this" was, it would play its course and eventually be over. Long-distance relationships didn't work. He knew that.

She's your soul mate. The *wacoi* confirmed it.

Redfoot's words echoed in his mind, but he tossed them into a mental blender. Not only did he not believe in that stuff, he knew himself better than any prophecy ever could. But did Shala? Did she know him enough to not expect much? Lucas had been right: Shala wasn't his normal type. His type didn't have that hint of innocence, that touch of vulnerability. His type wouldn't be misconstruing what had just happened.

Then again, Shala had practically told him she didn't want to get involved because of her ex. She'd implied she didn't want to go down that whole serious-relationship path. All he had to do was clarify that they both understood their limits, and then all these yin and yang feelings would fade. Right?

She plucked at the sheet again and tugged it higher. "Can I have the coffee?" she asked.

Realizing he'd been staring like an idiot, Sky moved. He set the tray down, sat, and handed her a cup. He took his own. "Did you sleep well, Blue Eyes?"

"When I was sleeping I did."

Her sexy grin pulled him closer. Damn, she was beautiful. "I hope that's not a complaint."

She chuckled. "Not at all." Her gaze shifted to her coffee, and when she looked up, her eyes held a different glint—one that reminded him of the "Wedding March" and *Jaws*. "Am I going to talk to the Texas Rangers today?"

"Yeah, it's set for ten." He looked at the time. "I'll probably just hang out here and take you in." He sipped his coffee and ached to touch her. Oh, hell, he ached to tug the sheet away and have a repeat performance of last night. The idea shot a lot of blood down south.

She nodded. "But after that I should probably get back to Houston."

He nearly choked. "Go? Are you freaking kidding? The idiot tried to run you down in a car and he shot Jessie. What in God's name are you thinking, woman?"

She blinked those vulnerable blue eyes at him. "You said it would only be a couple of days. That's passed, and—"

"That's before he tried to make roadkill out of you and

nearly murdered a friend of mine." When she dropped her head on her sheet-draped knees and groaned, he added, "I'm sorry, but there's no way I'm letting you walk away from here right now."

She raised her eyes. "I know you're right, but I have a life, my job, my house, a missing computer, and a police report to make, and it's all in Houston. And Lucas has been great, and you've been great, but what am I supposed to do? Put my whole life on hold until you catch the guy?"

The fact that he'd been referred to as great in the same sentence as Lucas—and came second in the lineup—bothered Sky more than he wanted to admit. Then another bothersome realization jumped into place: her leaving annoyed him on *many* levels, some of which had nothing to do with her being in danger. The whole thought process didn't make sense, because he'd just concluded distance from her would be a good thing.

Baffled, he pushed all his insane thoughts aside and tried to think like a cop. He set his cup on the bedside table and said, "Okay, let's look at the options. You can put your life on hold for a little longer, stay here where people are more than willing to watch out for you, or go home alone where there's a damn good chance you'll get killed. Now, which one seems like the better deal?"

Shala didn't get to answer, because Sky's phone rang. He picked it up from the bedside table and saw it was Trooper Pete Dickens. Holding up a silencing finger, he took the call.

"Yeah?"

"You want the good news or the bad news?" Pete asked.

"Both," Sky snapped, having no patience for games.

"I think I can explain the shots your friend heard."

"And?" Sky asked.

"And I found Charlie Rainmaker. Unfortunately, that's how I know about the shots."

"Shit! Is he—?"

"Dead?" Pete said. "Afraid so."

Sky moved off the bed. "I'm on my way."

Staring at the door, Shala pinched off a bite of buttered croissant, poked it into her mouth, and swallowed without tasting. Sky had kissed her and left, saying only that he had to go and would call. Something bad had happened—she'd gathered that. And from the way he'd looked at her, as if he had more ammunition to keep her in town, she gathered it had something to do with her neighborhood stalker.

"Lovely! Just lovely!" she muttered, Nana's favorite sarcastic saying. Then she dropped her plate on the bed and hugged her knees to her chest again.

What she wouldn't give for Nana to be alive right now, because she needed to talk to a woman. She needed someone she could talk to about the budding emotions causing hurricane-sized havoc in her heart. She could call her sister-in-law, Beth, but honestly, she'd never really bonded with her brother's wife. Calling her now to say, "I had awesome, multiple-orgasm, curl-your-toes-up, headboard-banging sex, and I'm afraid it's the biggest mistake I've made since I had mediocre sex with my ex-husband" . . . well, that just didn't feel right. Then again, she wasn't sure she'd have told Nana that, either.

I'm sorry, but there's no way I'm letting you walk away from here right now. Sky's words floated through her head. He was right about her safety, but seriously, how long could she stay? She had things to do, things to attend to . . . and more importantly, things to run from. And those didn't include her stalker. More like awesome, multiple-orgasm, curl-your-toes-up, headboard-banging sex.

* * *

"Everything is so freaking fucked up!"

Sky looked up from his desk at Maria, who charged into his office with all the subtlety of a pissed-off elephant.

"Yup."

Leaning back in his office chair, he agreed totally with her assessment. His last four hours had been spent staring at Charlie Rainmaker's corpse, combing over the crime scene with the Texas Rangers, and trying to make heads or tails of just how involved Charlie was with everything that had been going on. He knew Charlie was adamantly against bringing Shala into town, and finding several photos of her on the man's cell phone proved he'd been following her. Phillip had interviewed a group of people who'd attended one of Charlie's protest meetings, and they admitted that Charlie had insinuated that Shala could probably be "easily convinced" to up and leave town. And he knew the person willing to do it.

Contributing to Sky's bad mood was the phone call he'd just had with Candy Peterson about her reasons for not wanting to file charges against her abusive husband. Thankfully, he'd managed to talk her into it. Getting off the phone with Candy, he'd found missed messages on his cell: Jose wanting to talk to him about Maria, and Matt—Maria's married ex—presumably wanting to talk about her, too. The third message was from Redfoot, asking what Sky had done with his pills. And all this had been served up while he was still dealing with his emotions regarding Shala. Yup, Maria's assessment of "fucked up" pretty much described it all.

Maria slammed her purse on his desk and dropped down in the chair in front of him. The tears in her eyes kept Sky from handing her his cell phone and telling her to call someone who cared. Because he did care. He cared about Maria. He cared about Jose. He cared about Redfoot. He cared about Charlie Rainmaker's wife, whom he'd left sobbing in her living room. He even cared about Candy Peterson—well, he cared more about her little girl. And damn it to hell and back, he cared about Shala Winters. A lot. So much so that she was at the top of his list of worries.

"What's wrong?" He pushed a box of tissues toward Maria.

"I punched Matt. Hit him hard on the nose."

"Okay," Sky said, not knowing what else to say. Matt, unlike the others, didn't inspire even an iota of caring. "He hasn't filed charges against you, so I don't have to arrest you yet. A good thing, since I'm tired of having to lock up my own family." It was a bad joke, but he didn't have a lot of energy left. Seeing her tears, he wouldn't mind giving Matt a punch himself. He didn't know crap about relationships, but lying about being married always deserved a hammering.

"It hurt like hell," she sniffled. "But it felt fabulous."

He remembered how it had felt to hit Mr. Peterson last night. "As long as you don't make it a habit, it's fine."

"No, it's not fine! He lied to me, Sky. He's married, and now he comes into my kitchen and announces that I can't give Jose another chance because I still love him!"

"What?"

"He told Jose that I still love him," Maria said, and the fact that she didn't deny it said a whole lot more. "What makes it worse is I think Redfoot is the one that took Matt there. Why would he do that?"

Sky shook his head. "He wouldn't."

"Then Veronica comes charging in, saying that the tribal council is going to force her to marry Redfoot. Matt's all worried about my hand, and Jose just stands there with his pants filled with mustard and doesn't say a thing!"

Sky shook his head again. "What? You almost had me until you got to the mustard part."

"It's not important." Maria grabbed a tissue and blew her nose.

Sky scratched his chin. "Okay, Redfoot's not going to be forced to do anything he doesn't want to do. And I'm sure Ms. Cloud will—"

"But that's just it. Why didn't we know about that?"

Sky shrugged. "Redfoot obviously—"

"You know what I think?" she interrupted. "I think we didn't see it because we're so fucking busy burying our heads in the sand. I buried my head in the sand when it came to Matt and his weekends in Dallas. I buried my head in the sand about how Jose feels about us."

Sky didn't know whether to listen or ask. He decided to ask. "Uh, how does Jose feel about us?"

"He's jealous."

"Of us?"

"Mostly you."

"Of me? Please. The guy has a couple-hundred-thousand-dollar-a-year job, probably drives a hundred-thousand-dollar car, lives in—"

"That has nothing to do with it. You're more like Redfoot's son than Jose is."

"No. I refuse to take that on. When Jose was living here, I purposely didn't join in on anything those two did together. I didn't even do science projects, because that was their thing. I didn't go on those father-son camping trips . . ."

"You did the powwows," Maria accused.

"Only because Redfoot insisted!"

Maria sighed. "I'm not saying you did anything wrong, Sky. But remember that Redfoot insisted Jose do it, too, and he didn't because he hated it. And you enjoyed it."

"I didn't enjoy it. I respected it. There's a difference." Even today, Sky participated in the powwows only because he respected the culture. He didn't believe—at least, not in everything.

"Truth is, you've always had more in common with Redfoot than Jose. Jose is no fool. He could see that. I can see it, looking back. Jose is like Estella."

This was more crap to care about, and Sky didn't think he could handle it now. "If Jose wants to be close to his dad, he should move back here."

She shook her head. "He would be miserable."

"So it's my fault that he hates Precious?"

Maria rolled her eyes. "You're not listening. It's not your fault. It's not about you—it's about them. Estella used to be the link between them, and when she died they lost touch. I should have seen it. I should have done something a long time ago."

Sky shook his head. "It's not your job, or mine, to 'do something.'"

She crossed her arms over her chest. "I can't fix Matt, I can't fix Veronica and Redfoot, I can't fix you and Shala, but I can fix Jose and Redfoot. Or I can try."

"Me and Shala? How the hell did we get on your list?" He shook his head. "You can't go around trying to fix people."

"Really? For a guy who makes his living doing just that, that's a pretty big statement. You don't just run this town, you babysit it. Drunks call you to give them a ride home in the middle of the night. When you know I'm upset, you just drop by like you did yesterday. When I lost my client last year, and I was worried about money, I suddenly get a call from your friend in Austin to keep his books for him. If Redfoot's truck so much as hiccups you've got Ramon fixing it, and you pay for most of the bill and don't tell him . . ."

Sky just shrugged. "But I still don't stick my nose in other people's business."

"Yeah, right." Maria stood and walked around the desk to smother him in one of her hugs. "Thank you."

"For what now?" he asked, confused.

She pulled back. "For making me see I needed to

stop thinking about me and start thinking about other people."

"I did that?" he said. "Doesn't sound like me."

She smiled. "Okay, then, thank you for listening." She gave him another hug. "And for caring."

Caring—that might just be the death of him, Sky thought as he watched her leave.

He looked at the clock on the wall. In twenty minutes, Lucas was bringing Shala here to meet with Phillip and the rangers. Due to the discovery of Charlie's body, they'd rescheduled for the afternoon.

A sudden commotion from out front, raised voices and clatters, caught his attention. What was it now?

CHAPTER THIRTY

Sky jumped up, but the ruckus in the front of the station ended with the slamming of the front door. Footsteps echoed down the hall, and Sky expected to see Martha poke her head in and inform him of what was going on, but instead Matt appeared. Maria's Matt. And he had his hand over his bleeding nose.

"I need to talk to you," he said, and sat down in the chair Maria had just vacated.

"My sister again?" Sky asked, pushing the tissues to Matt.

"Yeah. She seems to have taken a liking to hitting me. As has Jose."

Sky leaned back. "To be honest, I'm thinking of doing it myself. You lied to her."

Matt pulled several tissues from the box and tried to stanch the bleeding. "I'm not guilty of what she thinks, and it's killing me. I can't sleep, eat. All I think about is her."

Sky crossed his arms on his chest. "Not thinking about your wife, huh?"

Matt shook his head. "I'm divorced."

"You got another woman in Dallas?"

"Yeah, I do." Matt pulled a picture from his shirt pocket and pushed it over. "She's my world."

Sky looked down at the little girl's face, so much like the man standing in front of him. "Your daughter?"

Matt nodded. "Beautiful, isn't she?" He let go of a deep breath through his mouth. "Redfoot came to see me this morning. He said I needed to tell Maria the truth. He assured me that whatever she had with Jose is over."

"Redfoot knew you were divorced?" Sky asked.

"Yeah, he said he dreamed it. How fucking weird is that? Anyway, I went to the house to explain, and Maria hit me then, too." He shuddered. "She's getting better at it. She hit me a lot harder this time. Next time she'll probably knock me out."

"I hope you're not here to press charges, because—"

"No," Matt said. "Redfoot suggested I talk to you about Maria."

Sky laughed. "Do I look like Dr. Phil? I'm so not the person to come to for relationship advice." He had his own problems. Huge ones.

Matt studied him. "So you're not going to help me?"

Sky leaned forward. "The only advice I can give is to tell her the truth."

"I would, if she didn't sock me every time I tried." Frustration echoed in his voice. "Can't you talk to her?"

"Me?"

"Just tell her to hear me out." Matt stood and walked to the door, fleeing as if he was afraid Sky would tell him no. "I appreciate it." He left.

Sky slumped back in his chair. He hadn't quite gotten

his head around Matt's request when another commotion exploded from the front office. Martha's scream brought Sky to his feet, but he was only halfway around his desk before footsteps sounded down the hall. Jose shot through the office door, also with a bloody nose.

Sky motioned. "Let me guess. Matt?"

"Yeah. Fucker hit me and walked off—the cowardly piece of crap."

Somehow, Sky didn't think it was so much cowardly as much as a territorial statement: Maria belonged to Matt and Jose had best back off. Sky went back to his desk, dropped into his chair, and pushed the tissues toward his brother. Then he looked at the clock. "You've got ten minutes, Jose. Then I've got a meeting."

Jose lowered himself into the other chair but didn't talk.

"What is it you need?" Sky took in his brother's beat-up face and felt sorry for him. When his mind turned to what Maria had said earlier, his gut tightened more.

Shoot, there had been a time when he had been jealous of Jose. Jose was Redfoot and Estella's real son, and while those two had never made Sky feel like a second fiddle, Sky had never felt anything but. Jose always seemed to know what he wanted out of life, while Sky had floundered, eventually joining the police force. It hadn't helped that Jose got the prettiest girls in high school. Hell, there had even been a time Sky envied Maria's affection for their brother.

"Time's ticking," he warned the still-silent Jose.

"It's Maria . . . and Dad." Jose went with what was clearly the easier topic. "I wouldn't put it past the tribal council to tell him he has to marry Ramon's mom."

Sky shrugged. "Since when has Redfoot done something he didn't want to do?"

"Since it involves his beloved culture," Jose snapped.

Sky shook his head. "He's loyal to the tribe, but if I had

a dollar for the times he said the council isn't about culture, it's about politics, I'd be rich. The only reason he's in the council is to try and keep politics out."

Jose grabbed another tissue for his nose. Changing the subject, he asked, "What are we going to do about Matt? Guy's married and still sniffing around Maria."

Sky didn't know how much to reveal, but he figured Jose might as well hear it all. "He's not married. The reason he's been hanging out in Dallas is because he has a daughter."

"A daughter?" When Sky nodded, Jose let out a big whoosh of air. "Maria loves him, doesn't she?"

Sky shrugged. "I think so, but hell, what do I know about relationships? I'm just as screwed up as the rest of you. Probably more."

"You mean you and Shala?"

Sky started to deny it, but then said, "Yeah."

"She's hot," Jose remarked.

"Yeah, that she is." Sky was remembering how she'd looked that morning, wrapped in only that sheet.

Jose grabbed another tissue. "I hope I didn't ruin it for you."

"Ruin it for me?" Sky asked.

"Yeah, her seeing me naked." Jose chuckled. "Once she's seen the best, and knows how a real man looks . . ."

Sky laughed. He and Jose might not have completely understood each other over the years, but they had bonded. "I'm not worried. I saw you naked, too. The pink robe was a nice touch."

"Sorry about being an ass the other morning," Jose said.

Sky shrugged. "From what I gather, you had a rough night."

"I have had a rough *three* nights."

"You do look like hammered shit," Sky said, studying him.

Jose chuckled. "I feel like hammered shit. Did Dad tell

you that I fell through a wall? My head went right through the Sheetrock. You can see the shape of my nose and everything."

"Really?" Sky couldn't help laughing.

"Yeah, and then this morning Maria spilled hot coffee all down the front of me. Burnt the shit out of my junk."

Sky laughed harder. "Ahh, that explains the mustard."

Jose shook his head. All humor had left him. "I screwed up."

"How's that?"

"With Maria. I should have snapped her up when I had a chance." He sighed. "Whatever you do, Sky, if you care about this Shala woman, don't let her walk away. You'll regret it."

"It's not like that," Sky said, but the words sounded and felt like a lie.

Jose stood. "Thanks for . . . hearing me out."

"Anytime," Sky said. As his brother started to leave, he added, "You know, Redfoot told me all about those buildings you designed. The one in Vegas and the one in New York. He's proud of you."

Surprise filled Jose's eyes. "He told you about it?"

"All about it. Said you took him on a tour of the one in New York when he visited. He brought those magazines back that had the article about you, and he passed them out everywhere."

The look on Jose's face told Sky that Maria was right: Jose and Redfoot needed to talk.

"Hey." Martha popped her head inside the office. "I've set Phillip and Ms. Winters up in the interview room." Her gaze shot to Jose. "You look as if you ran into Mr. Ugly and he attached himself to your face."

Jose smiled at Martha, who used to be his school nurse. For some reason, they'd always given each other a bit of hell. "Gosh, I was just about to say the same about you."

Martha snickered and gave his arm a pat. "You always had a smart mouth."

"Thanks, Martha." Sky left the pair talking and went to find Shala.

Redfoot knocked on Veronica's door. He had to talk to her, damn it! Ramon had called and insisted they go meet with the tribal council, but first he needed to talk to the man's mother.

He wouldn't put it past the old farts of the council to recommend he make the union legal between himself and Veronica. Frankly, considering his dream, he had assumed that was supposed to happen. After Veronica's temper tantrum, he wasn't so sure.

"Go away!" came a voice from behind the door.

"Not until you talk to me. I swear, I'll pitch a tent and sleep here tonight if you don't open up."

He meant it, and Veronica knew he didn't lie. The back door swung open. She stood there, her beautiful face red and puffy from what looked like hours of crying. Guilt speared Redfoot's heart. His goal had been to convince Veronica to marry him. He'd assumed she might waver, but if he thought she really didn't want this . . .

He reached for her, but she jumped back. It hurt. "What do you want me to do?" he asked. "Tell me what you want and I'll do it."

Tears welled up in her brown eyes. "What I wanted was to not climb into that hospital bed with you. What I wanted was to simply see you a couple of nights a week, to share a small part of myself with you. Now you've ruined everything."

"Nothing is ruined," he argued.

"Ramon plans to go to the council. You know what they'll say. They'll insist you do right by me. They could kick you out of their group."

Redfoot gritted his teeth. "I don't care. They can take that council position and shove it up their asses."

Veronica swiped at her tears. "That won't change anything. You don't have to look into your son's face knowing you're a whore."

"Don't you dare call yourself that!" Redfoot growled. "What we shared was not ugly." He slapped his chest. "I care about you. I want you to share my life. I want to get older with you."

"Is that why you did it? You set out to make me marry you, so I would belong to you. So I would have to take care of you."

He felt another wave of guilt, because he had indeed set out to make this happen. "You would never belong to me, Veronica. And caring is a two-way street."

Her face was stony. "I'm no fool, Redfoot. I lived this once."

"So it's true, isn't it? That bastard hurt you. And you judge me to be the same type of man."

"You're all alike." Fury brightened her eyes.

"No. We are not." Redfoot took a step closer, but the pain in her eyes halted him. "I will fix this."

She shook her head. "It's too late. Ramon is going to talk to the council, and he's going to think less of me if I don't marry you. I won't have my son think bad things about me. But don't you ever think that I will forgive you for this."

"It's never too late." He wanted so badly to touch her, to hold her, to spend the last years of his life proving to her that all men weren't bad. But if setting her free made her happy, that's what he would do. All he had to do was figure out how.

Shala twisted in her chair, frowning as the back of her thong climbed up between her butt cheeks. The door opened, and her heart made a leap of joy that bordered on pain. Sky! She had assumed he would be here, and when he hadn't come at the beginning, her nervousness had grown by leaps and bounds. Who liked to be interrogated by a Texas Ranger?

Okay, she knew she hadn't done anything wrong, but the man's direct question about her involvement in anything illegal gave her the heebie-jeebies. His mere presence demanded a confession, and she'd been about to admit cheating on her sixth-grade history test. Hey, he wanted a confession? He would get one.

"Sorry, I had someone in my office." Sky studied her. Sitting, he slipped his hand into hers and squeezed. It reminded her of how he'd held her hand at the hospital, how he'd naturally sensed her discomfort. Warmth and strength washed through her.

Leaning back in his chair, Sky looked at Phillip. "Have you already introduced yourselves?"

"Yes, we've gotten that far," the ranger said. "I was just asking Miss Winters if she's ever been connected to anything illegal."

"So, you're scaring her, huh?"

"Only if she's hiding something," the ranger replied.

Sky scowled. He gave her hand another squeeze.

Sensing his anger, Shala said, "It's okay."

"No, it's not," Sky snapped. "She's the victim, Phillip. I thought I made that clear."

"And some victims know more than they're letting on."

"Bullshit," Sky interrupted. "She's been nothing but cooperative. Just because you've got a high-ranking job with some fancy badge doesn't mean you can go around intimidating people. And unless you can pull your head out of your ass and be a gentleman, this interview is over!"

Shala stared at the two men, imagining them next throwing fists. "It's really okay," she repeated.

Phillip burst out laughing. "I'll be damned. Protective, aren't you?"

Sky didn't appear to appreciate the other man's mirth. He growled, "Play nice or she doesn't play at all."

The ranger leaned back in his chair and faced Shala, a smile still pulling at his lips. "Ms. Winters, if I came on too strong, I'm sorry. I've had a rough day. Murder does that to me, and the fact is, this case just keeps getting bigger and we don't have a clue where to start." He looked to Sky and then back at her. "But Sky's right, I might have taken my frustration out on you. So how about let's start over? My name's Phillip, and I've known Sky Gomez here for about seven years. I play poker with him three times a year, and any friend of his is a friend of mine." His gaze shifted back to Sky. "Better?"

"It's a start," Sky replied.

CHAPTER THIRTY-ONE

The chat went on for forty-five minutes. Sky felt pleased that his Texas Ranger friend hadn't asked any questions that he himself hadn't.

"Did you look at the images I told Sky about?" Shala asked.

"You mean the ones of Charlie Rainmaker and the man you think was driving the black sedan?" Phillip asked.

Shala nodded.

"Yeah. We're trying to get an identity on the driver."

"Do we know when we might get that?" Sky asked.

"These things take forever," Phillip said.

"What about the other image?" Shala asked. "The one of the couple . . . uh, getting busy in the car? Like I told

Sky, maybe one of them is married and they think I'm a PI."

Phillip shrugged. "With what we know about Rainmaker forming the petition, the pictures he had of you on his phone, and his talk about getting you scared out of town, we're leaning toward the theory that he hired some muscle to scare you off, and maybe when Rainmaker didn't pay up, or complained about the fact that you were still here, the guy turned on him."

Sky knew Phillip's theory had merit, but he still had his doubts.

"I guess it would appear that way," Shala admitted.

They were about to call the meeting done when the door popped open and Martha leaned her head inside. "Sky," she said frowning. "There's . . . You . . . I think you'd better come out here."

Sky stood up, almost scared to find out what was next. "Excuse me," he said. But he hadn't gotten out the door before Candy Peterson stormed up to him.

"I've decided not to press charges," she said.

Taking in her face, he couldn't remember her ever looking so bruised. Sky led her into his office and, gritting his teeth, forced calm into his voice. He shut the door. "Have you looked at yourself in the mirror, Candy?"

"He was drunk."

"Oh, does that make it okay? You should have told me that last night, and I'd have let him keep beating the shit out of you."

"He says your threat to take Amy from me is bullshit. You can't do that."

So she was already talking to the asshole. Sky remembered the look on the little girl's face last night. It made him want to explode. Even worse, it made him want to lie and say he'd witnessed Peterson beating her. But he hadn't. And his lying wouldn't stop Candy. She had to want to put a stop to this.

"You should know, Candy, I don't make idle threats. One more time . . . one more time, and I swear to God, I'll have Child Protective Services on your ass so fast your head will spin."

"I'm a good mother!" she snapped. "He's never hurt her!"

"Never *hurt* her? Did you see her last night? Didn't you see the pain in her eyes? You think that doesn't hurt her? Have you ever seen your mother get the crap beat out of her? Have you? I have, Candy! So, don't tell me it doesn't hurt!" Realizing he'd lost his cool, he pointed to the door. "Go! If you're not going to press charges, get the hell out of my office. But hear me loud and clear: this was your last chance."

He opened the door and waited for her to leave. Feeling the rage boiling inside him, he stormed to his desk and ran his hand across it, knocking everything to the floor. He was still staring at the mess he'd made when he heard someone behind him.

He swung around. "I told you to leave, Candy!" It wasn't Candy. "Sorry," he said.

Shala stepped closer. "That was the emergency you went to last night, wasn't it?"

"Yeah." She must have heard him through the door.

She put her hand on his chest. "I'm sorry."

"For what?"

"That you had to deal with that."

"It's my job."

She glanced down for a few moments before looking back at him. "I . . . When I was looking for my camera, I found—"

He put his finger over her lips. "I know."

"How?" she asked.

"You left the closet light on." He frowned. "I didn't appreciate it."

"Didn't appreciate me leaving the light on?" she asked,

a little teasingly. When he frowned again, in no mood for humor, she continued. "I know it was wrong, but I didn't mean to—"

Realizing he was taking his mood out on her, afraid she was going to start jabbering, he put his finger over her lips again. "Just shut up and kiss me," he said.

She smiled. "Okay."

Her lips were sweet and soft. He slipped his tongue inside her mouth, and her breasts pressed against his chest. Losing himself in the moment, he moved his hand down to cup her bottom. The kiss got hotter, fast.

She shifted closer, and he pressed one thigh between hers. Her pelvis brushed him ever so slightly. She tugged his shirttail out of his jeans and slid her hand up under his shirt. That soft palm caressed his chest. He went instantly hard. Opening his eyes, he spotted his clean desk and decided clearing it off hadn't been a bad thing after all.

After he took one step, however, sanity broke through his lust. His gaze shot to his open office door. "Shit. Where's Lucas?"

Shala blushed as if she'd just realized how far the kiss had gone. "Waiting to see if you want him to bring me home."

"Phillip?"

"He left." She buried her head on his chest as if embarrassed.

Sky released her and went to the door. "Lucas," he called. "I got Shala. I'll bring her home."

"Okay," his friend called back. "I'll see you at the cabin."

"Yeah. We'll be there . . . shortly. Did you pick up those items from the grocery store that I told you to get?"

"Got 'em," the man replied.

"Good. I'll cook us supper tonight. And, Martha?" Sky called. "You can head out."

He waited until he heard the tap of Martha's heels leaving before he shut his office door. When he looked back, Shala still wore embarrassment on her cheeks. But he had a feeling he could make it disappear. Or at least he hoped he could.

His gaze moved down her body, from her blue-jean skirt to the red button-down short-sleeved shirt that so perfectly accentuated her lush curves. He'd been so distracted at seeing her upset by Phillip that he hadn't noticed what she was wearing. Or that she looked so damn hot.

"Where did you get those clothes?" he asked.

"Lucas took me shopping."

Sky frowned. "I was supposed to do that."

"You were busy."

He moved in and wrapped his arm around her waist. When she leaned into him willingly, softly, he let his hand slide lower. "Are you at least wearing the underwear I bought?"

"Afraid so."

"Afraid so?" he repeated, puzzled.

She shrugged guiltily. "They kept sliding up places they shouldn't the whole time I was talking to Phillip. Thongs. Talk about uncomfortable."

He laughed. "You told me you wore them."

"I lied. I hate the stupid things."

"But you wore one anyway. For me?" His glaze slid downward, and he imagined her panties—and slipping into places he shouldn't. His jeans felt too tight.

"I forgot to buy any at the store. So it was wear the thong, wear dirty underwear, or go pantyless."

"We wouldn't want you wearing dirty underwear. But pantyless might work." He kissed her and, reaching down, found the zipper of her skirt. She didn't stop him as he slowly lowered it, but she did look up with a hesitant expression.

"Should we really . . . ? Here?"

"Not if you don't want you to," he said, prepared to call himself into check.

"No, I'm fine." She looked around. "But where are you planning to . . . have this event take place?"

He finished with her zipper. "Well, the most logical place would be my desk."

She looked over at it. He dropped her skirt, which fluttered to the floor. Her red panties had his heart racing. That little triangle of silky material barely covered her patch of blonde hair. The adjoining thin red straps hugged her hips.

Sky raised his gaze to her face and fought the need to adjust his pants. "Or we could use the chair. The rug?"

Her gaze shifted. "I'm not sure we'd both fit in the chair."

"We could manage." Still enjoying the view of her thong, he walked around her to get the whole picture. "Very nice." He ran his finger down the thin band, brushing her shapely ass. "Are you wearing the red bra?"

She rolled her eyes. "It's a matched set. You have to wear them together. It's a rule."

"Nice." He pursed his lips and moved his hand. "Do you think I could get a peek at this . . . matched set?"

"I suppose." She started fidgeting with the first button on her shirt. Then, grinning, she tilted her head to the side and released it. "You wouldn't want to turn around, would you?"

"Not on your life." He propped against the desk. His dick was already as hard as oak.

Shala let out a nervous chuckle. "I'm not used to being watched so closely."

"How about I start taking off my clothes and let you watch me while I watch you?"

She smiled. "That might help."

He pulled the rest of his shirt from his jeans and started unbuttoning. He did it slowly for her pleasure, but he never took his eyes off her. She slipped the second button free and then the third. Her red bra and all that sweet cleavage came into view, and he forgot about creating a show. He tore off his shirt and unbuttoned his jeans.

Finished, Shala slowly let her top fall away from her shoulders and to the floor. She stood before him in a red bra and red thong panties, and a pair of white sandals. His gaze lowered to her painted toenails, to the little daisies.

"Nice," he whispered.

He kicked off his shoes, shucked his jeans and underwear. When her gaze lowered to his sex, that took him to another degree of hardness.

One bra strap hung off her shoulder. He ran a finger down it, over the sweet orb the garment contained, but he stopped when he found her nipple pebbled against the fabric. Shala reached back to unhook her bra, but he stopped her.

"Not just yet."

He moved her to his desk, lifted her slightly, and carefully set her back down. She lay back. He withdrew an inch and stared. Her light blonde hair haloed her head on the dark stained oak, and the red underwear was a splash of hot color on her ivory skin. "Damn," he whispered, his gaze devouring her. "Now, whenever I sit at this desk I'll picture you."

She laughed and ran her hands up his forearms. "What am I supposed to do?" she asked. "I've never had desk sex."

He stared down at her, smiling. "Don't worry. You could just lie there and that'd be enough."

He brushed his palms up and down her waist. She caught one of his hands and brought it to her lips. As she slipped one of his fingers inside her mouth, sucking his finger in and then out, his gaze stayed riveted. It was almost more than he could bear.

Slowly, he pulled his hand free and lowered it to trace

the triangle of her panties. The sweet moisture there told him of her desire. "I think someone likes desk sex," he accused.

She chuckled. "I'm not complaining."

Slipping his finger inside her thong, he brushed her sex from side to side. Her hips rose. Eyes closing, she gave a first little moan.

"I love it when you do that," he said.

"Do what?"

"Make that sound."

He used his free hand to reach back and release her bra. She arched up as he gave a tug, and he withdrew the garment from beneath her. Her breasts shifted, so he leaned down to kiss them. A moment later he had her panties off and had found the condom in his wallet, glad he'd run by his house and replenished his supply.

Pulling her to the edge of the desk, he wrapped her legs around his waist and entered her. He moved slowly at first, easing his weight down upon her, but the pleasure was too intense to hold back. He placed his hand behind her head to pillow it and let his body take control. Her arms came around him. The bumping and grinding increased until at last he heard her sounds of pleasure in his ear. His own orgasm followed instantly. Not unlike last night, there was an emotional impact, too. The only awkward part came when they finished: he couldn't curl up beside her, and he couldn't stay bent over her. Pulling away would leave them both cold.

He suddenly realized he couldn't recall ever being worried about the moments after sex with any other woman. Forcing that thought from his mind, he picked her up and lowered her to the rug and stretched out beside her.

When he realized she hadn't opened her eyes, he ran a finger over her nose. "You okay?" he asked, his heart still racing.

"Perfect." She sounded just as breathless. Curled up in his arms, she pressed her cheek to his chest. They stayed like that for several minutes. "Is it always busy like this?"

"What?" he asked.

"I mean here, being chief of police in a small town. So much seemed to be going on here today."

"It's been a busy last few days." He laughed.

"So I did bring trouble with me, huh?"

"It's not you." He paused, and after a few minutes, when the silence grew long, he elaborated. "I have to deal with everything the way a big city would—on a much smaller scale, thank God. We've had a shooting, break-ins, domestic violence . . ." He said the last one with a certain amount of loathing. "There're the traffic violations, too damn many DUIs to contend with." His mind considered some of the oddest things his job required. "Then on any given day I might be called out to help Miss Gordon find her dog. Once I was called to help Mr. Thompson find his teeth. He was certain his neighbor stole them."

She laughed. "Did you find them?"

"What? The dog or the teeth?"

"Both," she said.

"Yeah. I did." He chuckled. "The dog was in the closet. The teeth in the microwave. And don't ask me to explain either one." They stayed there holding on to each other and laughed for a good three or four minutes.

They didn't talk for the next five minutes. The silence felt right this time. Then he caught her hand, the one with the large bandage covering her palm. "Damn, I was supposed to take you to get the stitches out."

"Doctor said three or four days. I'm sure tomorrow is fine." When he brought her palm to his lips, she rose up on her elbow and studied him. "Can I ask you something?"

A nervous tickle hit his gut. "I generally hate questions that start like that, but go ahead."

"How . . . how old were you when your parents died?"

See? He knew he'd hate it. He fought the desire to quash this line of questioning and found himself answering. "Ten."

"And did you come live with Redfoot right afterward?"

"No. I floated from foster home to foster home for about a year and a half."

She bit down on her lip and placed her hand on his chest. "That must have been terrible."

It had been. "I did okay."

Sky realized this might be the best time to set the record straight about his relationship barriers. Maybe she'd understand why he couldn't offer more. But then his foster brother's words played in his head like an old song. *Whatever you do, Sky, if you care about this Shala woman, don't let her walk away. You'll regret it.*

He shook his head and said, "You know, the past—mine and probably yours—it can make things hard."

"Hard?"

"Relationships and things," he babbled, knowing he was making a mess of this.

"I know," she said. She reached out and touched his chin. "I'm scared."

A weight suddenly lifted off his chest, and relief spilled into him. "Me, too! But I figure we can live for the day, enjoy it. Make the most of it. Right?"

She nodded. "I have to go back home sooner or later."

The weight crashed right back down. "When it's safe you can leave. Not until then."

"But whoever was after me or the camera hasn't tried anything for a couple of days. I've seen Lucas and you both looking for him, and he obviously isn't there. Maybe he's given up."

Sky took her chin between his fingers. "Are you nuts? This is the same guy who we think killed someone yesterday!"

She gazed up at him. "I know, but . . . Lucas and I were talking earlier, and it's like Phillip said. It appears Charlie hired someone to do all this. Now that Charlie is gone, this guy doesn't really have a reason to come after me. And Lucas thinks . . ."

He was going to have to tell Lucas to keep his friggin' thoughts to himself. "I've considered that, Shala, and yes, I admit that from what we know it appears as if this is what went down, but there's still a couple of things that don't make sense. Charlie lives on a fixed income. I just can't see him using what little money he had to hire someone to do his dirty work. We've looked over his bank account. No money was withdrawn. And everything that's happened still points to this guy wanting the camera." When Shala dropped back against his chest, he ran his hand over her naked back. "I know this is hard, Shala, but give me some time to figure it out before you go putting yourself back in danger. Please."

She rose up on her elbow, smiling. "Wow, you're not threatening to arrest me this time."

"No. But I'd probably follow you if you left town."

She shook her head. "You have a job."

"I know. That's why it would be hard." He touched her face. "Just a little more time."

She sighed. "Okay, but I need to start working while I'm here."

"Working?"

"Yeah, talking to the tribal council, meeting with Maria about starting an art program, talking to the mayor about the changes he'll need to make. If I'm here, I need to work. I can only play so many games of Scrabble before I lose my mind."

Sky laughed. "I'll talk to Johnson and we'll work things out." For the first time that day, breathing came easier.

Shala looked down at her legs. "I don't think I've ever had sex with just my shoes on."

"I'll have to get you a pair of leather boots," he said.

When they were done laughing, Shala sighed again.

She ran her hand down his chest and said, "Don't you think we should probably get going?"

"Going? I thought we'd give the chair a whirl."

She slapped him playfully. "Come on."

As Sky dressed, he watched her put on her clothes, and that chair started looking better and better. *Whatever you do, Sky, if you care about this Shala woman, don't let her walk away. You'll regret it.*

"Hey." He zipped up his jeans and then snagged her shirt from the floor. "When you do leave"—God, that was hard to say—"how often will you have to come back?"

She shrugged and stepped into her jean skirt. "It depends on how many press trips the Chamber can afford. I bring other writers with me, and Precious has to pick up the tab. Some of my clients can afford trips every few months, some every six months."

Every few months? That wasn't nearly enough. Would she come down more often if he asked? Considering he was on call 24/7, his leaving for a whole weekend would be hard. But she'd come if what they had was worth coming down for. Was he giving her what she needed right now, making it worth her while? Hell, how could he know for sure? Hadn't he admitted to himself that she was different from everyone he'd ever dated? More innocent, sweeter . . . He looked around his office. Had the whole sex-on-the-desk thing been too much? Remembering her hesitation in the beginning, a mess of emotions boiled to the surface. Was he already screwing things up?

"What?" he asked when she held out her hand.

"You have my shirt."

And I'm afraid you've got my heart.

He wasn't sure where that thought came from, but he refused to let it set in. He handed over her shirt and grabbed his own.

CHAPTER THIRTY-TWO

Shala looked up and caught Sky staring as she buttoned her blouse. "What?"

He ran a hand over his face. "You were okay with this, right?"

"Okay with what?"

He motioned to the desk. "What we just did."

Shala's insecurities surfaced like a school of hungry piranhas. She hadn't had sex in so long, and even back when she was having sex, her hubby obviously hadn't been satisfied. "Did I do something wrong?"

"Wrong? Why would you think...? God, no! I just realized that this was a bit—"

"Wild?" She tossed the word out.

He nodded. "Yeah."

Crazy as it seemed, Sky looked as if he was the insecure one. How cool was that? Real cool. People didn't feel insecure unless something mattered to them. She obviously mattered to Sky Gomez.

She tilted her head to the side. "It *was* wild." She remembered how he'd looked down at her sprawled on his desk, how his eyes had been so filled with desire that she'd gone instantly wet. "And a little crazy." She couldn't remember sex ever being so spontaneous. She hesitated, then added, "I loved every moment of it. Are you going to think less of me now?"

He laughed and pulled her to him. "We could still do the chair."

She rose up on tiptoes and kissed him. At that moment, Shala couldn't remember ever being happier.

* * *

"Redfoot's not here." Maria stirred the onion in the pan while she spoke to Sky on the phone. "He called and said he had business to handle. I'm worried."

"Stop worrying," Sky replied. "But have him call me when he gets home. Did you see Jessie today?"

"Yes, I was at the hospital most of the afternoon. She's good. Back to gossiping."

"Not about me, I hope," Sky said.

"Nah, but you do know there are pills for that . . ."

"Great!"

Maria laughed. "Silly rumor. No one will believe it. Anyway, I think she's going home tomorrow. I've got to get a client's payroll done in the morning, and then I told Sal I'd come over while he got caught up on work."

"Let me know if I can do anything. Oh, do you want to come over to Lucas's for steaks?"

"No. I'm cooking Spanish rice and chicken as we speak." Maria stirred in some peppers.

"Don't add too much garlic."

Maria grumbled good-naturedly. "I swear—you can't stay out of my kitchen, even when you're on the phone."

"Sorry, but you always add too much garlic."

"I like garlic," she replied.

"I know." He chuckled, and Maria couldn't remember him being quite so happy before. "Is Jose there?" he asked.

"No." She reached for the garlic powder, smiling as she did. "I don't know where he is, either." And she needed to see him, needed to do what should have been done two years ago.

"Has Matt visited again?"

Maria heard hesitation in his voice, and she thought she understood. "I'm sorry I hit him at the station."

"Yeah, about that. I think that instead of . . . hitting, maybe you should hear the guy out."

"I have no interest in hearing how his wife doesn't love him and—"

"What if that's not what he has to tell you?"

"What are you saying?" She gave the bottle of garlic powder a good shake as another thought suddenly occurred to her. "Why was he even at the station?"

Sky didn't answer. Instead he said, "Hey, I think my steaks are burning . . . and I think Shala's cheating at Scrabble again. I'd better run."

"Sky . . . ? Damn!" she muttered when he hung up.

"Something wrong?" someone asked. When Maria swung around, she saw Jose in the doorway behind her.

Something? Everything is wrong. "No. Just Sky still trying to tell me how to cook." She didn't want to get into a conversation with Jose about Matt right now, especially considering the conversation she needed to have. "Want some coffee?"

"No! No mustard, either." He grinned.

"Sorry about that." Adding water to her rice mixture, she put the lid on the pot. Then she turned. "We need to talk."

He studied her. "Why does your tone remind me of Mom when she found those *Playboy*s under my bed?"

Maria grinned and settled into a chair at the table. Jose sat across from her. When she met his eyes, guilt filled her chest. She should have told him, should have come clean before he left for New York. She should have told him when she lost the baby. Matt should even know. She should have told him about the baby and the possibility of her not being able to conceive when they started getting—Wait. That didn't matter anymore. Matt was a married bastard. But she should have called him on his weekends in Dallas. Should have. *Should have.* Her life was filled with too many should-haves.

She tried to think how to ease into the conversation, but subtlety had never been her strong point, so she decided to dive in headfirst. "When you left for New York I was pregnant."

His mouth dropped open. "You were . . . I . . . We have a child?"

A few tears slipped past her lashes. "No. I lost it."

It? She'd never known if she carried a girl or a boy. Maria put her fingers over her trembling lips and explained, "I had a tubal pregnancy. They said it wasn't my fault, but sometimes I think that if I would have dealt with things better, if I would have—"

"Why didn't you tell me?"

"At first it was pride. I thought that if you didn't want me, you wouldn't want the baby. Then you didn't even call me, and I got angry. About three weeks after you left, I started hurting. They had to operate and . . ." She wiped her face with the back of her hand. She didn't have to tell him everything. "I was wrong. I know that now. I'm sorry."

He buried his face in his hands. She heard the rice bubbling over and went to turn down the heat. The chair shifted behind her, and she thought he planned on leaving. She didn't blame him. Instead, she felt him move close.

"Why the hell are you apologizing when it's my fault?" He touched her shoulder. "I should have never left."

She turned. "No, Jose." Biting back her tears, she tried to explain. "You had to go. I know that now."

He shook his head. "I loved you. I think I'm still in love with you. If we could—"

"Don't say that." She put a finger over his lips. "Look, I love you, too. I will always love you, but it's not the right kind of love. When I came here, I wanted so badly to be a part of this family. You were so . . . hot, and I was so young, and I thought that if we fell in love, then I would really be a part of this family. And I think when Estella died . . ." She had to think how to say it. "When she died, I was the person who understood you like she did. I think you finally opened yourself up to me because I represented everything you'd lost."

Jose blinked. "Mom told me not to let anything happen. That it would cause a ruckus."

Maria grinned. "She was a smart woman."

"What if she was wrong?" He touched her face.

"She wasn't. You belong in New York. I'll never leave Precious. And right now I hate Matt, but what I felt for him . . . That was what love is supposed to feel like."

He cupped her chin in his hand. "I hate that bastard. If he doesn't treat you right, I'll rip out his heart."

"It's over between us," she assured him.

"Have you two talked?"

She shook her head. "No! And I don't plan on it."

Speak of the devil, a knock sounded at the door. Maria's insides started shaking, and she eyed the living room. Grabbing Jose by the arm she begged, "Answer it, please. If it's Matt, make him leave."

Jose walked out. Maria turned back to the stove and refused to listen, afraid that she'd be tempted by his voice if it was Matt. She was afraid she'd be tempted to tell him she didn't care that he'd lied to her, didn't care that he was married, because she'd loved him with all her heart and probably always would.

In spite of not listening, she heard the front door close. When Jose moved back into the kitchen she asked, "Was it Matt?"

"Yes." The voice wasn't as deep as Jose's, and it sounded too damn much like the man she loved. Closing her eyes, Maria sent up a prayer that she was wrong—a prayer to God, the Virgin Mary, to every saint she could remember, and just in case, she also added all the spirits Redfoot believed in. There was no reason not to cover all her bases.

"Look," Matt said, making her prayer futile. "If you're going to hit me, let's get it over with, because we need to talk."

Redfoot walked up to Ramon Cloud's porch, his heart heavy and whiskey on his breath. Before he'd left the

Funky Chicken, he'd doused himself with his last drink, hoping that too would help. Ramon's zero tolerance for drunks was a little-known fact. Redfoot figured there was a reason for that, and the obvious suspect was the young man's late father.

Reaching up, he banged on the door. This felt morally wrong, but he had gotten Veronica into this quandary, and he would get her out.

Ramon opened the door, and his gaze was filled with contempt—the contempt of a son who thought no man was good enough for his mother. Redfoot respected that.

"You said for me to come and . . . we'd go to the council." Redfoot drew his words out. "And I'm here." Purposely leaning close, he hoped the smell of whiskey on him was overpowering. Ramon stepped back.

"You damn well know the council has gone home for the day!"

Redfoot gaped at his watch. "Damn. Guess I lost track of the time."

"We'll go tomorrow."

"Sounds like a good plan." When Ramon tried to shut the door, Redfoot put his hand against it. "You know, at first I was mad. No way was I going to marry your skinny-assed mom!"

Ramon seethed. "Go home before I do something I'll regret."

"But you're not listening," Redfoot argued. "I've changed my mind. While I was at the Funky Chicken, it occurred to me. She put up with your daddy's ass for a quarter of a century, she can put up with mine for a while. I'm not much worse than your old man."

"You bastard!" Ramon stormed outside and threw him against the house.

"I'm not a bastard," Redfoot managed to say. And that was the truth, though the truth would end there. He forced himself to continue. "Yeah, it was probably wrong, all that crap I told her about how I cared, but you know how women are. They don't give it up until you make 'em *believe* it."

Ramon drew back his fist. Redfoot prepared himself for the blow, but the man dropped his arm and shoved him away instead. "Get the hell out of here. And stay the fuck away from my mother. You got that? Because I swear to God, old man, if you come anywhere near her, I'll beat the life out of you. She put up with one asshole; she'll not put up with two."

"What about g-g-going to the council?" Redfoot slurred.

"Not happening." Ramon stormed back inside the house and slammed the door.

As Redfoot walked away, adding a sway to his step just in case Ramon watched from the window, he muttered, "I fixed it." Veronica should be happy now. It didn't matter that he himself had never been more miserable.

"I'm not married."

Matt's words bounced around the yellow kitchen and had Maria catching her breath. She picked up the garlic powder and gave the rice mixture another good dousing before turning.

"Can I sit down?" He motioned toward the table. She nodded, and he dropped into a chair. "I was married. We're divorced. And before you say anything, I know I should have told you."

She crossed her arms over her chest, puzzled. "But you're still seeing your ex-wife."

"No. Not like you think."

"You called her when you thought you were arrested."

"Only because I couldn't get my ex-father-in-law. He's a lawyer and a nice guy. I thought I'd need him to get me out of jail."

Maria considered. "She lives in Dallas?" she asked.

"Yes."

"So all those weekends away, you weren't seeing her." She was feeling pretty dubious.

"I was, but—"

"Leave!" She pointed to the door.

Matt pulled something out of his shirt pocket and slid it across the table to her. "This is why I saw her."

Maria's gaze shifted. Unable to stop herself, she moved closer and stared at a photograph, at the precious face of a little girl who looked to be about three. She had big green eyes and sandy hair. Without a doubt, the child was Matt's.

"Brenda, my ex . . . We met in college. I was crazy about her, but she had a thing about this other guy. I became the person she cried on when the jerk did her wrong. And he did her wrong a lot. He left and ran off to Europe. One night she came over and we got drunk and she got pregnant. I convinced her to marry me, and I thought life was great." He raked a hand through his hair. "Great until about six weeks after we got hitched and the asshole came back. To make a long story short, we got a divorce and she married the other guy. All this happened before Brandy was born."

Maria heard the pain in his voice. "I'm sorry," she said.

"At first I thought I could just walk away, but I took one look at that girl and that's the day I knew what real love is. There's nothing like seeing your own child look up at you."

Maria swallowed the lump in her throat. She was seeing a new side of Matt. No, that wasn't right. She'd seen this all along. He had goodness in him, the kind of goodness that would make him a perfect family man. He was loyal, dependable, kind.

"Why didn't you tell me?" she asked.

"At first it was to protect Brandy."

"Protect her—from me?"

"Yes . . . I mean, no. Not just you. I didn't want to bring people into her life and then have them walk away. Brenda and the asshole got a divorce. I saw how it hurt Brandy, and I didn't want . . ." He leaned across the table. "I was going to tell you before things got serious. But it got serious so quick. Then one night you mentioned how glad you were that neither of us had been married. You said it brought a bunch of extra baggage into the relationship. I panicked. I convinced myself that if I let you fall in love with me, you'd understand."

Maria stood frozen, trying to understand her emotions. Matt hadn't been cheating on her. He loved her. Why wasn't her heart rejoicing?

He pressed his hand down on the table. "I was waiting until the right time, but the time never seemed right." He stood and walked to her on the other side of the table. "The idea of losing you was too much. But I was going to take you to meet Brandy next weekend. Remember I asked if you'd go away with me? I had this whole speech prepared about how I wanted you to marry me and I wanted us to have kids—to give Brandy a sister or a brother."

The lump in Maria's throat grew larger, and everything became clear. She recalled the gynecologist's words. *You lost one of your fallopian tubes. I also found some endometriosis. This could mean that you could have a very difficult time conceiving.*

Matt pulled her into his arms. She inhaled his scent at the same time she accepted the truth: he wanted something she couldn't give. In a crazy way, this was the same situation as with her and Jose—and a mistake. Her love for Matt was real, and deep down she knew him well enough to know he would say it was okay, her being unable to conceive, but would it? His words echoed in her heart. *And that's the day I knew what real love was.* She was going to miss out on that kind of love, and she would never wish that pain on Matt. He wanted more children, and a man like him should have them.

Pulling away, she met his eyes. "I'm sorry. Just go."

"Damn it. I know I was wrong for not telling you, but—"

"That's how I know this won't work." It wasn't the truth, but she knew Matt would want a reason.

"You still love Jose?" he asked.

She wouldn't lie about that. "No, but you obviously don't trust me enough to be honest. And any relationship that doesn't have trust isn't worth pursuing."

CHAPTER THIRTY-THREE

A week passed, and Shala lost herself in getting Precious whipped into shape. She'd met with just about everyone who belonged to the Chamber or who could help make the town the next big vacation spot in Texas. She'd offered recommendations, given her gotta-fix list to the mayor—heck, even her meeting down at the Funky Chicken had gone well, although she'd agreed to dance with Bo again if he did all the things on her list.

After reviewing all her images, she'd decided she didn't need any others, with the exception of the powwow, which was still against the rules. Tomorrow, however, was the big day. Tomorrow was the tribal-council meeting.

Not that she was too worried. She had no time to worry. She remained focused on the work. Well, she was focused on work when she wasn't focused on having curl-your-toes-up, headboard-banging sex with the chief of police. Or shower sex. A smile played over her face as she recalled the steamy scene from that morning. Who knew sex could be so much fun?

Maria walked into the bedroom that Shala and Sky were occupying at Lucas's. She held a box in her hands. "I got the pictures. Now tell me what they are for."

"Fantastic." Shala had asked Maria to see if the wives of the men on the tribal council might loan her some vacation photos.

When Maria and Shala had met about building the art community last week, and about possibly opening an art studio, they'd clicked like lost sisters. Maria had even discussed Matt, though Shala got the feeling she hadn't revealed the whole story. Not that Shala could blame her. She hadn't been forthcoming about Sky and herself, either. Maybe her feelings weren't as crazy and mixed up as she felt, but they certainly seemed so.

"So, what are they for?" Maria asked.

Shala glanced at the box. "They're for my presentation."

Maria looked puzzled. "What would pictures of the council's family vacations . . . Wait! I get it. This is your way of convincing them to let visitors take pictures, isn't it? You're good."

"Of course, she's good." Sky walked in and, pressing a knee on the mattress, leaned down to kiss Shala. A real kiss, too. He'd been doing that more lately. For a while he'd seemed the type who didn't go in for public displays of affection, but that had changed. Everything had changed. Except the sex. It was still toe-curlingly wonderful.

Oh, the other thing that hadn't changed was the investigation. So far, nothing had turned up. And the more time that passed, the more it seemed that Charlie Rainmaker was behind things. Apparently he and whomever he'd hired to do his dirty work had suffered a falling-out. With Charlie killed by him, the unidentified man had surely left town. There was no one to threaten her and no one to pay her assailant, which basically meant that Shala was no longer in danger. She could head back to Houston.

When she'd mentioned it to Sky, however, he'd hit the roof. For a minute there, she'd thought he was going to threaten to arrest her again. Shala wondered if he just didn't want her to leave. She didn't want to leave, either, but sooner or later they had to deal with the fact that they lived hundreds of miles apart. They needed to talk about how they intended to deal with a long-distance relationship, or better yet, needed to figure out exactly what kind of relationship they had.

Where her own emotions were concerned, she'd already done the figuring. If she wasn't perfectly in love with Sky, she stood on the verge. But in a relationship, one-sided figuring didn't work. It took two people wanting the same end for things to add up. Odd as it seemed, Sky never mentioned his feelings. Call her insecure, but she at least wanted a hint that she wasn't alone before she declared any love.

She looked at her watch. "You're early."

"Phillip and the others left, and I figured what the hell. I closed shop early. Just felt like taking another shower and calling it a day." His eyes twinkled with implication, and Shala blushed as she saw Maria smile.

Pulling away from the bed, Sky faced Maria. "How's the crew at your place?"

"The same," his sister said. "It's as if someone sucked the joy right out of the house. Redfoot just mopes around. Yesterday, he didn't even change out of his pajamas. Jose spends all his time on his laptop. If he has to work so much, why doesn't he just go back to New York?"

"Give them time, they'll work it out," Sky said.

Sky and Maria had each told Shala about the situation. Little did they know, she was secretly jealous of their family, even with the drama. Yesterday she'd called her brother, hoping to find some of the warmth from him that she felt between Sky and Redfoot's crew. Only it didn't happen. Her brother had given her two minutes before he had to run. She hadn't even begun to tell him about the danger she'd faced. Oh, she knew he loved her, but his life was too full for him to be concerned about her right now.

"I'm trying to give them time," Maria continued. "But I can't stand the dark cloud hanging over the house. Which is part of the reason I'm here. I thought after the council meeting tomorrow everyone could come over for dinner. Maybe company will pep things up."

Sky and Maria both eyed Shala. "Is that okay?" they asked at the same time.

Shala's heart swelled. They planned to include her in a family get-together! "Sounds great," she said with a smile. "The last time I visited Redfoot's, it was rather exciting."

"Don't worry." Maria laughed. "I'll make sure Jose is wearing clothes this time."

"So will I," Sky growled.

"I'd like some proof, is what I'd like," Sky practically yelled at Phillip the next morning. "Charlie lived here all his life. Where would he have reached out to hire this guy? And how the hell was he planning on paying him?"

His friend shrugged. "Look, I know this is personal for you, but we've done everything we can. Until some forensic evidence comes in—"

"We've got a murder, three attempted murders, and you're just walking away?" Worse, once Shala heard the rangers were gone, she'd be right on their coattails.

"The case has gone cold," Phillip said. "We got six people telling us Charlie practically admitted to having Shala scared out of town. Now Charlie's dead and we have nothing else to look at, zilch to go on. If we get something back from forensics, we'll pick it up then."

"I got something," boomed a voice from the doorway.

Sky turned to find Lucas. Phillip did, too. Although Sky had invited his reclusive friend many times to their poker parties, Lucas had always declined. Last week, the two men had met briefly for the first time. As a matter of fact, Sky was pretty sure that Lucas had met more people in the last few weeks than in the last five years. Surprisingly, Lucas hadn't seemed to mind.

The seriousness in the man's expression caught Sky's attention. "Where's Shala?" Had she already left town?

"She's here." Lucas motioned down the hall and slapped a manila envelope against his palm. "But I got something."

"What?" Phillip asked.

"Possibly your killer." Lucas focused on Sky. "I told you, I sent a few pictures to a friend. They did a face-recognition search and got a hit."

"We sent one in," Phillip said, looking confused. "But they're backlogged for months." He shook his head. "Who do you know that does that, anyway?" Phillip asked.

Respecting his friend's wishes, Sky hadn't told Phillip about Lucas's government ties.

Lucas shrugged. "A friend of a friend."

"A friend of whose friend?" Phillip insisted, obviously annoyed that Lucas had come through when his own boys were still chasing their tails.

"Doesn't matter," Sky interrupted. "What do you have?"

"It matters," Phillip interrupted. "I can't use—"

"Then don't use it," Lucas said, his tone dry.

"Damn it, Phillip," Sky said. "This isn't a big-dick contest. He's helping. Whatever information he gives us, I'll bet my life we can back it up as soon your guys get you their results."

Lucas handed Sky the envelope. "His name is Bradley Conners. He's got an arrest record longer than a PMSing woman's complaint list. Got out of the joint six months ago. Was in for nearly killing a guy in a bar. It was thought to be a hired hit, but that couldn't be proven. He got seven years, only served three." Sky pulled out the papers and began looking through them while Lucas continued. "Guess who Mr. Conners shared a cell with for a few months in Huntsville?"

"Who?" Phillip asked, now more curious than pissed.

"Rainmaker's brother," Lucas said.

"And now we have our connection," Phillip said.

Sky shook his head. "But why the hell was this Conners guy all worked up over Shala's camera?"

"Maybe they knew she managed to get Charlie's picture. Maybe Conners suspected she'd caught him on film," Lucas said.

"That makes sense," Phillip said.

"It still doesn't fit," Sky said. "I mean, I know Charlie didn't want Shala here, but to hire a hit man?"

"Maybe he didn't have to hire him," Phillip added. "Maybe this guy did it as a favor. Hell, maybe Rainmaker realized how far the guy was going to take it and told him to fuck off. That's probably what got Rainmaker killed."

"No." Sky pressed his hand on his desk. "I don't buy it."

Phillip said, "We'll talk to the guy's brother, maybe—"

"That's gonna be hard," Lucas interrupted. "He died about a month ago. My sources say natural causes, nothing suspicious."

"Who the hell are you, and who are your sources?" Phillip demanded.

"I just know the right people," Lucas replied.

"It just keeps getting worse," Sky seethed, ignoring them.

"Worse?" Lucas asked. "We know who he is. We got a connection with this guy and Charlie. With Charlie gone, Conners doesn't have a fight with Shala. Shala's no longer in danger. I wouldn't call that worse. I'd say we're a step further on."

"Did you tell Shala?" Sky's heart bumped around his chest.

"Of course I did. She's ecstatic."

Which meant she'd be going back to Houston.

"You have a talent, young lady. You owned that room," Redfoot said as Shala and Sky walked into his house half an hour after meeting the tribal council. Shala felt his praise all the way to her toes.

"Thank you. And thank you for being my ally. I couldn't have done it without you." She hugged him and hung on a few minutes because it felt so good. God, she missed her grandparents, missed the feel of older, wiser arms wrapped around her.

"Another hugger," Redfoot muttered.

"Get used to it," Maria said, bouncing into the room and hugging her as soon as Shala released her father. "Congrats. Redfoot said there's no way the council wouldn't give you everything you asked for."

"Really?" Shala met the older man's gaze. "You really think they'll agree to everything?"

Redfoot looked at Sky. "Your woman should have been a lawyer. You should have seen her. She charmed the socks off them."

"I would have seen, if you guys had let me come," Sky said.

Shala glanced at him. Sky had been tense all afternoon. She suspected it was about her going back to Houston. She'd told Lucas that she'd probably leave this weekend, but Sky hadn't mentioned it yet.

"You know the rules," Redfoot said. "Only the tribal council is present when—"

"Don't have to like them," Sky interrupted.

"Something smells good," Shala spoke up.

"Paella. Estella's recipe." Maria looked at Sky. "Don't start saying I added too much garlic."

"I'll make him behave." Shala reached for his hand.

"That's a pretty big promise," Lucas's voice boomed from the doorway. Shala turned and almost laughed at what he carried in his hands.

"Lucas!" Maria said and grinned. "Thank you for reconsidering."

Shala leaned in and mock-whispered, "What did you do, promise we'd play Scrabble?"

Maria giggled. "Just one game."

"Come in," Redfoot said.

As the men walked inside, Maria eyed Shala. "Redfoot's happier today. Thanks for agreeing to this."

"I wouldn't have missed it," Shala admitted. "Can I run to the bathroom, and then I'll help with dinner?"

"It's the second door on the left. Just past the hole in the wall that looks just like Jose's face." Maria grinned.

Shala hotfooted it down the hall, her bladder pinching. She had just grabbed the knob when the door swung open. And there was Jose, standing in front of her, naked. Well, he had a white towel wrapped around his waist.

"Oh fuck! Sky's going to kill me." He slammed the door.

Shala went back into the living room, trying not to laugh, and found Maria. "Is there another bathroom? I think that one is occupied." She almost told her friend the whole story, then decided Jose might prefer she didn't.

"My room, first door to the left."

"Thanks."

A few minutes later, bladder happy, she walked back out into the hall. At the same time, Jose exited the room next to Maria's. At least he had clothes on this time.

He shrugged guiltily and motioned. "I'm sorry. I didn't know anyone had arrived yet. I was just going to pop across the hall."

Shala grinned. "It's okay. I think we got here early."

Jose smiled. "We've met, but I don't think we've ever been properly introduced."

"Geez, without the pink robe, I almost didn't recognize you."

He laughed, and it sounded a lot like Redfoot. Shala decided she liked Jose.

Thirty minutes after they arrived, Sky was seated at the dining-room table with Jose, Redfoot, and Lucas. The men were playing Scrabble while Shala helped Maria in the kitchen.

"That's not a word," Lucas said.

"Is too. *Wacoi.*"

"What is it?"

"It's a sacred word," Redfoot said.

"You don't want to know," Sky muttered under his breath.

"You know what sacred word comes to my mind right now? *Bullshit!* You can only use English. Only English," Lucas insisted.

His friend and Redfoot were arguing about using Native American words. Sky laughed. In spite of worrying himself sick about Shala leaving, being here was fun. Every few minutes he'd peer into the kitchen, and something about seeing Shala in the kitchen of the house where he'd grown up felt perfectly right.

"Jose," Lucas said, "it's your turn. And don't be pretending to read the paper when I know you're looking for words."

Jose grinned. "This man takes his Scrabble serious, huh?" He stared down at the wooden bar with his letters, then started setting out his word. "I wasn't cheating, I was reading. An article about Senator Blanton. Did you know he went to high school in Bueford? Says here he was quarterback for the Bueford Bulldogs. Heck, we might have played against each other when I was on the football team."

"Put him down for eight points," Lucas said, counting Jose's points.

Sky tallied up the total. "He's a lot older than you, isn't he?"

Jose looked back at the newspaper as if checking the man's picture and guessing his age. "Yeah. But damn, it would have been pretty neat to think I knocked the president on his ass a time or two."

"With him having ties to this community, maybe if he runs for president he'll do something for Precious and the other small towns around here." Redfoot eyed the board with intensity. "I've read some good things about him."

"Don't tell Maria," Sky replied, glancing into kitchen again to get another peek at Shala. "She doesn't care for the guy."

"Maria has good taste," Lucas spoke up.

"You know some dirt on him?" Sky asked.

"Not really," his friend said. Then, "Are we playing Scrabble or talking politics?"

"You know who would make a good politician?" Redfoot looked at Sky. "Your woman. She shined today."

Sky looked through the doorway again. His woman. Why was it that hearing Redfoot refer to her as that bothered him less each time he heard it?

"Has Matt called?" Shala asked, sensing there was something on Maria's mind.

"No," Sky's sister replied. "Thank goodness."

"I know it's not my place to say anything, but if you two really love each other, then maybe—"

"Not happening." Maria looked away. Again, Shala got the feeling there was something going unsaid. "Can you get the salad dressing out?"

Translated, that meant "shut the heck up." And Shala had to respect Maria's wishes.

Laughter echoed from the dining room, and both Maria and Shala glanced that way. "You have no idea how good that is to hear," Maria said. "I swear, no one has laughed in this house all week."

"Does that include you?" Shala asked.

Before Maria could answer, Sky sauntered in. "I smell garlic," he teased.

Maria waved a spoon at him. "Get out of my kitchen."

He laughed. "Just came for tea." He refilled his glass and then moved behind Shala. Leaning down, he said, "I'm proud. Redfoot just keeps praising you."

She smiled back at him. "Thanks."

He kissed her and said, "We need to talk tonight."

"About?" She hoped he'd say that he figured it was time for them to put a name on what was happening between them. Sure, he acted crazy about her, but words made the feelings real. Shala needed real.

"It's not safe for you to leave yet," he said.

She didn't argue. Later, they'd talk. But it obviously wouldn't be about them. That hurt.

When Sky walked off, Shala saw that Redfoot had stepped into the kitchen. He stood by the stove talking to Maria. A moment later, the man walked over to her and put a hand on her shoulder. "You make him happy, Blue Eyes."

Shala smiled. "He makes me happy, too." And he did— *if he'd just open up a little,* Shala added to herself.

Soon they all sat at the dining-room table and were feasting. Dinner conversation was composed of funny stories about Jose, Maria, and Sky. There was a lot of laughter. Shala couldn't remember ever enjoying a meal more. It wasn't the food—not that it wasn't wonderful— but the company that she enjoyed most. Afterward, Redfoot poured them all shots of dessert wine. Lucas, Shala noticed, stuck with his tea.

Sitting at this table, Shala felt part of a family. Several times, tears threatened. She realized that not only was she inches away from falling for Sky, she was equally close to falling for his family and his friends.

Redfoot set filled glasses in front of everyone and raised his own. "A family toast. To more dinners where everyone is here," he announced, his gaze on Jose. Shala noted guilt flash in the younger man's eyes.

"To accepting our differences," Maria offered, almost to make a point.

"To Scrabble," Lucas said, and everyone laughed.

"To food without too much garlic." Sky grinned at Maria.

It was Shala's turn, but she didn't have to think too hard. "To family."

All eyes turned to Jose, the last person. He smiled. "To Sky finally accepting that Shala is his soul mate, just as Redfoot's spirits said."

CHAPTER THIRTY-FOUR

Everyone's arms remained raised, but no glass-tapping followed. Shala stared at Jose. "Say, what?" That's when she realized everyone stared at her.

Sky lowered his wineglass and glared at Jose.

"What?" his brother seemed surprised. "Don't tell me she doesn't know."

"Know what?" Shala set her glass down and gazed around the table. Not one person would meet her eye except Sky.

"It's nothing," he growled.

She chuckled nervously. "It doesn't feel like nothing."

"I made pie and coffee!" Maria said, drawing Shala's attention. Maria didn't look away this time but shrugged guiltily, as if admitting there was something she'd kept secret.

"I would love pie," Lucas said.

Shala studied him, wondering if he knew what they were talking about. When the man wouldn't look at her, she figured he did.

She shifted her focus to Redfoot. He looked at her, but he'd gone back into his wooden-statue mode.

"Well, why didn't someone tell me I wasn't supposed to say anything?" Jose hissed.

"Just shut your god damn mouth," Sky seethed. He rose from the table and eyed Shala. "Are you ready to go?"

Bam. Just like that, guilt chased away Shala's happy mood, though she couldn't quite figure out how this was her fault. Regardless, she couldn't stop herself from apologizing. "I'm sorry." She placed her napkin on her plate. "Maybe I should help with the dishes first."

"No," Maria said. "I've got them."

"Okay." Shala gave up. "Dinner was great." And as she walked out of the room, she realized that she no longer felt like a part of this family. How had it happened?

Redfoot sat at the table, staring at his wine. Awkwardness still permeated the air. Lucas got up to leave next. "You are welcome in my home anytime," Redfoot said to him.

"Thank you," Lucas answered, and Maria walked him to the door.

Jose sat on the opposite side of the table, looking uncomfortable, as he probably should. "I swear to God, no one told me not to say anything."

Redfoot felt bad for his son, but he also felt sorry for Sky, who no doubt now faced the hardest part of his journey with Shala Winters. The dream last night had told Redfoot that Sky and Shala's path was not fully walked. The same went for Matt and Maria. Yet to be seen was where their roads and hearts would lead them.

As for Veronica, the spirits had not answered his question. Redfoot surmised they were angry that he had lied.

Not that Redfoot would change anything. He would not force Veronica into marriage, even if it meant going against them.

"All someone had to do was tell me," Jose continued.

Redfoot sipped his last bit of wine. "I suppose we all understood that no one likes to be told that their destiny is set."

"Really?" Jose leaned forward, pushing his arms on the table. "Then why is it you do that to me all the time?"

Redfoot reclined. "How do I do this to you?"

Jose held out a hand. "It's not important. Forget it." He stood up and walked out, leaving Redfoot alone at the table.

"What isn't important?" Redfoot asked the empty room. Then he looked inside his heart to find the answer.

Shala sat quietly in Sky's truck for five minutes before the words and frustration just came bubbling out. "Are you really not going to explain? How can you just sit there and not explain? How could—?"

"Stop!" Sky held up his hand. "For God's sake, woman, please don't start jabbering!"

His anger, his tone, raked over her like broken glass. "Jabbering? Do I . . . jabber?"

"Yes, you jabber! When you're nervous, when you're upset, and sometimes even when you're happy. And it hurts my ears."

She felt herself lose it, but she didn't care. "Well, maybe I jabber because you just sit there and never say a freaking word while the elephant squats in the middle of the room, hikes up his tail, exposes his pink little asshole, and takes a big crap. Maybe I jabber because I'm trying to figure out what's going on inside your head about *us*. Maybe . . ." She slammed her body back against the seat. "Is my car fixed yet?"

Sky let go of a deep growl and yanked the truck over to

the side of the road, coming to a sudden, tire-screeching halt.

"Do you want me to get out?" Shala faced him, adrenaline doing marathons through her bloodstream.

"No!" He reached for her but she pulled away. "It's stupid," he said.

"What's stupid?" Tears climbed up her throat. "My jabbering, or the fact that you and your whole family have some secret about me and are obviously laughing behind my back!"

"No one is laughing."

"You said it was stupid."

He raked a hand over his face. "It is stupid, but we're not laughing at you." He leaned back and stared at the roof of his truck. "Okay, here it is. Redfoot believes that the People's spirits send him dreams. He believes these dreams told him you and I are soul mates."

Shala brushed her palm over her jean skirt, remembering the odd meeting she'd had with Redfoot when she first met him. "He dreamed that I was your soul mate?"

"Yes. I told you it was stupid."

"When did he have this dream?"

"It's not important."

"When did he have this dream?" she insisted.

"About three weeks before you came into town."

She sat there taking everything in. Or tried to. "Is that why you were so rude to me when I first—"

"I wasn't rude, I—"

"You followed me around and took my camera."

"You took a picture."

"I did *not* take a picture!"

"Okay. I thought you took a picture. And I followed you around because . . ." He fisted his hands around the steering wheel. "Okay, maybe I followed you instead of introducing myself because I didn't want Redfoot to start believing in his own nonsense."

"Then why did you change your mind? Because someone was after me?"

"Yes and no. Mostly because I realized how stupid it was."

"What was stupid?"

"The whole freaking thing! I don't believe in this."

"Believe in what? The dreams, or that we're soul mates?"

"Both. Relationships play their course. They last as long as they last. I'm not a soul-mate type of person. I don't believe in that crap."

He didn't believe? She tried to wrap her mind around what he really meant. "You don't believe in love."

He sat there staring at her. "Come on, Shala. We talked about this."

Her mind raced. "We did?"

"Yes."

"When? Because I don't recall us ever—"

"The afternoon at my office. I told you I wanted to just live for the moment, enjoy . . . I told you this was hard."

The emotional upheaval in Shala's chest was imploding her heart. "Yes, you said it was hard, you said we just needed to enjoy it, but somehow you left off that little part about you thinking it wouldn't last and that you didn't expect it to ever lead anywhere. Or that you'd never really care—"

"I care!"

"Until that plays its course," she muttered. "Until the newness wears off the sex." She closed her eyes and felt used. Everything they had shared now looked different. Tainted. She breathed around the huge empty hole in her chest. "Well, it's played its course."

"No, it hasn't. Damn it! I didn't mean . . . I don't . . ."

Sitting straighter, she faced him. She was done arguing. She was done, period. They were done. "Take me to my car. Wait—just take me back to Lucas's house, and he can take me." She bit down on her lip and refused to cry. "I need to get my things."

"It's late. You can't drive back to Hous—"

"I'm not. I'll rent a room at the hotel."

He stared out the windshield. "The hotel is still closed because of Jessie."

Her mind raced. "Then I'll drive to the closest town and—"

"Damn it, stay at Lucas's tonight. I'll get your car in the morning and . . ." He stared at her. "If you don't want me sleeping with you, I won't."

Logic said he was right about driving tonight, and no matter how hurt she was, she needed to keep her head. Logic was the key to survival, and she would survive this gaping pain. Look what she'd survived before. Sky Gomez was nothing compared to her past losses. Besides, she didn't even love him, not really. Not yet.

So explain why it hurt so much.

She looked away and felt her first tear—one of many, she was afraid—slip down her cheek. "Fine, I'll leave in the morning. But you're right, I don't want you sleeping with me."

Jose stared at the computer screen, at the "buy now" button that would give him his ticket back to New York.

He'd never planned to stay this long. He'd had three weeks of vacation and called after that first day and put in for it. Never mind that he'd worked these last few days. Hell, he enjoyed his work. He enjoyed living in New York, so why the heck was he hanging out here? He'd accepted that he and Maria were over. He hated admitting it, but what she'd said about their relationship was true. She'd been the one thing in Precious that he felt connected to.

The thought that she had carried his child—*lost* his child—stuck to his heart like gum to a shoe on a hot day. He tried not to think about it, but it wouldn't go away. While he couldn't exactly name the emotion running through him, it felt a lot like grief, the same pain he'd felt when his mom died.

Thinking about his mom made him realize how little time he might have left with his dad. Which brought him back to why he hadn't left yet. Jose couldn't see moving back to Precious, but he suspected the physical distance wasn't truly what bothered him about their relationship.

Closing the screen without buying the ticket, he walked into the living room. Redfoot wasn't there. His dad was sitting at the dining-room table, the same place Jose had left him over an hour ago, and so Jose walked into the dining room and sat down across from him, unsure what to say but knowing they had to talk.

Redfoot cleared his throat. "You are so much like your mom."

"Am I?" Jose asked. "I always thought she was prettier."

His old man ignored his attempt at humor. "She had big dreams. More dreams than could fill one life." Redfoot paused, and his voice shook a little. "I was damn lucky she decided that I was part of her dream. I sometimes wonder if she regretted it. She could have been so much more if she'd left Precious."

Jose's heart clutched. "Mom loved you and this town."

"I hope so," Redfoot replied. "But you do not?"

Jose considered. "I don't hate it—not always," he confessed. "I love the people here. I love the memories. But I've never felt as if I fit."

Redfoot nodded. "Maria reminded me last night of the story your mother used to tell. Of how our parents were totally against our getting married."

"I remember," Jose said. "Mom said you guys met by the creek and eloped."

"Your mother, she was my destiny then. We were right to rebel against our parents." Redfoot paused. "And you are right to make your dreams come true. I'm sorry that I have made you feel as if they are not important. Your destiny is your own, Jose. I can only ask that you come back often and share your dreams with me as your mom did."

Emotion tightened Jose's chest. "I will. And you'll visit me in New York, too."

"Yes," his father agreed, "I will visit often."

Both men stood. "Son," Redfoot said. "Your mom would be so proud of you. As am I."

Air froze in Jose's lungs. "Thank you," he finally said. Turning to walk away, at the last minute he changed his mind. "I feel as if I should hug you."

"We are not huggers," Redfoot said, laughing.

"Maybe I am." Returning, Jose embraced him. "I love you, Dad."

Redfoot hugged him back. "I love you, too, son. I love you, too."

CHAPTER THIRTY-FIVE

Sky sat on Lucas's porch—the same spot he'd sat all night before Shala found him and doused him with milk—hoping like hell he could find the words to stop her from leaving. To stop her from being so damn angry. After several hours, he still hadn't found them.

He stared at her car. It was parked out front; Lucas had gotten up at the crack of dawn and driven Sky to the hotel to pick it up. All Sky could think about was being forced to watch Shala leave.

The door opened. Sky's heart jumped into his throat. He shot to his feet, thinking it was her. Lucas stepped outside and handed him a cup of coffee.

"Thanks," Sky said. When Lucas didn't look away, he shrugged. "Go ahead and say it."

"Say what?" Lucas asked.

"Whatever is on your mind. You're gritting your teeth to keep it in."

Lucas nodded. "You're an idiot if you let her leave."

"Fine. Now all you have to do is tell me how to stop her."

Lucas sighed. "If you don't know, you're more of an idiot than I suspected." He walked back inside.

Thirty minutes later, Shala came out. She didn't meet his gaze, but that didn't stop him from noticing the dark circles under her eyes.

"Are you sure you're up to driving?" he asked.

"I'm fine." She stepped off the porch.

He followed. "Your camera and things from the hotel are in the car."

"Thanks." She didn't sound very grateful.

"I'll call you," he said, having no other words.

"I'd appreciate it if you didn't."

She got into her car and drove off. He held his breath, praying she'd stop, turn around, and come running back into his arms. He remembered the line of a country-western song that said, "I'd have been happy for a slow-down." He'd never realized how powerful that line was. When Shala left, she hadn't slowed down. She hadn't glanced back. She'd simply driven away as if leaving didn't hurt at all.

Three days after leaving Precious, Shala sat at her brother's kitchen table. Beth, her sister-in-law, was pouring a round of decaf coffee. Shala had arrived that afternoon, calling from LAX to tell them she'd arrived. They'd been a little surprised. She'd spent four glorious hours playing board games and computer games with her nephew and niece, and she'd had a blast. Five minutes after the children were down for the night, she booked the six A.M. flight back to Texas. She suspected explaining her unexpected and very short trip might be difficult.

Beth set the cups down and dropped into a chair. Cory said, "Okay, sis, don't you think it's time you come clean?"

"Clean?" she echoed.

"What's up? If it's money, I can help out some."

"No." Shala shook her head. "I don't need—"

"You're not pregnant, are you?" he asked.

"No!"

"Oh, shit, you didn't kill your ex-husband like you threatened, did you?" Beth asked.

"*No!*" And just like that, the tears started flowing. "I just needed to see you guys, to have family around me." She'd spent the last three days crying about Sky and his family and feeling sorry for herself because she had no one. Then it hit her that the reason she didn't have anyone was because she'd put up barriers. Her family's standoffishness was a status quo that Shala herself had mandated.

She wiped her cheeks, and her breaths were short. "I'm sorry."

"What's wrong, sis?" Cory leaned in, concern etching his brow. That only made her sobs come faster, harder, and deeper.

"Don't," she managed to say. "Don't look at me like that."

"How am I looking at you?"

"I'm sorry," she repeated. "It's been a rough few weeks."

Beth got up and passed Shala a box of tissues. "What happened?"

"I went to Precious and . . . some people didn't want me there."

"Precious?" her brother asked.

"Precious, Texas." She hiccupped, and it all came pouring out. Even though she knew she was jabbering, just like Sky accused her of, she couldn't stop. "I picked up a stalker, and then Sky thought I took his picture and he stole my camera."

"Who did what?" her brother asked, but Shala couldn't stop to explain.

"Then I went to the Funky Chicken to find out—"

"You went where?"

"I had to find out where he lives, but first I had to dance disco with this other guy. I finally found where Sky lives and I went there. I called the police, but he is the police. Then a stalker showed up and I grabbed a knife and cut myself." She held out her palm. Cory looked at it and frowned.

"Then Sky forced me to go the hospital"—her tears were rolling faster down her face—"and you two know that I can't stand hospitals. But it was almost okay because he was so nice. Then the stalker tried to run me over, and Sky saved me, but then a friend of his got shot. The Texas Rangers showed up. Then things really got crazy, and we had curl-your-toes-up sex on top of his desk and . . ."

"You had sex with the Texas Rangers?" Beth asked, clearly shocked.

"No." Shala blew her nose. "With Sky. And then they found the dead man and I found out that Sky's foster father thought I was Sky's soul mate, and Sky accused me of jabbering, but the worst part is that he doesn't believe in love." She dried her eyes. "And I think I'm *this* close to being in love with him." She looked up at the befuddled expressions on Beth's and Cory's faces. "I know—I do jabber, don't I?"

They didn't say anything, but their heads bobbed up and down in unison.

"I'm sorry. It's a lot to digest, isn't it?"

Their heads bobbed again. Shala's sister-in-law held up a finger. "Someone tried to run you over?"

Her brother followed with, "You had sex on a desk?"

Beth elbowed him. "Please, someone is trying to kill your sister and you're worried about her having sex?"

He shook his head. "It's the top-of-the-desk part that disturbs me."

Beth rolled her eyes. "We had sex on your desk."

"You wouldn't have if I'd stolen your camera," he insisted.

Suddenly, Shala started laughing and Beth and Cory joined in. They laughed for a good five minutes. Afterward, she answered a few questions. Okay, a lot of questions—she'd obviously done a terrible job explaining.

They were still at the kitchen table when Shala's phone rang. She reached for her purse, looked inside at the number, and tossed it back.

"Don't tell me," her brother said. "That was the camera-thief, sex-on-the-desk guy?"

She nodded.

"You're not taking his calls?" Beth asked.

"No."

Beth grinned. "The sex must not have been *that* curl-your-toes-up good."

Shala sighed. "I can't chance getting my heart broken again."

"I think it's too late for that. If this isn't you suffering from heartbreak, I'd hate to see you when it happens."

Shala ignored that. "I should tell you, I'm leaving in the morning."

"You just got here," Cory and Beth said at the same time.

"I know, but I'm miserable."

"I thought misery loves company," her brother replied.

She shook her head. "I promise to come back soon. When I'm not miserable."

Her brother called her the next day as she stood in the crowd, waiting for her luggage at Bush Intercontinental Airport. She'd checked the screen to be sure it was him. "Hello."

"You make it to Texas?"

"Lovely flight," she muttered.

"You still sound miserable."

"I'll be okay."

"Yeah. Well, I don't know if you want to hear this but . . . we've gotten two messages on the home phone this morning from a Sky Gomez."

"Sorry," she replied.

"That's the camera-thief sex-on-the-desk guy, right?"

"Right." She heaved a sigh of dejection.

"Well, I'm not going to get into your business, but he sounded worried about you."

"He doesn't have a right to worry," Shala snapped. "I'm not his soul mate."

They talked a few more minutes and hung up. She was still holding her phone when it rang again. She checked the screen. It wasn't Sky, but did she want to talk to Maria? No. Yes. No—

"Hello?" she answered.

"I'm so glad you picked up," Maria said. "Sky's so worried."

"I've been in California, visiting my brother and his family."

"Sky drove to Houston yesterday, and if one of your neighbors hadn't said she saw you leaving with your bags, I think there'd be a missing-persons report on you right now."

"Is he still in Houston?" Shala asked, and actually looked around.

"No, he came home last night. But . . . I know it's none of my business, but it's so hard to see him hurting like this. All he does is go around growling. He's miserable, Shala."

"You're right. It's none of your business." Shala tempered her words with a soft tone. "I've got to take care of myself right now."

"It's just—"

"Maria, I didn't interfere with you and Matt."

"You're right. I'll shut up." There came a pause. "How was your brother's family?"

"Good, thanks."

They talked a few minutes before Maria asked, "Can I at least tell Sky that I spoke to you and that you're okay?"

"Sure," Shala said.

"One more thing." Maria paused. "You're not going stop working with the Chamber because of this, are you?"

Shala had spent the entire flight contemplating that very question. In the end she'd decided that she wasn't going to let Sky stop her from doing her job. She would just have to pull up her big-girl panties—which would *not* be a thong—and avoid him at every turn, crosswalk, and stop sign.

"No, I'm not quitting." Saying it made it official. Mentally, she reached down and yanked up her big-girl panties.

Damn it, it felt like a huge string had crawled right up into her mental crack.

"She'll take Maria's calls but not mine," Sky muttered, sitting on his front porch and staring out into the darkness. "What the fuck is up with that?" When he dropped his cell phone beside his leg, Butch and Sundance looked up at him and whined. "You miss her, too, don't you?" he asked them.

Sky closed his eyes. Misery, his constant companion, bumped around his chest. Everywhere he looked, he saw Shala: on his desk at work, at Lucas's place. Yesterday, when he drove by the hospital, he'd visualized Shala standing out there, teasing him about not being a Hollywood cop. Hell, right now she was standing on the porch demanding he return her camera.

The visual got interrupted as Redfoot's truck pulled into his driveway. Sky watched him and . . . was that Matt? Each man carried a six-pack. When they got to the porch, Redfoot chose the swing and Matt dropped down on the planks beside Sky.

"Did I send out BYOB invitations and forget?" He was definitely not in the mood for company.

Redfoot opened a beer and started drinking. Matt handed Sky a beer and—oh, what the hell—Sky took it.

"So we're all gonna get drunk and pout, huh?" he asked.

"No," Redfoot said. "We're gonna get drunk and come up with a plan."

"A plan to do what?" Sky took a sip of cold beer.

"To get your women back," Redfoot said.

"What about your woman?" Sky asked. Not since Estella passed away had his foster father been this depressed.

Redfoot glanced into the night sky. "My case is hopeless. I think I pissed off the spirits."

CHAPTER THIRTY-SIX

That night, Shala lay in bed pretending to watch television but mostly watching her phone. He'd called again this afternoon. This time, he'd left a message. She wasn't going to listen to it, though. Why hadn't she deleted it?

"Oh, screw it."

She picked up the phone to get rid of the message, but her hand didn't obey her command. Instead, it hit the message button. She needed a good cry anyway, since it had been a whole ten minutes since her last. She put the phone to her ear.

Her heart lurched at his voice. "Hi, Blue Eyes. I know you're not answering my calls, and I didn't even expect you to this time. Thing is, something happened today. Something good, and I wanted to tell someone, and it occurred to me that the person I wanted to tell was you. Because . . . I don't know, I think you'd understand." He paused, and Shala's grip on the phone tightened.

"Candy Peterson—the woman whose husband beat her—she came in today and signed the papers to press charges. She'd just come from a divorce lawyer, too. She said that something I told her had finally sunk in, that she didn't want her little girl to grow up and let some man hit her." He cleared his throat. "I know she could change her mind, but I think . . . I think I made a difference. It felt good, you know? Anyway, I wanted to tell someone who—"

His time ran out, and the message ended.

Shala dropped her phone, curled up against her pillow, and cried herself to sleep.

On Friday morning, three days later, Sky was over at Redfoot's. He'd taken the day off to help set up. The mayor had also seen fit to help with their plan. His help had included calling Shala and insisting she come down for a town meeting and the night's spur-of-the-moment pow-wow. Of course, Sky's threatening to hand the mayor his resignation had probably increased the man's help-fulness.

Sky looked at his watch. Shala was probably already on the road. His heart swelled at the thought of seeing her again, and he hoped Redfoot was right about this plan. So far, it was bringing Shala back to him. That in itself felt like a miracle.

His cell phone rang. Probably it was Matt wanting to know how things were going. Sky looked around for Maria before answering, but when he glanced at the screen, it wasn't the right number.

"Hey, Lucas." These last few weeks, his loner friend had changed. He'd even agreed to help set up the powwow.

"Where's Shala?" Lucas's tone was gut-clenchingly serious.

"On the way here. Why?"

"We were wrong. Not you, but your buddy Phillip and I. Charlie Rainmaker wasn't behind those attempts on Shala's life."

"What do you mean?" Sky demanded.

"She's not out of danger yet, Sky."

"Fuck! Who is it?"

"I'm not supposed to say, because the investigation is ongoing, but . . . ah, screw the investigation. It's Senator Blanton and his people."

"What? Why? And how long have you known this, Lucas?" Fear was rioting through Sky's heart.

"I just found out. I mean, I knew he's being looked at for some nasty stuff. Let's just say, when he travels, he's not real particular as to the type of brothels he visits. He likes girls young, and he doesn't care how they got to him. Doesn't much care what condition they are in when he leaves them, either. The guy was going to be renouncing his run for presidency and stepping down from the senate in a few weeks. He just hadn't gotten that memo yet."

Sky felt sick just listening. He also felt confused. "What does that have to do with Shala?"

"It appears the married senator spent a weekend in a rented cabin outside of Precious, accompanied by his play toy. It was the same week Shala was taking pictures. I'm not even sure if she got him on camera, but remember the shot she took of two people going at it in a car? I think that's our man. They are running that image now, seeing if they can get anything for sure."

"Aw, shit," Sky said. "All this because the guy couldn't keep his dick in his pants?"

"I'm afraid it's more than that."

"What do you mean?" Sky's grip on the phone tightened.

"You heard about the girl's body that was found about sixty miles west of Precious."

"Yeah, but I hadn't heard they'd indentified her. I'm assuming you're saying that the girl was the play toy."

"That's what I'm saying.

"It hasn't been leaked yet, but when they checked her place, well let's just say she wasn't as discreet as the good senator would have liked. There's evidence linking him and the girl in an earlier affair. But . . . no evidence putting him with the girl the week she died."

"Except Shala and her pictures," Sky said, and gritted his teeth.

"Right. And while the senator is scum, it may not even be him connected with Conners. They leaned hard and heavy on some of his hired bodyguards, mostly idiots with guns, figuring someone helped him make 'the problem' disappear. The FBI has been watching and waiting for one of them to screw up."

"And?" Sky asked.

"They got one of them on tape, talking to a Bradley Conners. They couldn't say for sure, because they talked in mumbo jumbo. But the FBI said from the conversation, they surmised that the man had originally just hired Conners to steal something, but due to some new discovery, the stakes went up. Which is probably because they now have the senator connected to the girl. And while they couldn't swear on it, it sounded like the guy on the line was ordering a hit."

"Shala?" Sky asked.

"He called her a reporter," Lucas said. "But yeah, we think it's her."

Sky still was trying to grasp it. "How the hell do you know all this?"

"When they ran a check on Conners, it came up that my friend had just done the same thing. They called him, and he told them it had been for me, and then I got pulled in for questioning."

Sky tried to think. "Okay, I'll find out exactly where she is and send state troopers to find her."

"Which way is she coming? I can start that way," Lucas suggested.

"I think she'd take the freeway. I'll have to call her."

He hung up, his heart thudding against this breastbone, and started dialing Shala's number. Then he remembered she wouldn't answer. Instead he dialed Pete with the highway patrol, who was still at his office, and told him what he was going to need. With Pete on hold, he yelled out, "Maria?" She called back, and he followed her voice to the kitchen, finding her sitting at the table. "Give me your phone," he ordered.

She frowned. "Why?"

"I need to talk to Shala," he growled.

"No! I'm not tricking her like that."

"Get me your god damn phone! She's in danger!"

Maria's eyes grew round. Running to the counter, she snatched up her phone. She started to hand it over, then pulled it back. "One condition. When she gets here, you tell her you love her."

"Deal." He grabbed the phone and started punching in her number. "But for the record, I was going to do that already."

He started outside. Shala's line rang, and he prayed she'd answer. Her voice spilled over the airways. "Hi Maria, I'm about an hour from Precious now. Do you want to meet me at the café?"

"Shala? Don't hang up. We just found out that Charlie Rainmaker wasn't behind those attempts to take the camera or to hurt you. We know who it is, and he could be following you. Shala?" He repeated her name when she didn't answer. Reaching his car, he dove behind the wheel.

"I'm here," she said. "But I swear, if this is a trick—"

"It's not." He heard her inhale. "Where are you at right now? What road, and I need a mileage marker."

"I . . . don't see one." Her voice sounded tight, scared. He pulled out of Redfoot's driveway, his own gut a pretzel of fear.

"Wait, there's one." She called it out. "Do you want me to pull over?"

"No, just keep driving." Sky headed toward the freeway, tallying in his mind where she'd be by the time he met up with her. "And I need you to hang on one second—don't hang up, okay? I've got DPS on another phone and need to let them know where you are, okay?"

After hearing her weak agreement, he switched phones and spat out the mileage marker to Pete. He heard Pete repeating the information into a radio. Then he told the trooper to call Lucas on another line and give him the info, too.

"Sky," Pete said a few seconds later. "There's a car within a few miles of her. He's going to catch up and escort her here."

"Great! I'm already on the road, too. Tell them to look out for my truck and Lucas's."

"We don't need a motorcade," Pete grumbled.

"Well, you're getting one."

Shala could hear Sky on the line, and just his voice sent mixed waves of pain and calm into her. Pain, because she'd given up trying to convince herself that she didn't love him. She was undoubtedly in love with this man who wanted nothing to do with commitment or happily ever after. Calm, because somehow he helped her forget that one of the four cars behind her on the freeway could have a man with a gun in it who was thinking her head made a good target.

"Shala?"

"Yes?"

"We've got a trooper only a few miles off. He should be pulling up any minute. And I'm on my way. Lucas is, too. It's going to be okay."

"Sky?" Even saying his name hurt.

"Yes?"

"Who is trying to kill me and why?"

He explained some, but she assumed he didn't tell her everything. Silence filled the line.

All of a sudden, a car pulled up next to Shala, close. Too close. "Oh, God," she muttered.

"What?" Sky asked.

"A car's trying to pass me, coming up along the median. I think he's trying to run me off the road."

"Is it a DPS car?" Sky asked, sounding panicked.

"No." Shala saw the man reach down, and when his hand came back up, he held something out. Shala didn't look carefully. She just punched the gas.

"Where the fuck is your guy?" she heard Sky yelling right before she dropped her cell.

"I said, where the fuck are your guys?" Sky shouted into the phone.

"He's there," Pete answered. "She's running from him. Tell her slow down. The guy is trying to show her his badge."

"Is he not in a squad car?" Sky demanded. Pete didn't answer. Sky heard him talking into a radio.

"No." Pete came back. "He's off duty. He's driving a blue Saturn."

"Shala!" Sky yelled into his phone. "Listen to me, is the car trying to pull you over a blue Saturn? If it is, he's a trooper, baby. Talk to me, Shala. Talk to me."

Seeing the WELCOME TO PRECIOUS sign should have eased the burning in Sky's stomach, but it didn't. This wasn't just about saving Shala's life; this was about convincing her to share her life with him. But Sky would still love to kick the trooper's ass for neglecting to inform Pete that he wasn't in a black-and-white. The idiot had put everyone through some unneeded panic.

Shala's phone was low on battery, so after the situation calmed down, and after he'd met up with her, they both hung up. Sky had since called Phillip, who was going to meet them at the station house in a few hours.

Sky's gaze kept shifting to Shala driving behind him. He'd run onto the curb twice trying to catch glimpses of her in her car.

The trooper escort phoned and said he'd let Sky take it from there, which was fine. Sky called Shala back and told her to head to the police station/jailhouse.

"I'm supposed to meet Maria at the café," she argued.

"Not until we know it's safe," he snapped.

He heard her sigh, but she turned down Main Street the right way. All he could think about was getting her out from behind the wheel and into his arms. And into his life. Permanently.

When she parked, Sky leaped out of his car to meet her. His heart lurched at the sight of her. She wore jeans that fit like an oiled glove, and the same red shirt he'd once watched her slowly strip off in his office. Awestruck at the sight of her, he didn't even acknowledge Lucas walking up. As Shala got closer, Sky ached to touch her. Then Sky watched as Shala ran straight into his friend's arms.

He swallowed a lump of disappointment when he heard Lucas whisper, "It's going to be okay. I got you."

It hurt like hell to know she'd turn to Lucas and not him, but he deserved the pain. Lucas was her friend, and Sky would bet his right arm that never once had Lucas told her that he was just a temporary fixture in her life, that as soon as the new wore off the relationship he was out the door. And that's exactly what Sky had told her—maybe not in those words, but after replaying their argument in his head, he begin to see how Shala would view his fucked-up excuses.

"We should get her inside," Sky said, hoping his jealousy didn't show. Then he looked around again to make sure it was safe.

He obviously didn't look hard enough. The moment they turned for the door, the bullets began.

CHAPTER THIRTY-SEVEN

"Down!" Sky yelled, and threw himself on top of Shala. He rolled them behind his truck. Another shot rang out. The *ping* sound told Sky his truck had taken the hit. He saw Lucas duck behind his truck's front wheel. They both pulled their weapons at the same time.

Rising up, Sky peered over the bed of his truck and saw the shooter. He was across the street, leaning over the top of a Dodge Charger. The sun caught a glint of metal, and Sky saw the rifle was propped on the roof of the car. "Cover me," he said to Lucas.

"No!" Shala grabbed Sky's arm. Electricity from her touch shot through him, and he forgot to breathe. He leaned down and pressed his lips to hers for a quick kiss.

"I love you," he said.

"That's real romantic, guys," Lucas said, "but—"

Sky shot out from behind the truck. Shala yelled again, and Lucas started popping off shots, trying to give him some cover.

Sky felt a bullet move past his ear. He ducked behind Martha's Cadillac. When he heard the pings hitting her car, he was more frightened of his secretary learning about the damage than at taking any himself. Swearing like a sailor, he shot out from behind the vehicle.

More pops from Lucas's gun echoed through the hot, humid air. The shooter remained behind the Charger,

which gave Sky enough time to get closer. He pelted
across the paved parking lot. Close. Almost close enough.
Sky only had to cross the street when he saw the killer
pile into the car.

"No!" He raised his gun.

Unfortunately, the man had the car moving almost immediately. The roar of the engine rang in Sky's ears.
Aimed right at him, the vehicle burst forward. Sky jumped
straight up in the air. His feet hit the hood. He fought to
remain standing as he unloaded his weapon into the
windshield. The car swerved, and so did Sky. Sky knew
he was about to hit the pavement. Probably hit hard. He
hated being right.

He twisted in midair, hoping to protect his head when
he went down. Air gushed out of his lungs when his elbow hit the concrete, and then his shoulder landed, followed by the rest of him. He hadn't stopped rolling, the
pain hadn't even registered, when he heard the crash. He
glanced up toward the sound, thankful he could still move
his neck, and saw that the Dodge Charger had T-boned
Martha's Cadillac. Martha was going to have—

And then the pain registered. "Son of a bitch," he
growled.

He didn't try to move again. He wasn't even sure
he could. He saw Lucas, gun drawn, moving toward the
crash site. A mental flash of the guy taking a chest full of
bullets filled Sky's mind, and he felt confident about what
Lucas would find. Then he saw Shala on her knees beside
him.

"Oh, God." She pressed her hand to her trembling lips.

"It's just my arm," he managed to say, and he hoped it
was true, but honestly he wasn't sure where all the pain
was coming from.

Her blue eyes, wet with tears, met his. God, he loved
this woman! Right then, his pain—with the exception of
his arm—faded.

"Is that how the Hollywood cops do it?" he asked, and tried to smile.

Redfoot adjusted Matt's headdress. It was late afternoon, and everything had gotten a little behind, with Sky being hurt, but the spirits had taken care of him. From the look on Blue Eyes's face, maybe Sky's injury had even helped her see past the issues keeping them apart. Redfoot hoped so, because he didn't think Sky would be up to taking part in the plan tonight. He certainly wouldn't be performing.

Now, if he could only fix things with Matt and Maria.

"Do I really have to wear this thing?" Matt touched the cascade of feathers on his shoulder.

Redfoot frowned. "Do you want to win her back or not?"

"Yes," Matt muttered.

"Then you have to wear it. And you have to dance properly. Have you been practicing like I showed you?"

"Yes, but I have two left feet."

Redfoot glanced down and grinned. "You are slightly bowlegged, as well."

"Oh, please," Matt argued. "With your skinny legs, you shouldn't be criticizing mine."

"Ahh, but my skinny legs are not so pale, hairy, or bow-legged." Redfoot gave Matt a pat on the shoulder. "You will do fine." This last week, Redfoot had discovered that Maria had good taste. The white boy had spirit, and a good spirit at that.

"I'm going to make an ass out of myself, aren't I?" Matt asked despondently.

Redfoot hid a grin. "That is yet to be seen." And it was. In his vision, he had heard the spirits howling with laughter, but he had also seen Maria with love in her eyes.

"You lied! Why would you lie?" Veronica's voice rang

out behind Redfoot. He turned. She stood there, arms crossed, dressed in a colorful beaded dress that hugged her body perfectly. Seeing her sent a spasm of pain to his heart.

"I did what I had to do," he said.

"You made yourself look bad so my son wouldn't force me to marry you."

"I told you I would fix it. And I did."

"But now my son thinks badly of you."

Redfoot met her gaze. "What does it matter?"

"It matters to me." Anger filled her voice.

"Should I leave?" Matt asked.

"No!" Redfoot snapped, and then looked back at Veronica. "Woman, you are difficult. I fix it so you do not have to marry me, and now you are mad at how I fix it."

"But why? You never lie."

"I did it for the reason that I didn't care that they were going to push us into getting married. I did it because I love you."

"You are the most stubborn old coot I know," she muttered.

"And you are the most stubborn old hag!"

Someone cleared their throat at the entrance of the tent. Redfoot, Veronica, and Matt all turned. Ramon stood there. "You're a stubborn old coot, she's a stubborn old hag, and I'd say that makes you two perfect for each other."

Redfoot nodded. He'd left a message on the young man's phone, inviting him to participate tonight, but Ramon hadn't returned the call and Redfoot hadn't known if he would come.

"I wish that was true," Redfoot said. "But your mother does not see it that way."

"How do you know how I see it?" Veronica asked.

"You told me," Redfoot insisted.

"That was last week. A woman has a right to change her mind."

"She does?" The heaviness that had taken up residence in Redfoot's chest began to fade.

Ramon said, "We need to get out there. You two can plan your future later." The drums had started playing, and he motioned for Matt to follow him.

Redfoot smiled at his beloved. "Yes, we can plan later." When he moved past her, he slipped his hand into hers for a brief squeeze. A lightness filled his chest as she let him. As Veronica smiled sweetly, one thought gave him pause as he walked out: he really needed to get his pills back from Sky.

"Where are you, damn it?" Shala muttered, using her close-up camera lens to try to find Sky in the crowd. The male dancers were gathered to the side of the arena. Sky wasn't among them. The drums were playing, and she could see Redfoot and the other elders about to walk out.

"Who are you looking for?" Sky's deep voice fluttered against her neck.

She turned. He wore his powwow garb, minus his headdress. Her gaze swept down his hard, muscle-corded body, but her gaze didn't linger very long, because she focused on the cast on his arm.

"Is that a camera in your hands?" A teasing glint filled his eye.

"I've heard the rules have changed," she replied.

"Yup." He ran his uninjured hand down her arm, and his touch sent shivers of pain into her heart. "Some blue-eyed angel came to town and changed everything."

She motioned to his arm. "It was broken?"

She'd gone to the hospital with Sky, but when Phillip arrived he took her back, fighting and screaming, to the police station. She suspected Sky had told him to take her because he remembered how she felt about hospitals. What Sky didn't know was that being away from him hurt more than any memory of the past. Phillip had released her to Lucas about an hour ago, and he'd brought her here, saying Sky would show up.

"Yup, broken," he said.

She leaned in a little. "That's what you get for trying to act like a Hollywood cop."

"Hey, my girl asks for Hollywood, she gets Hollywood." He took her hand in his. "Let's go somewhere we can talk."

"What about taking pictures?"

"What about it?" he asked.

When he led her away, she didn't hesitate. *I love you.* All afternoon she'd replayed what he said to her before running out from behind his truck. She was almost afraid she'd imagined it.

Jose studied his father, who was proudly holding his place amongst the elders, talking about the People's culture and their beliefs. Amazement filled him. How many times had he stood here and watched his father address the crowd? Why had he never felt this pride and sense of belonging before?

He could still remember the first day he refused to be a part of the ceremonies. His father had been angry and hurt, and he had demanded Jose get dressed and do his part. It had been his mom who had stood up for him, saying Jose had to find his own way. At this moment, Jose wasn't so sure his path had been the right one. He didn't regret who he was or what he did or didn't believe, but at this moment he knew he'd missed out on something important.

The tribesmen started moving away, and Jose turned to where Maria had been standing beside him. Damn it! He'd been given one lousy job tonight, and that was to ensure that Maria saw Matt dance. Now she was gone. He took off into the crowd to find her.

Maria crouched near the concession stand, talking to a prospective client on her phone. Redfoot would be angry if he knew she'd brought her cell phone to the powwow, but this was important.

"There you are!" a voice bellowed.

Maria heard Jose and then felt his arm latch around her elbow. He was suddenly pulling her through the crowd of people, who were all laughing about something. She covered her phone with one hand and said, "Stop. This is an important call."

Jose held up his palms as if to comply, then snatched the phone right out of her hands and cut it off. "Come on!"

He dragged her through the crowd. Before she could even think to stop him, it struck her that something was different. It took her a few minutes to figure it out: the spectators' laughter. Powwows were not famous for laughter. Nonetheless, her fury at Jose's rude behavior was stronger than her curiosity.

"Why did you do that?" she seethed.

"I guess this pretty much proves it, huh?" He waved to the arena.

"Proves what?" she snapped.

"That white men can't dance." He waved again to the arena.

Maria looked up and— "What the hell is he doing?"

Matt. It was Matt. As she stared, his headdress dropped to the ground, and when he reached to pick it up, his loincloth rode high on his backside. Another howl of laughter spilled from the audience. Maria covered her mouth to hold her giggles back.

When she saw the look of embarrassment in Matt's eyes, her laughter died. "Why did Redfoot do this?" she hissed.

"Redfoot didn't. Matt wanted to do it. It seems he'd do anything to get his girl back."

Right then, Matt's gaze found hers and Maria knew Jose was telling the truth. Matt's headdress slipped again, this time over his face. Maria's heart wrenched for him. "Stop this," she told Jose.

"I can't. But you could," he told her. "Of course, if I remember correctly, if a woman walks out and gets a man from the soul mate dance, she's pretty much announcing their engagement to the tribal council."

Maria looked back up at Matt and saw his headdress slip again to the ground. If he bent over for it, he'd moon the audience again.

"Oh, screw it!" She jumped over the rope, head held high, and marched right into the center of the arena. She grabbed Matt by the hand and led him away. Hoots and hollers filled the crowd, but Maria ignored it all.

"Where are we going?" Matt asked as the noise decreased.

She moved him inside the women's tent. Then, facing him, she snapped her hands onto her hips. "Why did you do this?"

He crossed his arms over his wide chest. In spite of being pale and somewhat ridiculous in the outfit, he looked sexy as hell to her. She fought that back.

"Why do you think I did it?" He took a step closer. "I love you."

She blinked back tears and tried to think of how to ease into the conversation she needed to have. There didn't seem to be a way, and she needed to believe he truly understood what was going on. "What if I told you that . . . that there's a chance I might not be able to give you a baby?"

He stared at her, looking befuddled. "Why would you ask that?" he said.

She sighed and then just blurted everything out. She told him it all. She told him about her and Jose, about the baby, and about what the doctor had told her after the operation. She saw the look on his face, which was shock. "I'm sorry," she said. Everything inside had told her that he would say it didn't matter. Right now, the look on his face said different. It told her he cared very much. So she turned again and walked away.

He caught her arm, but she flung off his hand. "You don't have to do this, Matt. I know you're a good guy, but you deserve—"

"Stop it!" He pressed a hand to his forehead. "You . . . you don't understand. Am I shocked right now? Hell, yes. But mostly I'm pissed at you for not telling me about losing a child. I'm not upset about your problem. I don't care about your problem. But *damn*, Maria—you lost a child, which had to have hurt like hell. You don't keep something like this from someone who cares about you."

"I guess it's like *having* a child, huh?" she asked, standing up to him.

Understanding filled his eyes. "I'd say it was exactly like that." He sighed. "Is this why you pushed me away?"

She swallowed her fear. "No. You said you wanted us to have kids. And it wasn't fair . . ."

He pinched the bridge of his nose. "Damn it, Maria. Do I want to have baby with you? Yes. But if for some reason we can't, then so the hell what? We'll adopt from the foster program. Look at you, look at how much you love Redfoot. We can do the same for some other kid out there. Heck, maybe we can do both."

She didn't know she was crying until he brushed the tears from her cheeks. She looked up at him as she put her other fear into words. "What if your daughter doesn't like me?"

He scoffed. "She's going to love you. I'm getting her next weekend, and I'd love it if you'd agree to meet her." He leaned down and stared into her eyes. "So would you please say it?"

"Say what?"

"That you love me. I think I've said it three times, and you've yet to say it back."

She smiled and pulled her paleface close. "I love you, Matt Goodson. I loved you from our second date, but tonight, seeing you out there . . ."

"Making a fool out of myself?"

She grinned. "Yeah, making a fool out of yourself. I fell in love with you all over again."

"I guess it's true then," he said.

"What?" She giggled. "That white men can't dance?"

He leaned his head back and laughed. "No, that love makes fools out of us all."

"I don't mind being that kind of fool," she said, and kissed him.

CHAPTER THIRTY-EIGHT

Jose stood watching the powwow continue, feeling damn proud that he'd managed to do exactly what Redfoot wanted. It seemed like a first. Then, suddenly, his father was standing beside him.

"I think we did it, son." He dropped his hand on Jose's shoulder.

"I think we did," Jose agreed, his gaze on the women moving center stage of the arena. "When's the next powwow?"

"In October. Maybe you can visit then."

"Yeah, maybe I can."

Jose wiped his brow. The temperature felt as if it had just risen ten degrees, and the drums changed to a different rhythm. He looked up. The sun hung low in the horizon and was painting the sky a bright pink and purple. His gaze slowly shifted back to the dancers, who were again standing tall and proud.

The drum tempo increased, and the women now began to move to the sound. Golden sunlight spilled everywhere, making them seem to glow, but one woman stood out from the rest. He recognized her: Poncha Rivers. The girl he'd taken to his senior prom, and the waitress who'd been so glad to see him at the diner.

Watching her graceful movements, the way her breasts jiggled ever so lightly, the way her hips moved in little circles, he was mesmerized. His chest grew heavy, and he tried to remember if he'd gotten further than second base with her. Damn, he had a vague memory of being extremely drunk and naked, but if anything had happened, he couldn't recall.

"Son?"

Jose tried to look away from Poncha but couldn't. "Yeah?"

"Nothing," his dad said and chuckled. He left Jose there to watch Poncha finish her dance.

Redfoot saw the Scrabble player standing a few feet away and went to join him. "Please tell me the bulldog has been arrested."

"The bulldog?" Lucas repeated.

"The senator."

"They've brought him and his men in for questioning. Their asses are ours."

Redfoot nodded. "That's good."

Lucas reared back on his heels. "How did you know that Sky and Shala would hit it off?"

"The spirits told me when I sleep."

"Seriously?" Lucas said.

"Seriously," Redfoot answered. "And the other night, I saw you in a *wacoi*."

"*Wacoi?*" Lucas laughed. "The sacred word?"

"Right." Redfoot said. "Maybe next time you'll let me use it."

"I doubt it. But what is a *wacoi*?" Lucas asked. "Or is it still too sacred to share?"

Redfoot dropped a hand on the young man's shoulder. "Like Sky, you too will find your way."

"What way?" Lucas asked. "Wait a damn minute. If

you've seen me with a soul mate in some weird-ass dream, then I know you are batty as shit."

Redfoot just laughed. When he saw Veronica, he left the Scrabble player to his stupidity. Like Jose, this man would know his fate soon enough.

"Where are we going?" Shala asked Sky when he finally got off the phone with the mayor.

"To the only air-conditioned spot around here. The ticket booth."

She saw the sweat rolling off his brow. "Are you sure you should be out here after all you've been through?"

"I'm fine," he grunted.

"I'll bet you were told to go home and go to bed, weren't you?" she asked.

"Maybe."

"That's it, I'm taking you home! Where's your truck?"

"I didn't drive. Phillip dropped me off." He opened the door to the ticket booth and motioned her inside.

She frowned. "I'll go find Lucas."

"Shala, please step inside and let's talk."

Seeing the determined way he looked at her, she walked inside. The booth was no bigger than a concession stand, but it was cool from the air conditioner humming in the corner. "Here." She pulled out a chair and motioned for him to sit.

He did so, and then motioned to a chair at the side. "You sit down, too."

"Why?" she asked. "Do you have more bad news? Is there another hit man out for me?"

"No. It's about us."

She sighed. "Can't we worry about that when you're better?" She was beginning to get worried about Sky walking around at the powwow after just leaving the hospital.

"No. Sit down," he ordered.

"Fine, but it's not fair to do this right now."

"Why not?" he asked.

"Because I'm feeling sorry for you and grateful that you played Hollywood cop to save my life, and it will be hard for me to be objective."

"Then this is definitely is the right time," he said. "Because I need all the ammunition I can get. Now, please sit, before I stand up."

She dropped into the chair. He met her gaze, and she saw something in Sky Gomez she'd never seen. Fear.

"I screwed up, Shala. I know that. I accused you of jabbering and said that I didn't believe—"

"I do jabber," she interrupted.

"I know, but it was mean of me to say it. And here's the thing. I didn't think I believed in love, I didn't think I'd find anyone who made me feel . . . whole, right, complete. I—"

She held up her hand. "Are you on pain medicine?"

"Yes, why?" He sounded annoyed that she'd stopped him.

"Then maybe you should wait until you're clearheaded to—"

He shook his head. "I'm very clearheaded about what I'm about to say. So just listen." When she nodded, and he continued. "I was saying . . . that I don't know if it's because you lost your parents the way I did, or if . . . hell, maybe there's something to this whole soul-mate thing. The first time I saw your picture, I think I fell for you. Then, the day you arrived in Precious and I followed you, I fell harder. When I kissed you and we made love . . . well, I just keep falling for you harder and harder. I know I told you that I didn't think it would last, but I was lying. Lying to you, lying to myself. Hell, I was lying to Sundance and Butch—who, by the way, miss you something terrible."

"Sky—"

"No, let me finish. I know you live in Houston. And I don't like the idea of moving, but if Precious isn't your type of town, then I'll do it. I'll follow you anywhere, because Precious hasn't been so precious since you left. I love you and—"

"Sky—"

"I'm not finished," he growled. "I need—"

She leaned in and put a finger over his lips. "Sky, I love Precious. I love you. Now would you please . . . just shut up and kiss me?"

National Readers' Choice Award Winner

GEMMA HALLIDAY

THE PERFECT

A Hollywood
Headlines
Mystery Romance

SHOT

Cameron Dakota is the *L.A. Informer*'s staff photographer and paparazzi to the stars. Her latest subject, Trace Brody, is an A-list actor and half of America's favorite Hollywood couple. He's about to get married in the wedding of the century, and Cam is determined to get the first shots of the bride and groom. But when Cam takes pictures of what looks like Trace being kidnapped at gunpoint, she suddenly finds herself smack in the middle of a scandal more sensational than even she could invent. On the run, under fire, and in serious danger of falling in love with one leading man, Cam must get to the bottom of this story . . . before the story gets to her.

Can't wait for all the good celebrity gossip?

Check out
www.LAInformerOnline.com
to get your fix.

Dorchester Publishing is proud to present

⊰ PUBLISHER'S PLEDGE ⊱

We GUARANTEE this book!

We are so confident that you will enjoy this book that we are offering a 100% money-back guarantee.

If you are not satisfied with this novel, Dorchester Publishing Company, Inc. will refund your money! Simply return the book for a full refund.

To be eligible, the book must be returned by 7/25/2010, along with a copy of the receipt, your address, and a brief explanation of why you are returning the book, to the address listed below.

We will send you a check for the purchase price and sales tax of the book within 4-6 weeks.

Publishers Pledge Reads
Dorchester Publishing Company
11 West Avenue, Ste 103
Wayne, PA 19087

Offer ends 7/25/2010.

JANA DeLeon

WHO KILLED HELENA HENRY?

Actually, considering her past, a better question would be: who didn't want her dead? Prying, spying, pushy, pesky—she was the most meddlesome mother-in-law in all of Louisiana.

Of course, mortals such as self-proclaimed psychic Raissa Bordeaux believe there are more important mysteries to be solved. One involves a rash of child kidnappings. Another is New Orleans Detective Zach Blanchard: why do such fine behinds always end up on such uptight men? If only her crystal ball really gave answers. Instead, she'll have to rely on Mudbug's garrulous ghost, her own dark past and a Bayou boy-in-blue who might turn out to be her very own frog prince.

Showdown in Mudbug

ISBN 13: 978-0-505-52849-0

✂ # ☐ **YES!**

Sign me up for the Love Spell Book Club and send my
FREE BOOKS! If I choose to stay in the club, I will pay
only $8.50* each month, a savings of $6.48!

NAME: _____

ADDRESS: _____

TELEPHONE: _____

EMAIL: _____

☐ I want to pay by credit card.

☐ **VISA**   ☐ **MasterCard.**   ☐ **DISCOVER**

ACCOUNT #: _____

EXPIRATION DATE: _____

SIGNATURE: _____

Mail this page along with $2.00 shipping and handling to:
Love Spell Book Club
PO Box 6640
Wayne, PA 19087
Or fax (must include credit card information) to:
610-995-9274
You can also sign up online at **www.dorchesterpub.com**.
*Plus $2.00 for shipping. Offer open to residents of the U.S. and Canada only.
Canadian residents please call 1-800-481-9191 for pricing information.
If under 18, a parent or guardian must sign. Terms, prices and conditions subject to
change. Subscription subject to acceptance. Dorchester Publishing reserves the right
to reject any order or cancel any subscription.